MAYDAY

Story & letters: Alex de Campi
Line art: Tony Parker
Color art: Blond
Editor: Brendan Wright

Rights inquiries: Sean Berard, APA

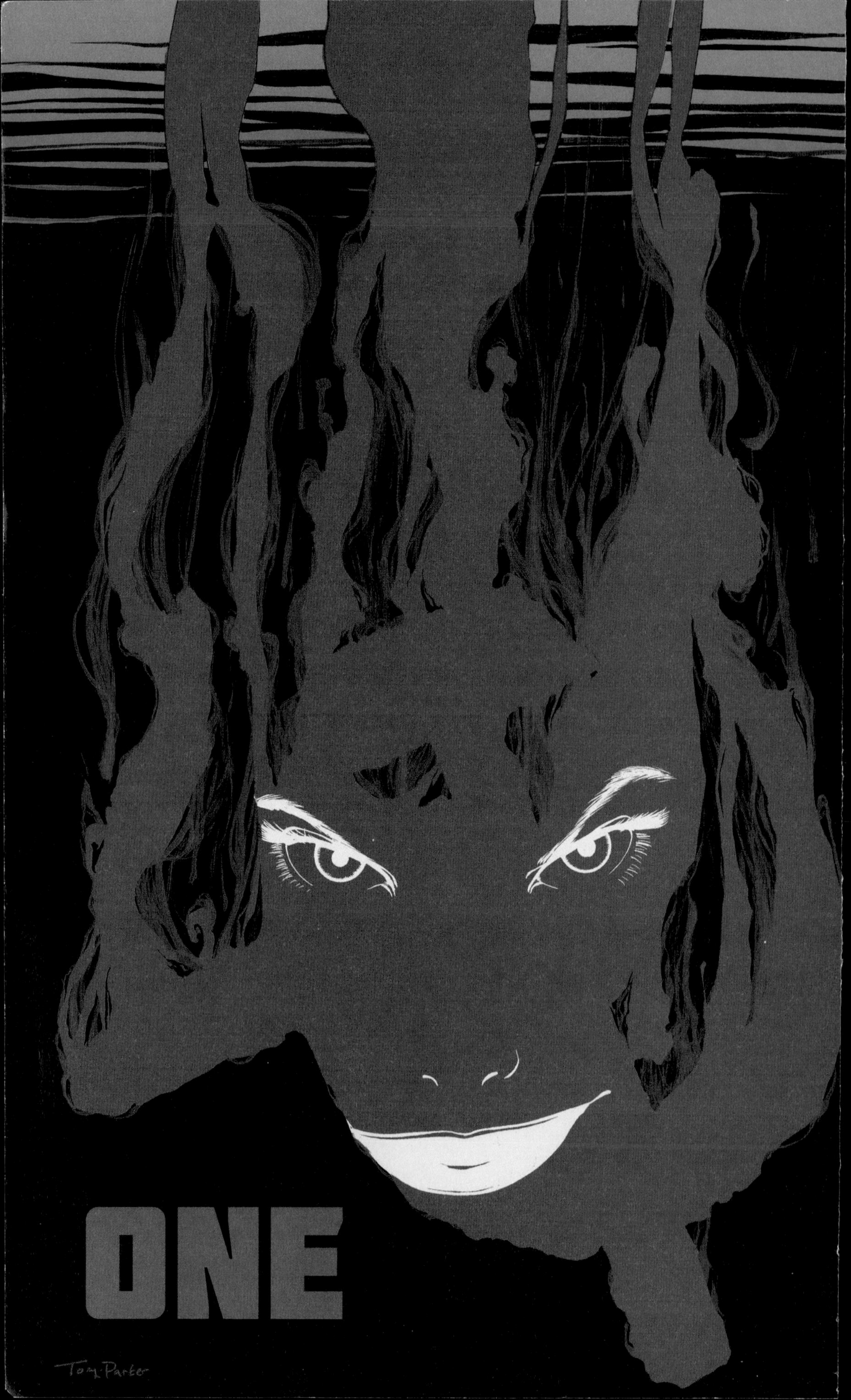
ONE
Tom Parker

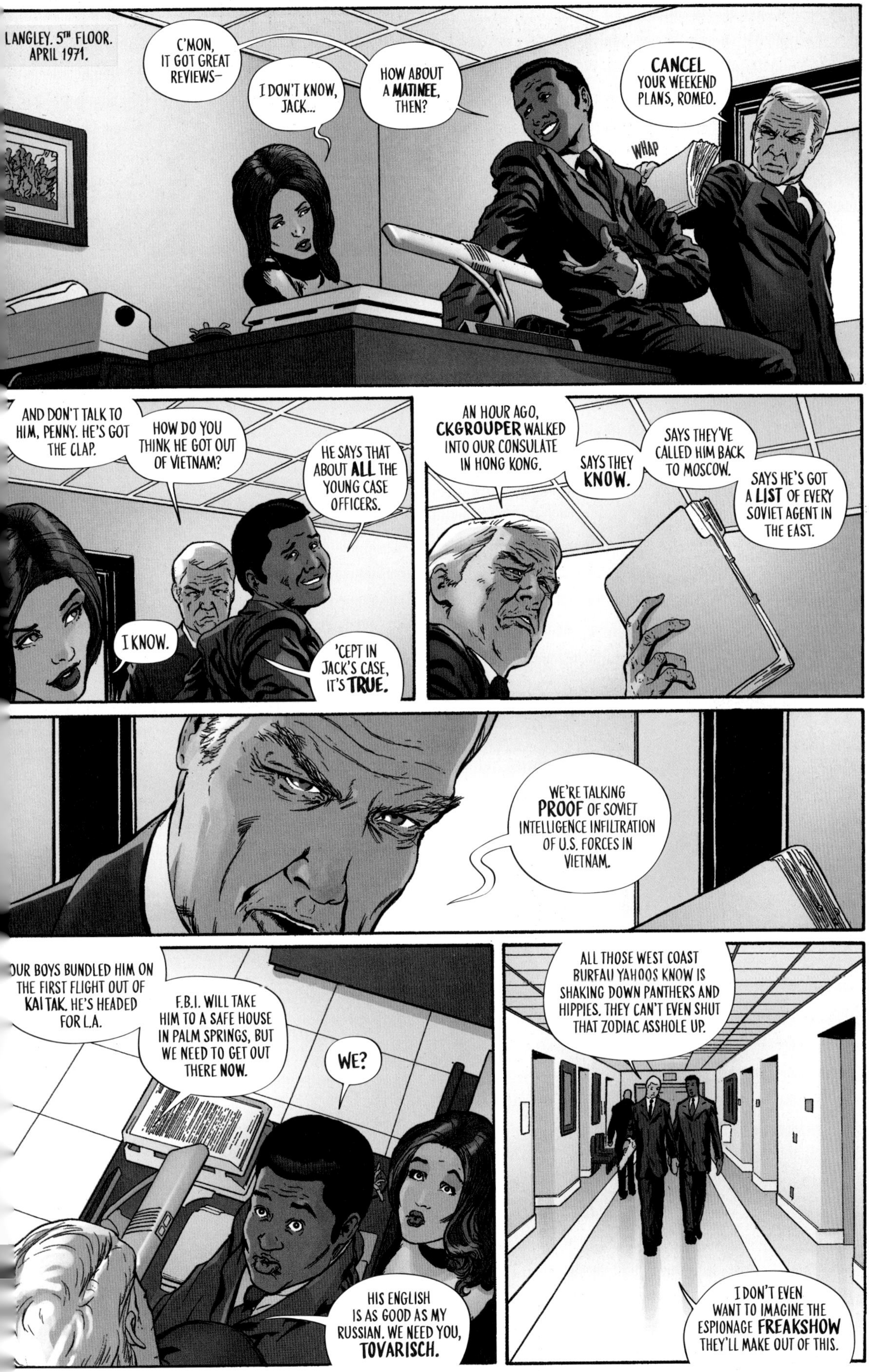
LANGLEY. 5TH FLOOR. APRIL 1971.
C'MON, IT GOT GREAT REVIEWS—
I DON'T KNOW, JACK...
HOW ABOUT A MATINEE, THEN?
CANCEL YOUR WEEKEND PLANS, ROMEO.
WHAP
AND DON'T TALK TO HIM, PENNY. HE'S GOT THE CLAP.
HOW DO YOU THINK HE GOT OUT OF VIETNAM?
HE SAYS THAT ABOUT ALL THE YOUNG CASE OFFICERS.
I KNOW.
'CEPT IN JACK'S CASE, IT'S TRUE.
AN HOUR AGO, CKGROUPER WALKED INTO OUR CONSULATE IN HONG KONG.
SAYS THEY KNOW.
SAYS THEY'VE CALLED HIM BACK TO MOSCOW.
SAYS HE'S GOT A LIST OF EVERY SOVIET AGENT IN THE EAST.
WE'RE TALKING PROOF OF SOVIET INTELLIGENCE INFILTRATION OF U.S. FORCES IN VIETNAM.
OUR BOYS BUNDLED HIM ON THE FIRST FLIGHT OUT OF KAI TAK. HE'S HEADED FOR L.A.
F.B.I. WILL TAKE HIM TO A SAFE HOUSE IN PALM SPRINGS, BUT WE NEED TO GET OUT THERE NOW.
WE?
HIS ENGLISH IS AS GOOD AS MY RUSSIAN. WE NEED YOU, TOVARISCH.
ALL THOSE WEST COAST BUREAU YAHOOS KNOW IS SHAKING DOWN PANTHERS AND HIPPIES. THEY CAN'T EVEN SHUT THAT ZODIAC ASSHOLE UP.
I DON'T EVEN WANT TO IMAGINE THE ESPIONAGE FREAKSHOW THEY'LL MAKE OUT OF THIS.

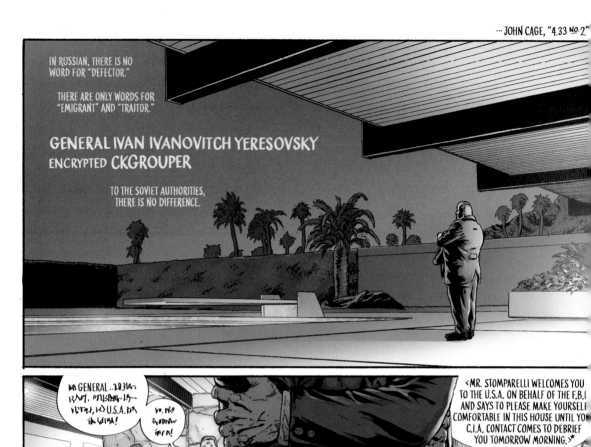

IN RUSSIAN, THERE IS NO WORD FOR "DEFECTOR."

THERE ARE ONLY WORDS FOR "EMIGRANT" AND "TRAITOR."

GENERAL IVAN IVANOVITCH YERESOVSKY
ENCRYPTED CKGROUPER

TO THE SOVIET AUTHORITIES, THERE IS NO DIFFERENCE.

<MR. STOMPARELLI WELCOMES YOU TO THE U.S.A. ON BEHALF OF THE F.B.I AND SAYS TO PLEASE MAKE YOURSELF COMFORTABLE IN THIS HOUSE UNTIL YO C.I.A. CONTACT COMES TO DEBRIEF YOU TOMORROW MORNING.>

<HE SAYS THERE IS VODKA FOR YOU.>

* <RUSSIAN

ДА, ДА.

СПАСИБО.

THIS IS BIG, BARRY, **REAL** BIG.

OL' PETE STOMPARELLI IS GONNA MAKE HIS MARK WITH THIS ONE, YES HE IS!

TAKE GOOD CARE OF HIM, LEWIS!

YES SIR, MR. STOMPARELLI!

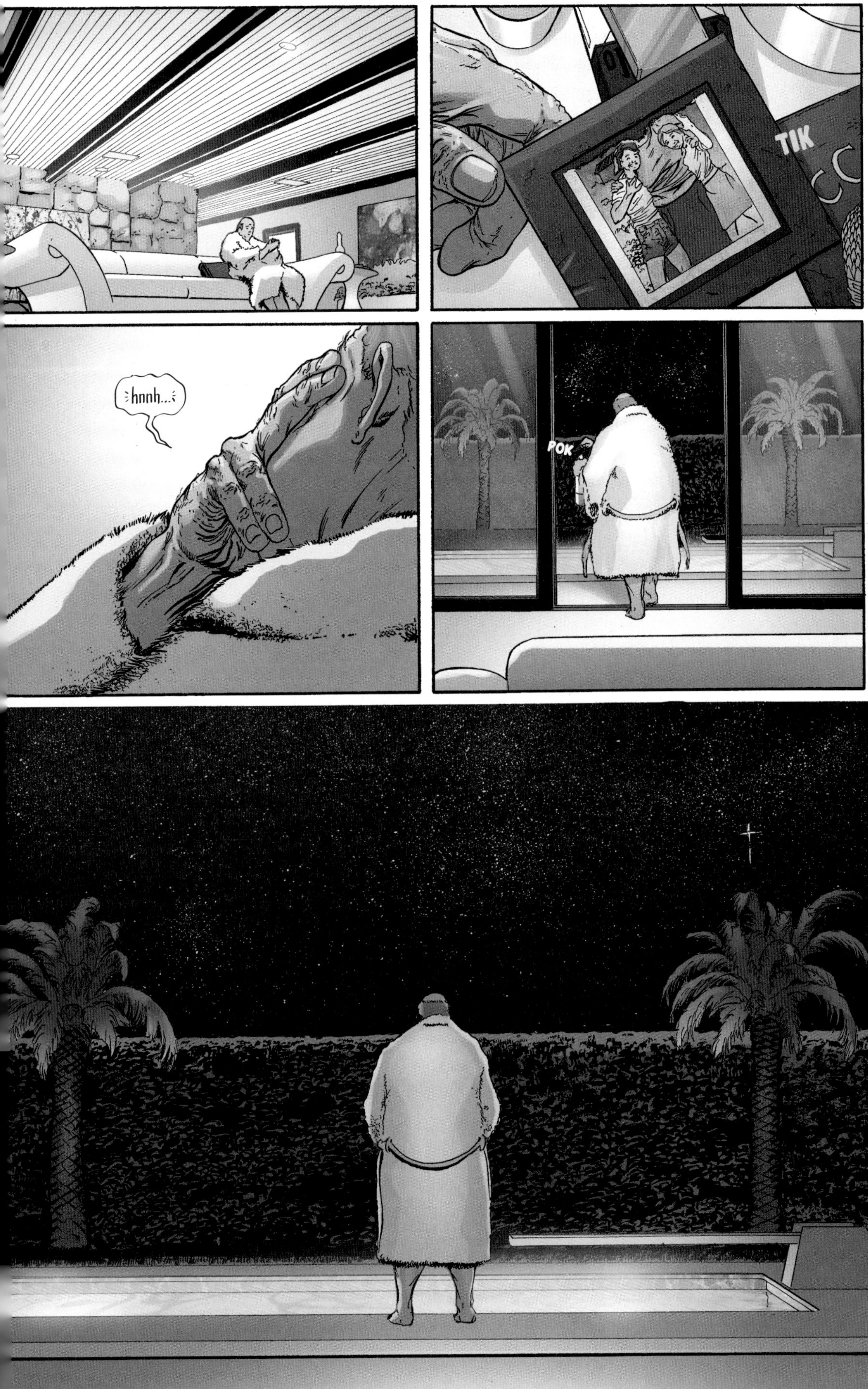
TIK
hnnh...
POK

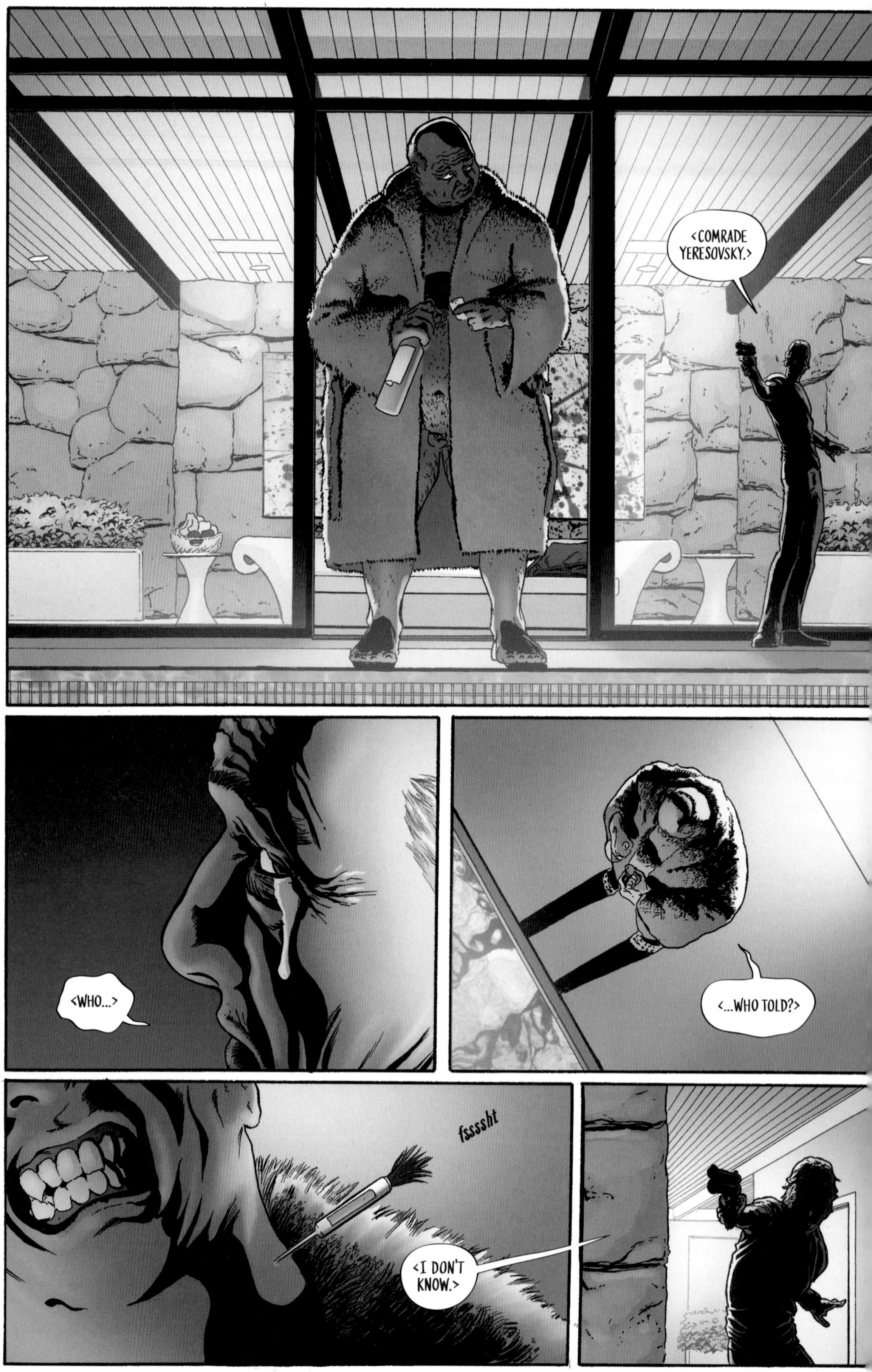
<COMRADE YERESOVSKY.>
<WHO...>
<...WHO TOLD?>
fsssssht
<I DON'T KNOW.>

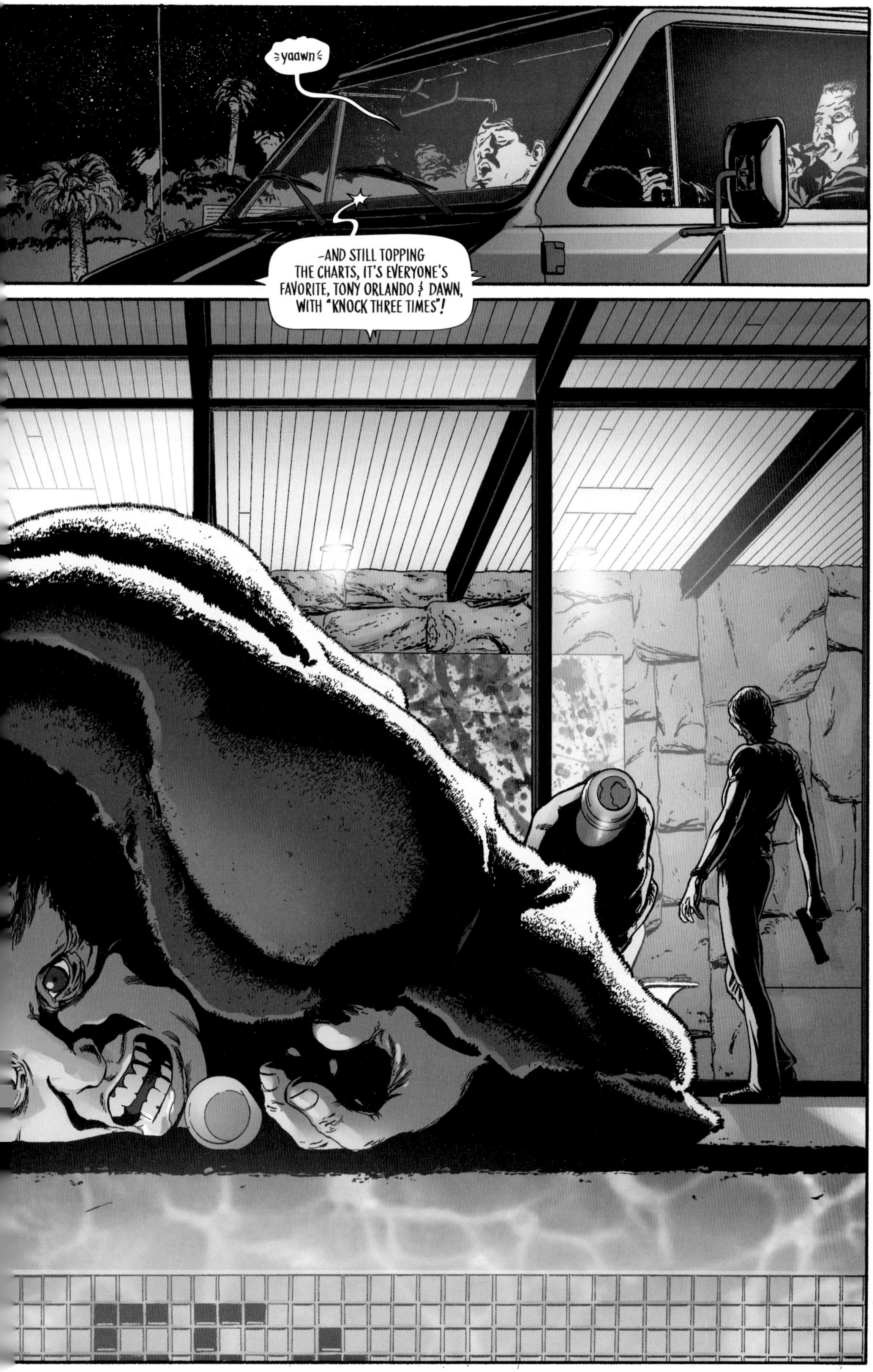

yaawn
-AND STILL TOPPING THE CHARTS, IT'S EVERYONE'S FAVORITE, TONY ORLANDO & DAWN, WITH "KNOCK THREE TIMES"!

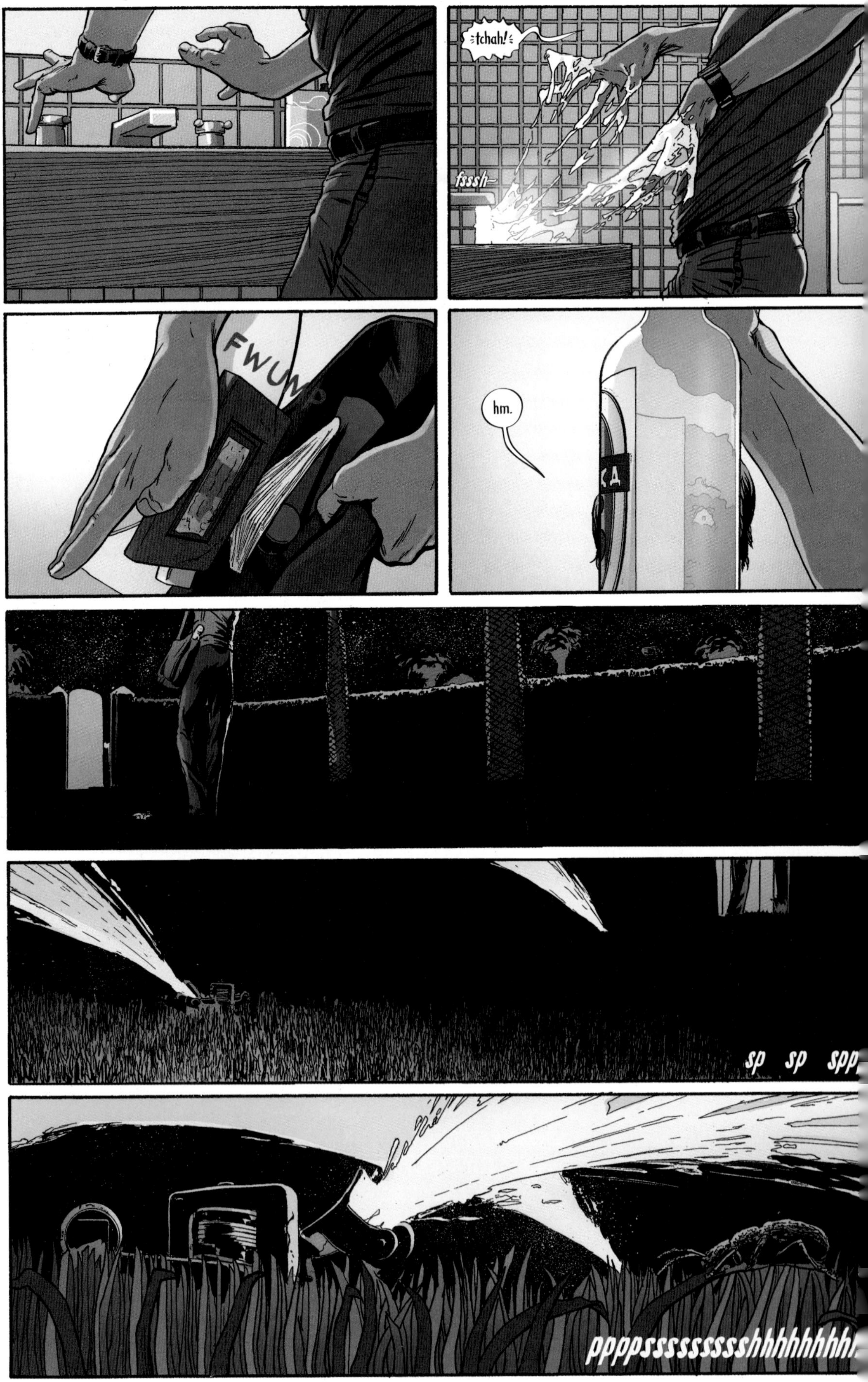
tchah!
fsssh~
FWUMP
hm.
sp sp spp
pppppsssssssssshhhhhhhh

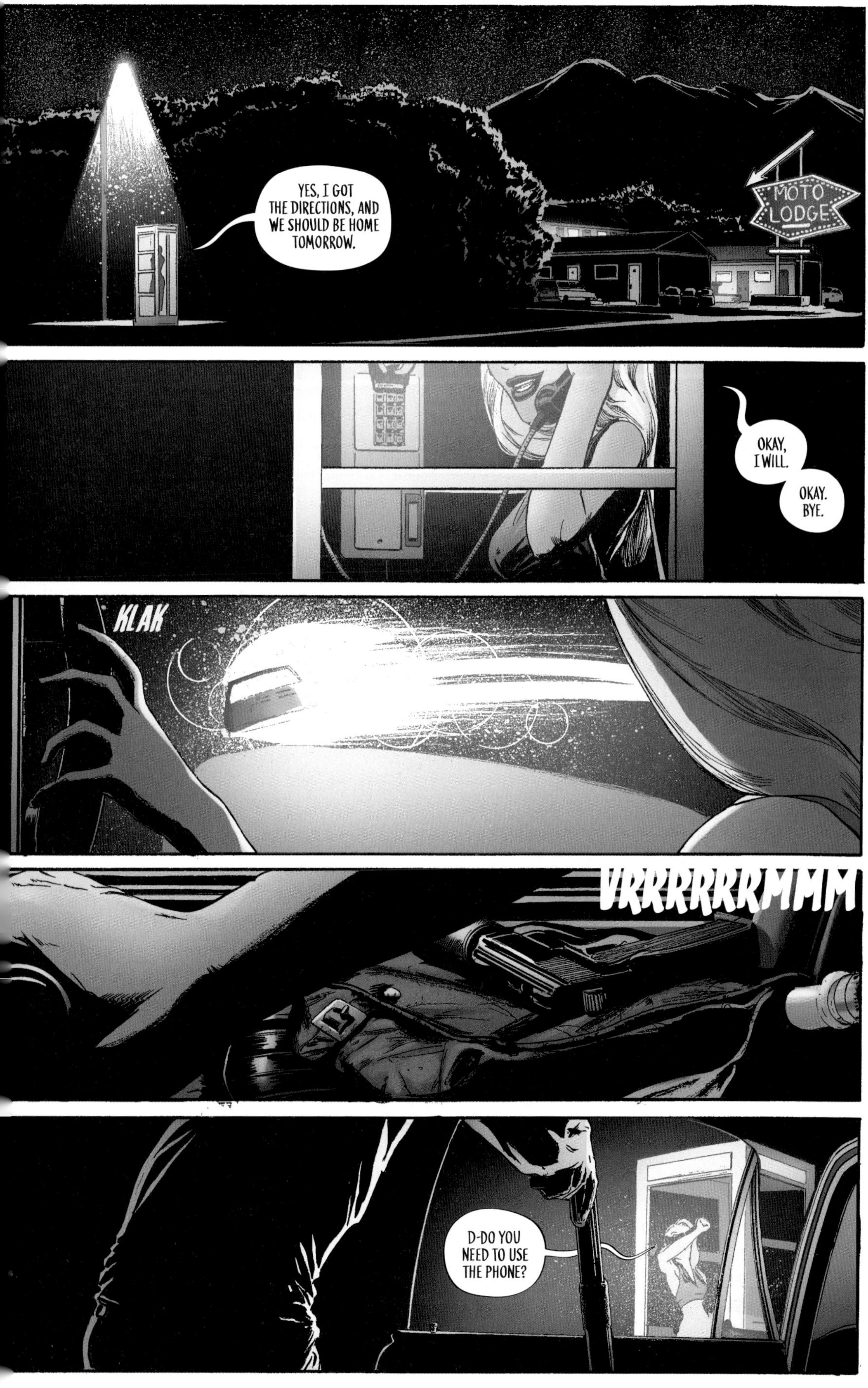
MOTO LODGE
YES, I GOT THE DIRECTIONS, AND WE SHOULD BE HOME TOMORROW.
OKAY, I WILL.
OKAY. BYE.
KLAK
VRRRRRRRMMM
D-DO YOU NEED TO USE THE PHONE?

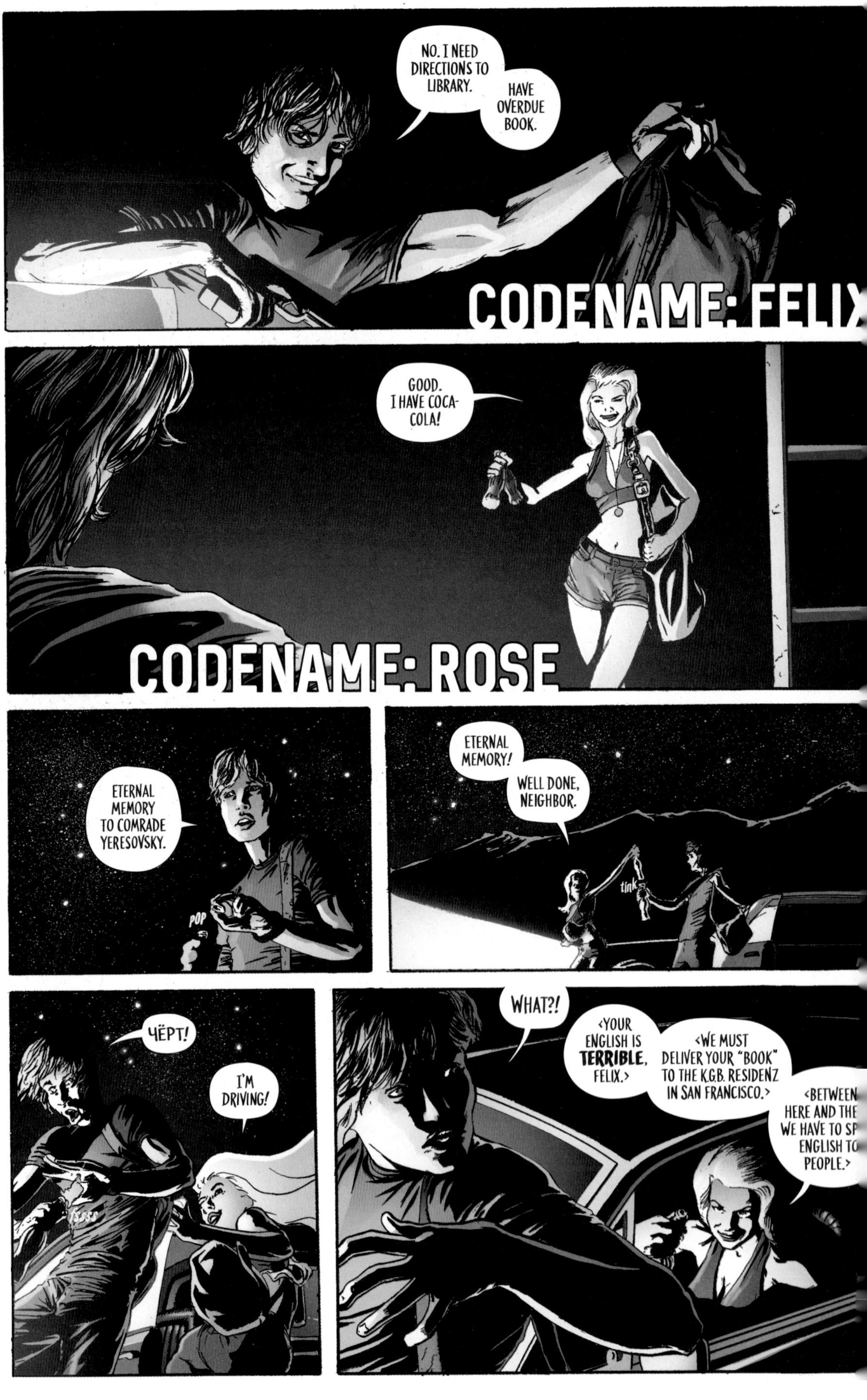

NO. I NEED DIRECTIONS TO LIBRARY.
HAVE OVERDUE BOOK.
CODENAME: FELIX
GOOD. I HAVE COCA-COLA!
CODENAME: ROSE
ETERNAL MEMORY TO COMRADE YERESOVSKY.
POP
ETERNAL MEMORY!
WELL DONE, NEIGHBOR.
tink
ЧЁРТ!
I'M DRIVING!
fssss
WHAT?!
‹YOUR ENGLISH IS **TERRIBLE**, FELIX.›
‹WE MUST DELIVER YOUR "BOOK" TO THE K.G.B. RESIDENZ IN SAN FRANCISCO.›

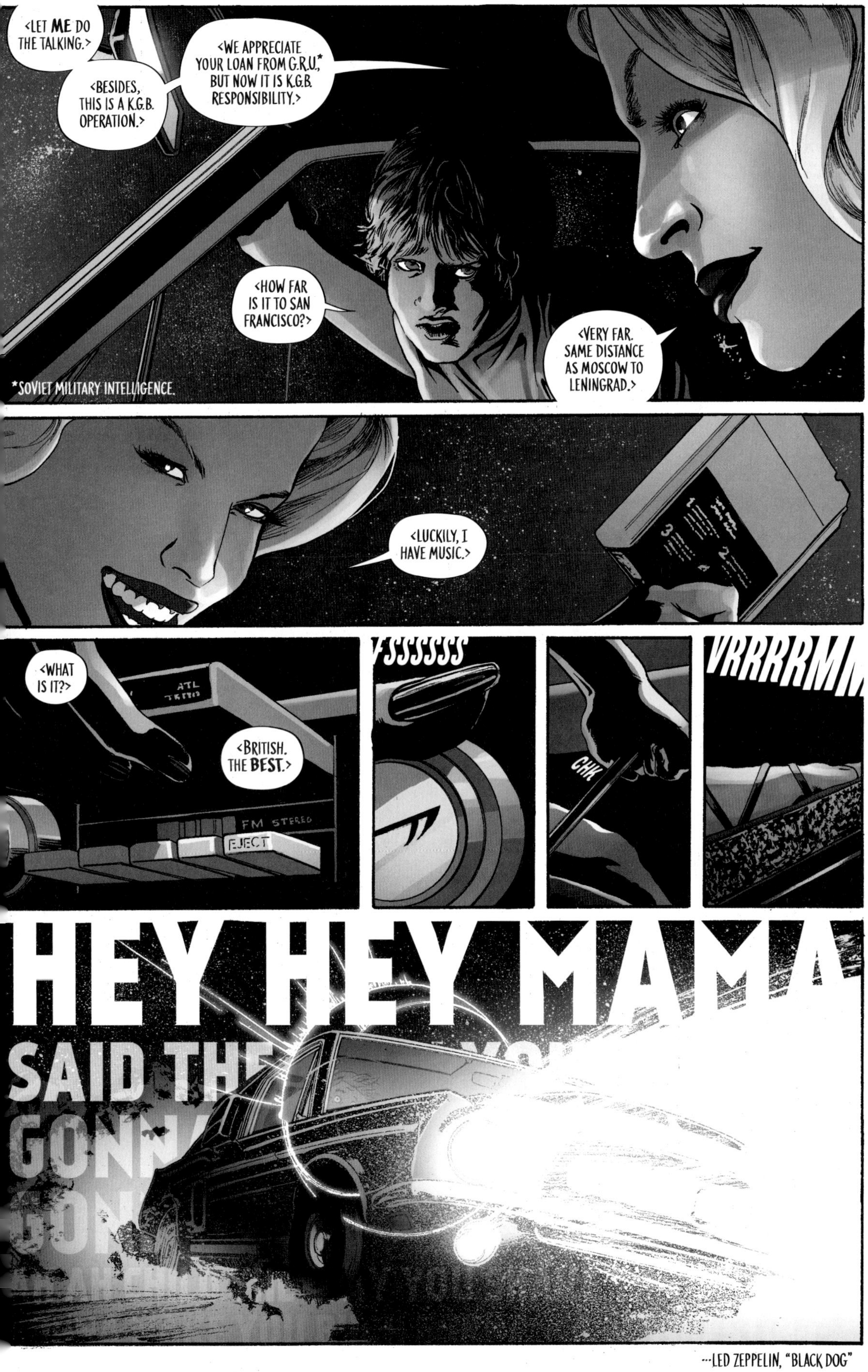
<LET ME DO THE TALKING.>
<BESIDES, THIS IS A K.G.B. OPERATION.>
<WE APPRECIATE YOUR LOAN FROM G.R.U.,* BUT NOW IT IS K.G.B. RESPONSIBILITY.>
<HOW FAR IS IT TO SAN FRANCISCO?>
<VERY FAR. SAME DISTANCE AS MOSCOW TO LENINGRAD.>
*SOVIET MILITARY INTELLIGENCE.
<LUCKILY, I HAVE MUSIC.>
<WHAT IS IT?>
<BRITISH. THE BEST.>
FM STEREO
EJECT
SSSSSS
CHK
VRRRRM
HEY HEY MAMA
SAID THE

—LED ZEPPELIN, "BLACK DOG"

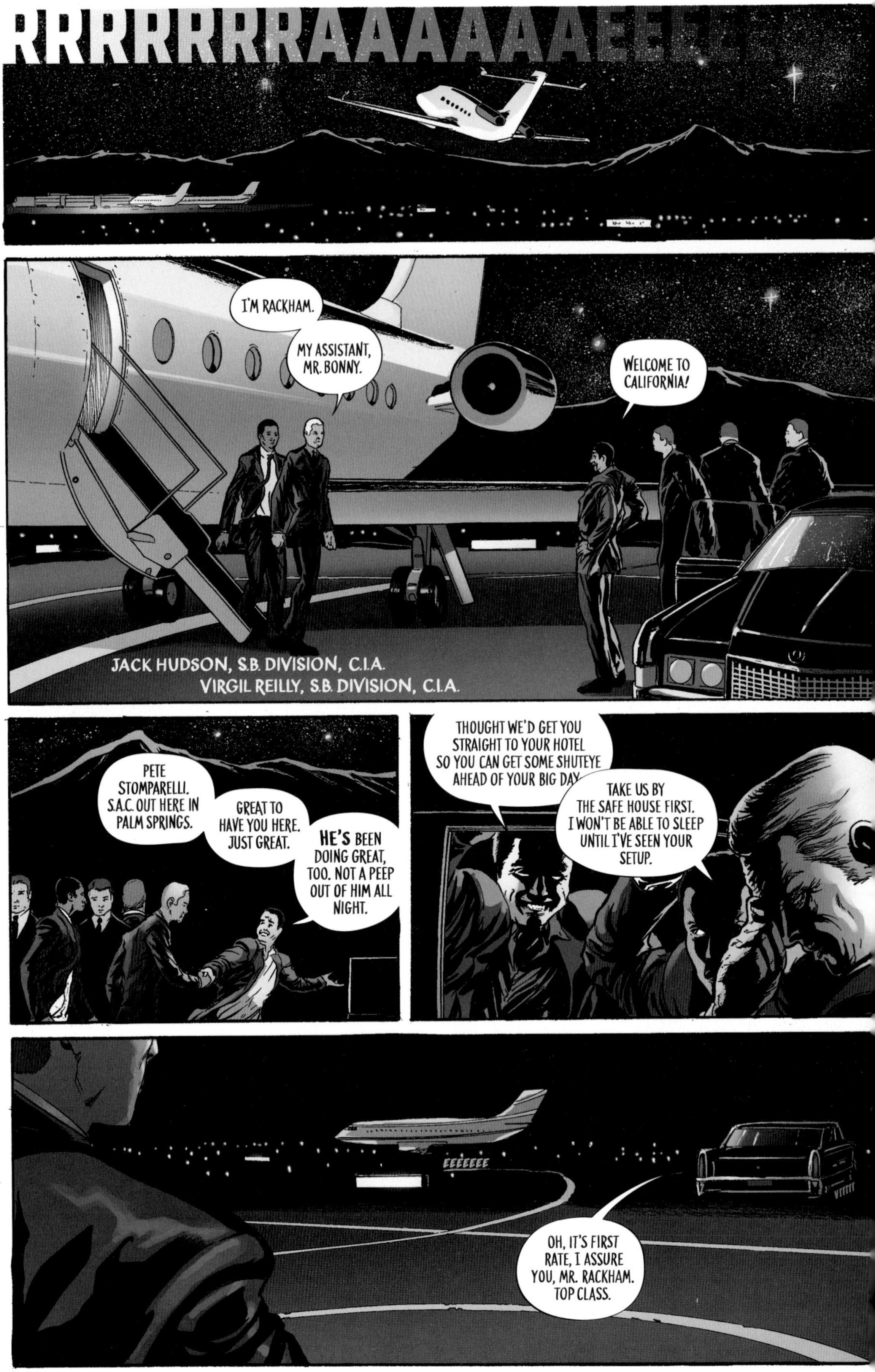
RRRRRRRAAAAAAEEE
I'M RACKHAM.
MY ASSISTANT, MR. BONNY.
WELCOME TO CALIFORNIA!
JACK HUDSON, S.B. DIVISION, C.I.A.
VIRGIL REILLY, S.B. DIVISION, C.I.A.
PETE STOMPARELLI. S.A.C. OUT HERE IN PALM SPRINGS.
GREAT TO HAVE YOU HERE. JUST GREAT.
HE'S BEEN DOING GREAT, TOO. NOT A PEEP OUT OF HIM ALL NIGHT.
THOUGHT WE'D GET YOU STRAIGHT TO YOUR HOTEL SO YOU CAN GET SOME SHUTEYE AHEAD OF YOUR BIG DAY.
TAKE US BY THE SAFE HOUSE FIRST. I WON'T BE ABLE TO SLEEP UNTIL I'VE SEEN YOUR SETUP.
EEEEEEE
OH, IT'S FIRST RATE, I ASSURE YOU, MR. RACKHAM. TOP CLASS.

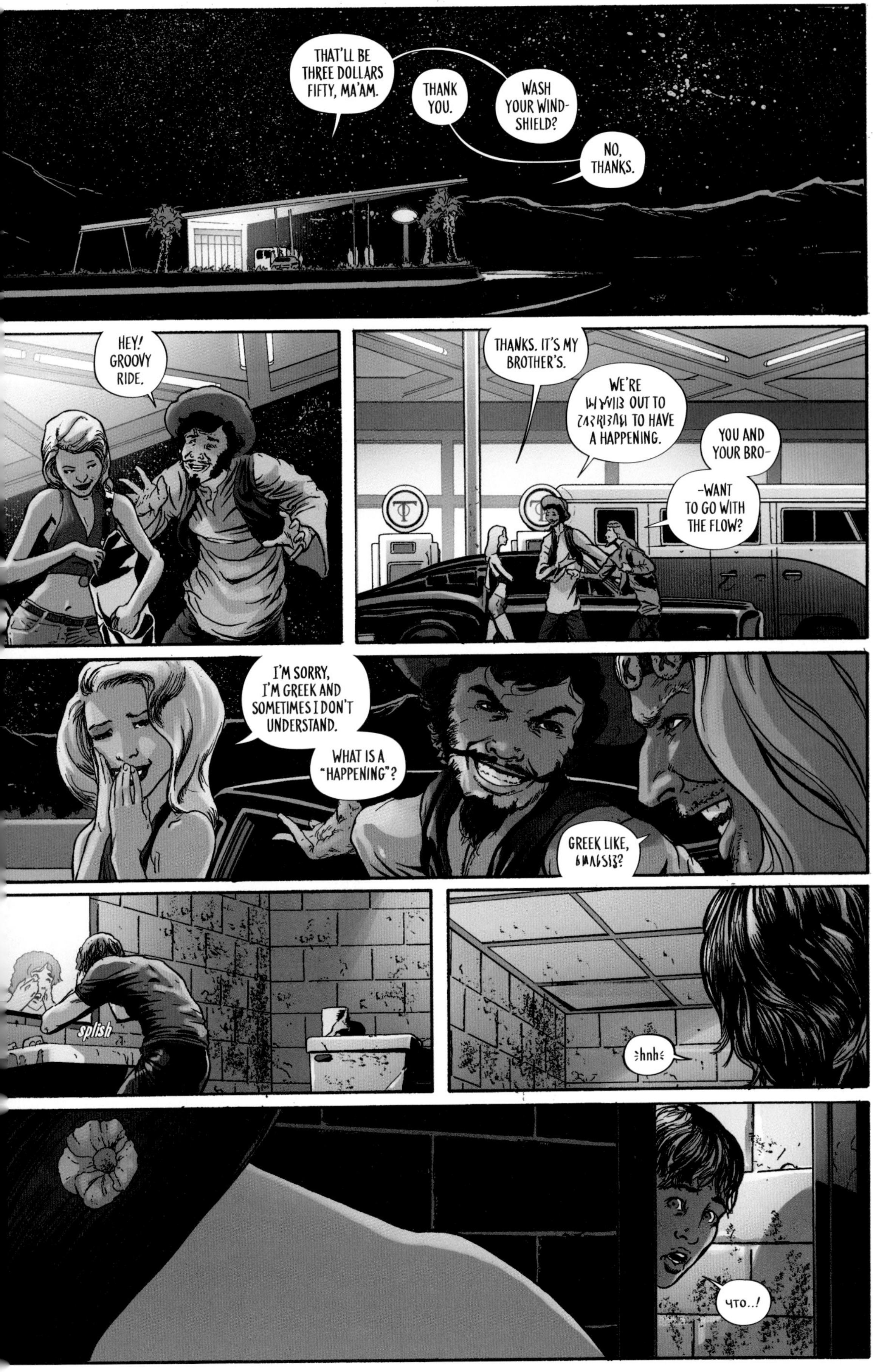
THAT'LL BE THREE DOLLARS FIFTY, MA'AM.
THANK YOU.
WASH YOUR WIND-SHIELD?
NO, THANKS.
HEY! GROOVY RIDE.
THANKS. IT'S MY BROTHER'S.
WE'RE OUT TO TO HAVE A HAPPENING.
YOU AND YOUR BRO-
-WANT TO GO WITH THE FLOW?
I'M SORRY, I'M GREEK AND SOMETIMES I DON'T UNDERSTAND.
WHAT IS A "HAPPENING"?
GREEK LIKE,
splish
hnh
ЧТО..!

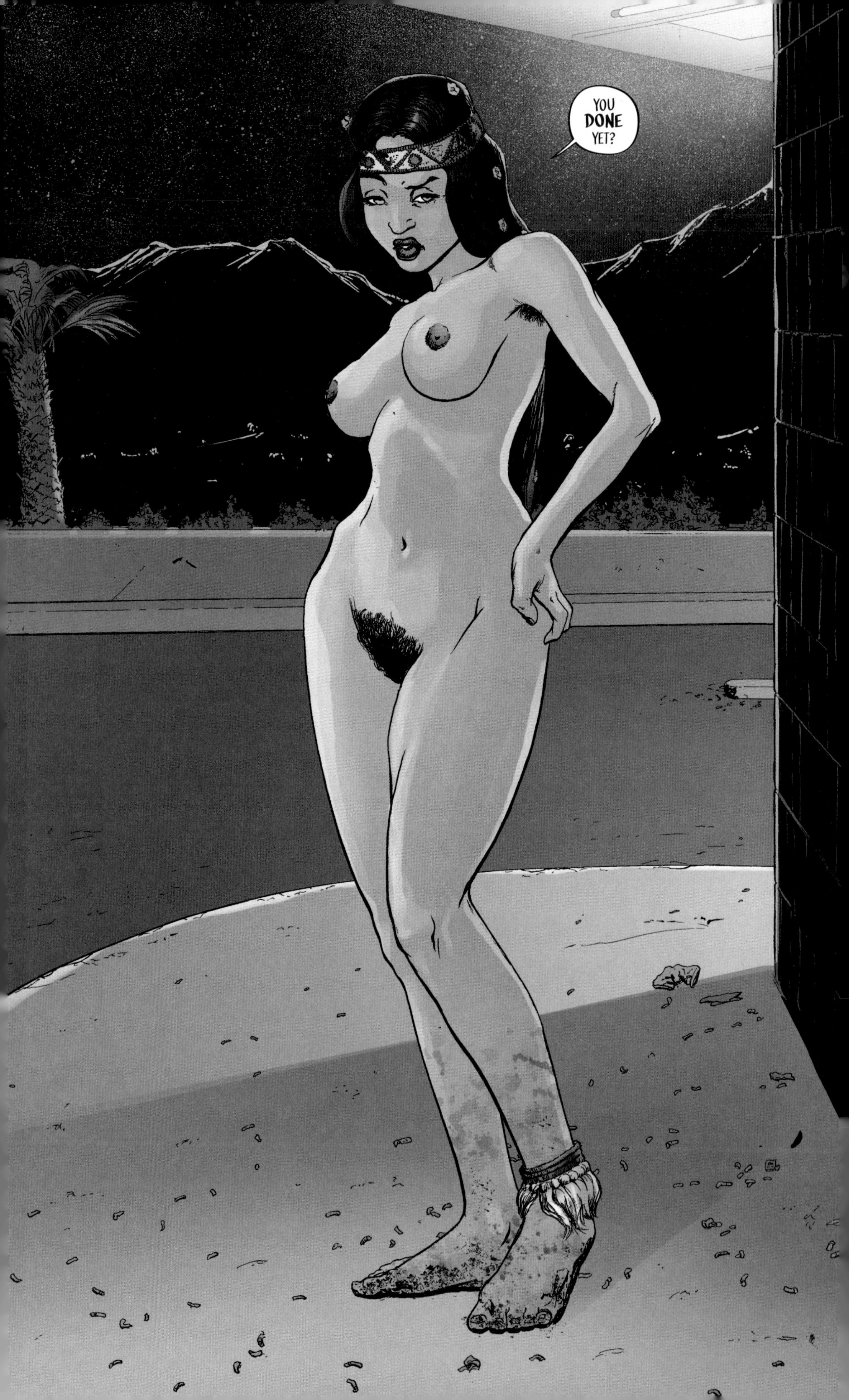
YOU DONE YET?

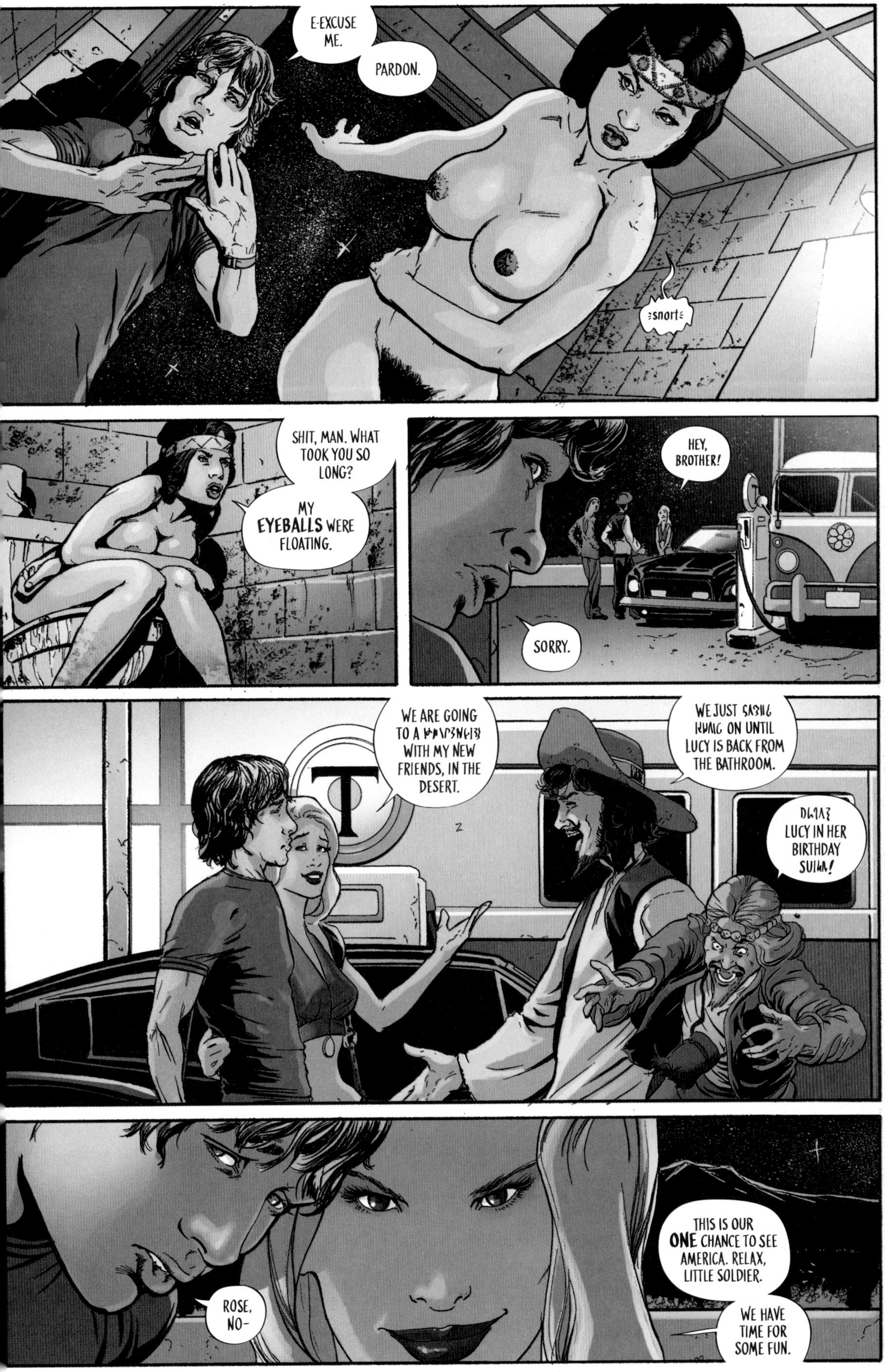
E-EXCUSE ME.
PARDON.
snort
SHIT, MAN. WHAT TOOK YOU SO LONG?
MY EYEBALLS WERE FLOATING.
HEY, BROTHER!
SORRY.
WE ARE GOING TO A
WITH MY NEW FRIENDS, IN THE DESERT.
WE JUST
ON UNTIL LUCY IS BACK FROM THE BATHROOM.
LUCY IN HER BIRTHDAY
THIS IS OUR ONE CHANCE TO SEE AMERICA. RELAX, LITTLE SOLDIER.
ROSE, NO-
WE HAVE TIME FOR SOME FUN.

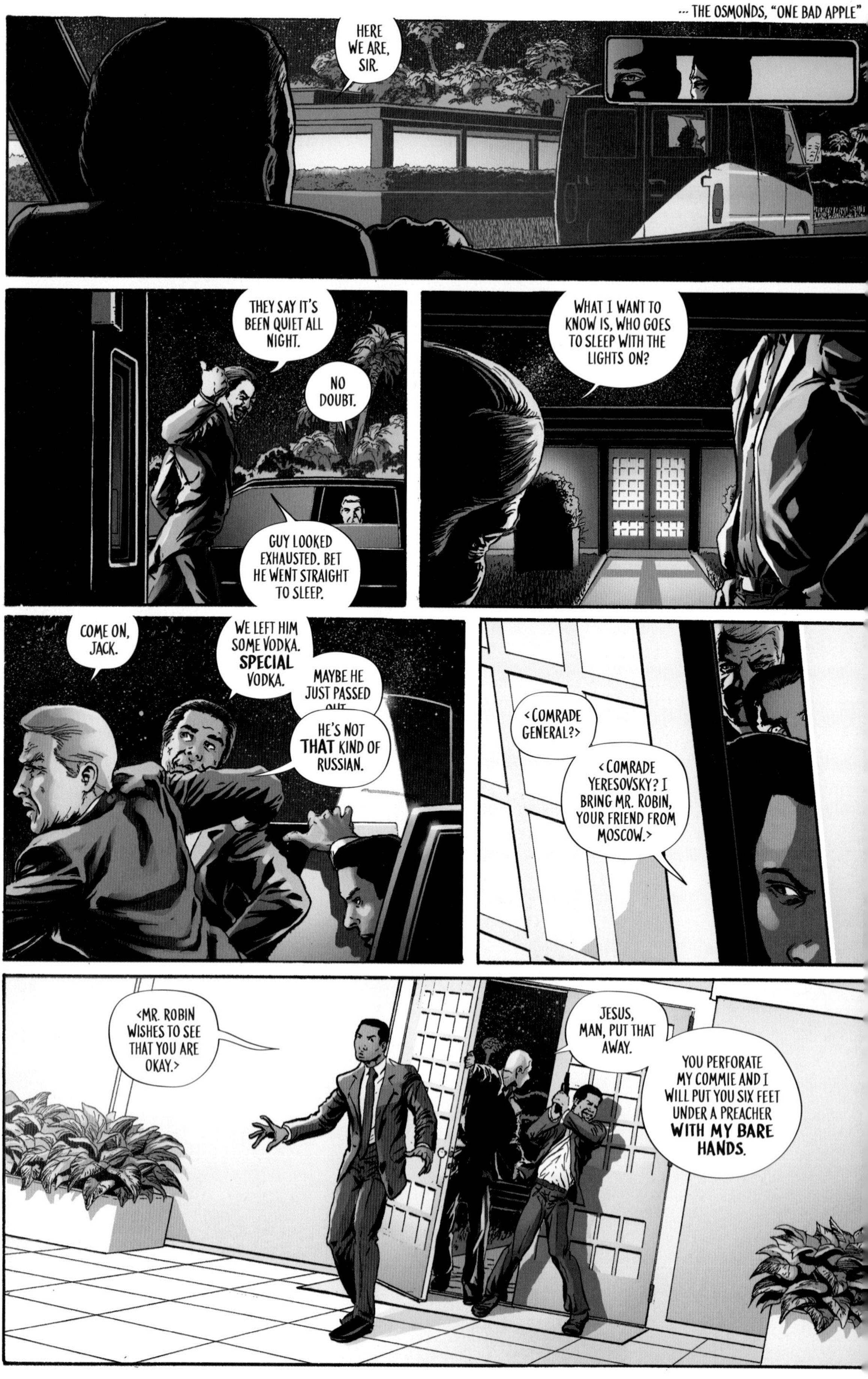
HERE WE ARE, SIR.
THEY SAY IT'S BEEN QUIET ALL NIGHT.
NO DOUBT.
GUY LOOKED EXHAUSTED. BET HE WENT STRAIGHT TO SLEEP.
WHAT I WANT TO KNOW IS, WHO GOES TO SLEEP WITH THE LIGHTS ON?
COME ON, JACK.
WE LEFT HIM SOME VODKA. **SPECIAL** VODKA.
MAYBE HE JUST PASSED
HE'S NOT **THAT** KIND OF RUSSIAN.
<COMRADE GENERAL?>
<COMRADE YERESOVSKY? I BRING MR. ROBIN, YOUR FRIEND FROM MOSCOW.>
<MR. ROBIN WISHES TO SEE THAT YOU ARE OKAY.>
JESUS, MAN, PUT THAT AWAY.
YOU PERFORATE MY COMMIE AND I WILL PUT YOU SIX FEET UNDER A PREACHER **WITH MY BARE HANDS**.

OUR GAME HAS TWO RULES, COWBOY.

ONE, WIVES AND KIDS ARE OFF LIMITS.

<COMRADE..?>

TWO, WE DON'T SHOOT AT EACH OTHER'S OPERATIVES.

BECAUSE ONCE WE LET THAT DEVIL OUT OF THE BOTTLE, WE'LL NEVER GET HIM BACK IN.

WHERE DOES A MAN WHO SPEAKS NO ENGLISH GO, IN THE MIDDLE OF THE NIGHT, WITH NO CLOTHES, A BAG OF STATE SECRETS, AND A BOTTLE OF VODKA?

UM... A REALLY GOOD PARTY?

WHEREVER HE IS, WHOEVER HAS HIM, THEY WON'T GET FAR IF THEY CRACKED OPEN THAT VODKA.

NO SIREE BOB.

IT'S LACED WITH MY OWN SPECIAL RECIPE.

SODIUM PENTOTHAL AND L.S.D.

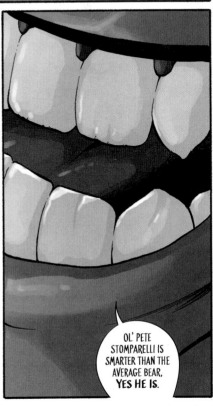

OL' PETE STOMPARELLI IS SMARTER THAN THE AVERAGE BEAR, YES HE IS.

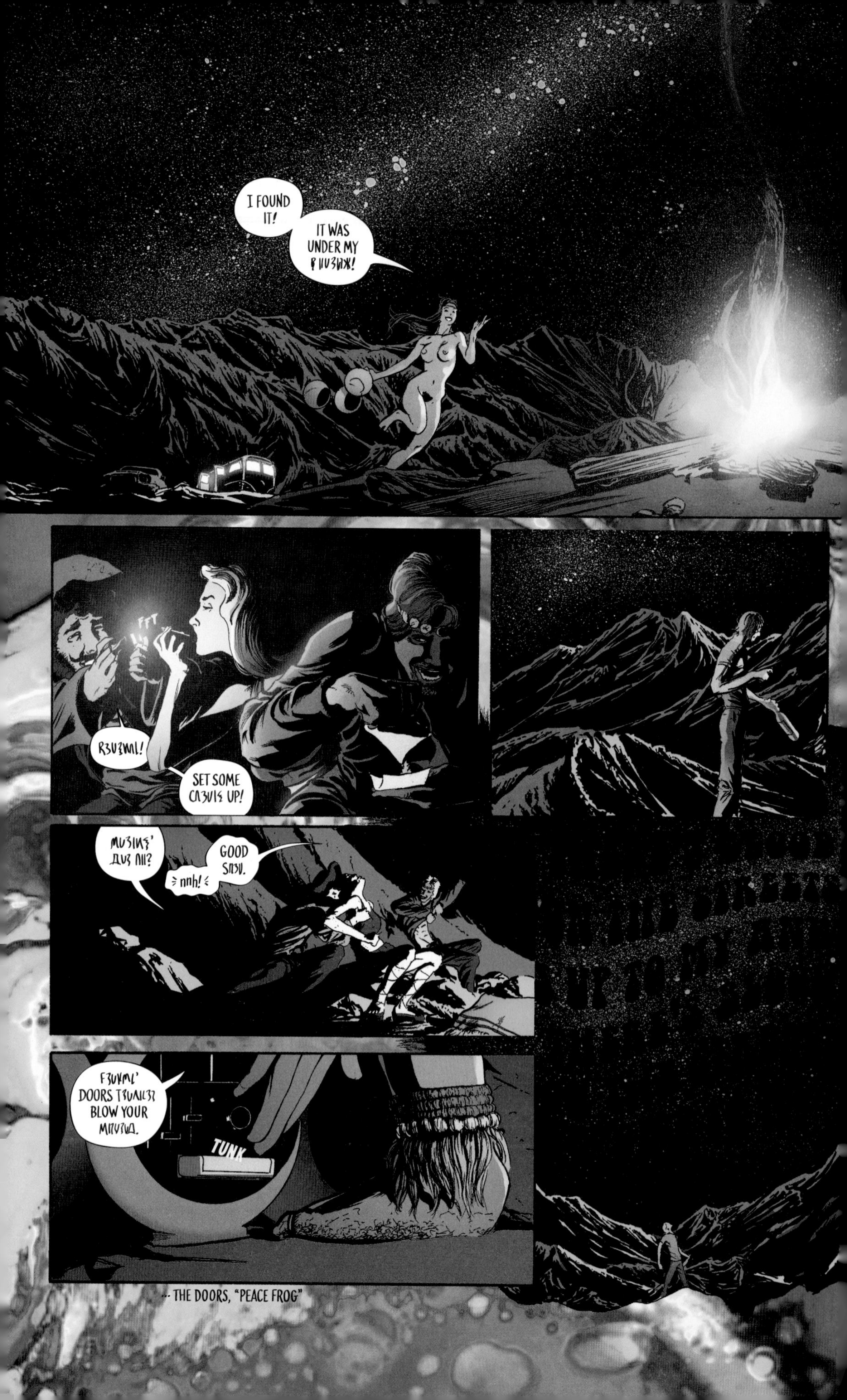
I FOUND IT!
IT WAS UNDER MY
SET SOME
UP!
GOOD
nnh!
DOORS
BLOW YOUR
TUNK
... THE DOORS, "PEACE FROG"

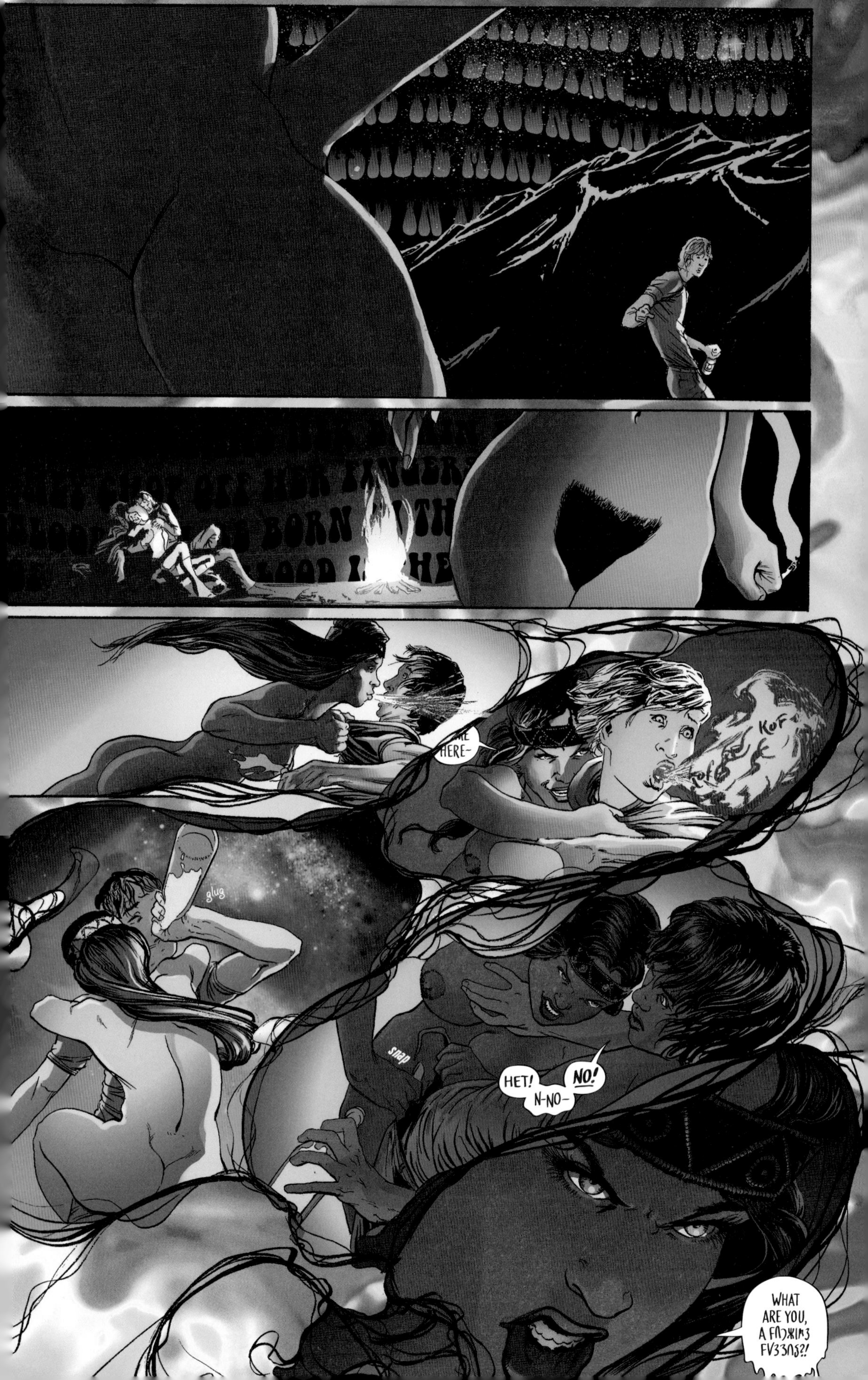
ME HERE-
KOF KOF
glug
snap
HET!
N-NO-
NO!
WHAT ARE YOU,

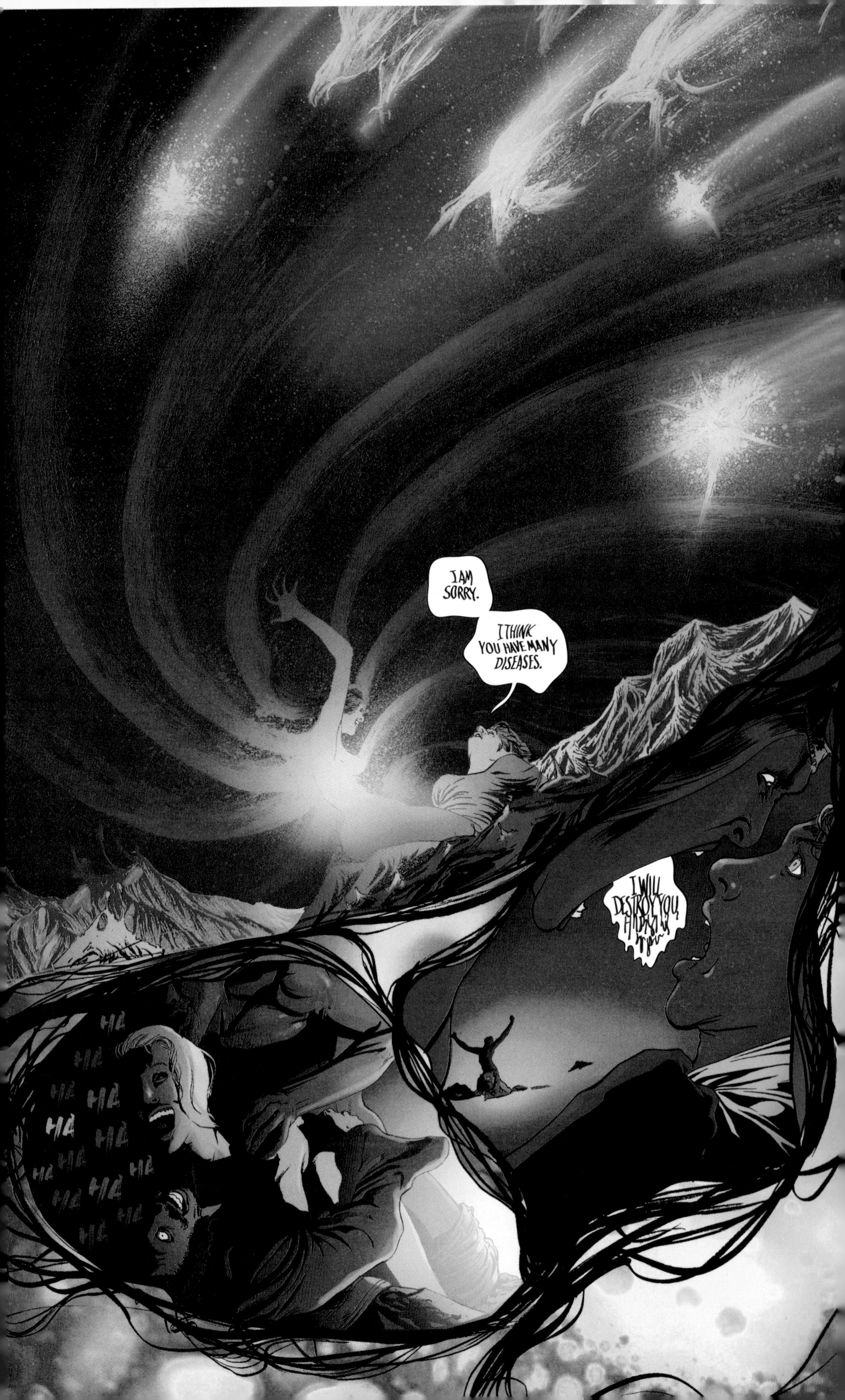
I AM SORRY.
I THINK YOU HAVE MANY DISEASES.
I WILL DESTROY YOU,
HA HA HA HA HA HA HA HA HA HA HA HA HA

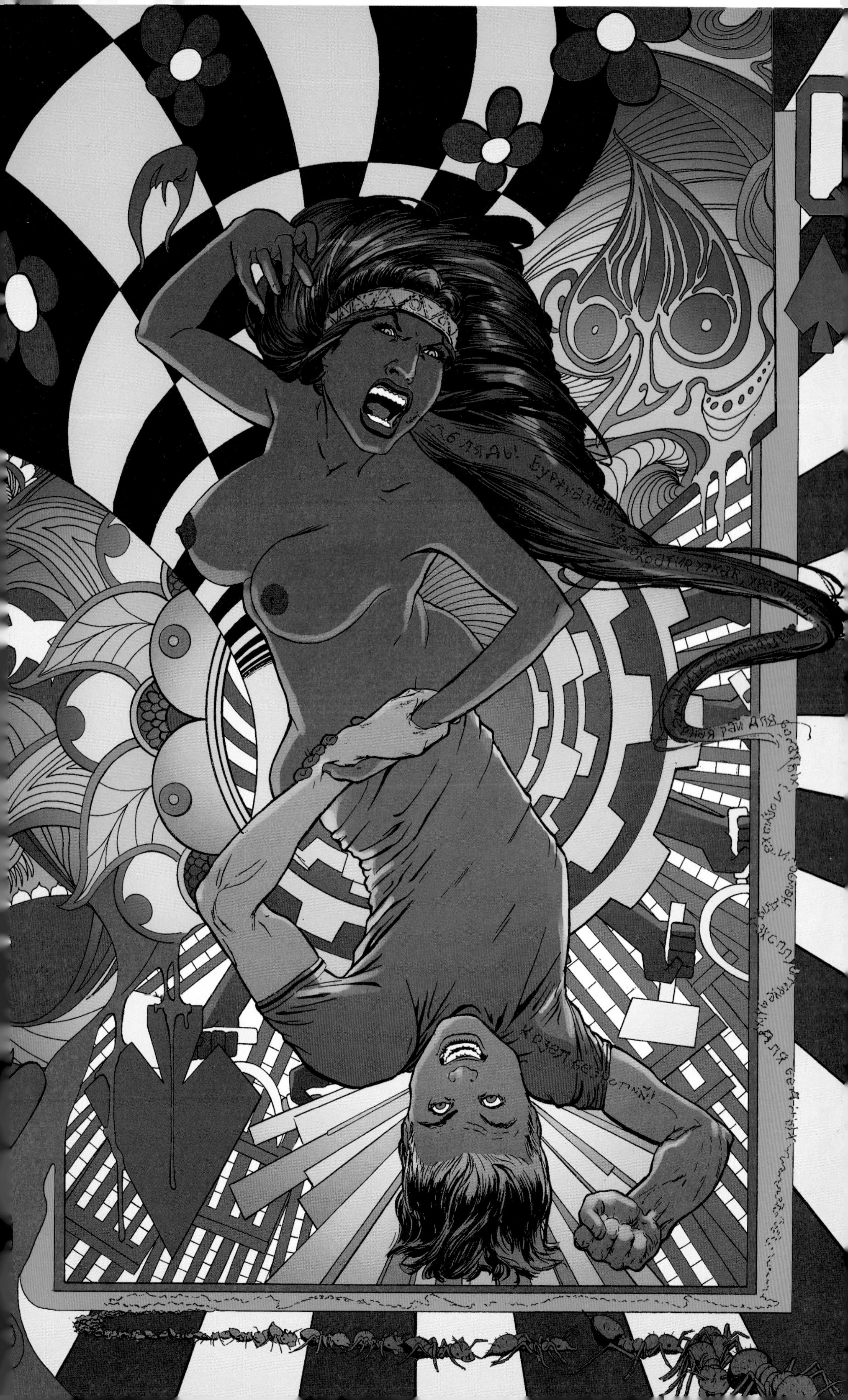

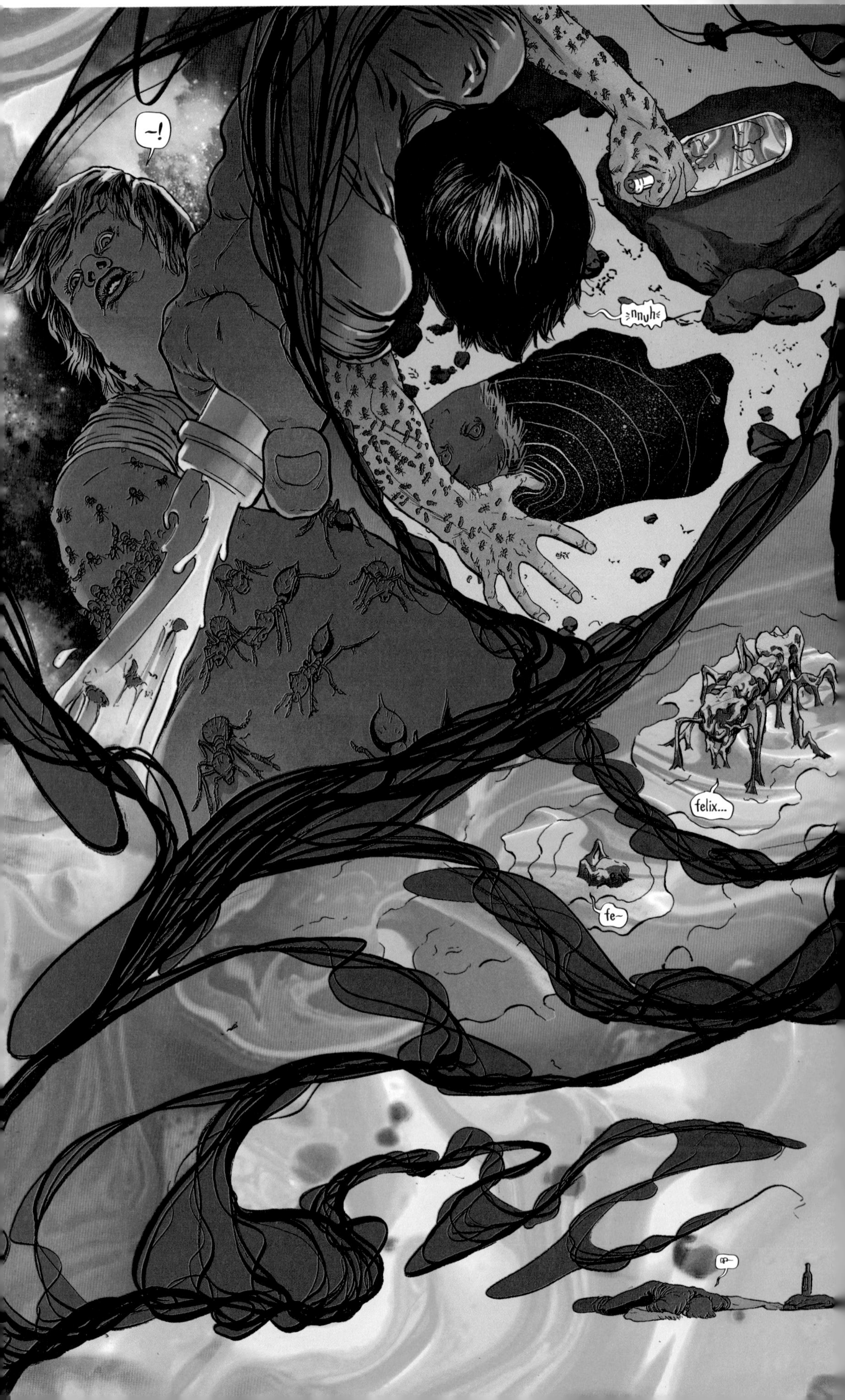
~!
nnuh
felix...
fe~

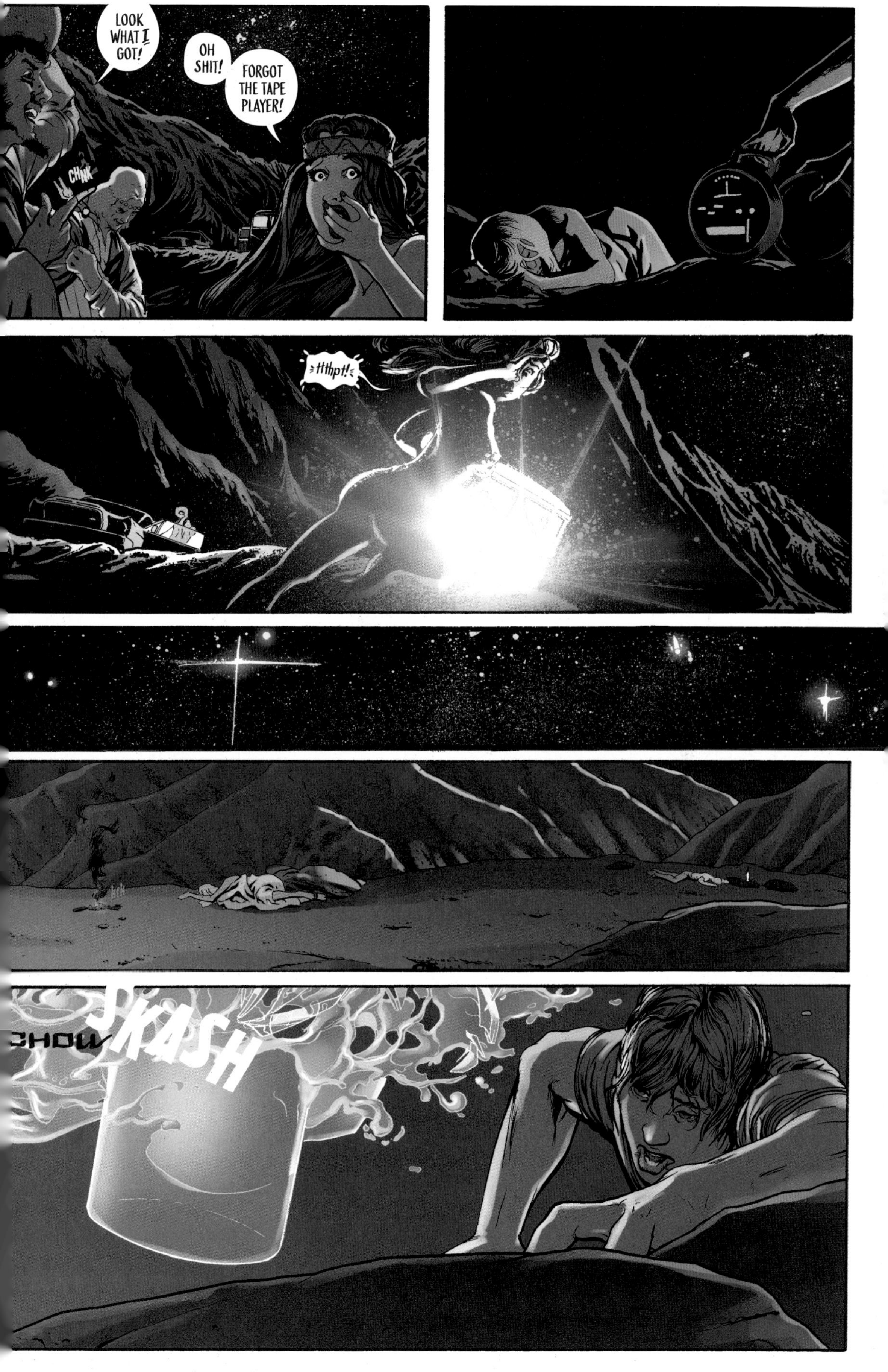
LOOK WHAT I GOT!
CHINK
OH SHIT!
FORGOT THE TAPE PLAYER!
ttthpt!
CHOW
SKASH

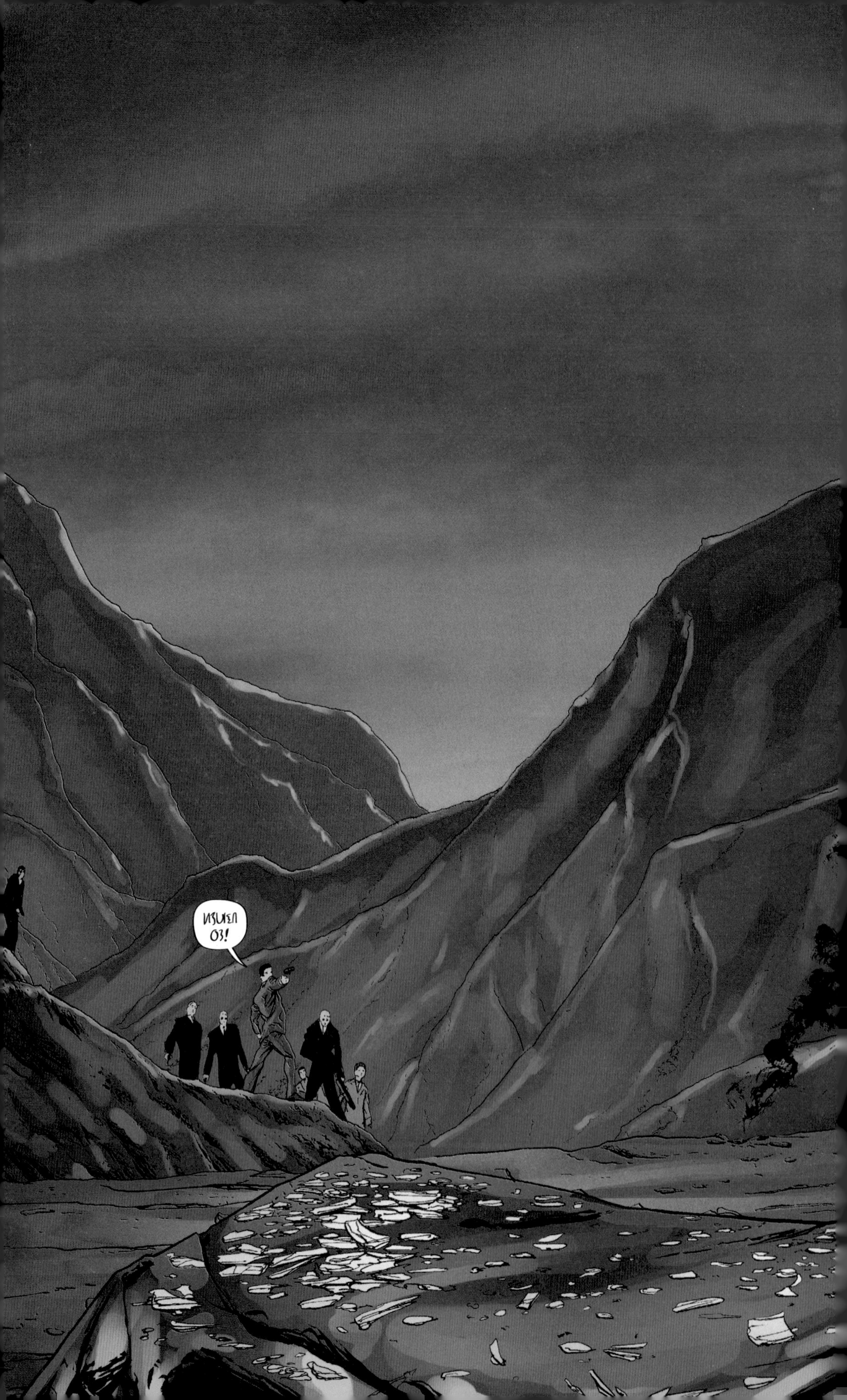

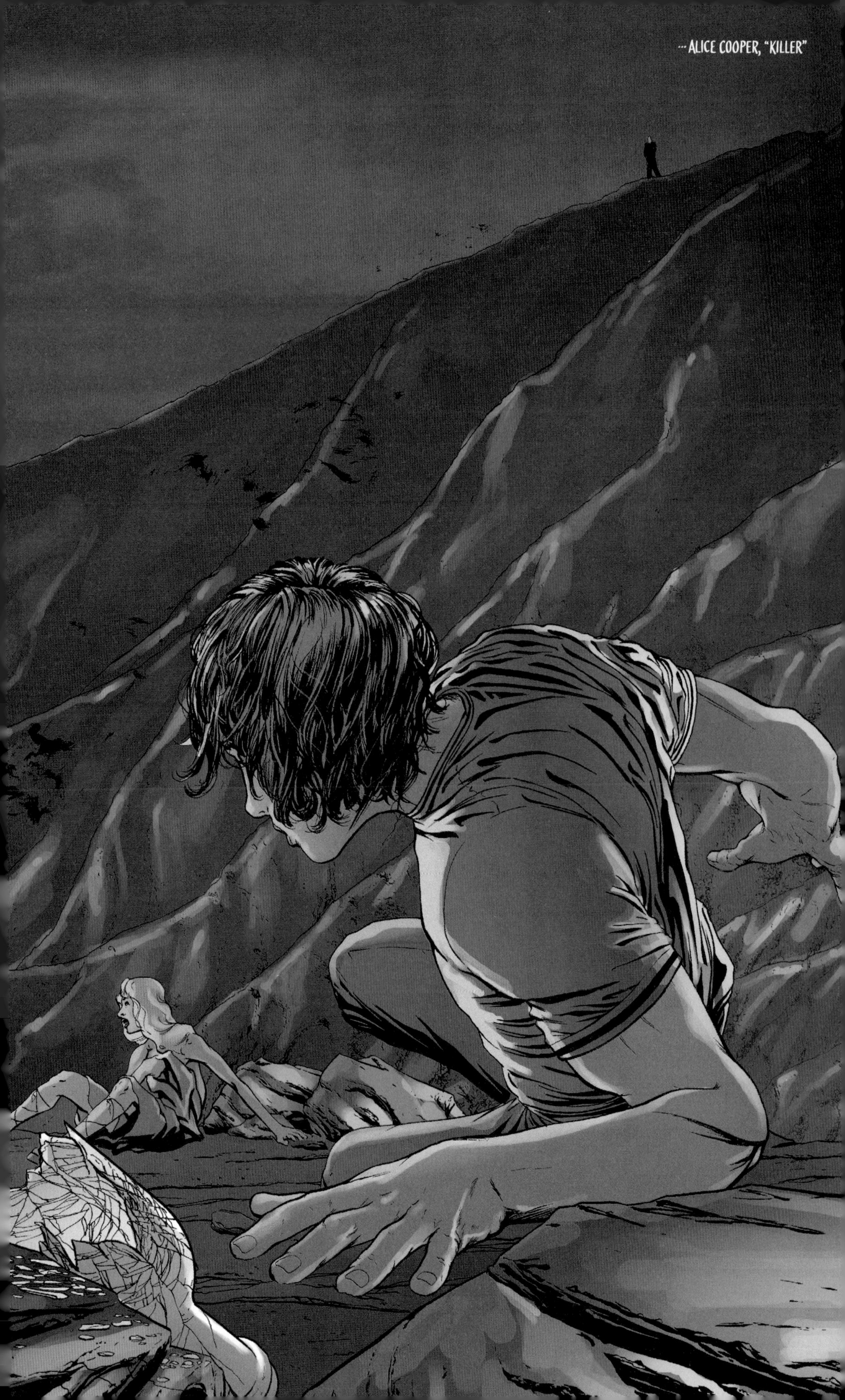
... ALICE COOPER, "KILLER"

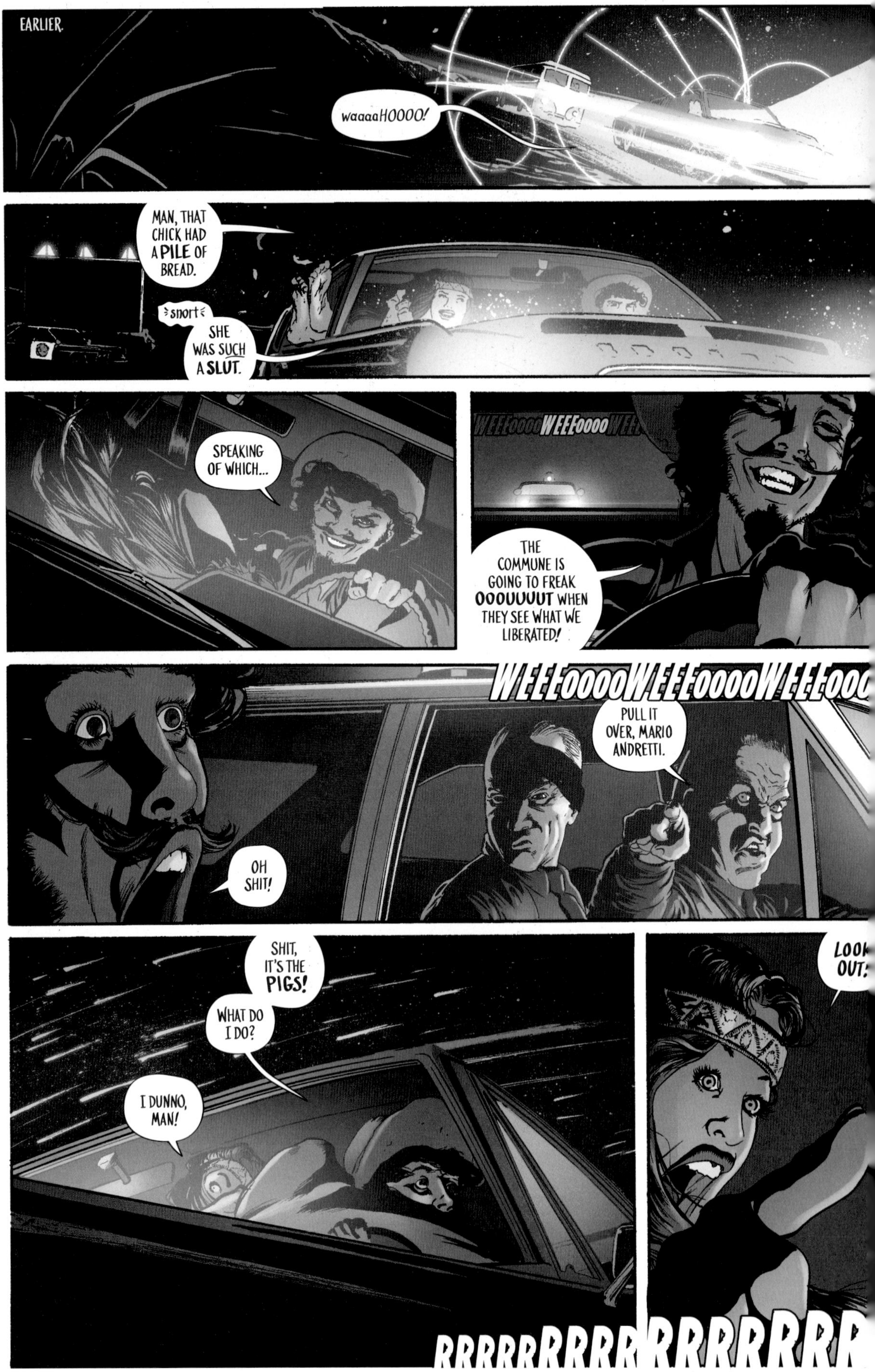

EARLIER.
waaaaHOOOO!
MAN, THAT CHICK HAD A PILE OF BREAD.
snort
SHE WAS SUCH A SLUT.
SPEAKING OF WHICH...
WEEEooooWEEEooooWEE
THE COMMUNE IS GOING TO FREAK OOOUUUUT WHEN THEY SEE WHAT WE LIBERATED!
WEEEooooWEEEooooWEEEooo
PULL IT OVER, MARIO ANDRETTI.
OH SHIT!
SHIT, IT'S THE PIGS!
WHAT DO I DO?
I DUNNO, MAN!
LOOK OUT!
RRRRRRRRRRRRRRRRRR

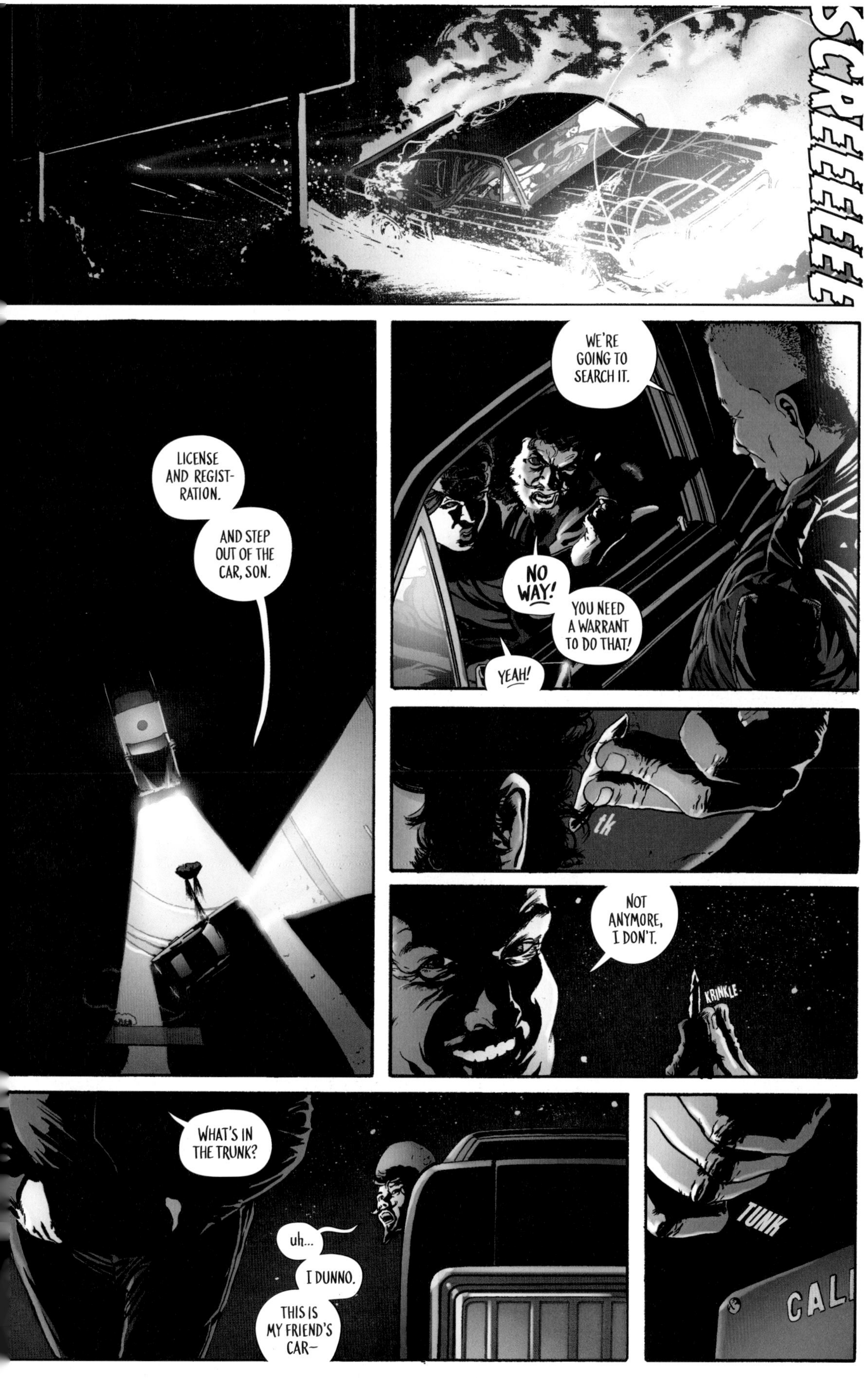
SCREEEEEE
LICENSE AND REGISTRATION.
AND STEP OUT OF THE CAR, SON.
WE'RE GOING TO SEARCH IT.
NO WAY!
YOU NEED A WARRANT TO DO THAT!
YEAH!
tk
NOT ANYMORE, I DON'T.
KRINKLE
WHAT'S IN THE TRUNK?
uh...
I DUNNO.
THIS IS MY FRIEND'S CAR–
TUNK
CALI

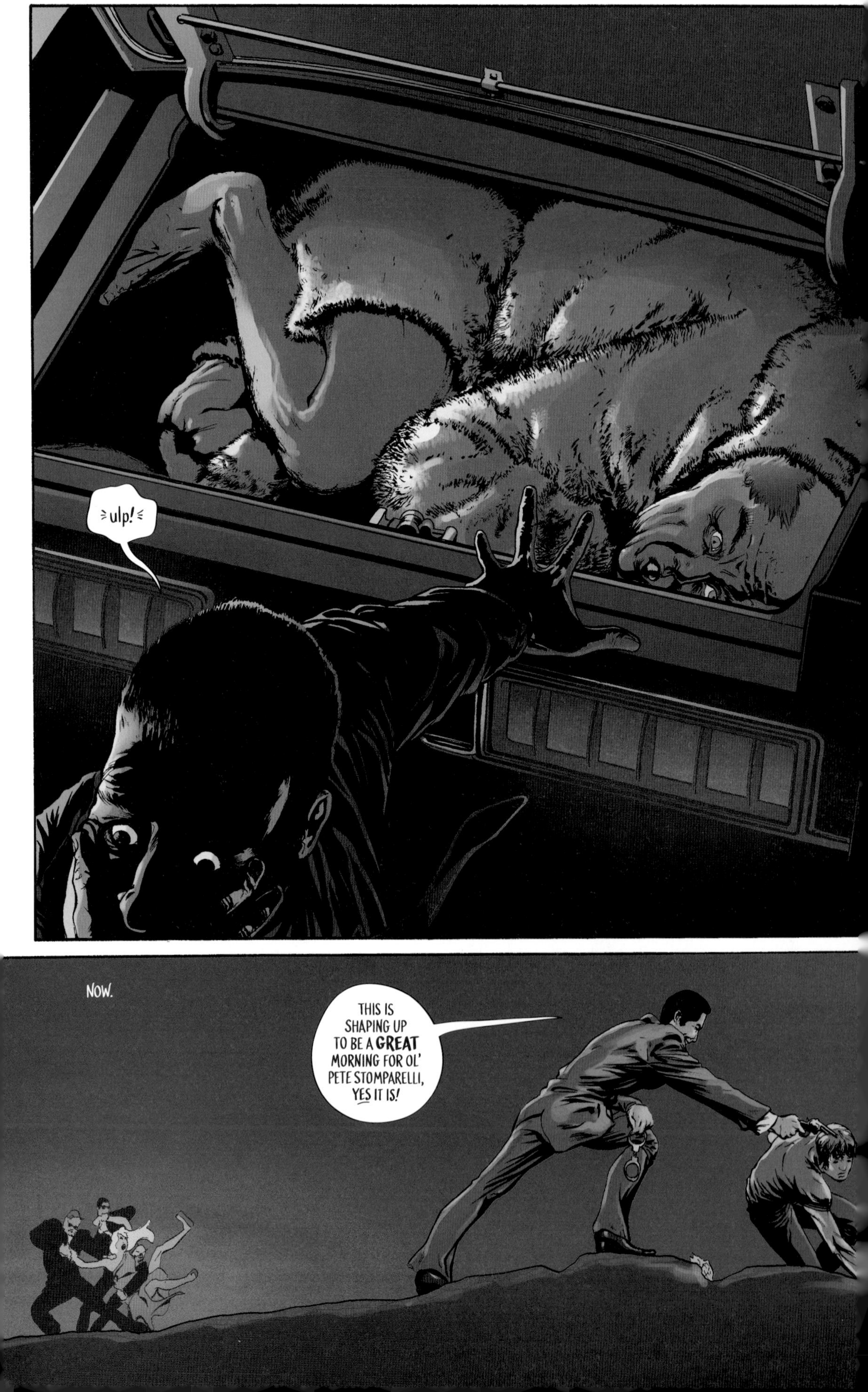
ulp!
NOW.
THIS IS SHAPING UP TO BE A GREAT MORNING FOR OL' PETE STOMPARELLI, YES IT IS!

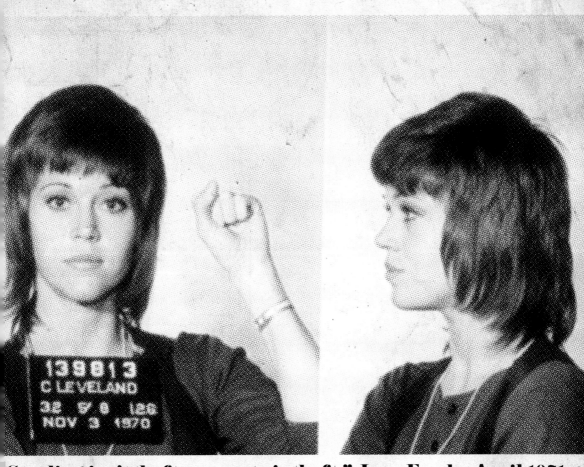

Stealing isn't theft; property is theft." Jane Fonda, April 1971

TWO

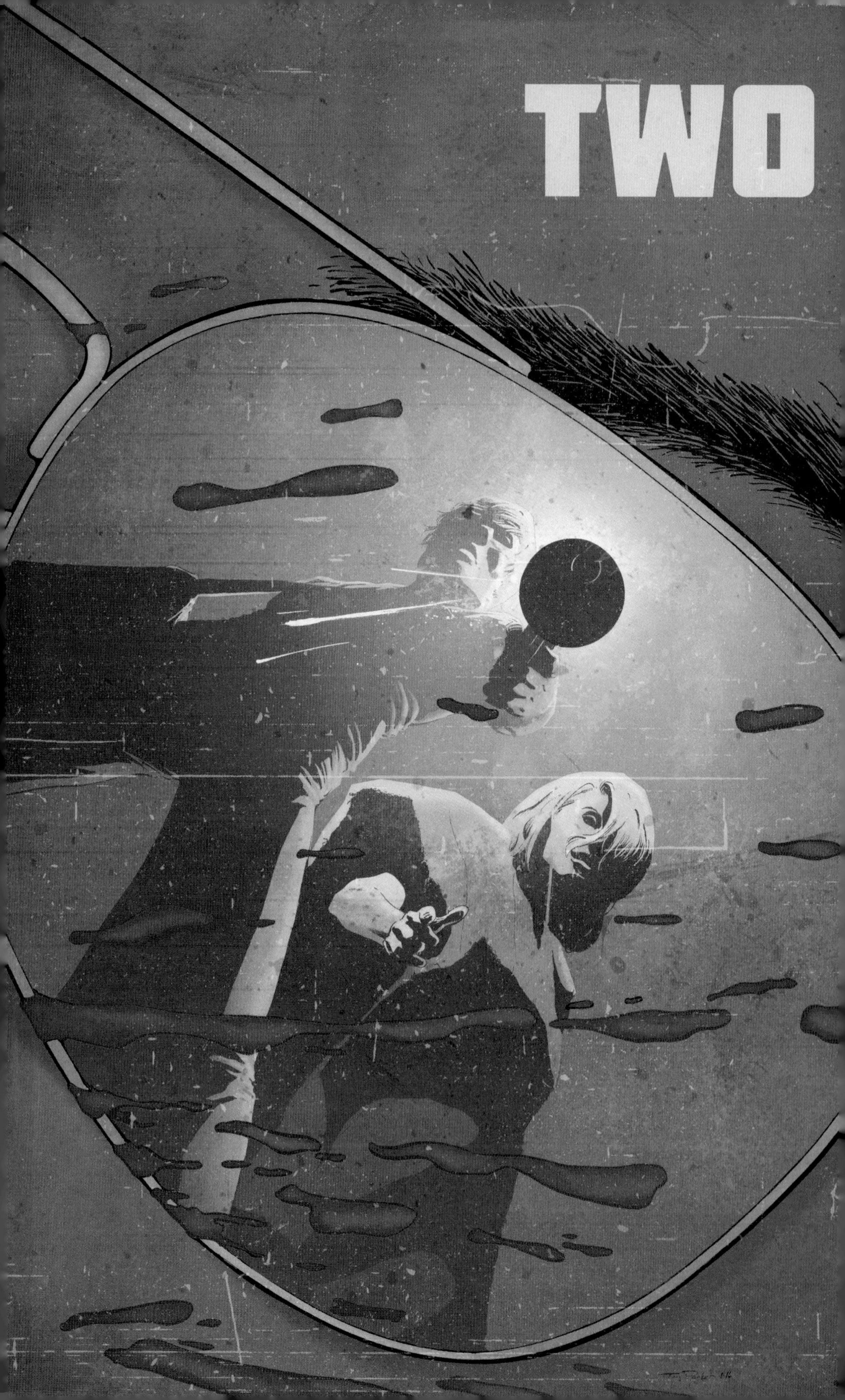

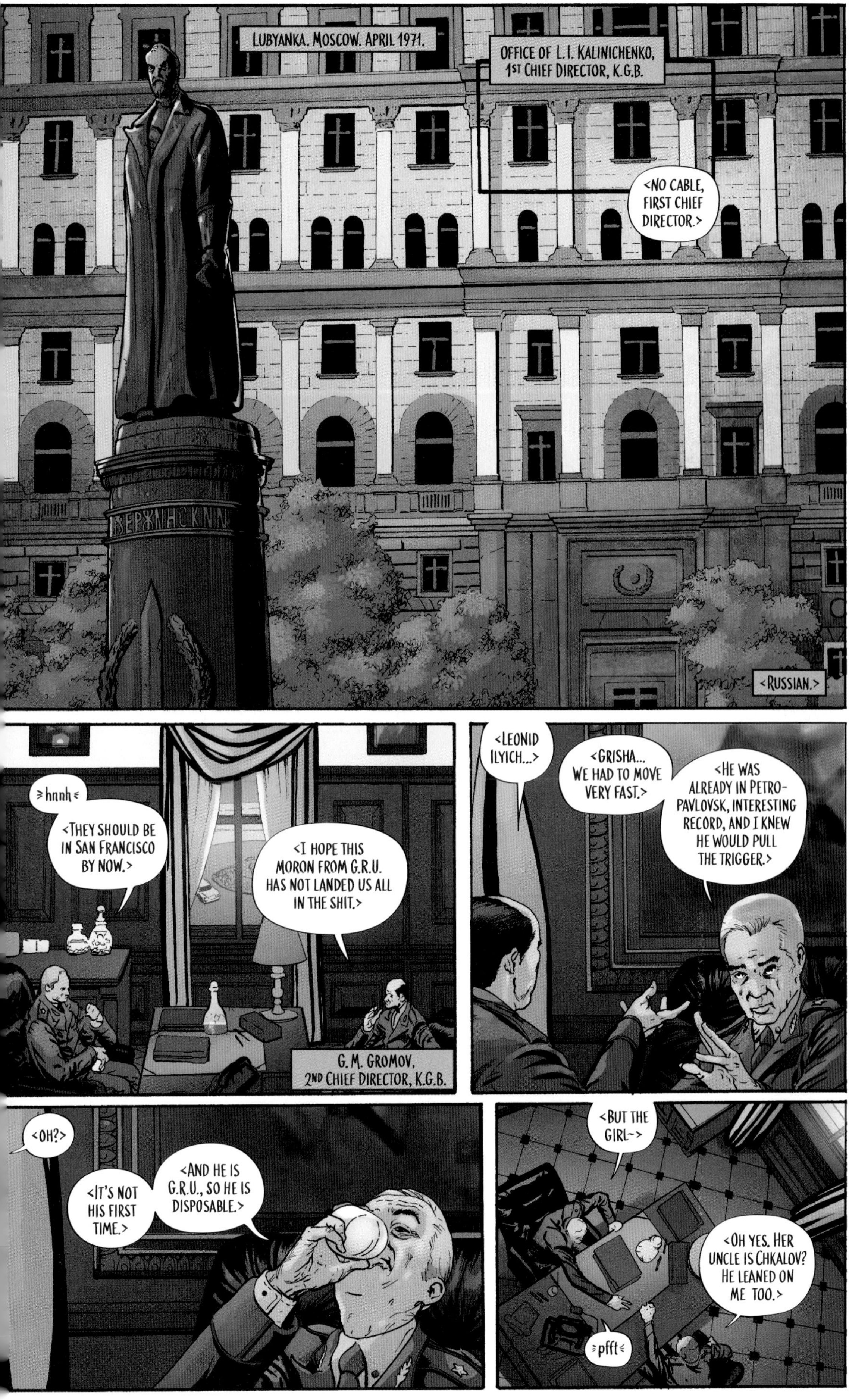
LUBYANKA. MOSCOW. APRIL 1971.
OFFICE OF L. I. KALINICHENKO, 1ST CHIEF DIRECTOR, K.G.B.
<NO CABLE, FIRST CHIEF DIRECTOR.>
<RUSSIAN.>
hnnh
<THEY SHOULD BE IN SAN FRANCISCO BY NOW.>
<I HOPE THIS MORON FROM G.R.U. HAS NOT LANDED US ALL IN THE SHIT.>
G. M. GROMOV, 2ND CHIEF DIRECTOR, K.G.B.
<LEONID ILYICH...>
<GRISHA... WE HAD TO MOVE VERY FAST.>
<HE WAS ALREADY IN PETRO-PAVLOVSK, INTERESTING RECORD, AND I KNEW HE WOULD PULL THE TRIGGER.>
<OH?>
<IT'S NOT HIS FIRST TIME.>
<AND HE IS G.R.U., SO HE IS DISPOSABLE.>
<BUT THE GIRL~>
<OH YES. HER UNCLE IS CHKALOV? HE LEANED ON ME TOO.>
pfft

<ON THE ONE HAND, IF YERESOVSKY HAD NOT BEEN MAKING PASSES AT HER, WE WOULD HAVE KNOWN **NOTHING**.>

<ON THE OTHER, THE DEVIL KEEP US FROM AMBITIOUS WOMEN.>

<SHE THINKS SHE HAS A CAREER **HERE**?>

<SHE IS LINE X IN HONG KONG. DOES OKAY, ACTUALLY.>

<BUT, GRISHA... THESE APPARATCHIKS WILL BE THE DEATH OF US.>

<DON'T TELL ME. YOU SHOULD SEE THE IDIOT I HAD TO TAKE YESTERDAY.>

<I'M NOT SURE HE CAN **READ**.>

<K.G.B. IS THE BEST COVERT AGENCY IN THE WORLD BECAUSE RUSSIAN PEOPLE KEEP SECRETS FROM THE CRADLE.>

<WE LIVE LIFE IN THE SHADOW OF THE GULAG.>

<BUT THESE YOUNG APPARATCHIKS... THEY DO NOT UNDERSTAND THIS.>

<THEY CANNOT EVEN CONCEIVE OF THE POSSIBILITY OF LOSS.>

<SO SHE DOES NOT KNOW YET ABOUT CHKALOV, THEN?>

<ONLY THE CENTRAL COMMITTEE KNOWS.>

<AND US, OF COURSE. ALWAYS US.>

≥tchaa≤

<WHY IS THERE NO CABLE?>

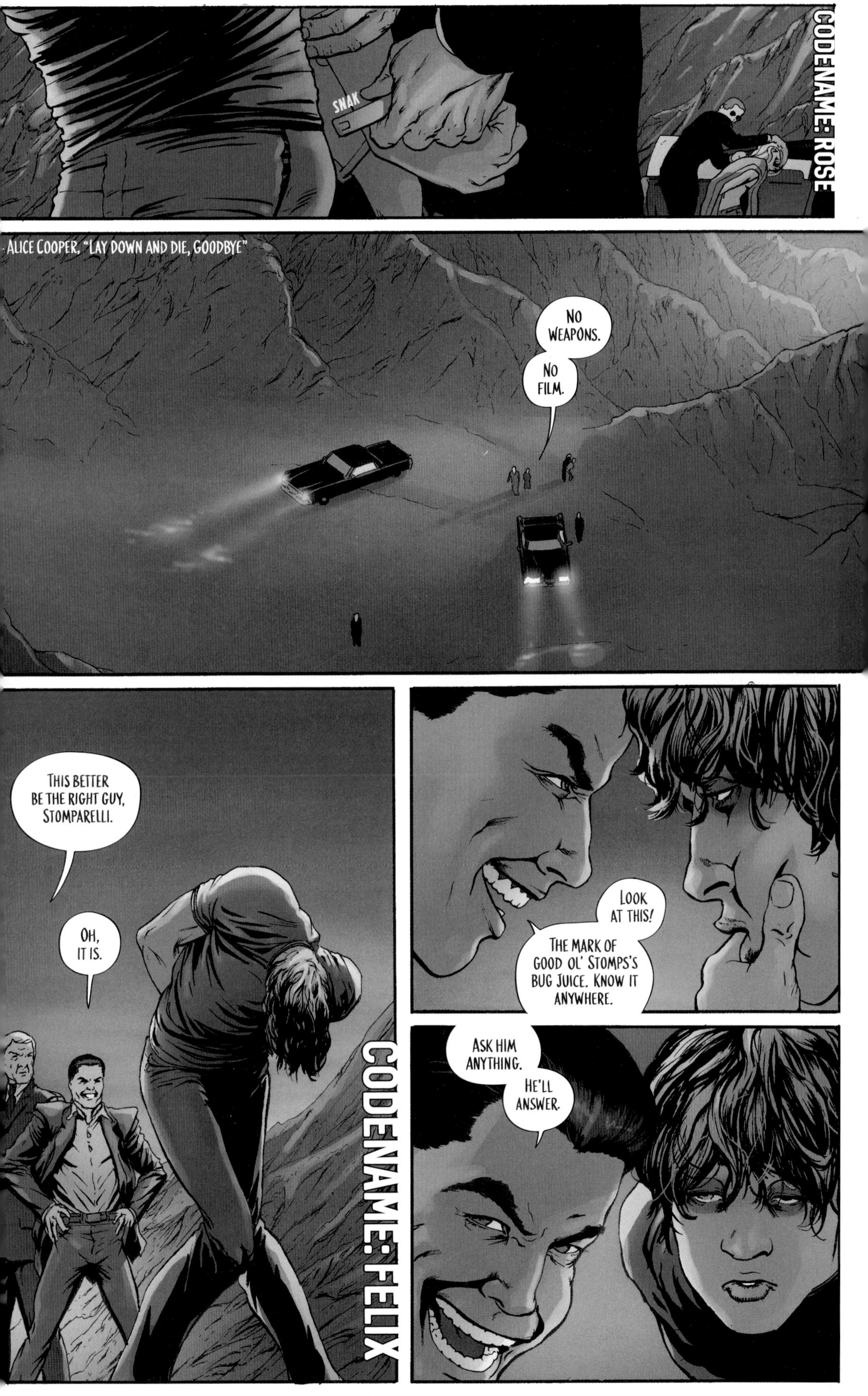
SNAK
CODENAME: ROSE
- ALICE COOPER, "LAY DOWN AND DIE, GOODBYE"
NO WEAPONS.
NO FILM.
THIS BETTER BE THE RIGHT GUY, STOMPARELLI.
OH, IT IS.
CODENAME: FELIX
LOOK AT THIS!
THE MARK OF GOOD OL' STOMPS'S BUG JUICE. KNOW IT ANYWHERE.
ASK HIM ANYTHING.
HE'LL ANSWER.

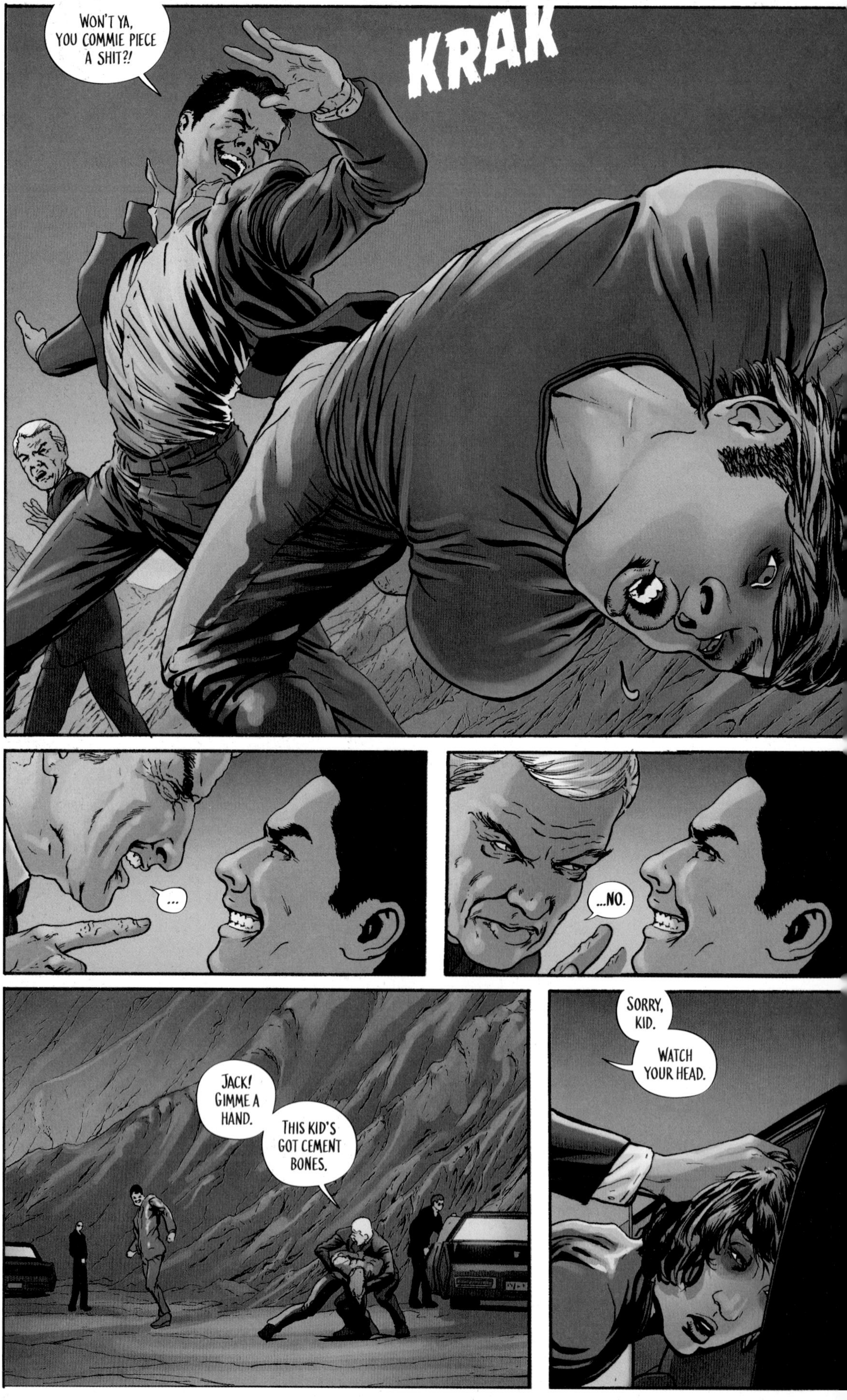
WON'T YA, YOU COMMIE PIECE A SHIT?!
KRAK
...
...NO.
JACK! GIMME A HAND.
THIS KID'S GOT CEMENT BONES.
SORRY, KID.
WATCH YOUR HEAD.

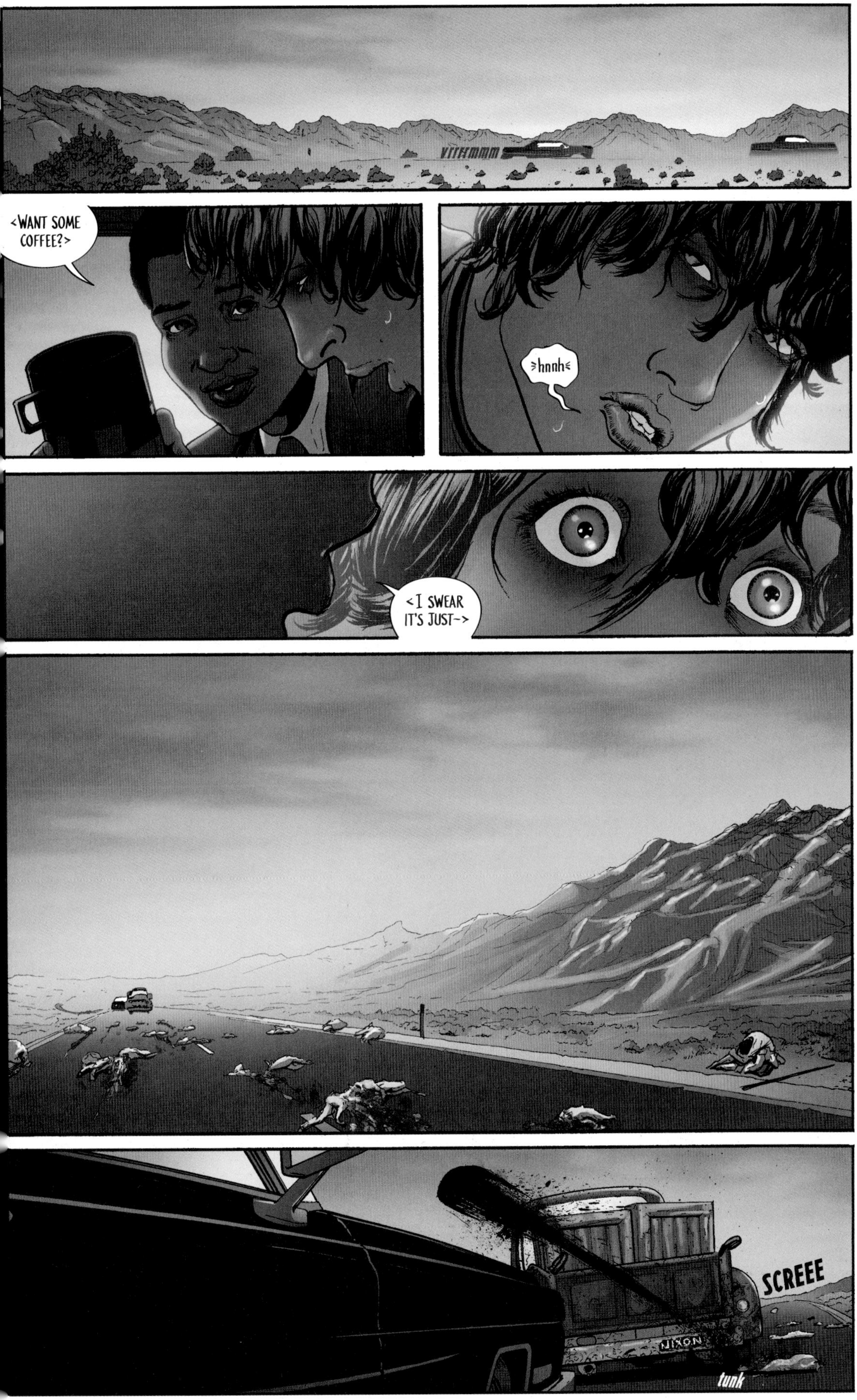
VRRRMMM
<WANT SOME COFFEE?>
hnnh
<I SWEAR IT'S JUST->
SCREEE
NIXON
tunk

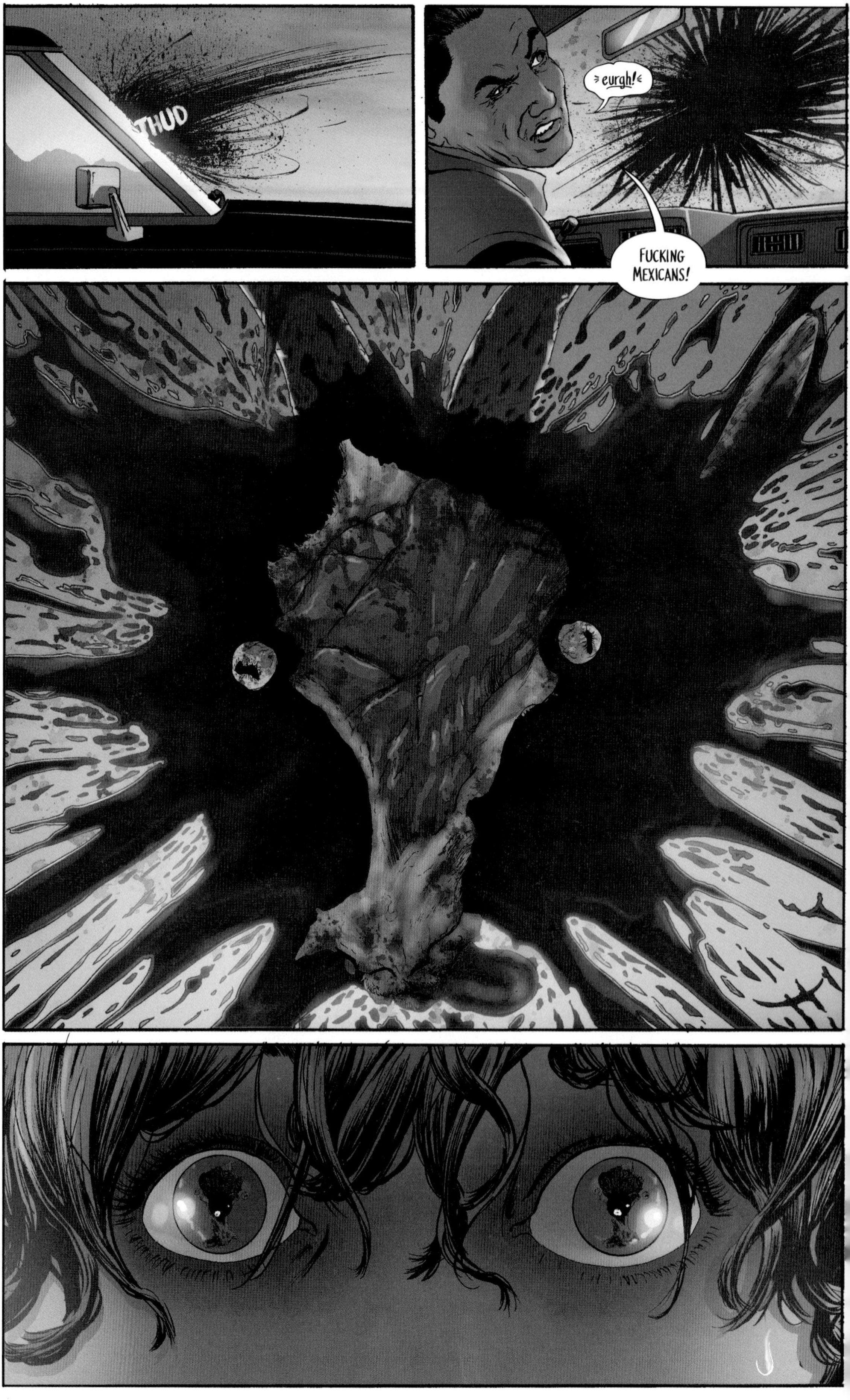
THUD
eurgh!
FUCKING MEXICANS!

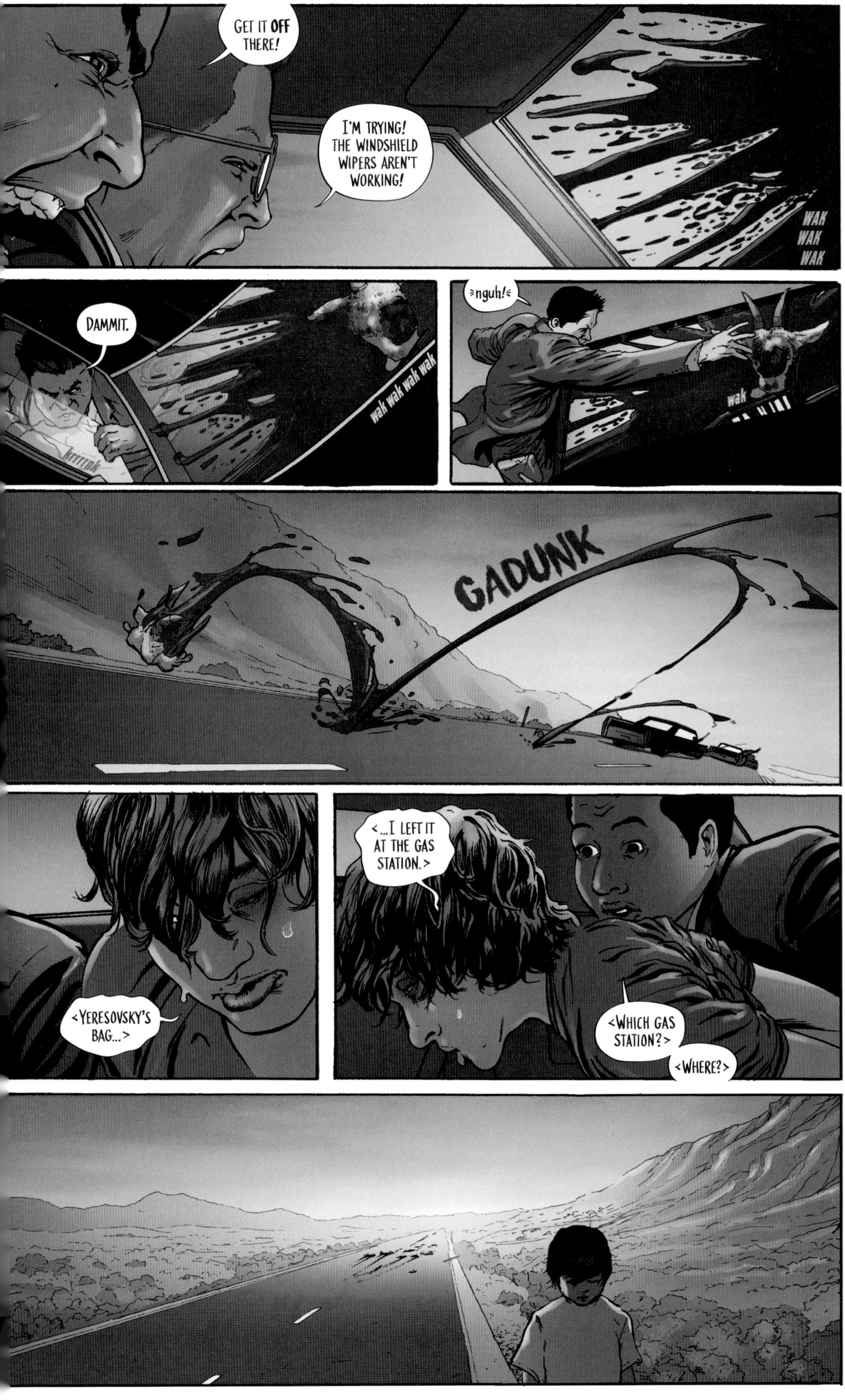
GET IT OFF THERE!
I'M TRYING! THE WINDSHIELD WIPERS AREN'T WORKING!
WAK WAK WAK
DAMMIT.
wak wak wak wak
krrrak
nguh!
wak
GADUNK
<...I LEFT IT AT THE GAS STATION.>
<YERESOVSKY'S BAG...>
<WHICH GAS STATION?>
<WHERE?>

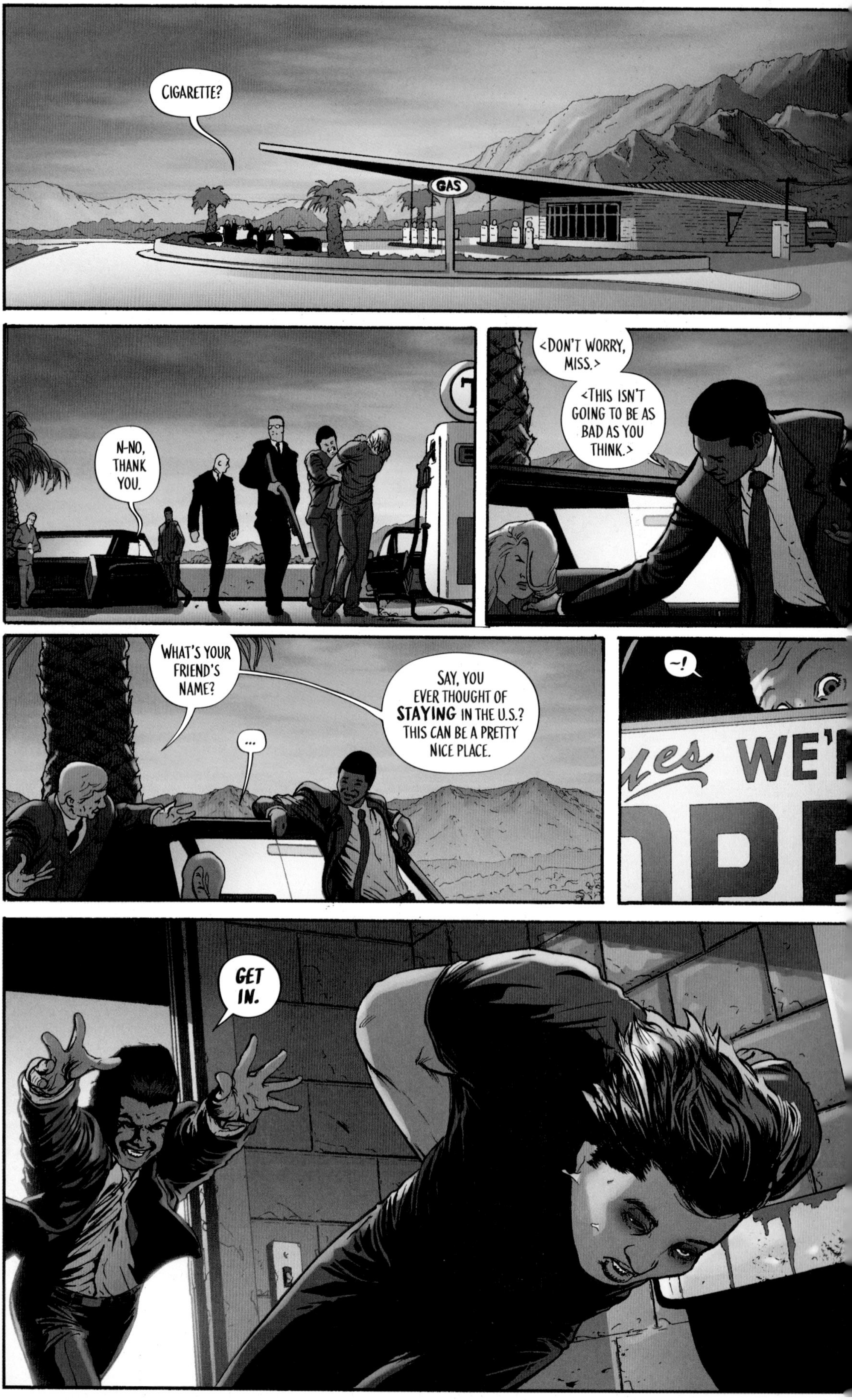
CIGARETTE?
N-NO, THANK YOU.
<DON'T WORRY, MISS.>
<THIS ISN'T GOING TO BE AS BAD AS YOU THINK.>
WHAT'S YOUR FRIEND'S NAME?
...
SAY, YOU EVER THOUGHT OF **STAYING** IN THE U.S.? THIS CAN BE A PRETTY NICE PLACE.
~!
GET IN.

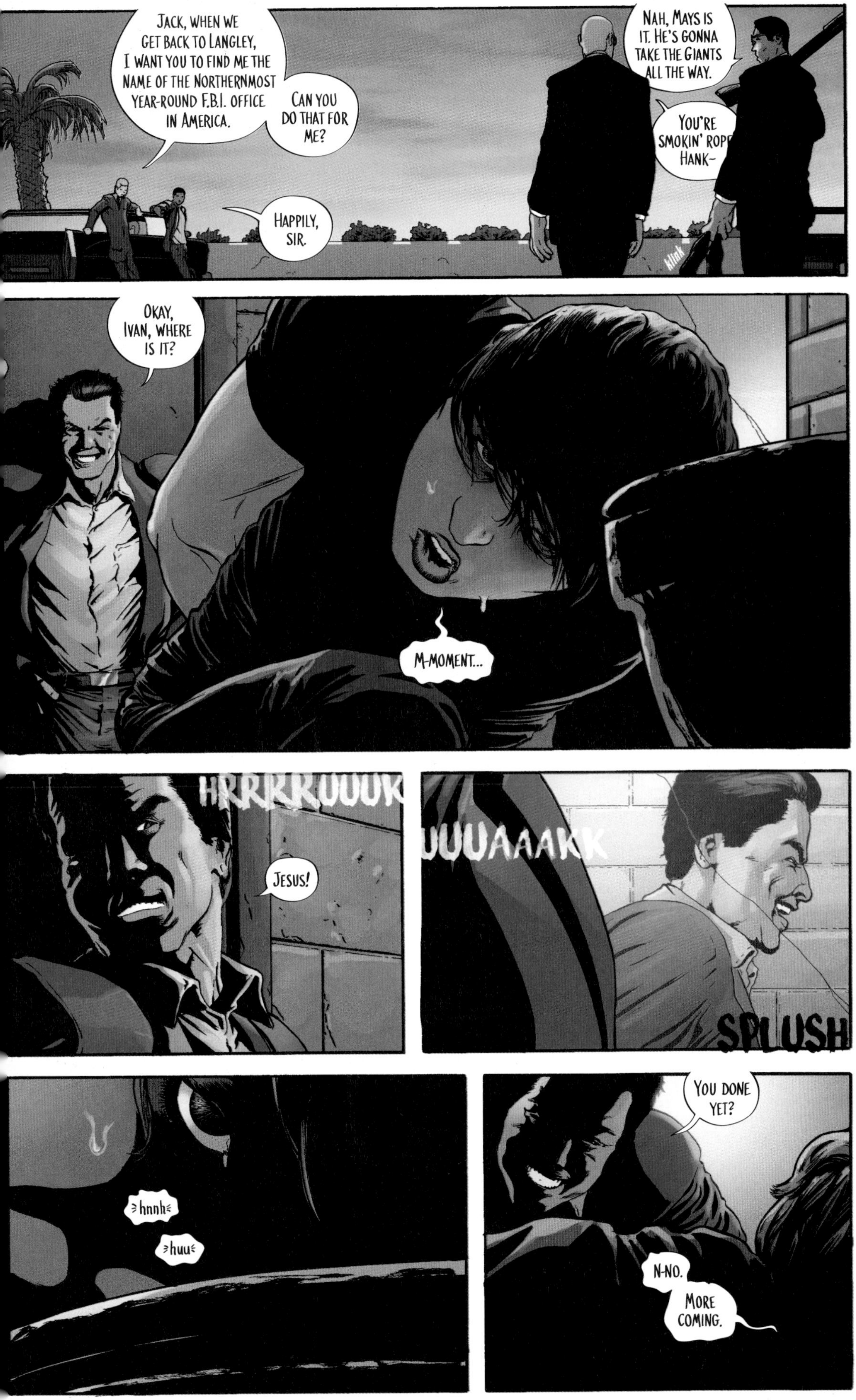
JACK, WHEN WE GET BACK TO LANGLEY, I WANT YOU TO FIND ME THE NAME OF THE NORTHERNMOST YEAR-ROUND F.B.I. OFFICE IN AMERICA.
CAN YOU DO THAT FOR ME?
HAPPILY, SIR.
NAH, MAYS IS IT. HE'S GONNA TAKE THE GIANTS ALL THE WAY.
YOU'RE SMOKIN' ROP HANK-
klink
OKAY, IVAN, WHERE IS IT?
M-MOMENT...
HRRRRRUUUK
JESUS!
UUUAAAKK
SPLUSH
hnnh
huu
YOU DONE YET?
N-NO.
MORE COMING.

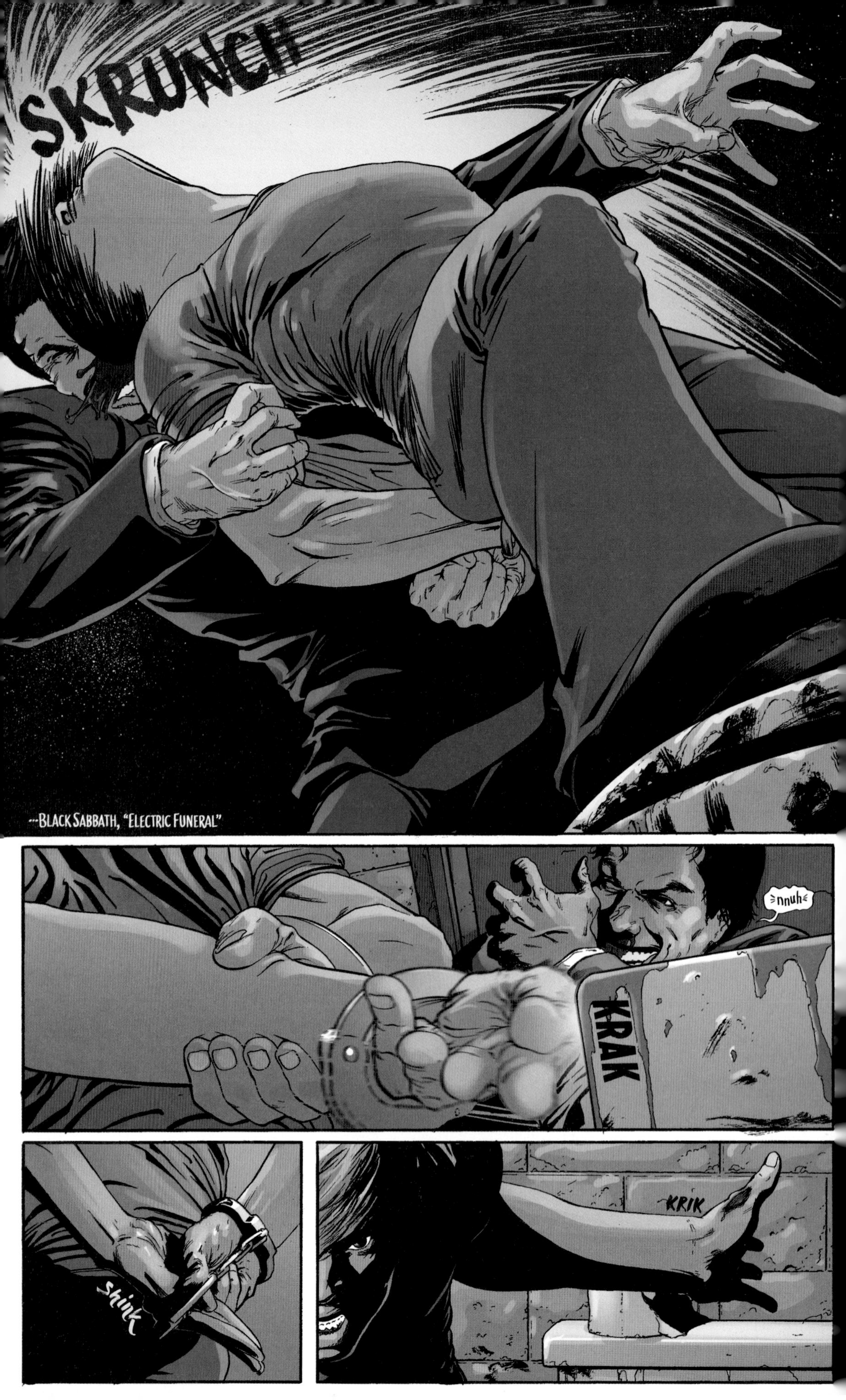
SKRUNCH
--BLACK SABBATH, "ELECTRIC FUNERAL"
nnuh
KRAK
shink
KRIK

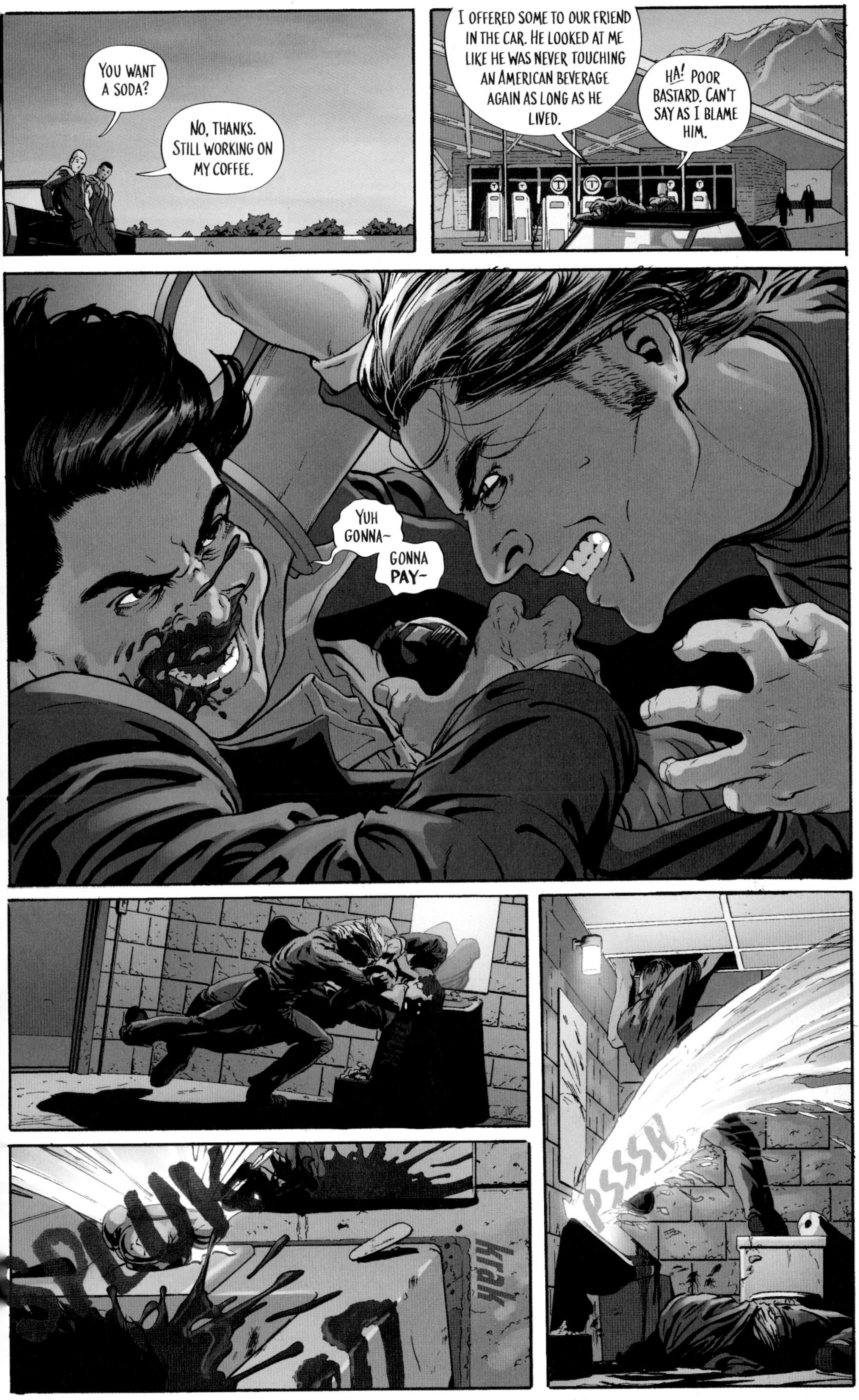
YOU WANT A SODA?
NO, THANKS. STILL WORKING ON MY COFFEE.
I OFFERED SOME TO OUR FRIEND IN THE CAR. HE LOOKED AT ME LIKE HE WAS NEVER TOUCHING AN AMERICAN BEVERAGE AGAIN AS LONG AS HE LIVED.
HA! POOR BASTARD. CAN'T SAY AS I BLAME HIM.
YUH GONNA-
GONNA PAY-
SPLUK
krak
PSSSH

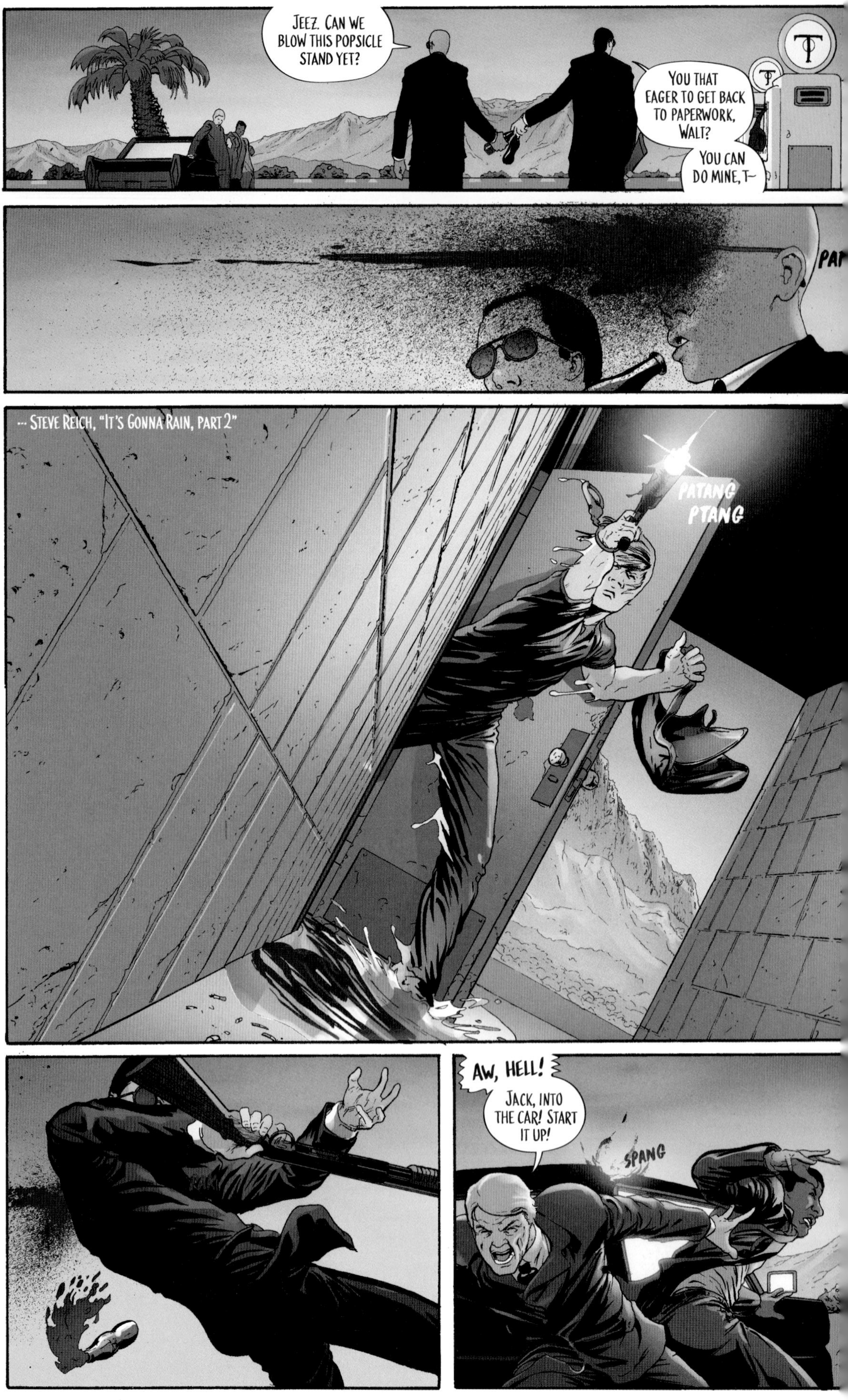
JEEZ. CAN WE BLOW THIS POPSICLE STAND YET?
YOU THAT EAGER TO GET BACK TO PAPERWORK, WALT?
YOU CAN DO MINE, T–
--- STEVE REICH, "IT'S GONNA RAIN, PART 2"
PATANG
PTANG
AW, HELL!
JACK, INTO THE CAR! START IT UP!
SPANG

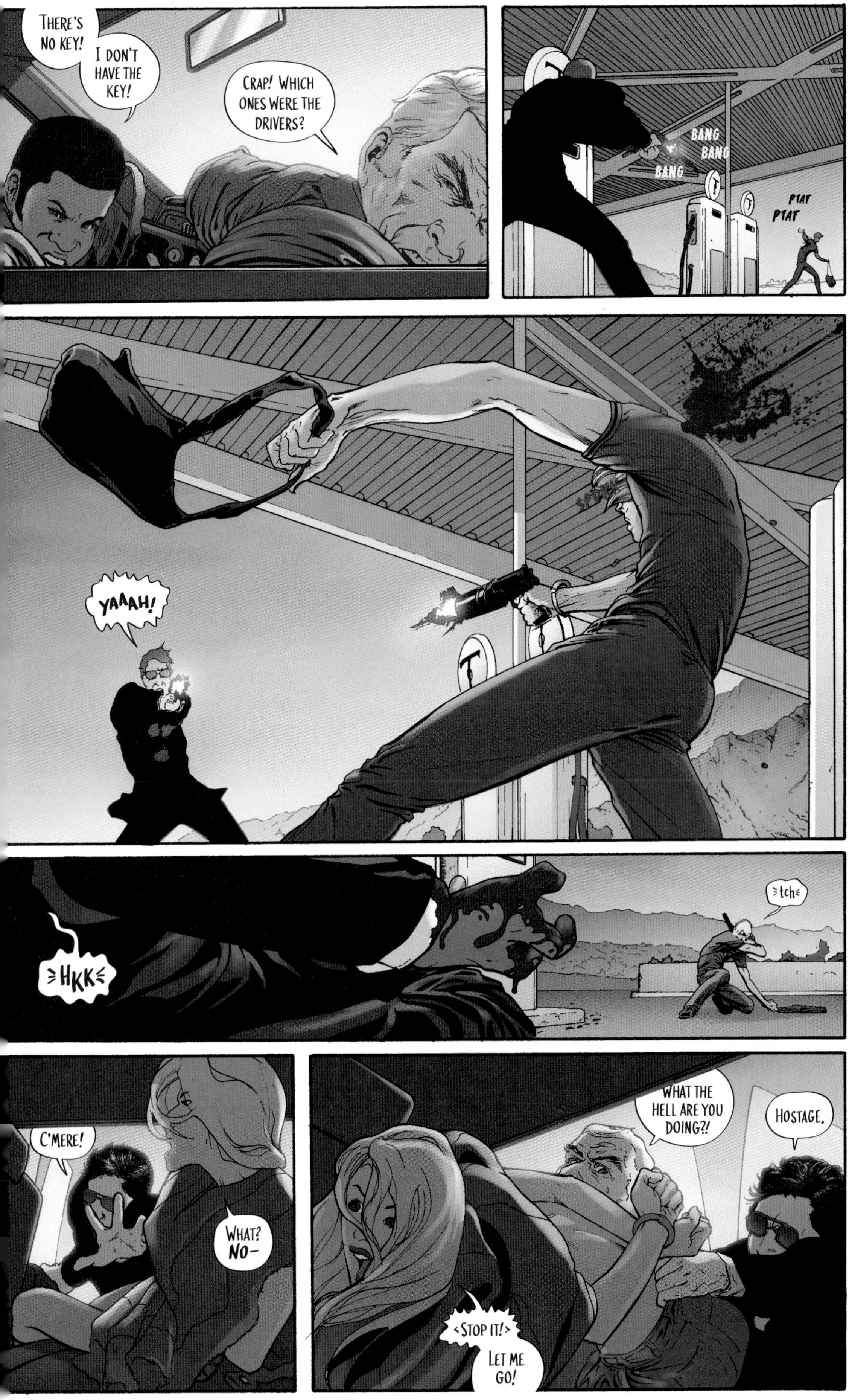

THERE'S NO KEY!
I DON'T HAVE THE KEY!
CRAP! WHICH ONES WERE THE DRIVERS?
BANG
BANG
BANG
PTAF
PTAF
YAAAH!
HKK
tch
C'MERE!
WHAT? NO-
WHAT THE HELL ARE YOU DOING?!
HOSTAGE.
<STOP IT!>
LET ME GO!

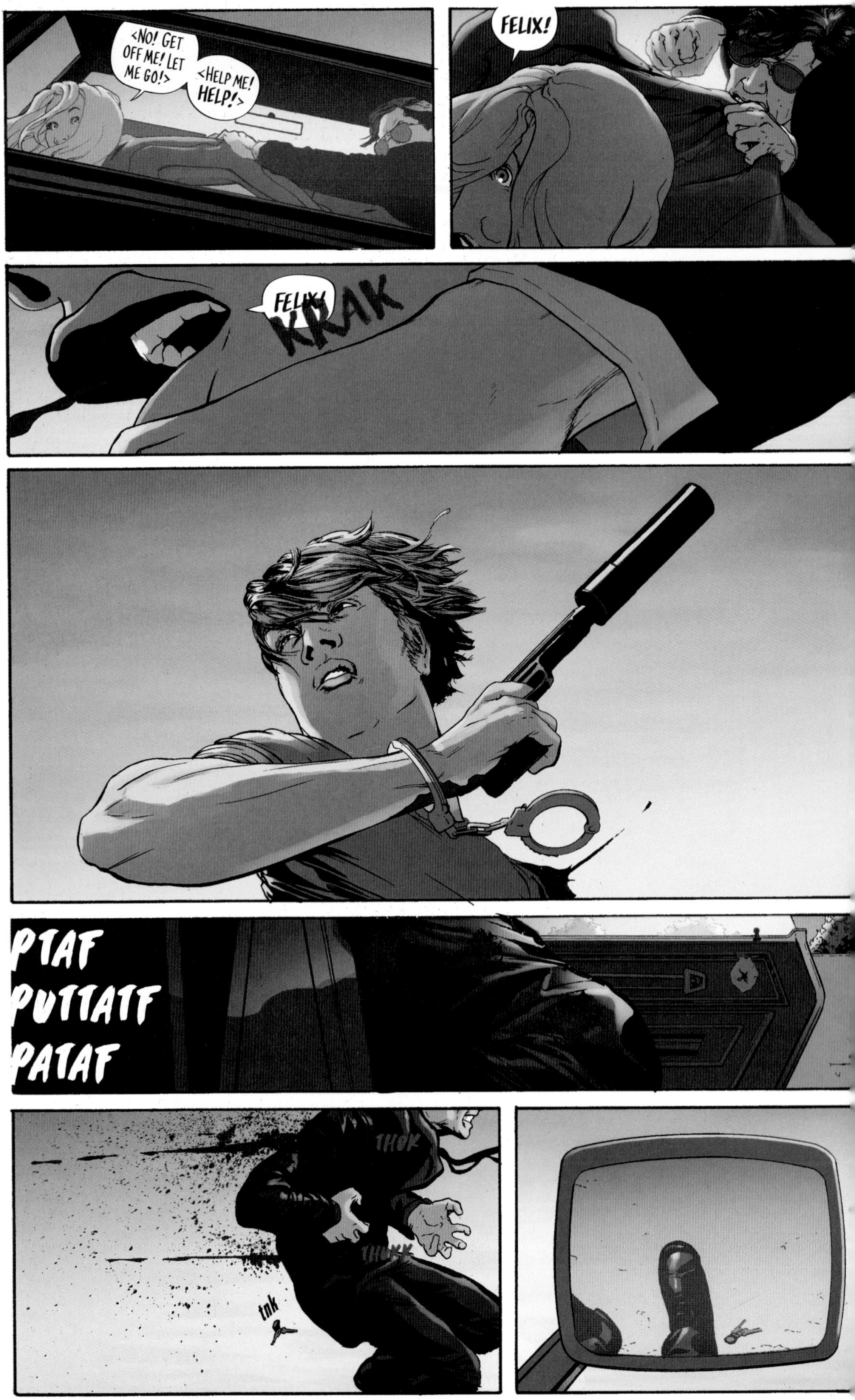
<NO! GET OFF ME! LET ME GO!>
<HELP ME! HELP!>
FELIX!
FELIX!
KRAK
PTAF
PUTTATF
PATAF
THOK
THOKK
tnk

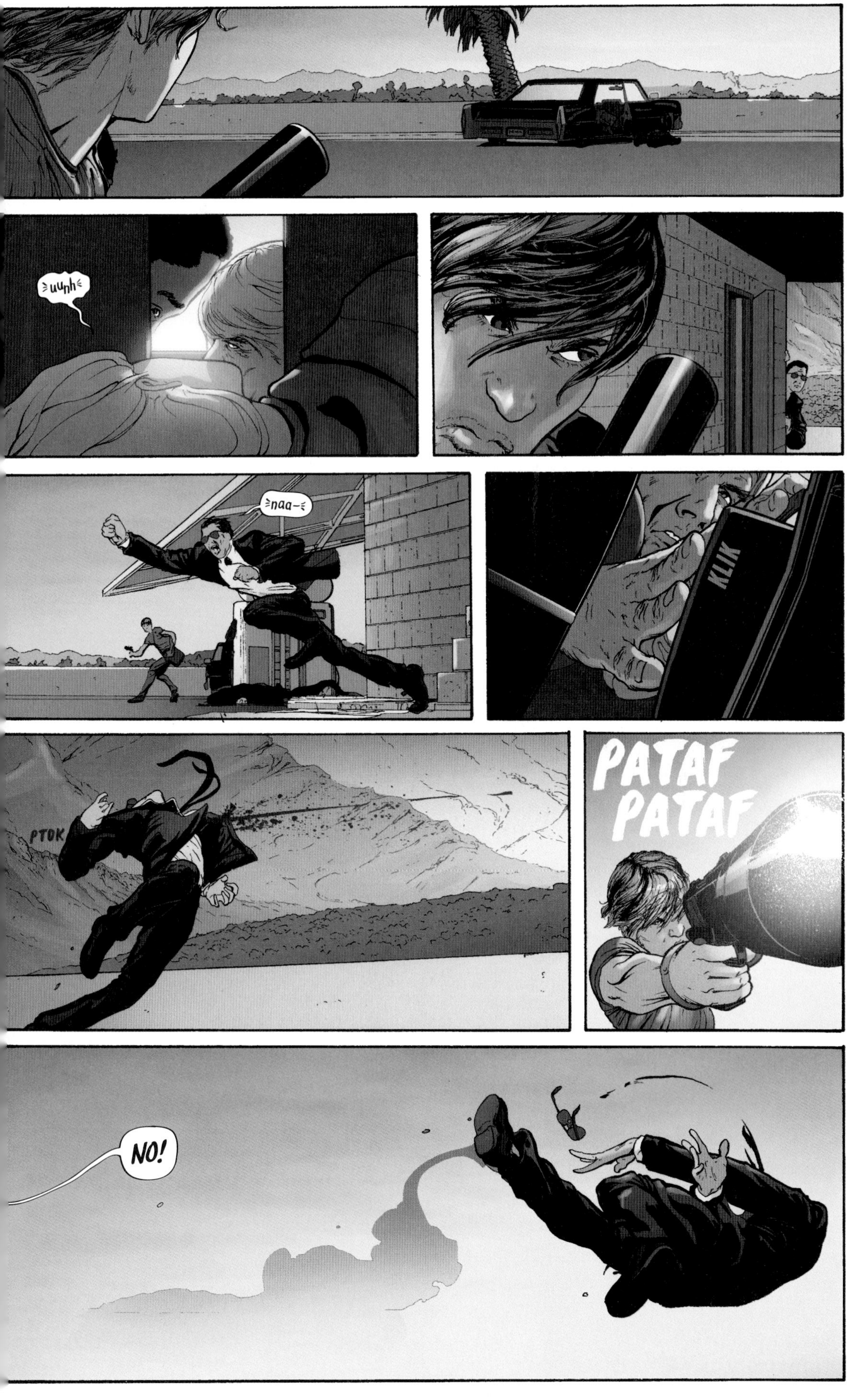
uunh
naa–
KLIK
PTOK
PATAF
PATAF
NO!

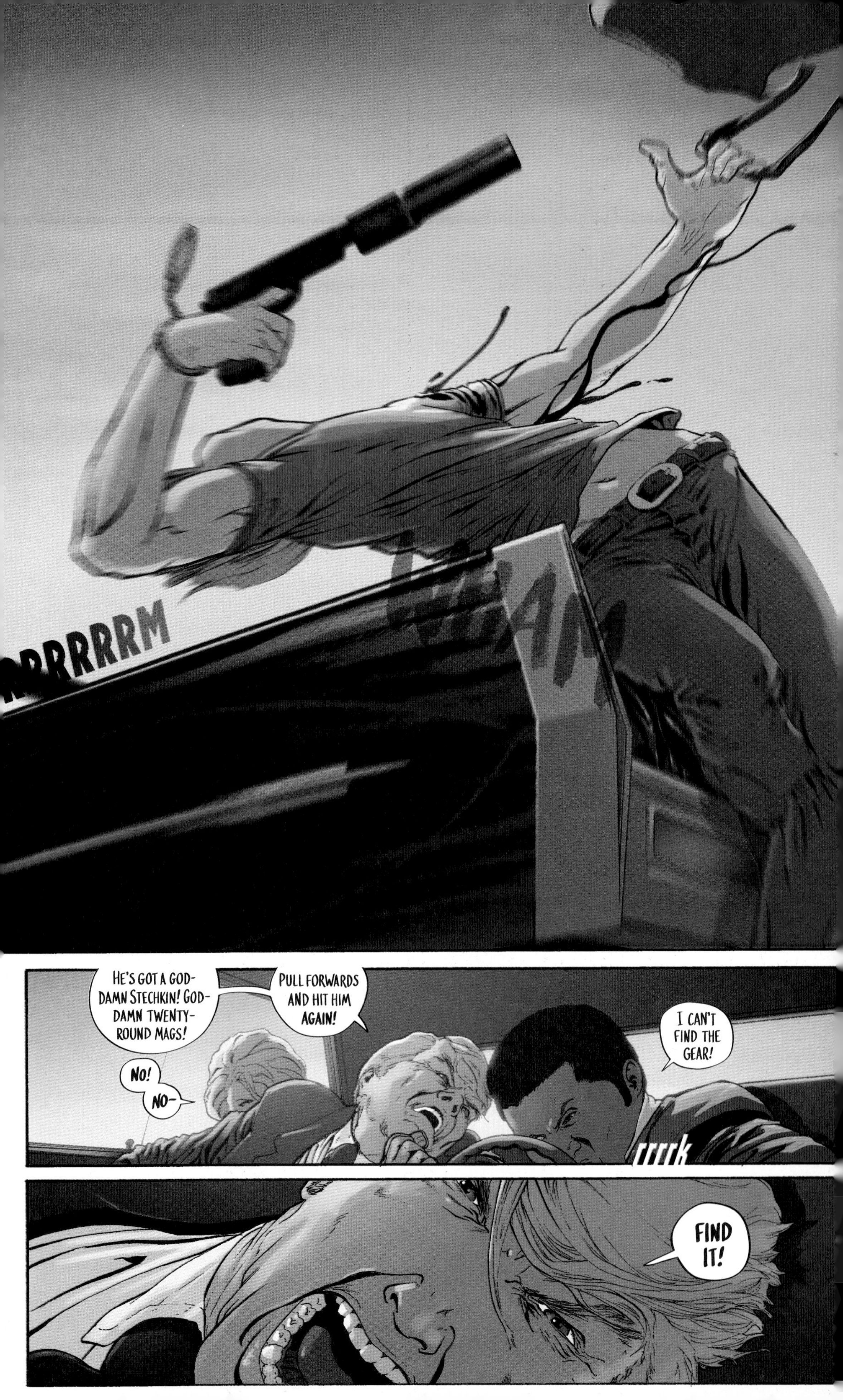
RRRRRRM
HE'S GOT A GOD-DAMN STECHKIN! GOD-DAMN TWENTY-ROUND MAGS!
PULL FORWARDS AND HIT HIM AGAIN!
I CAN'T FIND THE GEAR!
NO!
NO-
rrrrk
FIND IT!

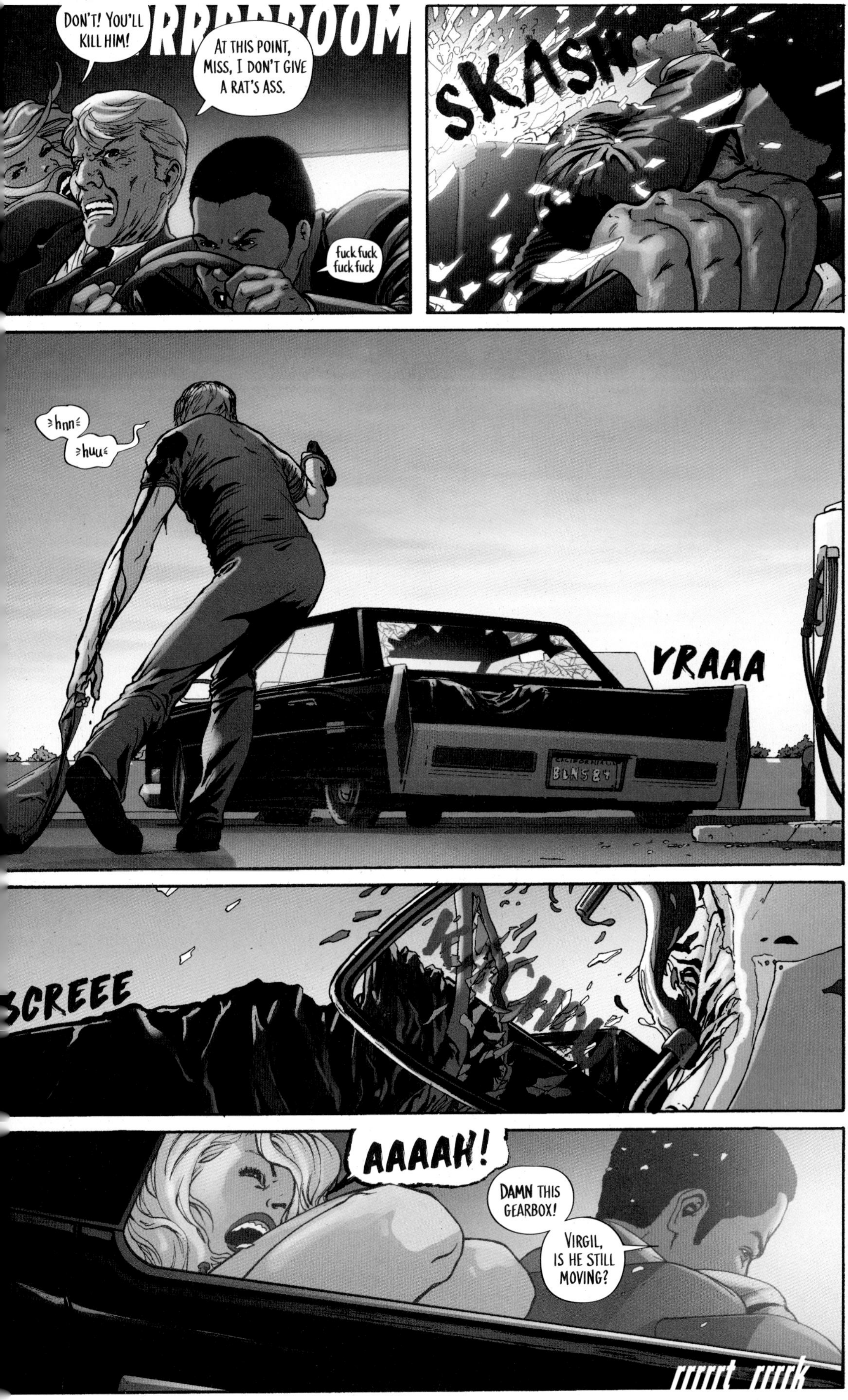
DON'T! YOU'LL KILL HIM!
AT THIS POINT, MISS, I DON'T GIVE A RAT'S ASS.
fuck fuck fuck fuck
SKASH
hnn
huu
VRAAA
SCREEE
AAAAH!
DAMN THIS GEARBOX!
VIRGIL, IS HE STILL MOVING?
rrrrrt rrrrk

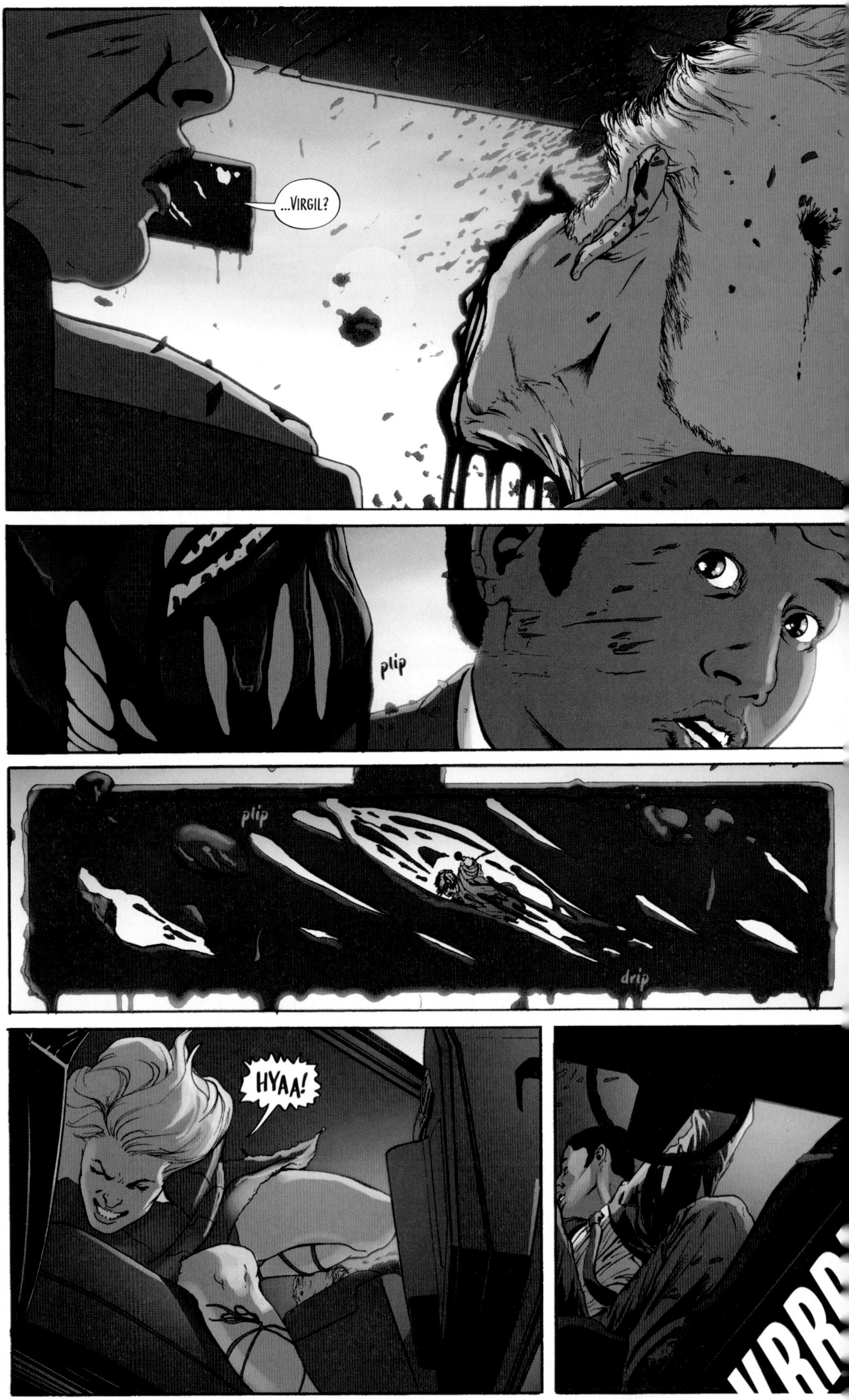
...VIRGIL?
plip
plip
drip
HYAA!

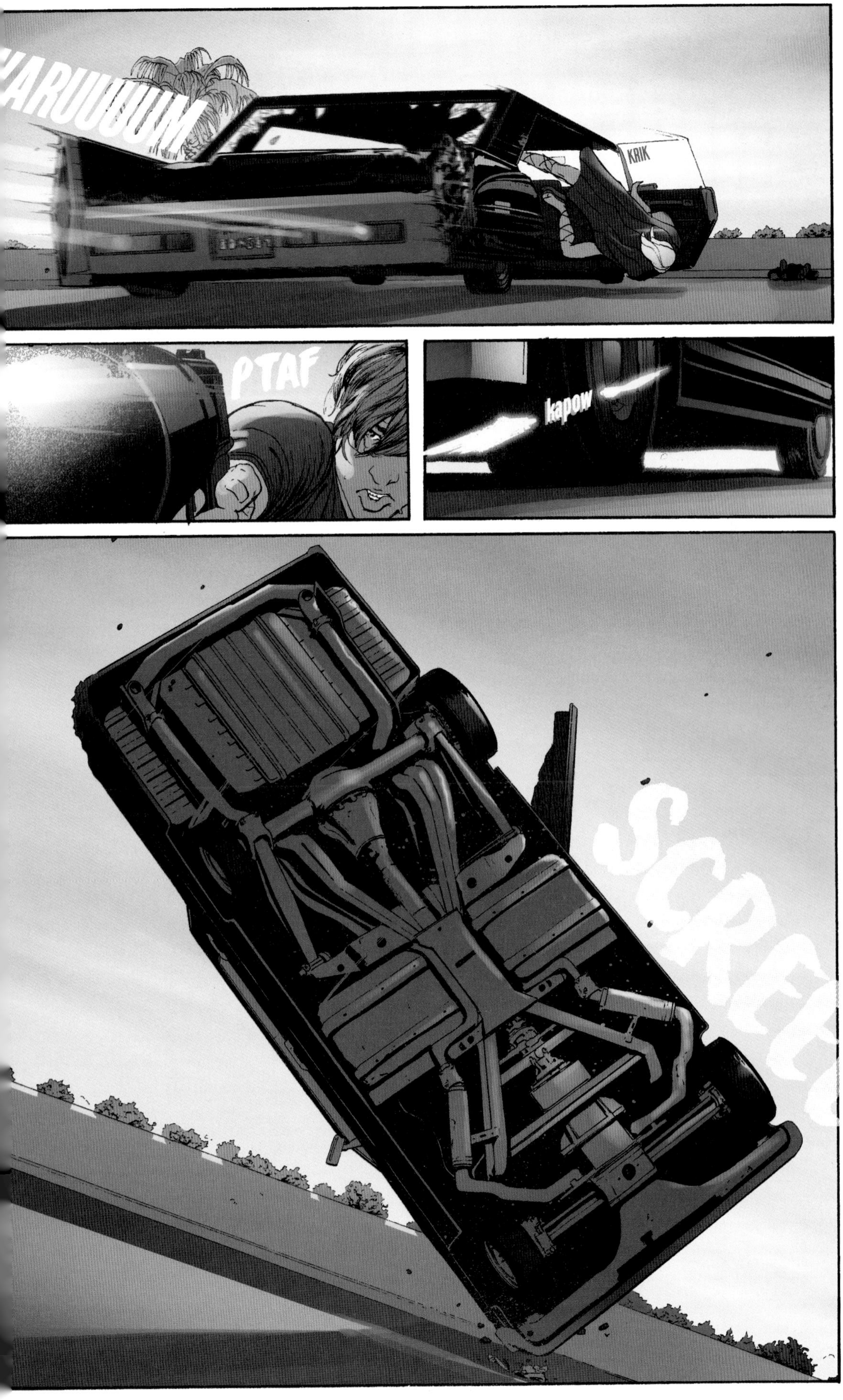

ARUUUUUM
KRIK
PTAF
kapow
SCREE

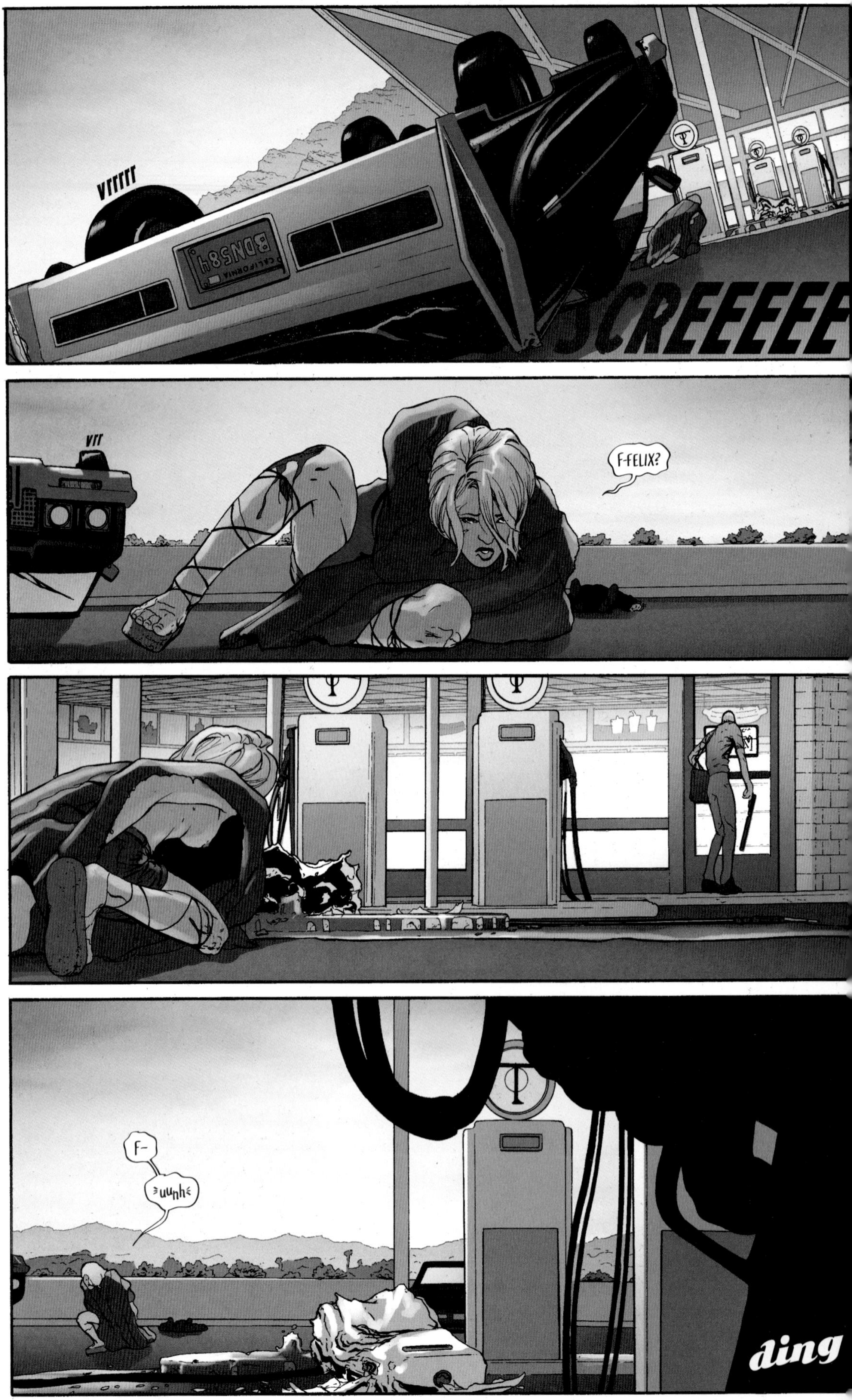
vrrrrr
SCREEEEE
vrr
F-FELIX?
F-
uunh
ding

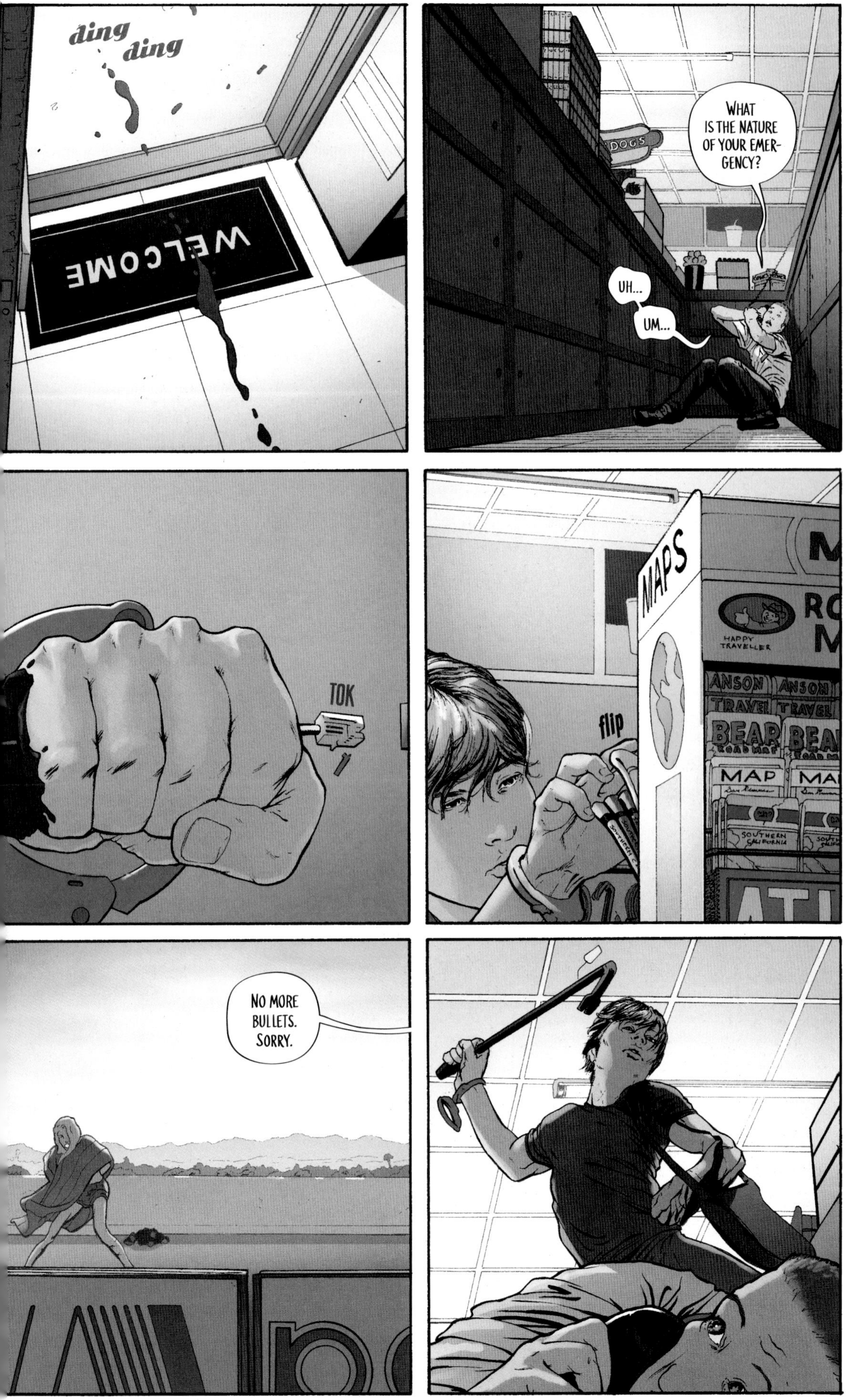
ding
ding
WELCOME
WHAT IS THE NATURE OF YOUR EMERGENCY?
UH...
UM...
DOGS
TOK
MAPS
HAPPY TRAVELLER
flip
ANSON TRAVEL
BEAR ROAD MAP
MAP
SOUTHERN CALIFORNIA
NO MORE BULLETS. SORRY.

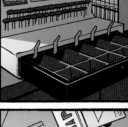

<COME. THE
WORKER'S TRUCK
IS BEHIND THE
STORE.>

...

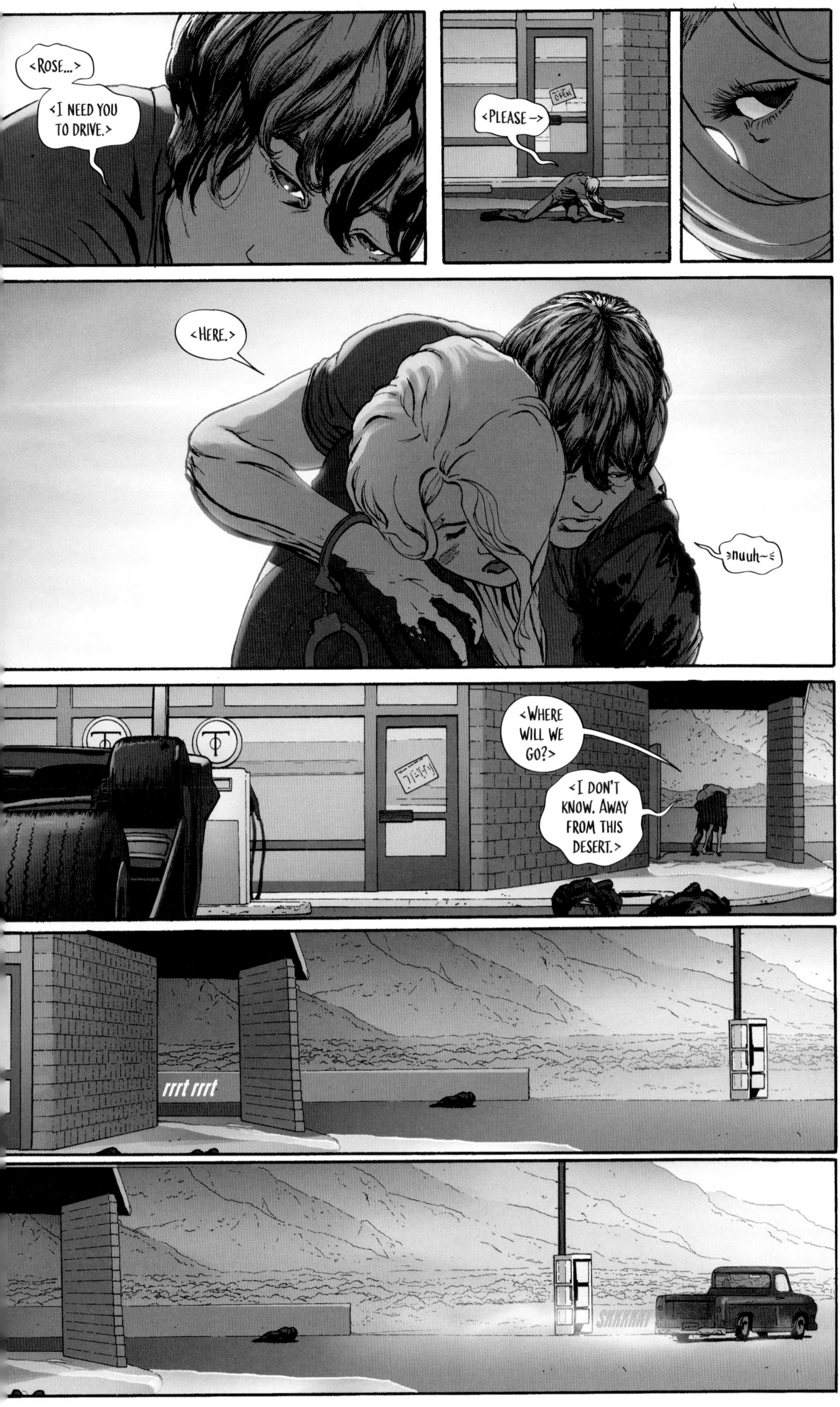

<ROSE...>
<I NEED YOU TO DRIVE.>
<PLEASE –>
<HERE.>
nuuh~
<WHERE WILL WE GO?>
<I DON'T KNOW. AWAY FROM THIS DESERT.>
rrrt rrrt
SKKKRRT

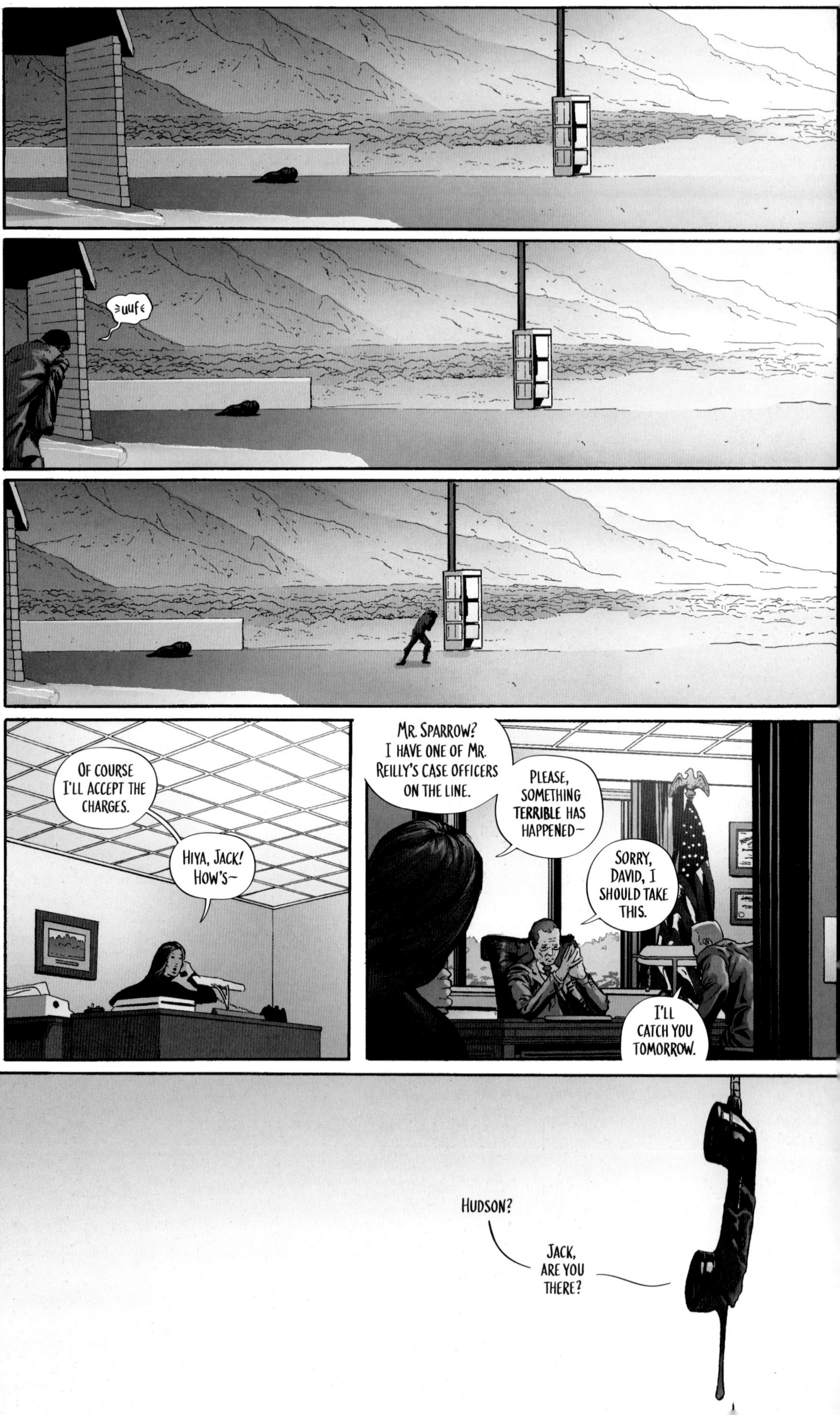
uuf
Of course I'll accept the charges.
Hiya, Jack! How's~
Mr. Sparrow? I have one of Mr. Reilly's case officers on the line.
Please, something terrible has happened~
Sorry, David, I should take this.
I'll catch you tomorrow.
Hudson?
Jack, are you there?

"I am you, and when you can admit that, you will be free.
I am just a mirror." Charles Manson, June 1970

THREE

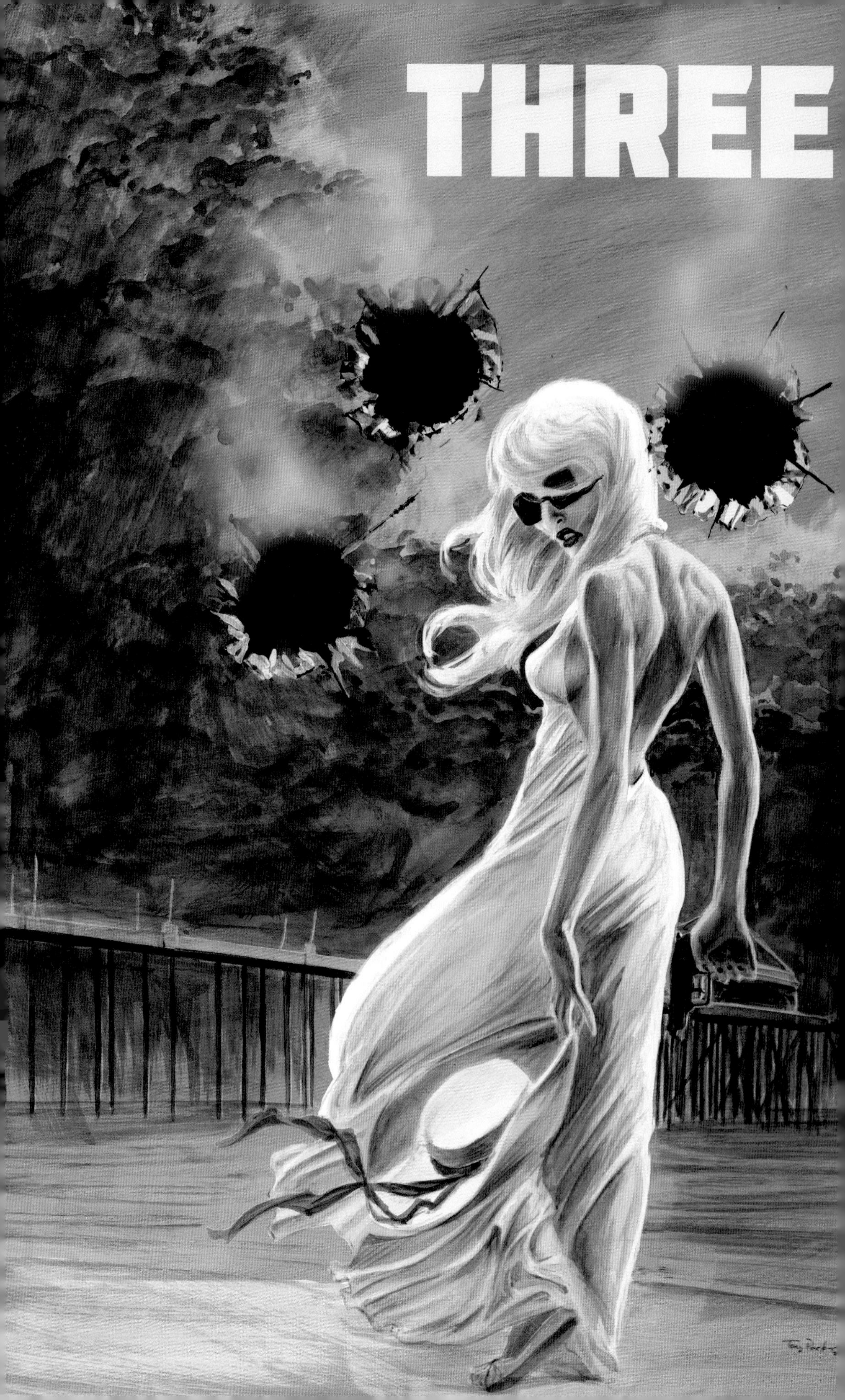

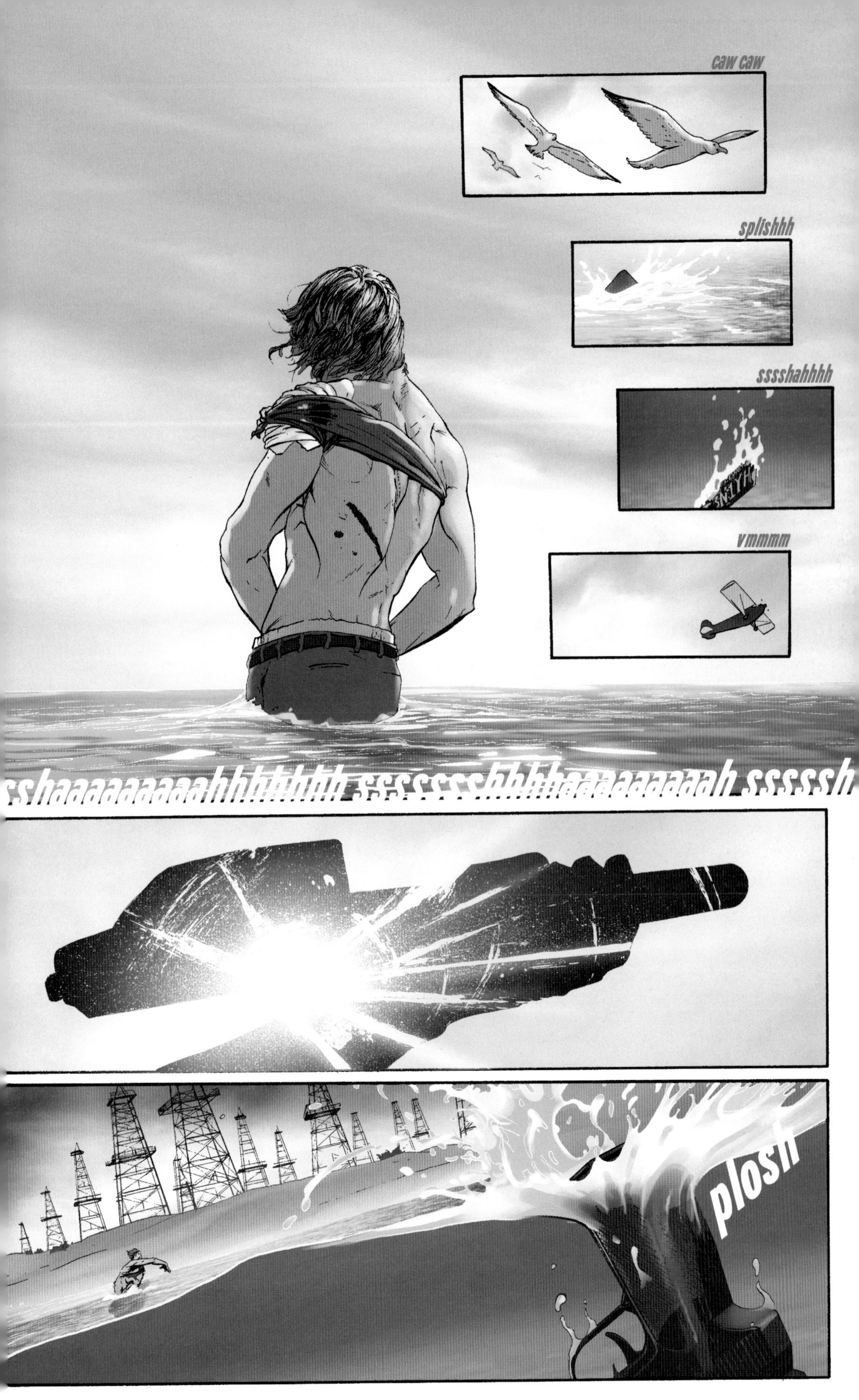
caw caw
splishh
sssshahhhh
vmmmm
sshaaaaaaaaaaahhhhhhhh sssssshhhhaaaaaaaaaah sssssh
plosh

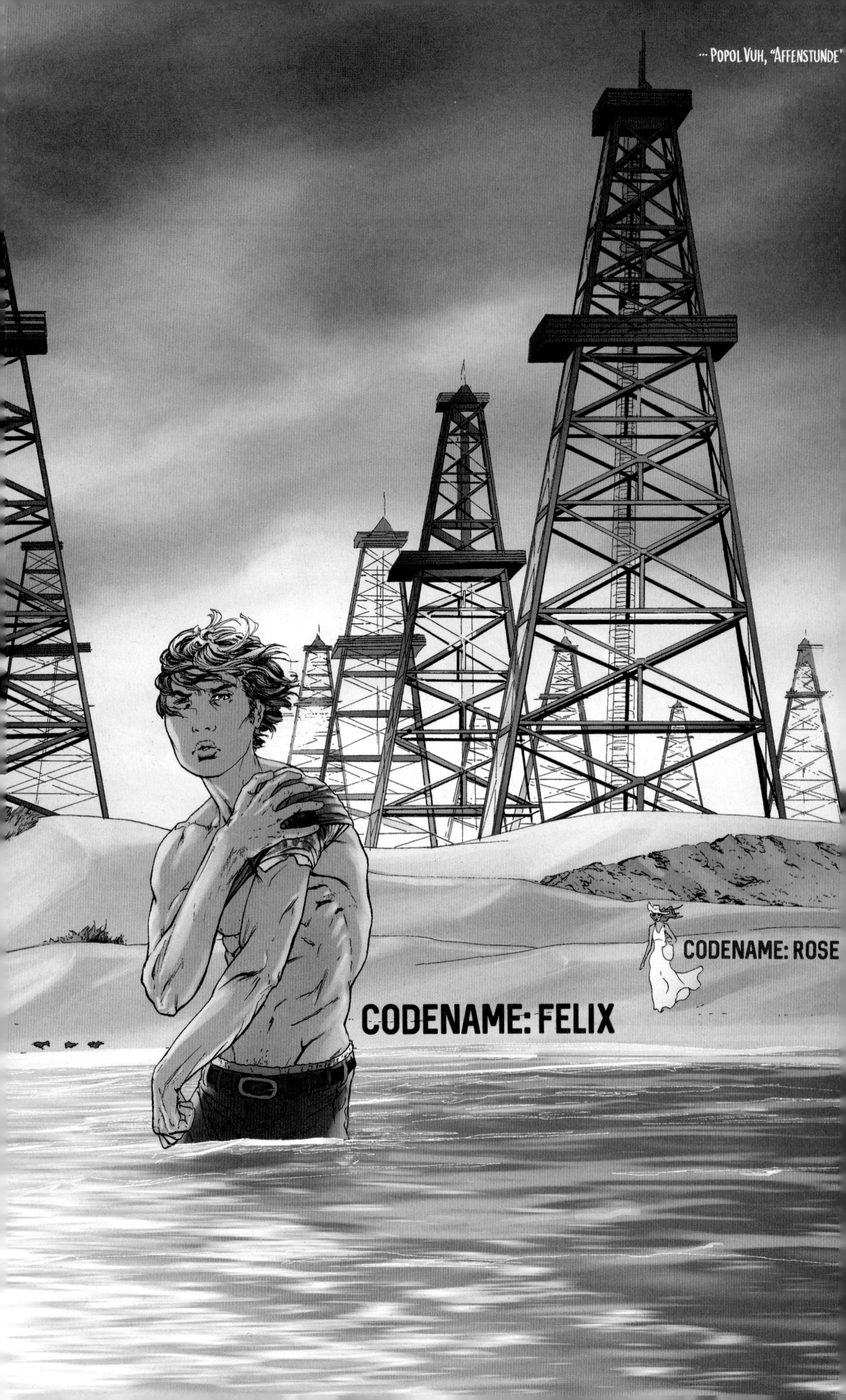
... POPOL VUH, "AFFENSTUNDE"
CODENAME: FELIX
CODENAME: ROSE

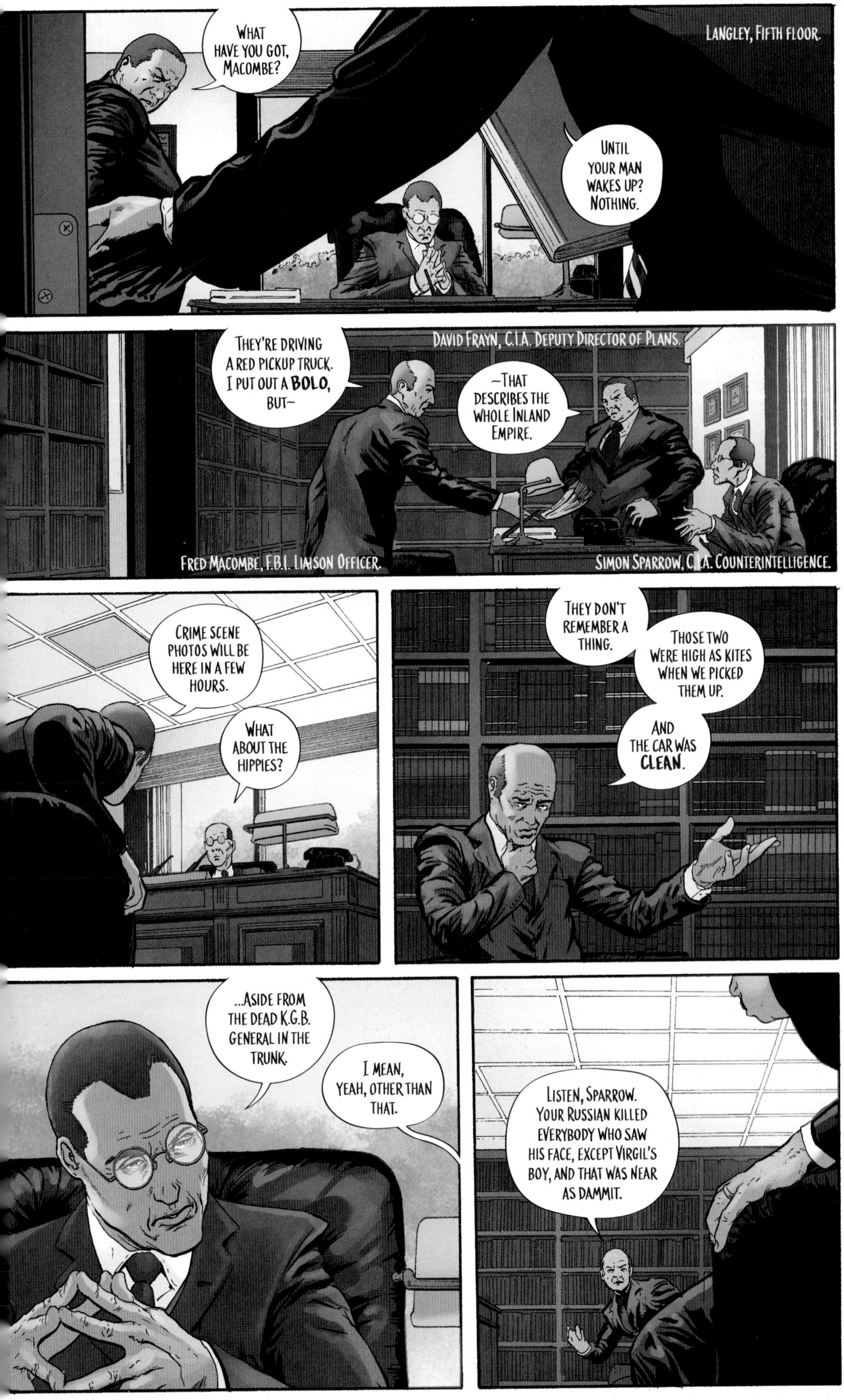
LANGLEY, FIFTH FLOOR.
WHAT HAVE YOU GOT, MACOMBE?
UNTIL YOUR MAN WAKES UP? NOTHING.
DAVID FRAYN, C.I.A. DEPUTY DIRECTOR OF PLANS.
THEY'RE DRIVING A RED PICKUP TRUCK. I PUT OUT A BOLO, BUT~
~THAT DESCRIBES THE WHOLE INLAND EMPIRE.
FRED MACOMBE, F.B.I. LIAISON OFFICER.
SIMON SPARROW, C.I.A. COUNTERINTELLIGENCE.
CRIME SCENE PHOTOS WILL BE HERE IN A FEW HOURS.
WHAT ABOUT THE HIPPIES?
THEY DON'T REMEMBER A THING.
THOSE TWO WERE HIGH AS KITES WHEN WE PICKED THEM UP.
AND THE CAR WAS CLEAN.
...ASIDE FROM THE DEAD K.G.B. GENERAL IN THE TRUNK.
I MEAN, YEAH, OTHER THAN THAT.
LISTEN, SPARROW. YOUR RUSSIAN KILLED EVERYBODY WHO SAW HIS FACE, EXCEPT VIRGIL'S BOY, AND THAT WAS NEAR AS DAMMIT.

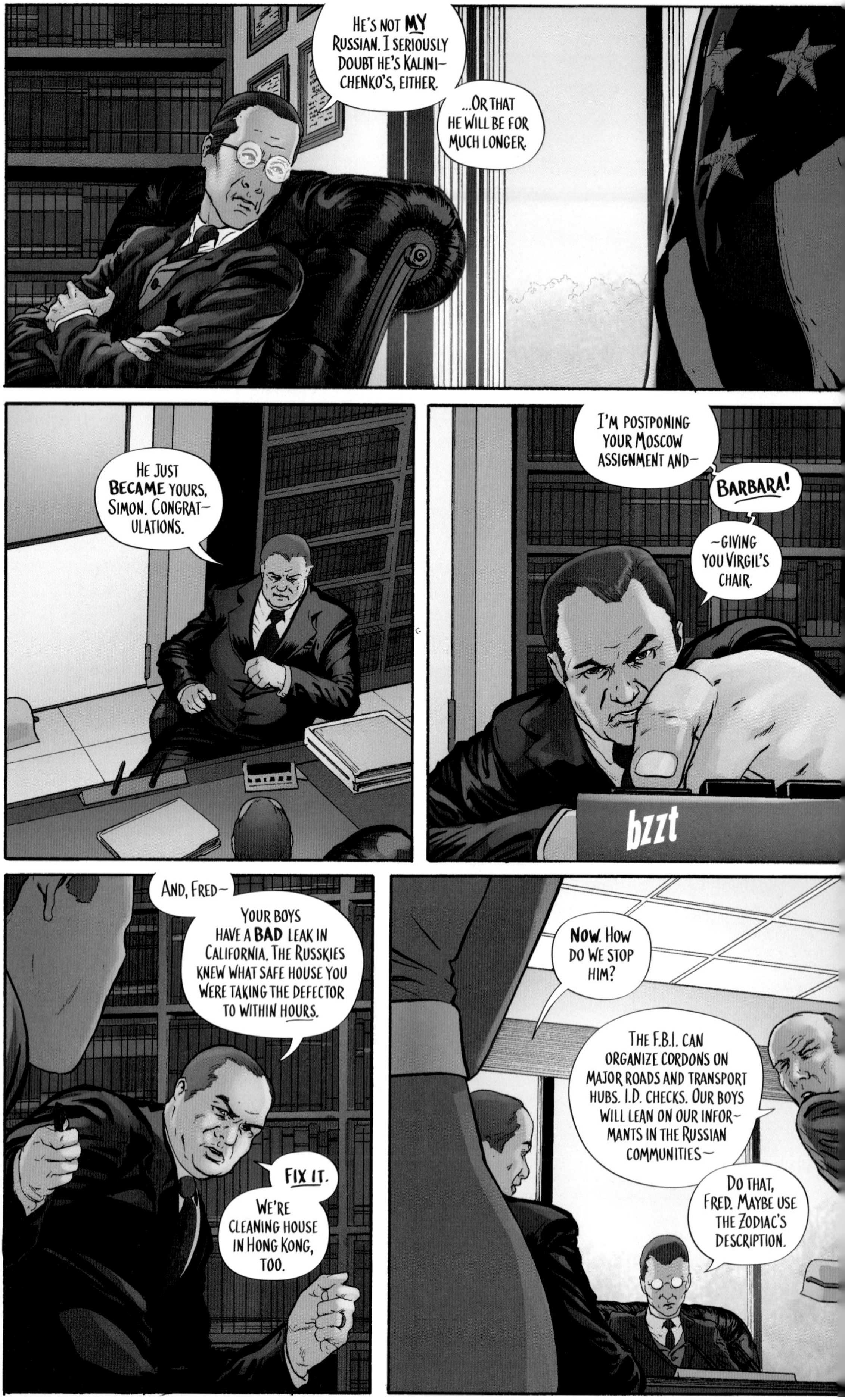

HE'S NOT MY RUSSIAN. I SERIOUSLY DOUBT HE'S KALINI-CHENKO'S, EITHER.
...OR THAT HE WILL BE FOR MUCH LONGER.
HE JUST BECAME YOURS, SIMON. CONGRAT-ULATIONS.
I'M POSTPONING YOUR MOSCOW ASSIGNMENT AND–
BARBARA!
–GIVING YOU VIRGIL'S CHAIR.
bzzt
AND, FRED–
YOUR BOYS HAVE A BAD LEAK IN CALIFORNIA. THE RUSSKIES KNEW WHAT SAFE HOUSE YOU WERE TAKING THE DEFECTOR TO WITHIN HOURS.
FIX IT.
WE'RE CLEANING HOUSE IN HONG KONG, TOO.
NOW. HOW DO WE STOP HIM?
THE F.B.I. CAN ORGANIZE CORDONS ON MAJOR ROADS AND TRANSPORT HUBS. I.D. CHECKS. OUR BOYS WILL LEAN ON OUR INFOR-MANTS IN THE RUSSIAN COMMUNITIES–
DO THAT, FRED. MAYBE USE THE ZODIAC'S DESCRIPTION.

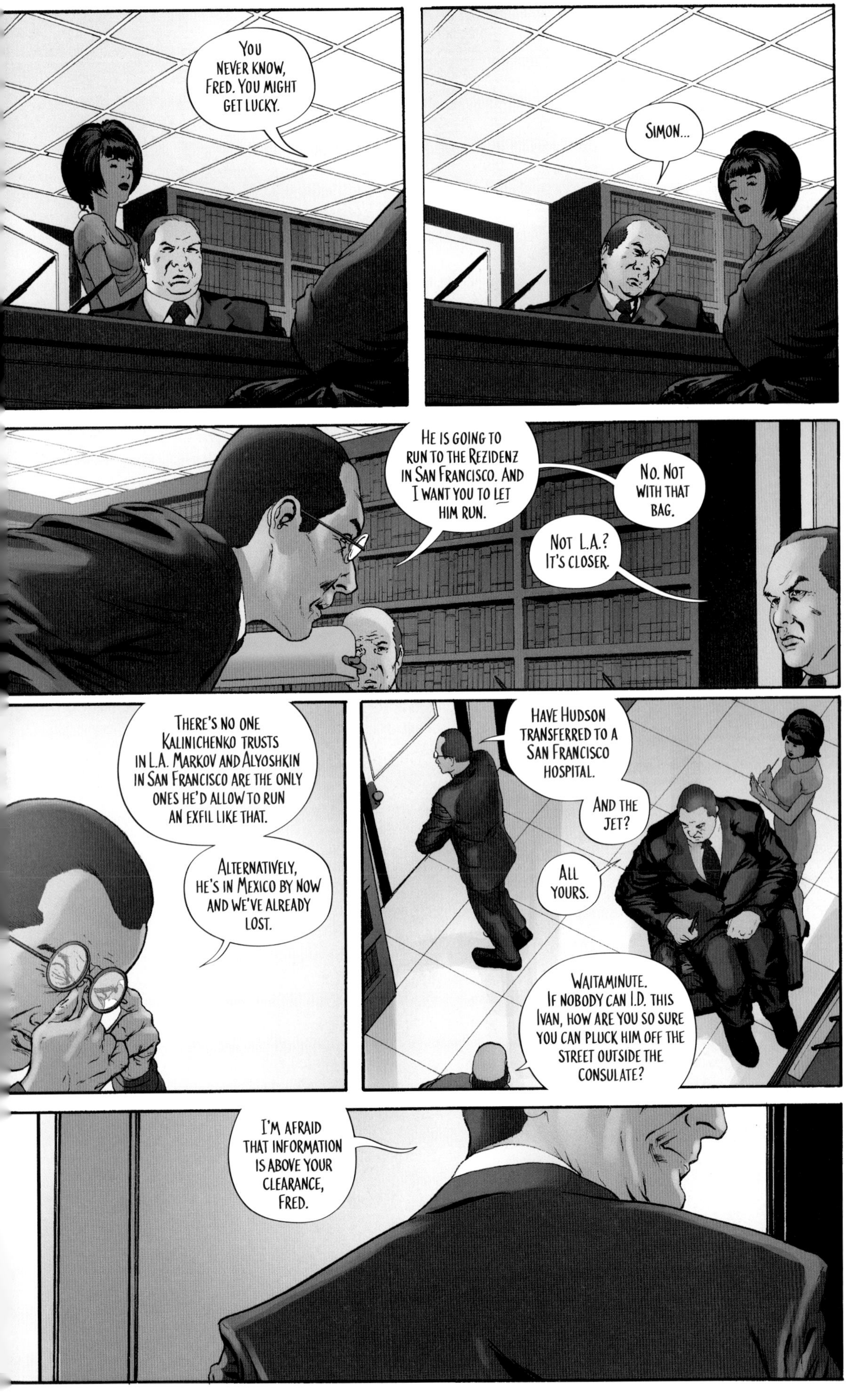
You never know, Fred. You might get lucky.
Simon...
He is going to run to the Rezidenz in San Francisco. And I want you to let him run.
No. Not with that bag.
Not L.A.? It's closer.
There's no one Kalinichenko trusts in L.A. Markov and Alyoshkin in San Francisco are the only ones he'd allow to run an exfil like that.
Alternatively, he's in Mexico by now and we've already lost.
Have Hudson transferred to a San Francisco hospital.
And the jet?
All yours.
Waitaminute. If nobody can I.D. this Ivan, how are you so sure you can pluck him off the street outside the consulate?
I'm afraid that information is above your clearance, Fred.

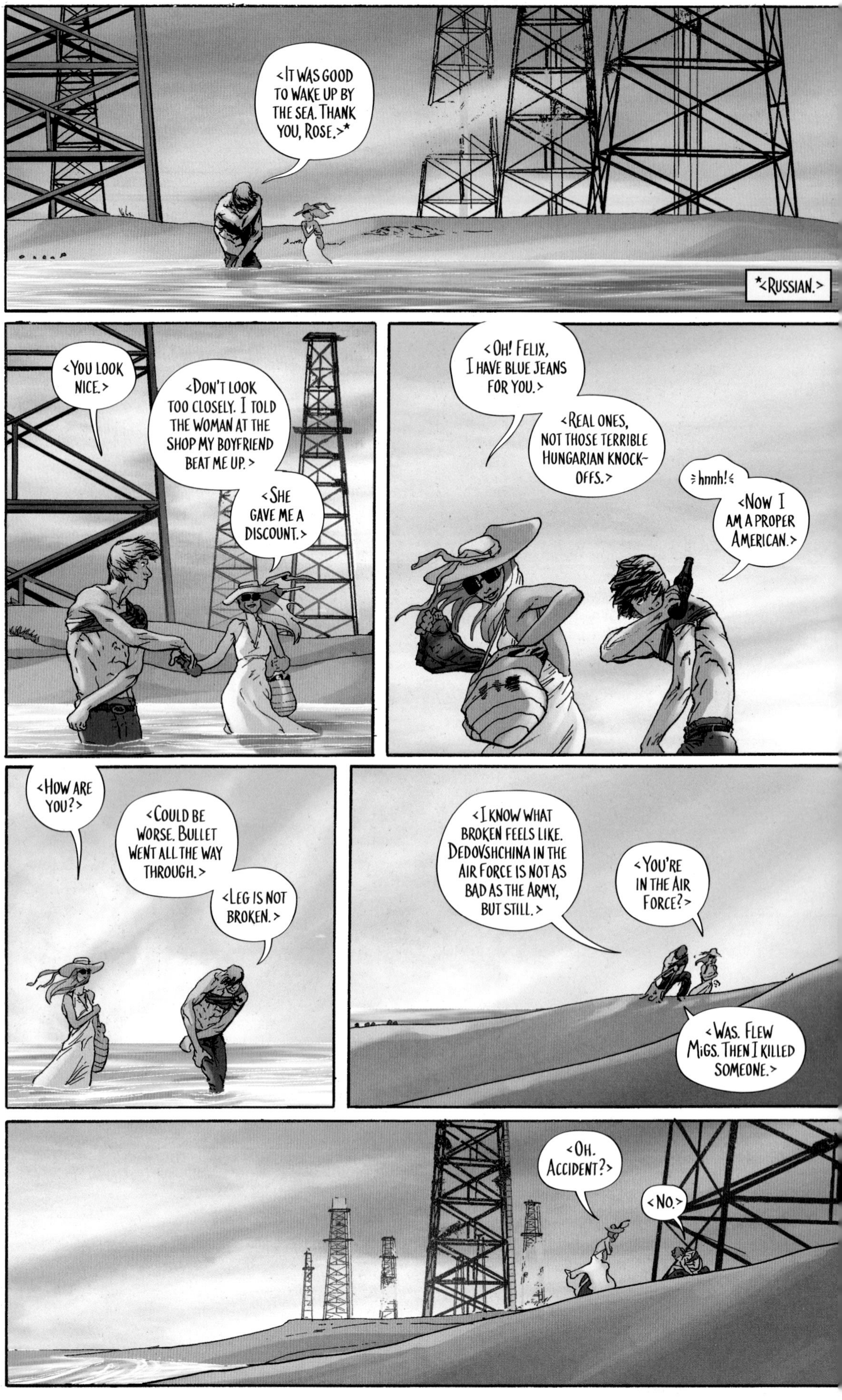

<IT WAS GOOD TO WAKE UP BY THE SEA. THANK YOU, ROSE.>*
*<RUSSIAN.>
<YOU LOOK NICE.>
<DON'T LOOK TOO CLOSELY. I TOLD THE WOMAN AT THE SHOP MY BOYFRIEND BEAT ME UP.>
<SHE GAVE ME A DISCOUNT.>
<OH! FELIX, I HAVE BLUE JEANS FOR YOU.>
<REAL ONES, NOT THOSE TERRIBLE HUNGARIAN KNOCK-OFFS.>
hnnh!
<NOW I AM A PROPER AMERICAN.>
<HOW ARE YOU?>
<COULD BE WORSE. BULLET WENT ALL THE WAY THROUGH.>
<LEG IS NOT BROKEN.>
<I KNOW WHAT BROKEN FEELS LIKE. DEDOVSHCHINA IN THE AIR FORCE IS NOT AS BAD AS THE ARMY, BUT STILL.>
<YOU'RE IN THE AIR FORCE?>
<WAS. FLEW MIGS. THEN I KILLED SOMEONE.>
<OH. ACCIDENT?>
<NO.>

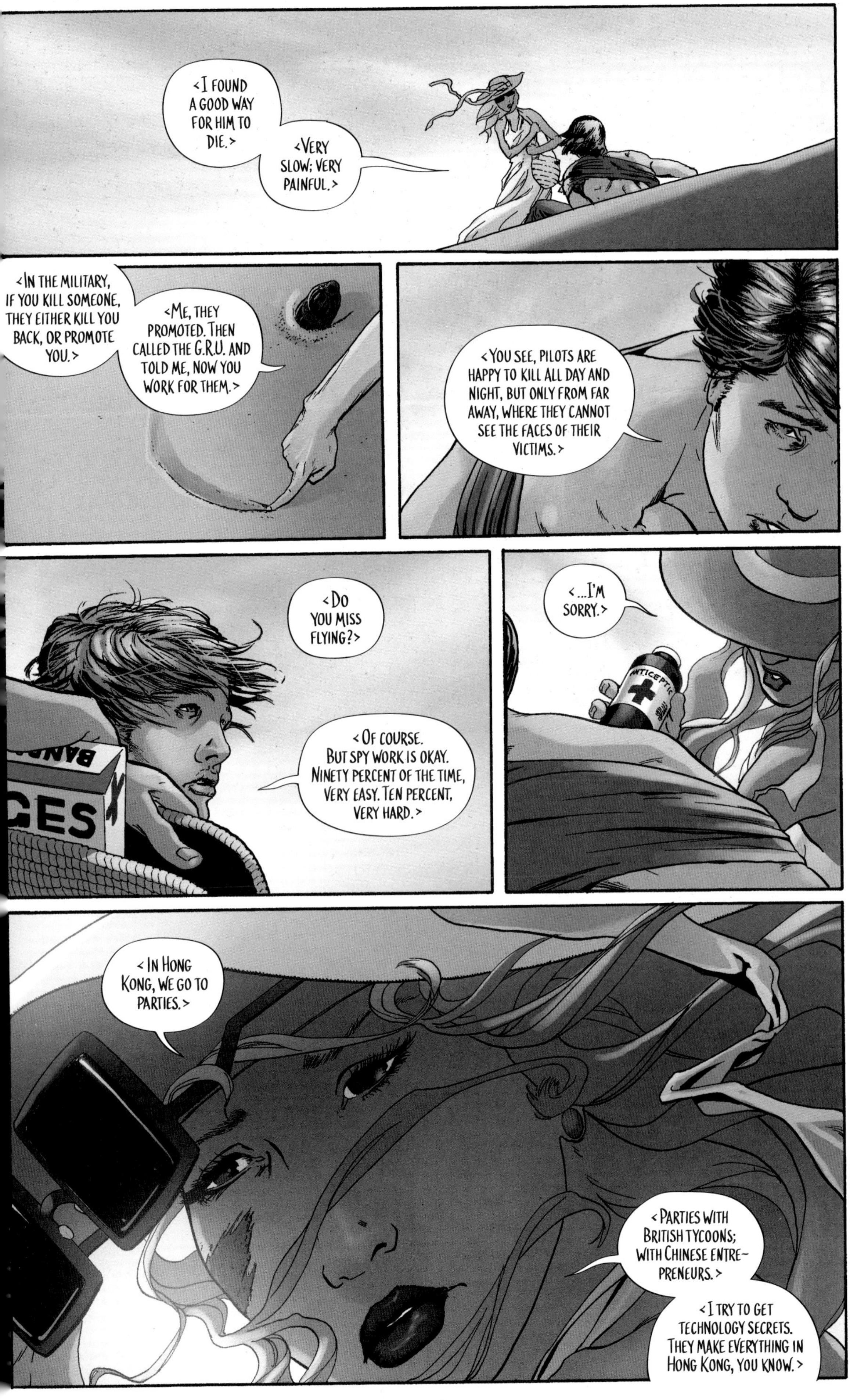
<I FOUND A GOOD WAY FOR HIM TO DIE.>
<VERY SLOW; VERY PAINFUL.>
<IN THE MILITARY, IF YOU KILL SOMEONE, THEY EITHER KILL YOU BACK, OR PROMOTE YOU.>
<ME, THEY PROMOTED. THEN CALLED THE G.R.U. AND TOLD ME, NOW YOU WORK FOR THEM.>
<YOU SEE, PILOTS ARE HAPPY TO KILL ALL DAY AND NIGHT, BUT ONLY FROM FAR AWAY, WHERE THEY CANNOT SEE THE FACES OF THEIR VICTIMS.>
<DO YOU MISS FLYING?>
<OF COURSE. BUT SPY WORK IS OKAY. NINETY PERCENT OF THE TIME, VERY EASY. TEN PERCENT, VERY HARD.>
<...I'M SORRY.>
ANTICEPTIC
<IN HONG KONG, WE GO TO PARTIES.>
<PARTIES WITH BRITISH TYCOONS; WITH CHINESE ENTRE-PRENEURS.>
<I TRY TO GET TECHNOLOGY SECRETS. THEY MAKE EVERYTHING IN HONG KONG, YOU KNOW.>

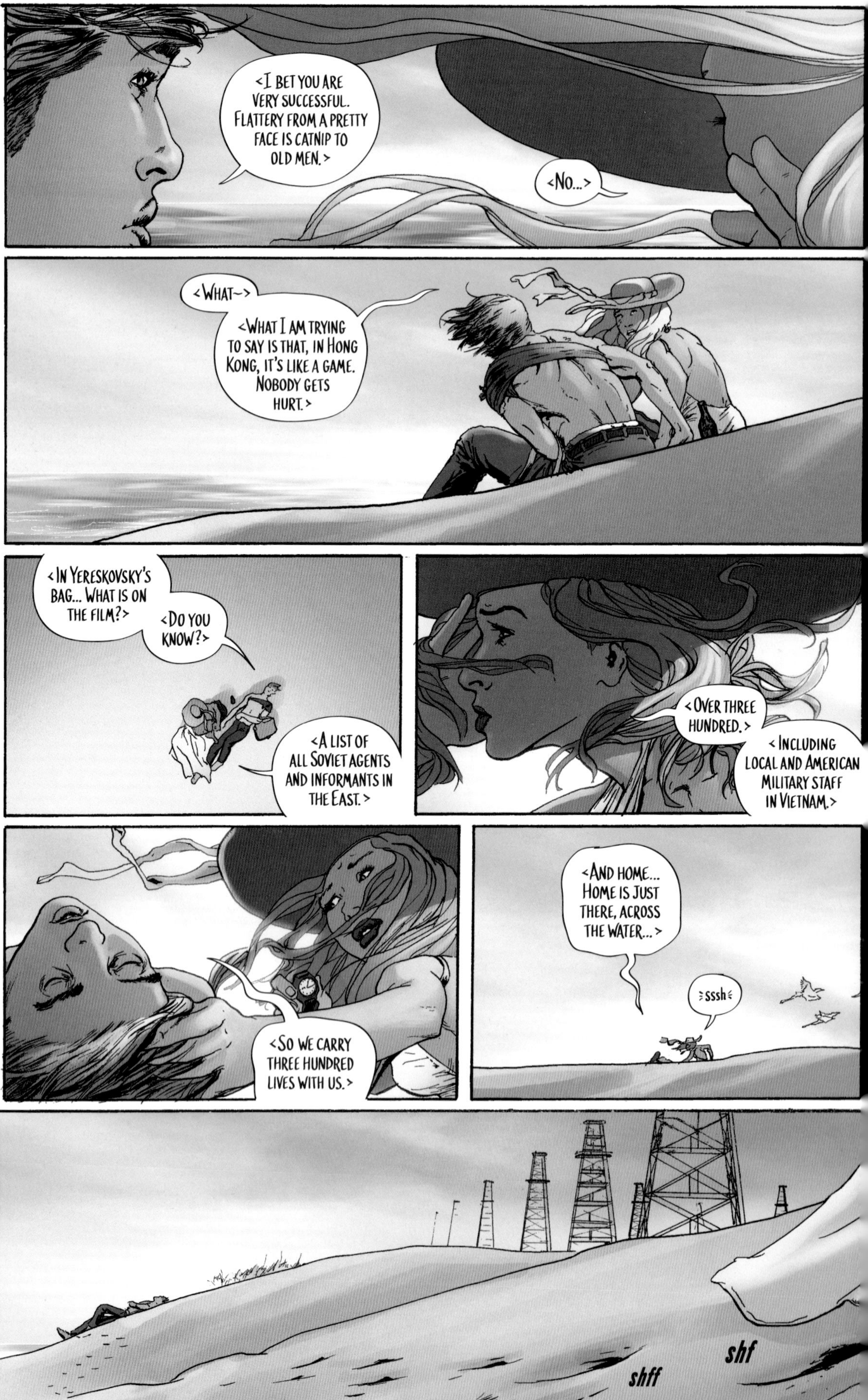
<I BET YOU ARE VERY SUCCESSFUL. FLATTERY FROM A PRETTY FACE IS CATNIP TO OLD MEN.>
<NO...>
<WHAT–>
<WHAT I AM TRYING TO SAY IS THAT, IN HONG KONG, IT'S LIKE A GAME. NOBODY GETS HURT.>
<IN YERESKOVSKY'S BAG... WHAT IS ON THE FILM?>
<DO YOU KNOW?>
<A LIST OF ALL SOVIET AGENTS AND INFORMANTS IN THE EAST.>
<OVER THREE HUNDRED.>
<INCLUDING LOCAL AND AMERICAN MILITARY STAFF IN VIETNAM.>
<SO WE CARRY THREE HUNDRED LIVES WITH US.>
<AND HOME... HOME IS JUST THERE, ACROSS THE WATER...>
sssh
shff
shf

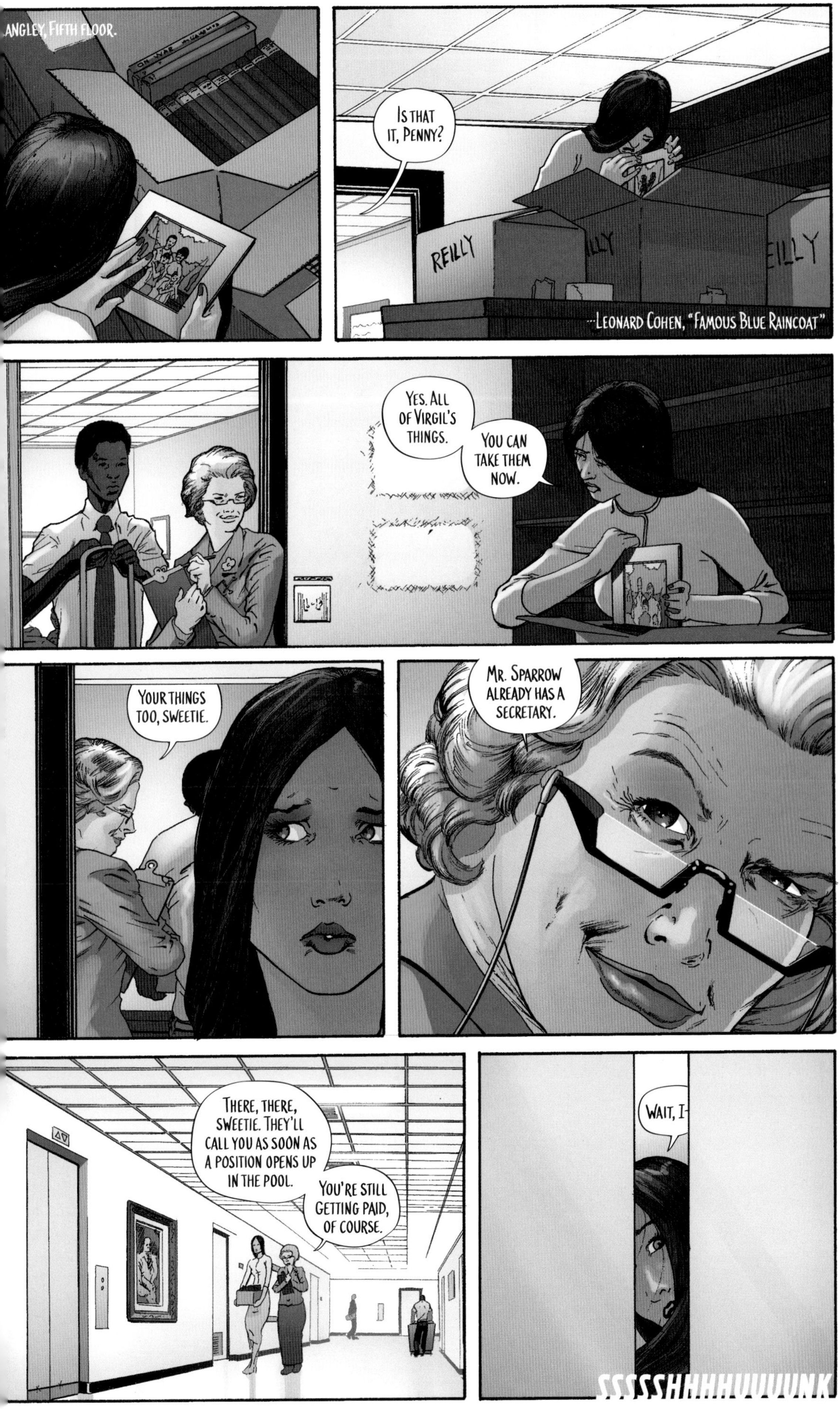
ANGLEY, FIFTH FLOOR.
IS THAT IT, PENNY?
...LEONARD COHEN, "FAMOUS BLUE RAINCOAT"
REILLY
YES. ALL OF VIRGIL'S THINGS.
YOU CAN TAKE THEM NOW.
YOUR THINGS TOO, SWEETIE.
MR. SPARROW ALREADY HAS A SECRETARY.
THERE, THERE, SWEETIE. THEY'LL CALL YOU AS SOON AS A POSITION OPENS UP IN THE POOL.
YOU'RE STILL GETTING PAID, OF COURSE.
WAIT, I-
SSSSSHHHHUUUUNK

hnnh

bing

—THOSE FREAKS GOT THE GAS CHAMBER—

OPERATIONS IN LAOS—

WE COULD HAVE A DRIN

TEE TIME AT THE CONGRESSIONAL

—ABOUT "BANGLADESH"

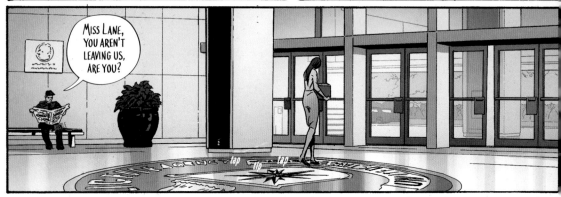

MISS LANE, YOU AREN'T LEAVING US, ARE YOU?

tap tp tap

tok tok

V.A. MEDICAL CENTER, SAN FRANCISCO.

NO—

JACK HUDSON, SOVIET BLOC DIVISION, C.I.A.

~VIRGIL!

≥nngh≤

VIRGIL IS **DEAD**, MR. HUDSON.

HELP ME CATCH HIS KILLER.

SIMON SPARROW. LATELY OF COUNTER-INTELLIGENCE.

YES...

I'VE HEARD OF YOU...

WHEN YOU FEEL SUFFICIENTLY RESTED, I'D LIKE TO DEBRIEF YOU ON WHAT HAPPENED AT THE GAS STATION.

I'M READY NOW.

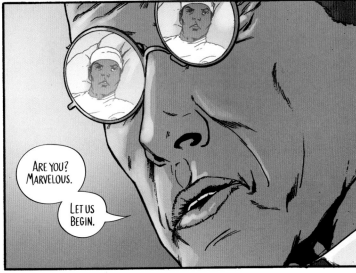

ARE YOU? MARVELOUS.

LET US BEGIN.

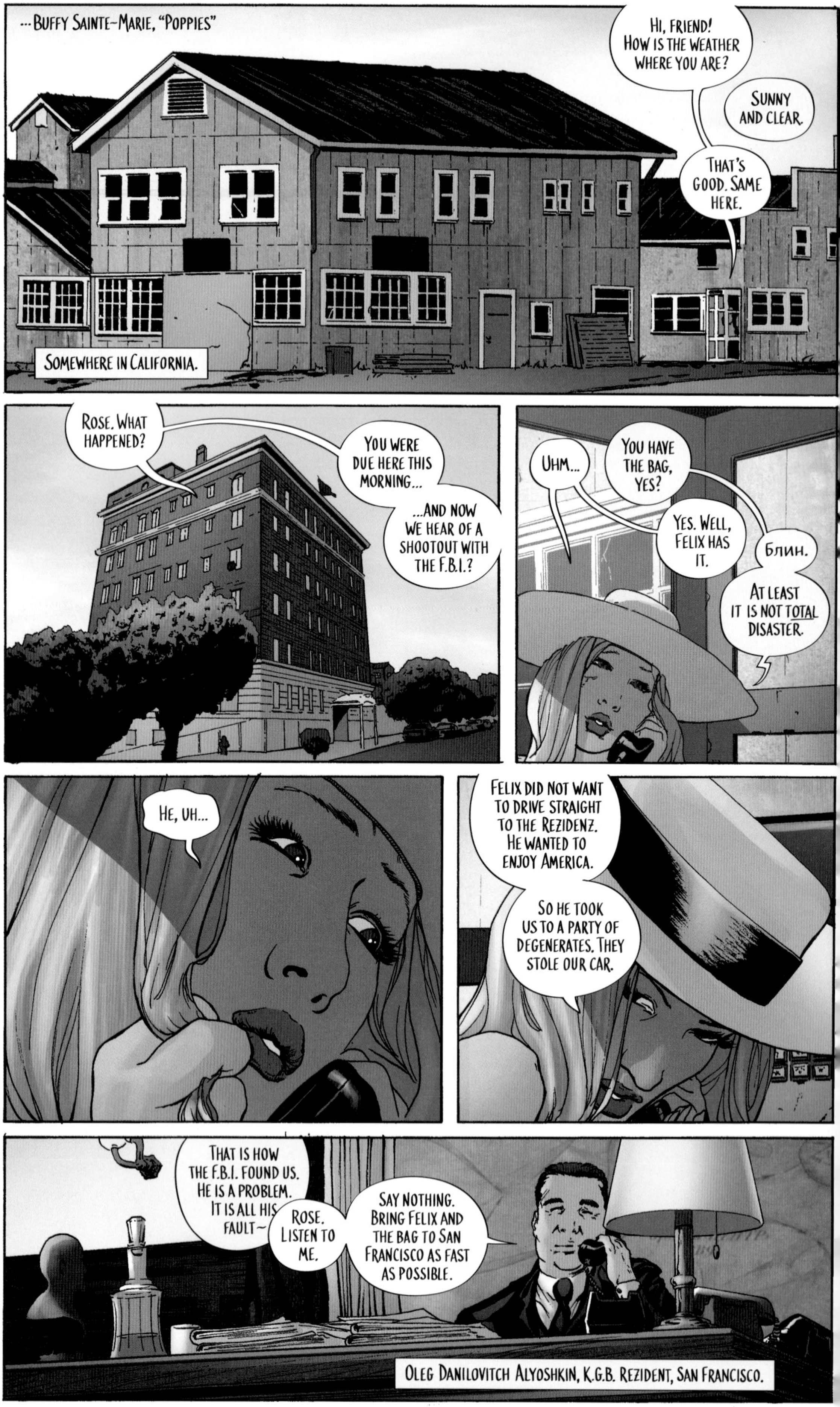
...Buffy Sainte-Marie, "Poppies"
Hi, friend! How is the weather where you are?
Sunny and clear.
That's good. Same here.
Somewhere in California.
Rose. What happened?
You were due here this morning...
...And now we hear of a shootout with the F.B.I.?
Uhm...
You have the bag, yes?
Yes. Well, Felix has it.
Блин.
At least it is not total disaster.
He, uh...
Felix did not want to drive straight to the Rezidenz. He wanted to enjoy America.
So he took us to a party of degenerates. They stole our car.
That is how the F.B.I. found us. He is a problem. It is all his fault—
Rose. Listen to me.
Say nothing. Bring Felix and the bag to San Francisco as fast as possible.
Oleg Danilovitch Alyoshkin, K.G.B. Rezident, San Francisco.

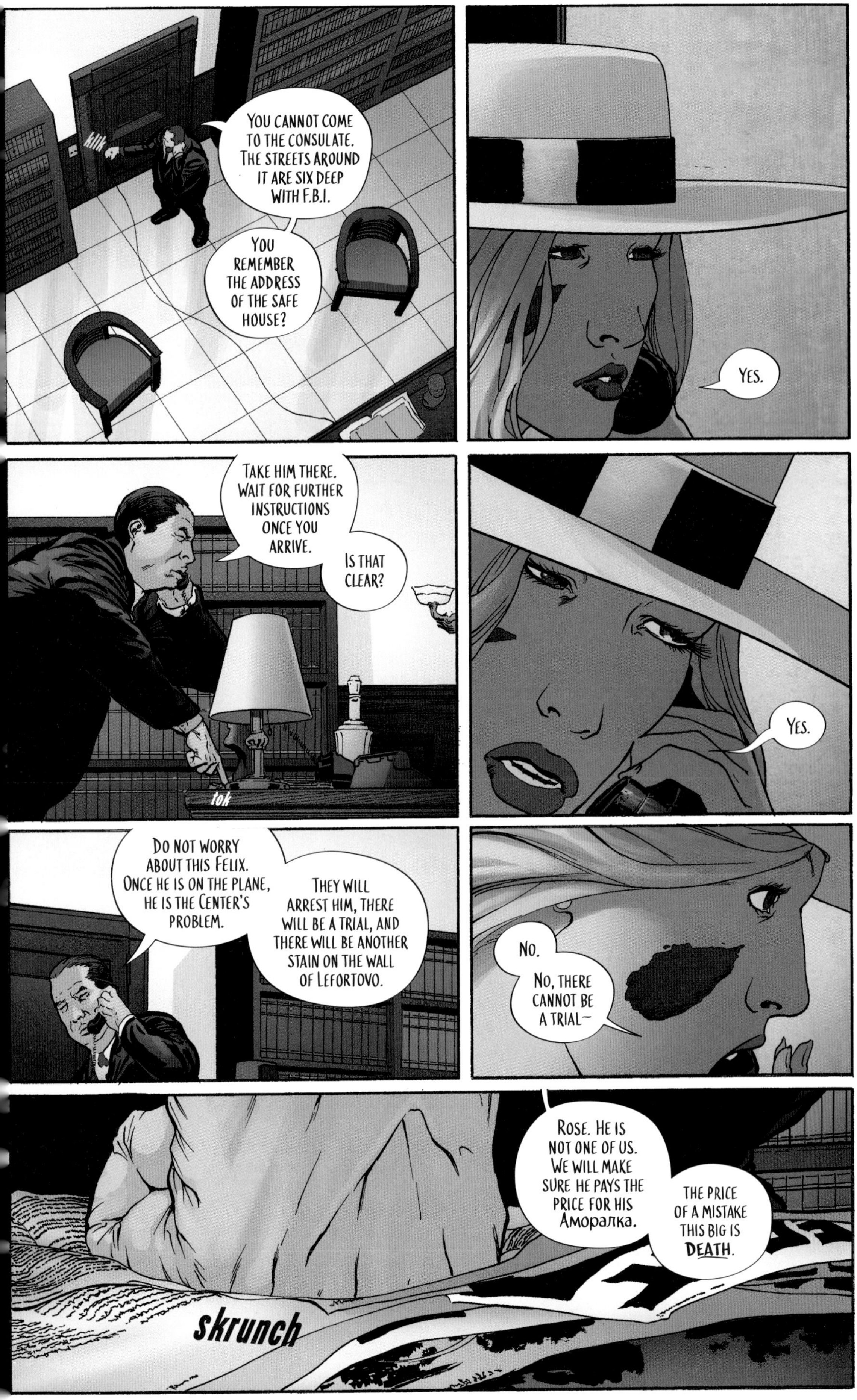
klik
YOU CANNOT COME TO THE CONSULATE. THE STREETS AROUND IT ARE SIX DEEP WITH F.B.I.
YOU REMEMBER THE ADDRESS OF THE SAFE HOUSE?
YES.
TAKE HIM THERE. WAIT FOR FURTHER INSTRUCTIONS ONCE YOU ARRIVE.
IS THAT CLEAR?
tok
YES.
DO NOT WORRY ABOUT THIS FELIX. ONCE HE IS ON THE PLANE, HE IS THE CENTER'S PROBLEM.
THEY WILL ARREST HIM, THERE WILL BE A TRIAL, AND THERE WILL BE ANOTHER STAIN ON THE WALL OF LEFORTOVO.
NO.
NO, THERE CANNOT BE A TRIAL–
ROSE. HE IS NOT ONE OF US. WE WILL MAKE SURE HE PAYS THE PRICE FOR HIS Аморалка.
THE PRICE OF A MISTAKE THIS BIG IS DEATH.
skrunch

...ROSE?

SKREEK

W-WHAT IF HE DIES HERE?

≥ehn≤ IT'S BETTER FOR YOU IF THEY ARREST HIM FROM THE PLANE.

YOU LOOK MORE INNOCENT THAT WAY.

BESIDES, LUBYANKA PREFERS TO DO THE PUNISHMENTS THEMSELVES. LOTS OF TROUBLE FOR ME IF THEY DON'T GET THEIR MAN.

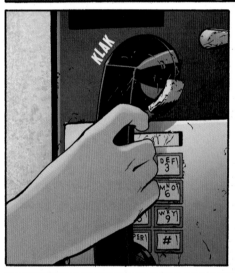

KLAK

DEF 3
MNO 6
WXY 9
PER1 #1

R D

HL 5E

-!

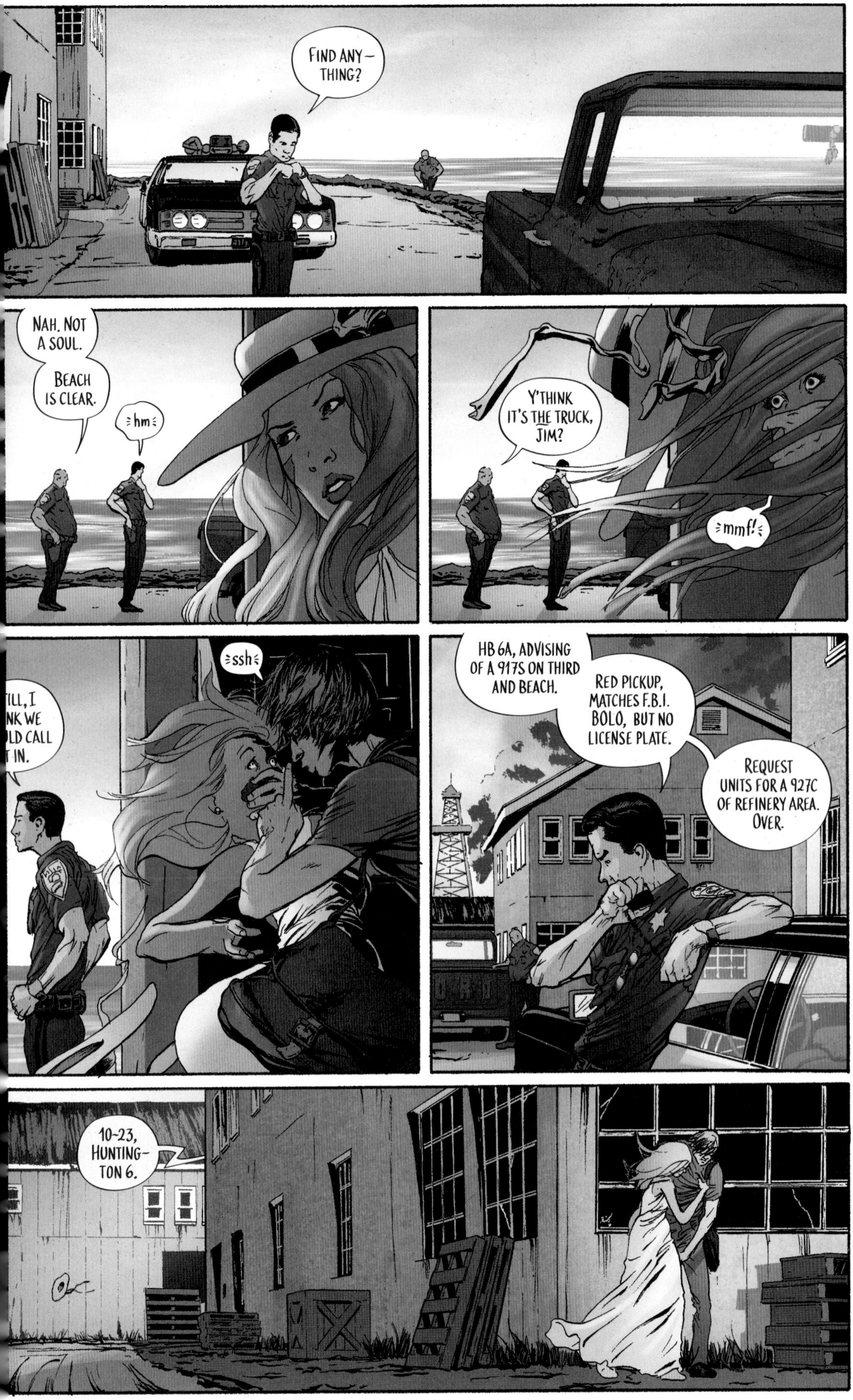
FIND ANY-THING?
NAH. NOT A SOUL.
BEACH IS CLEAR.
hm
Y'THINK IT'S THE TRUCK, JIM?
mmf!
ssh
TILL, I NK WE ULD CALL T IN.
HB 6A, ADVISING OF A 917S ON THIRD AND BEACH.
RED PICKUP, MATCHES F.B.I. BOLO, BUT NO LICENSE PLATE.
REQUEST UNITS FOR A 927C OF REFINERY AREA. OVER.
10-23, HUNTING-TON 6.

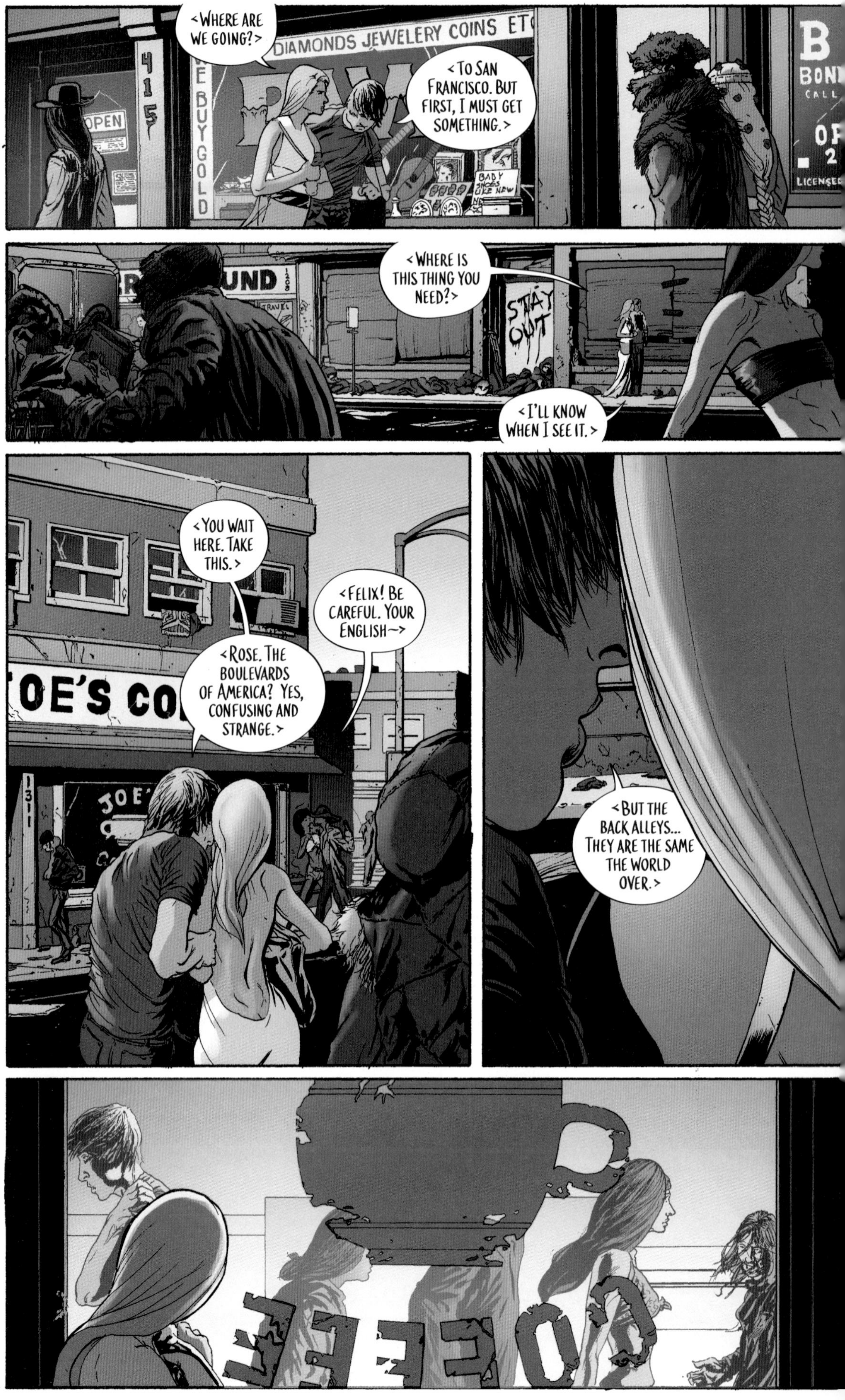

<WHERE ARE WE GOING?>
DIAMONDS JEWELERY COINS ET
WE BUY GOLD
415
OPEN
<TO SAN FRANCISCO. BUT FIRST, I MUST GET SOMETHING.>
BABY SHOES LIKE NEW
<WHERE IS THIS THING YOU NEED?>
STAY OUT
<I'LL KNOW WHEN I SEE IT.>
<YOU WAIT HERE. TAKE THIS.>
<FELIX! BE CAREFUL. YOUR ENGLISH~>
<ROSE. THE BOULEVARDS OF AMERICA? YES, CONFUSING AND STRANGE.>
1311
<BUT THE BACK ALLEYS... THEY ARE THE SAME THE WORLD OVER.>

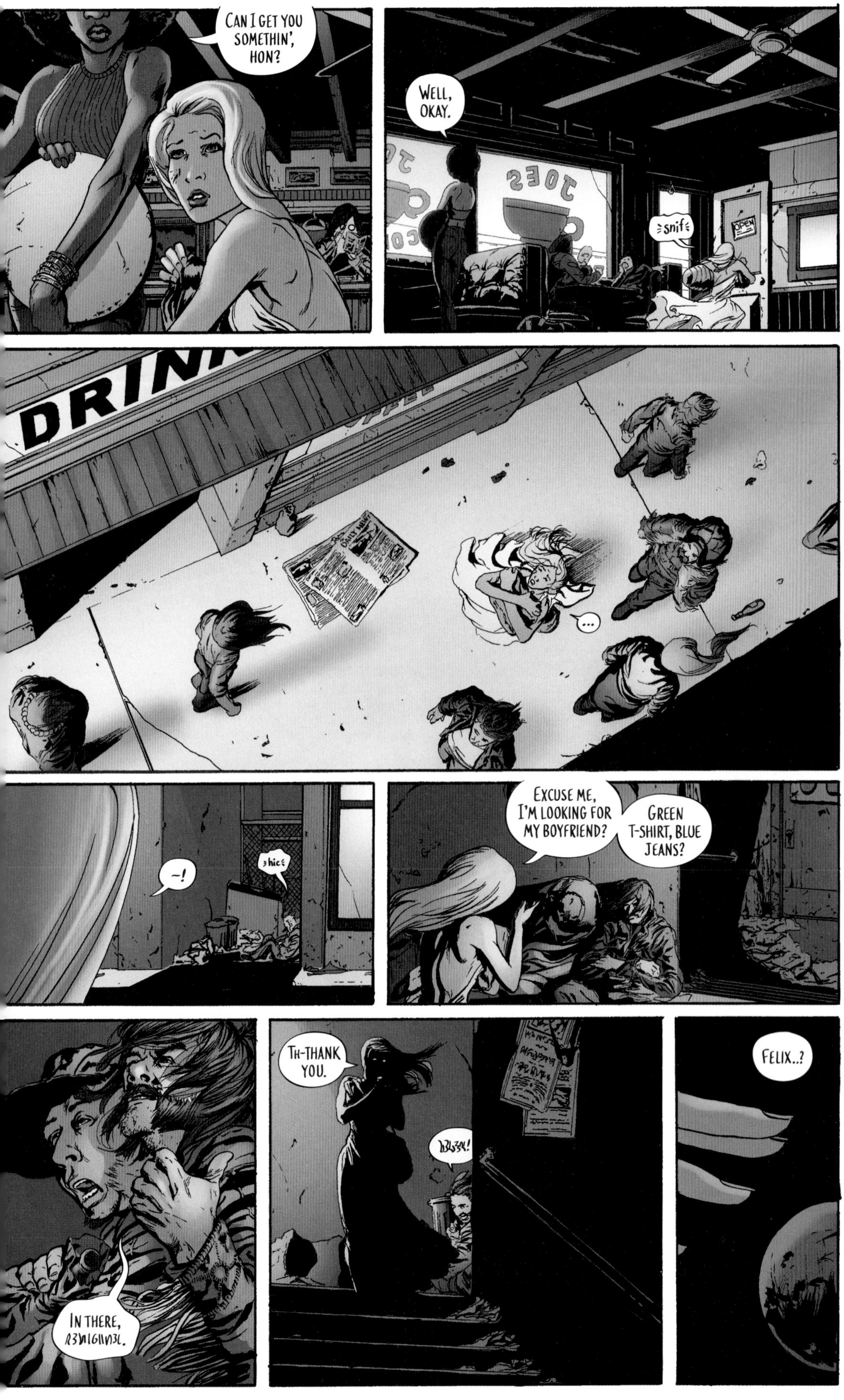
CAN I GET YOU SOMETHIN', HON?
WELL, OKAY.
OPEN
snif
...
~!
hic
EXCUSE ME, I'M LOOKING FOR MY BOYFRIEND?
GREEN T-SHIRT, BLUE JEANS?
IN THERE,
TH-THANK YOU.
FELIX..?

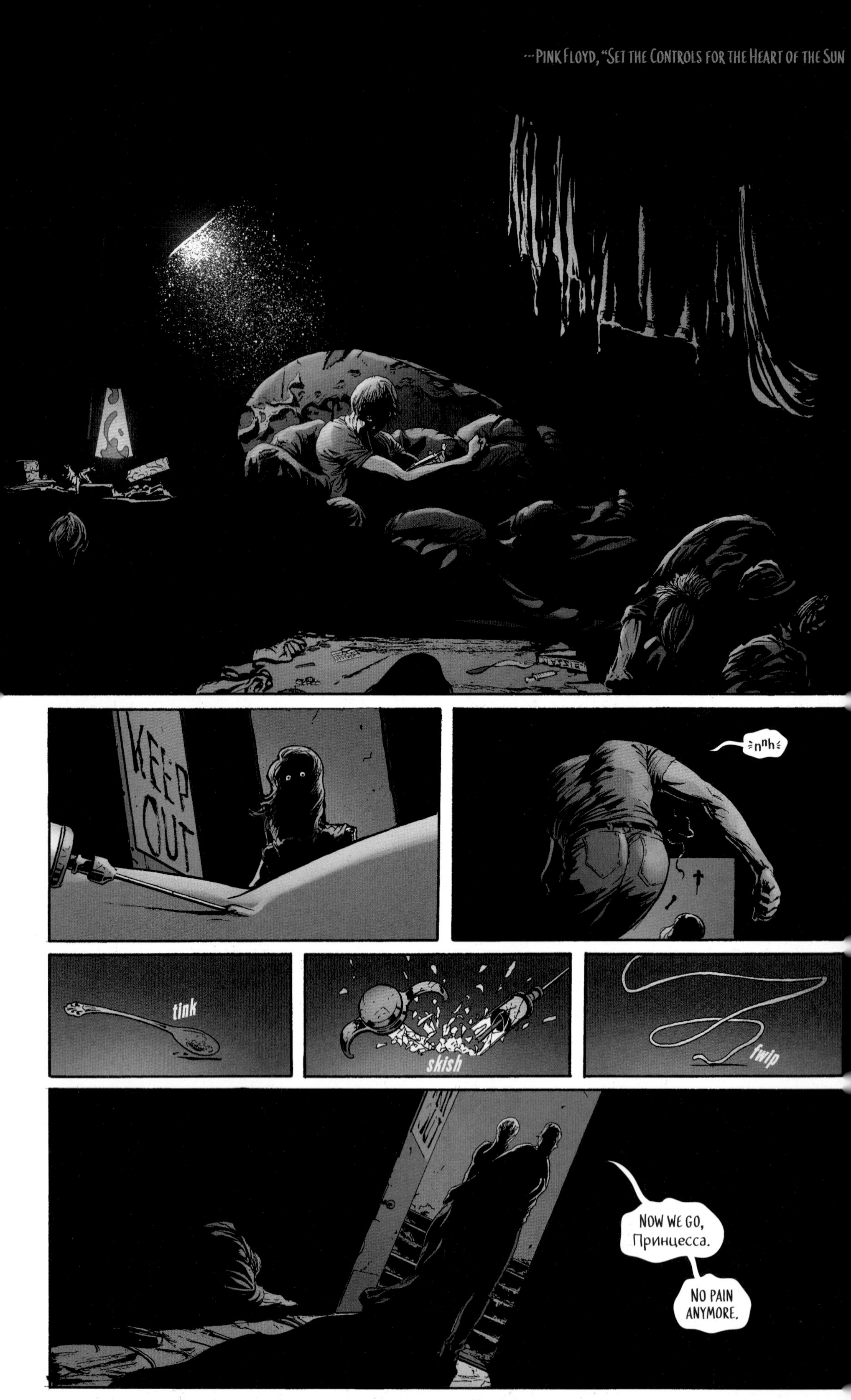
...PINK FLOYD, "SET THE CONTROLS FOR THE HEART OF THE SUN
nnh
tink
skish
fwip
NOW WE GO, Принцесса.
NO PAIN ANYMORE.

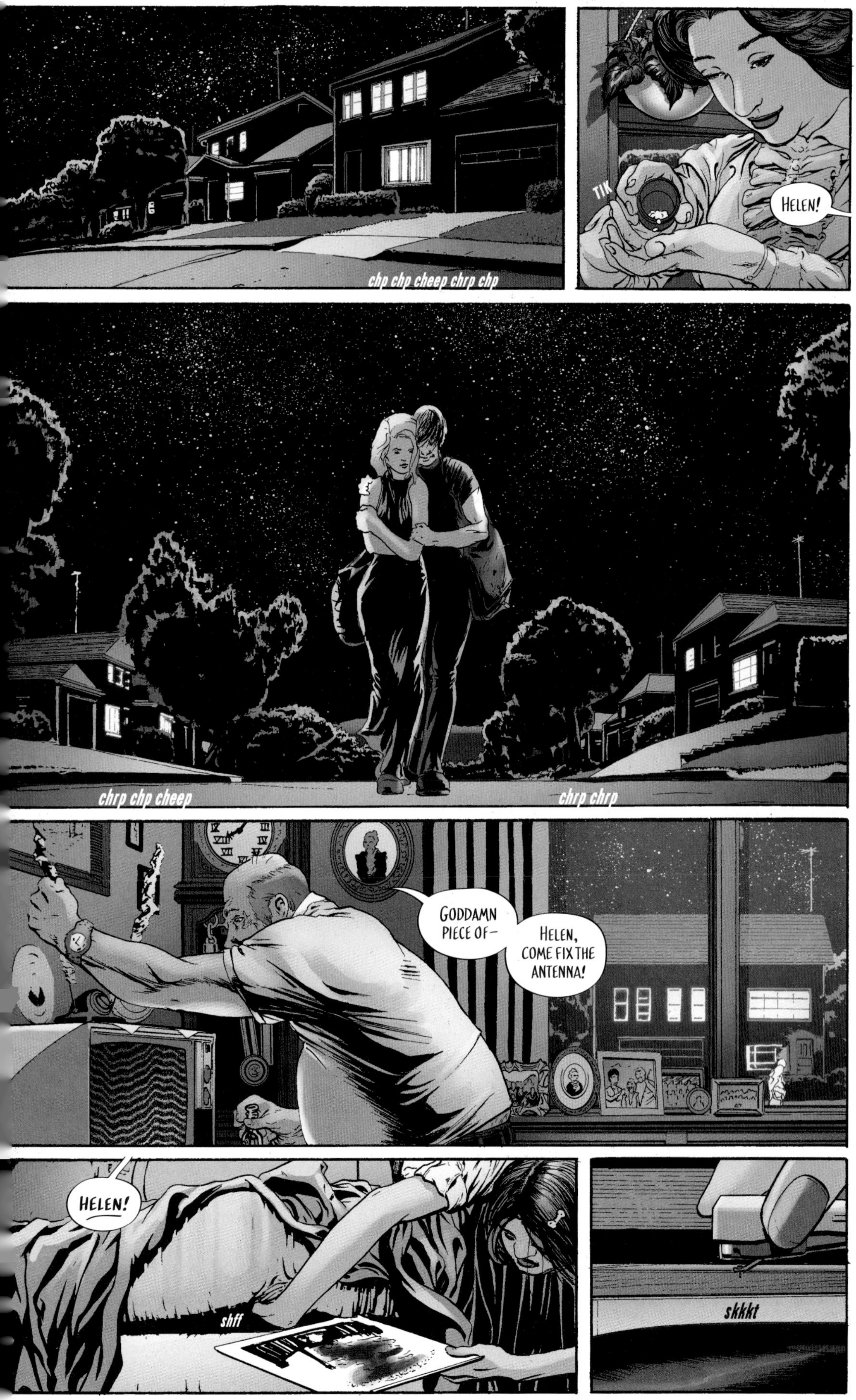
chp chp cheep chrp chp
TIK
HELEN!
chrp chp cheep
chrp chrp
GODDAMN PIECE OF—
HELEN, COME FIX THE ANTENNA!
HELEN!
shff
skkkt

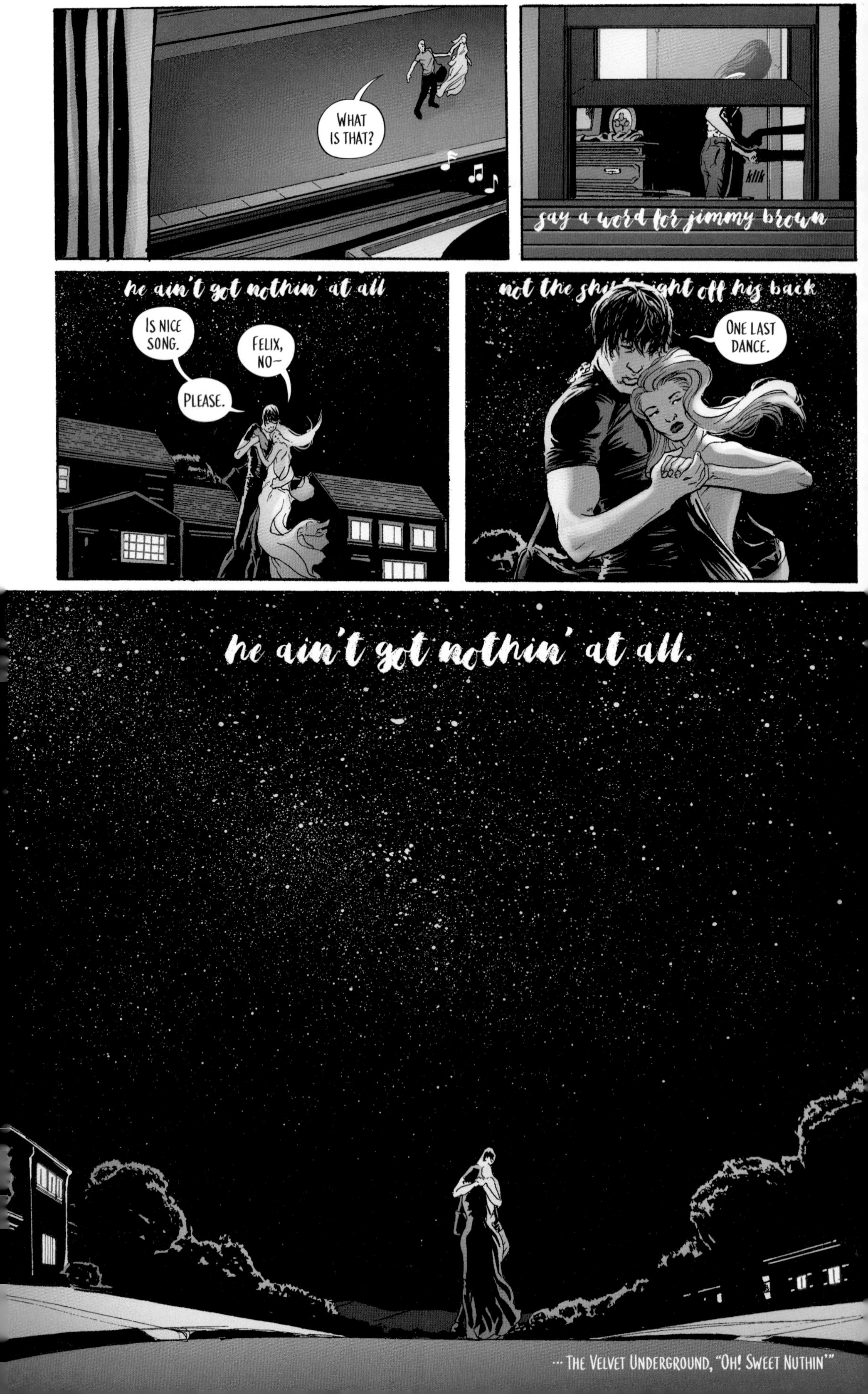

WHAT IS THAT?
klik
say a word for jimmy brown
he ain't got nothin' at all
IS NICE SONG.
FELIX, NO–
PLEASE.
not the shi ight off his back
ONE LAST DANCE.
he ain't got nothin' at all.
··· THE VELVET UNDERGROUND, "OH! SWEET NUTHIN'"

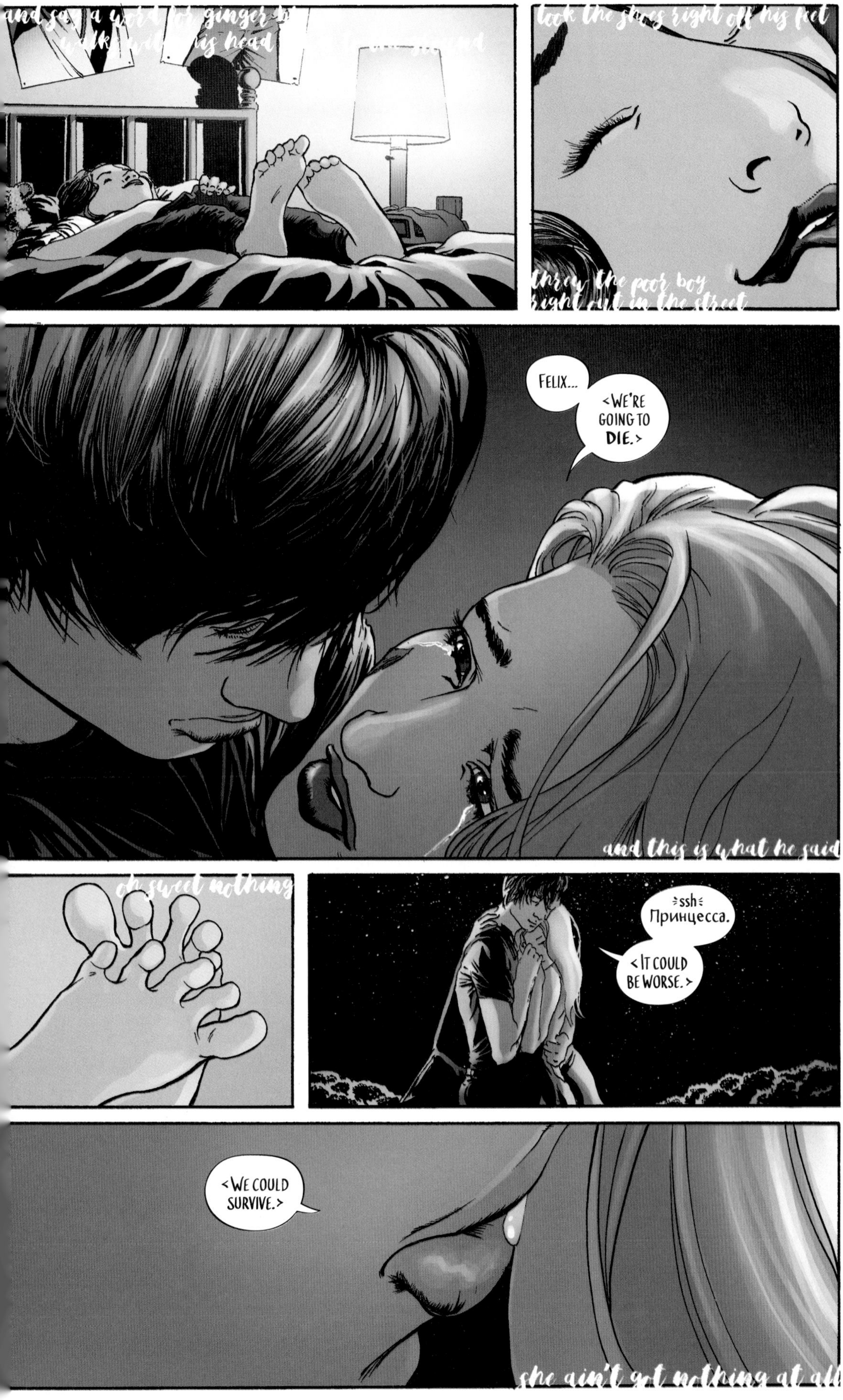

and say a word for ginger
took the shoes right off his feet
threw the poor boy right out in the street
Felix...
<We're going to die.>
and this is what he said
oh sweet nothing
ssh Принцесса.
<It could be worse.>
<We could survive.>
she ain't got nothing at all

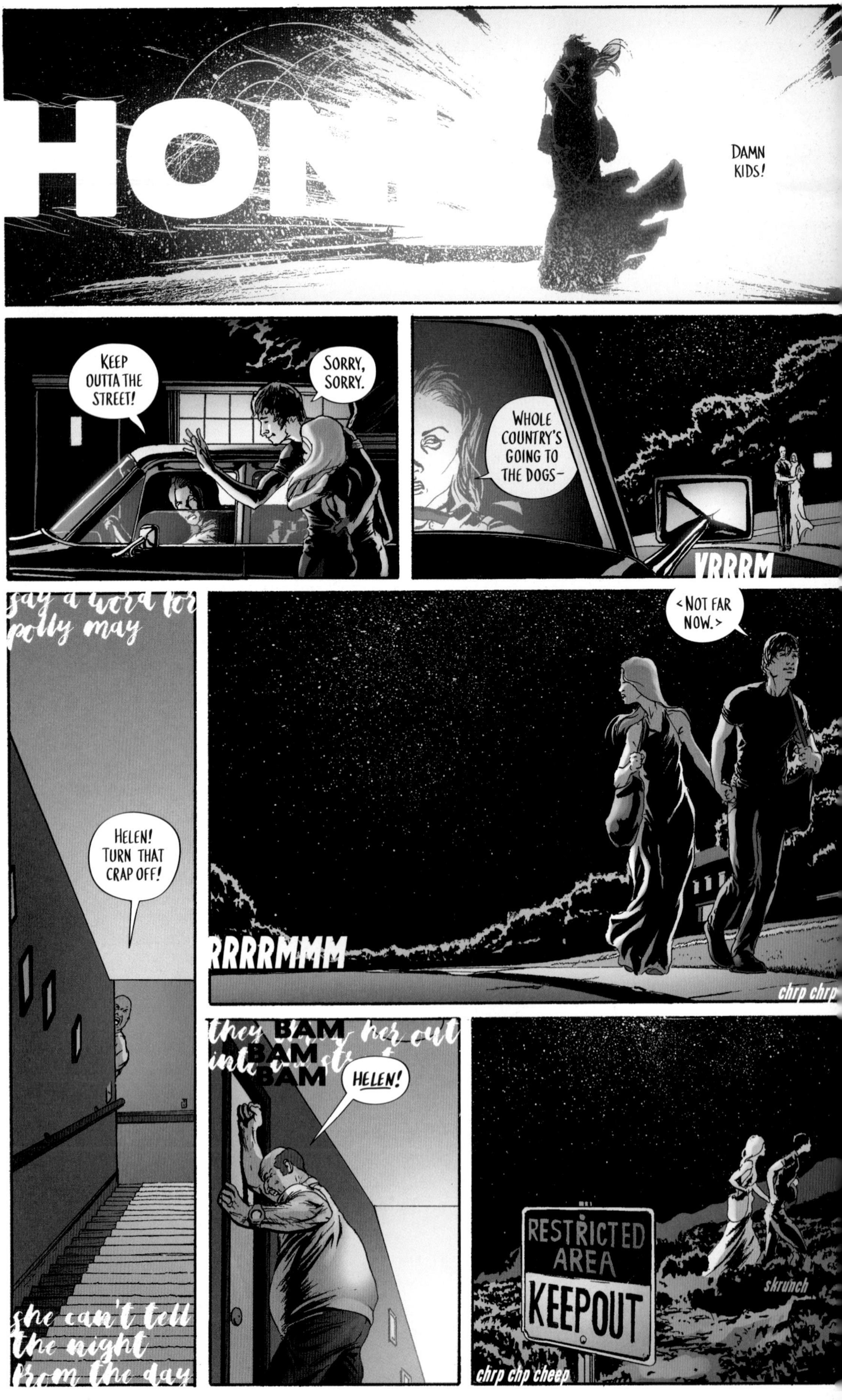
HON
DAMN KIDS!
KEEP OUTTA THE STREET!
SORRY, SORRY.
WHOLE COUNTRY'S GOING TO THE DOGS-
VRRRM
say a word for polly may
HELEN! TURN THAT CRAP OFF!
<NOT FAR NOW.>
RRRRMMM
chrp chrp
they
her out
BAM
BAM
BAM
HELEN!
RESTRICTED AREA
KEEPOUT
skrunch
chrp chp cheep
she can't tell the night from the day

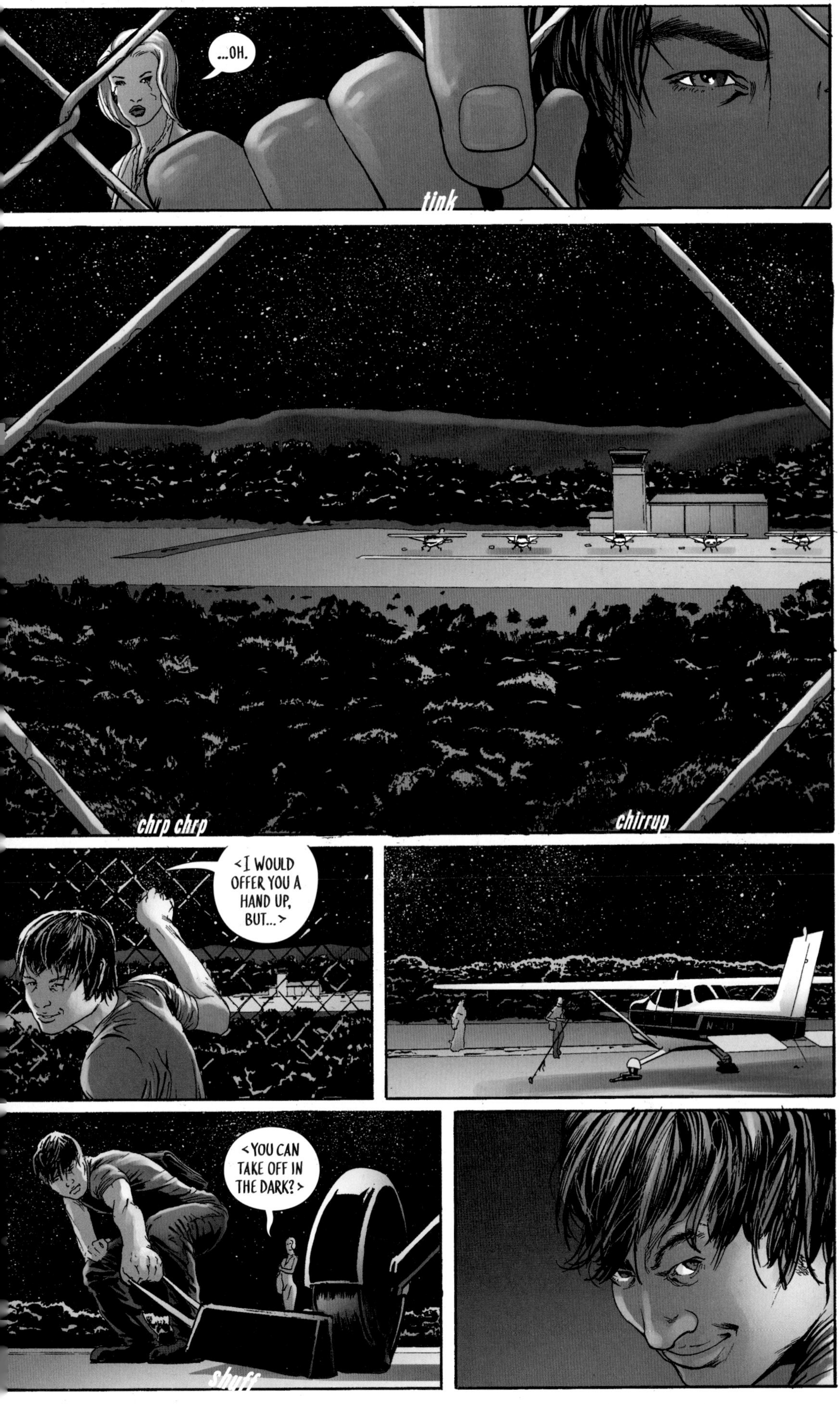
...OH.
tink
chrp chrp
chirrup
<I WOULD OFFER YOU A HAND UP, BUT...>
<YOU CAN TAKE OFF IN THE DARK?>
shuff

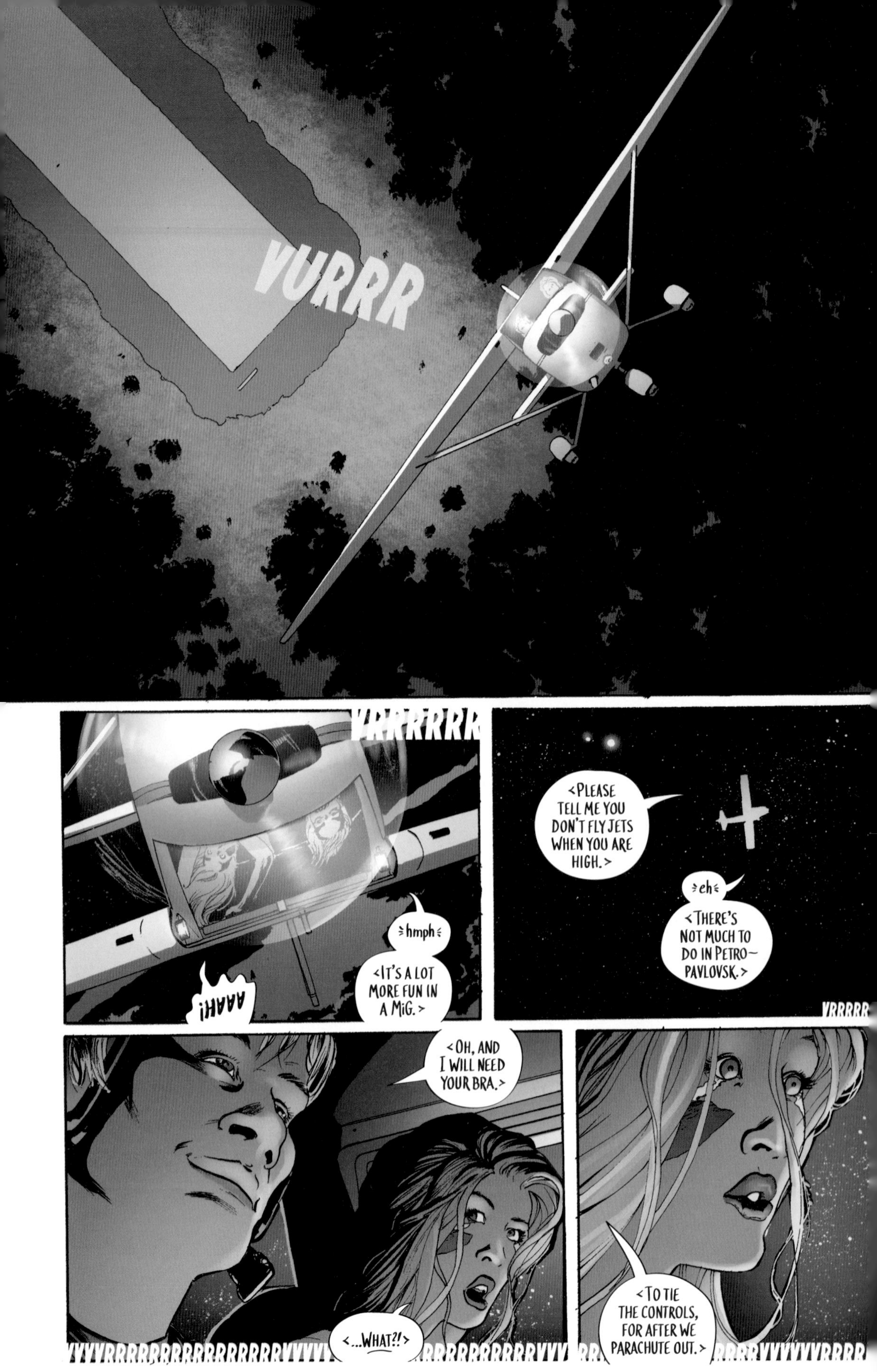
VURRR
VRRRRRRR
hmph
<IT'S A LOT MORE FUN IN A MiG.>
AAAH!
<PLEASE TELL ME YOU DON'T FLY JETS WHEN YOU ARE HIGH.>
eh
<THERE'S NOT MUCH TO DO IN PETRO-PAVLOVSK.>
VRRRRR
<OH, AND I WILL NEED YOUR BRA.>
<...WHAT?!>
<TO TIE THE CONTROLS, FOR AFTER WE PARACHUTE OUT.>
VVVVRRRRRRRRRRRRRRRRRVVVVV
RRRRRRRRRRRRVVVV
RRRRVVVVVVVRRRR

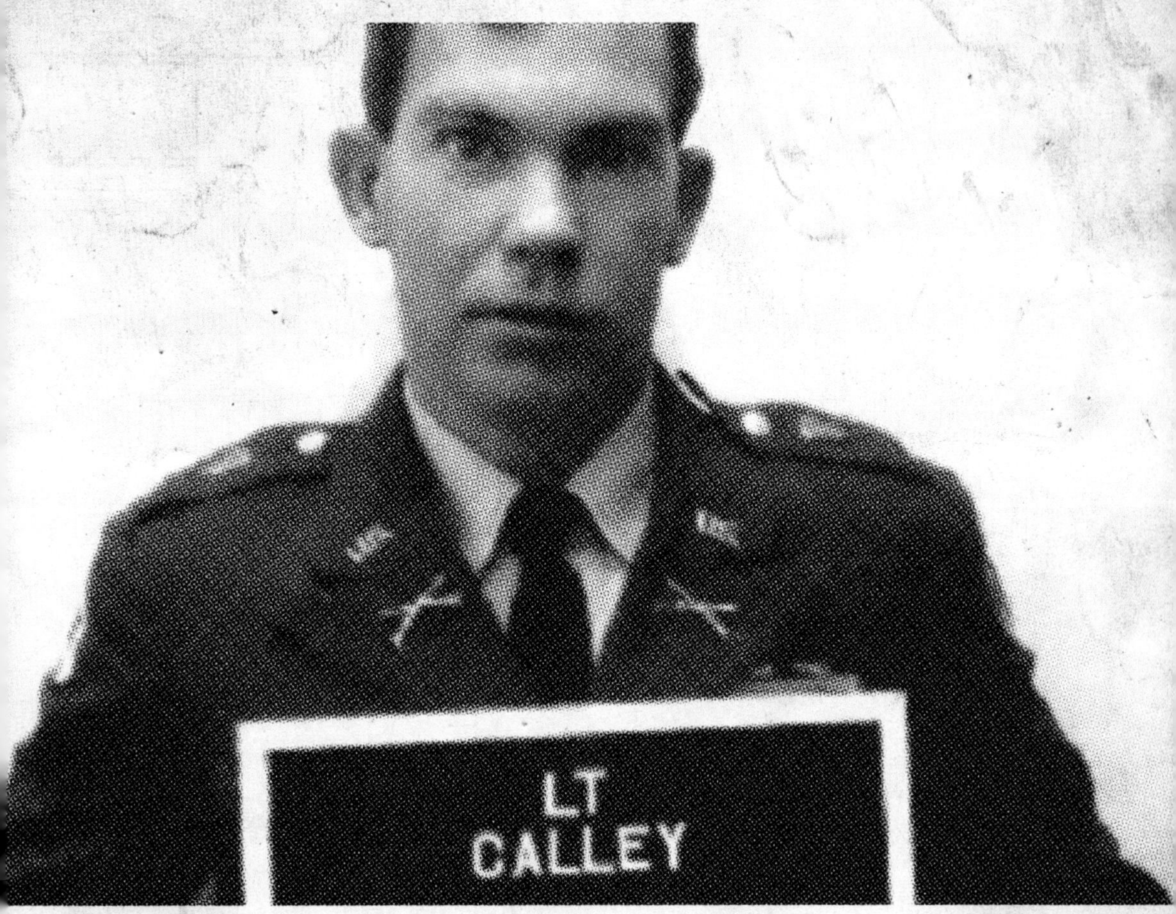
LT
CALLEY

“Well, I was ordered to go in there and destroy the enemy... I did not sit down and think in terms of men, women, and children. They were all classified the same, and that was the classification that we dealt with, just as enemy soldiers.”
Lt. William Calley, February 1971

If the Government doesn't stop the war, we will stop the Government.

DEMONSTRATE
APRIL 24
Washington, DC
San Francisco

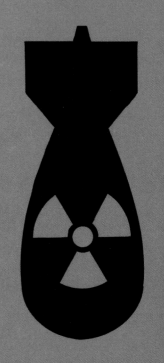

End the Killings NOW

FOUR

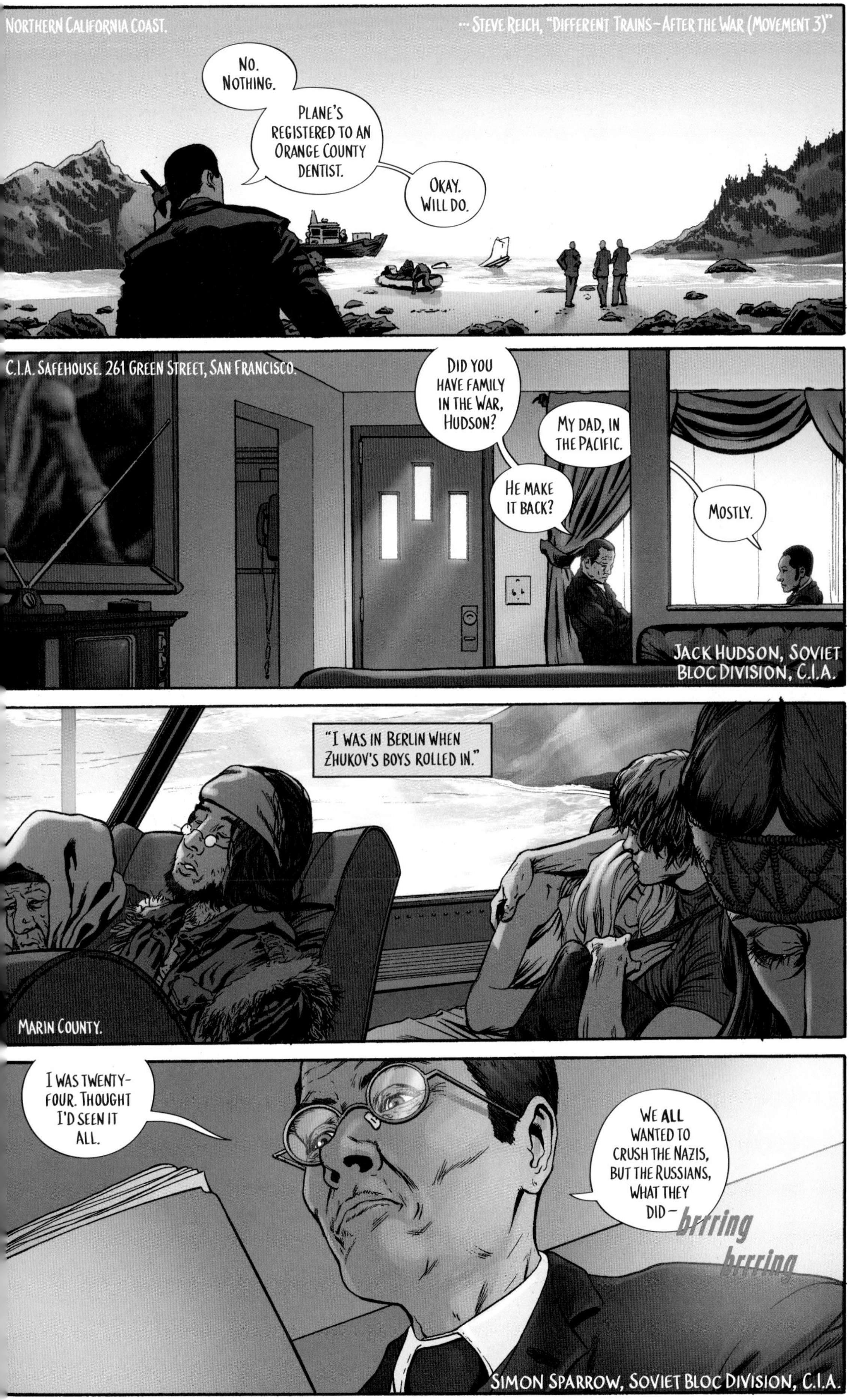
NORTHERN CALIFORNIA COAST.
... STEVE REICH, "DIFFERENT TRAINS–AFTER THE WAR (MOVEMENT 3)"
NO. NOTHING.
PLANE'S REGISTERED TO AN ORANGE COUNTY DENTIST.
OKAY. WILL DO.
C.I.A. SAFEHOUSE. 261 GREEN STREET, SAN FRANCISCO.
DID YOU HAVE FAMILY IN THE WAR, HUDSON?
MY DAD, IN THE PACIFIC.
HE MAKE IT BACK?
MOSTLY.
JACK HUDSON, SOVIET BLOC DIVISION, C.I.A.
"I WAS IN BERLIN WHEN ZHUKOV'S BOYS ROLLED IN."
MARIN COUNTY.
I WAS TWENTY-FOUR. THOUGHT I'D SEEN IT ALL.
WE ALL WANTED TO CRUSH THE NAZIS, BUT THE RUSSIANS, WHAT THEY DID–
brrring
brrring
SIMON SPARROW, SOVIET BLOC DIVISION, C.I.A.

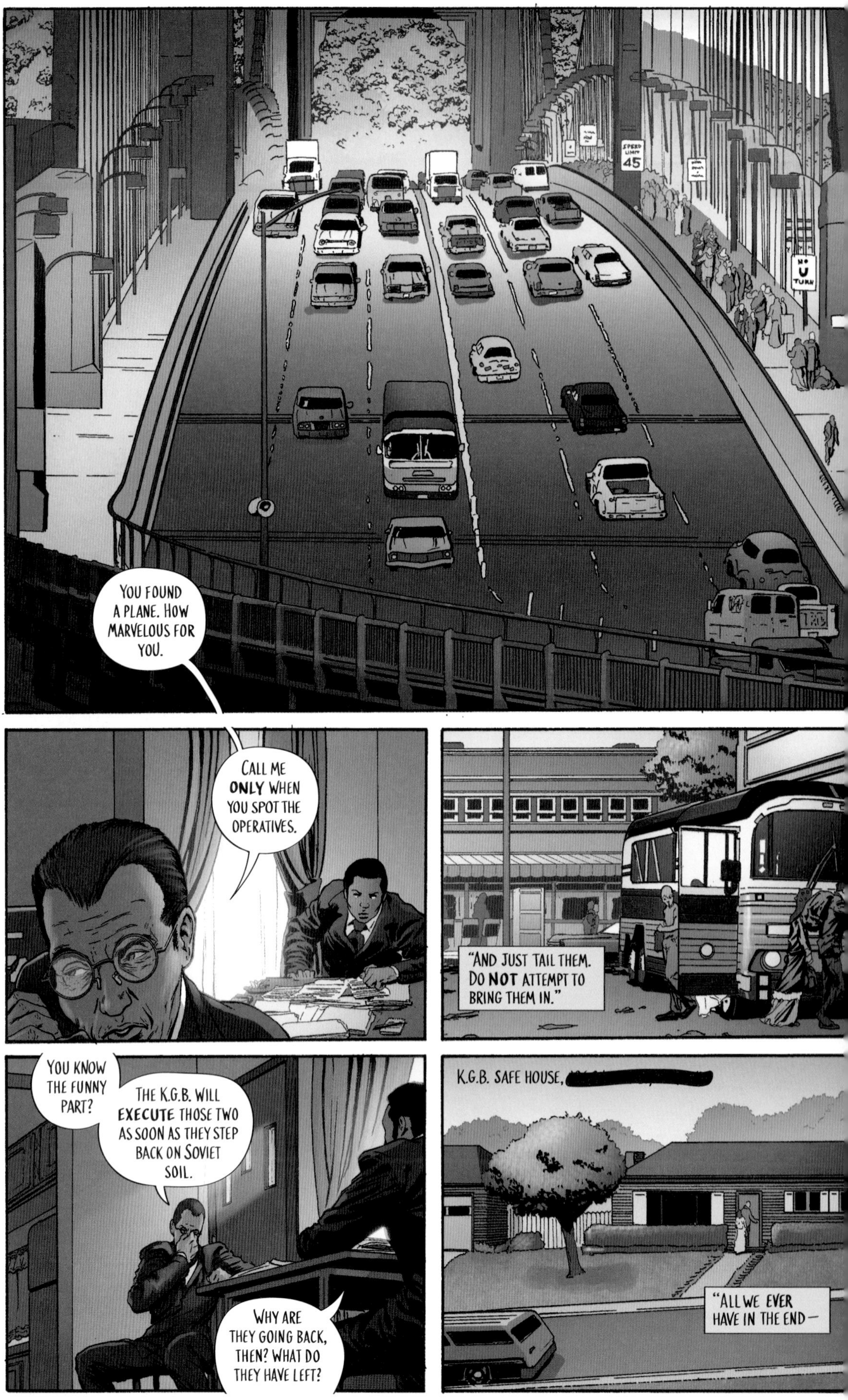
YOU FOUND A PLANE. HOW MARVELOUS FOR YOU.
CALL ME ONLY WHEN YOU SPOT THE OPERATIVES.
"AND JUST TAIL THEM. DO NOT ATTEMPT TO BRING THEM IN."
YOU KNOW THE FUNNY PART?
THE K.G.B. WILL EXECUTE THOSE TWO AS SOON AS THEY STEP BACK ON SOVIET SOIL.
WHY ARE THEY GOING BACK, THEN? WHAT DO THEY HAVE LEFT?
K.G.B. SAFE HOUSE, [redacted]
"ALL WE EVER HAVE IN THE END—

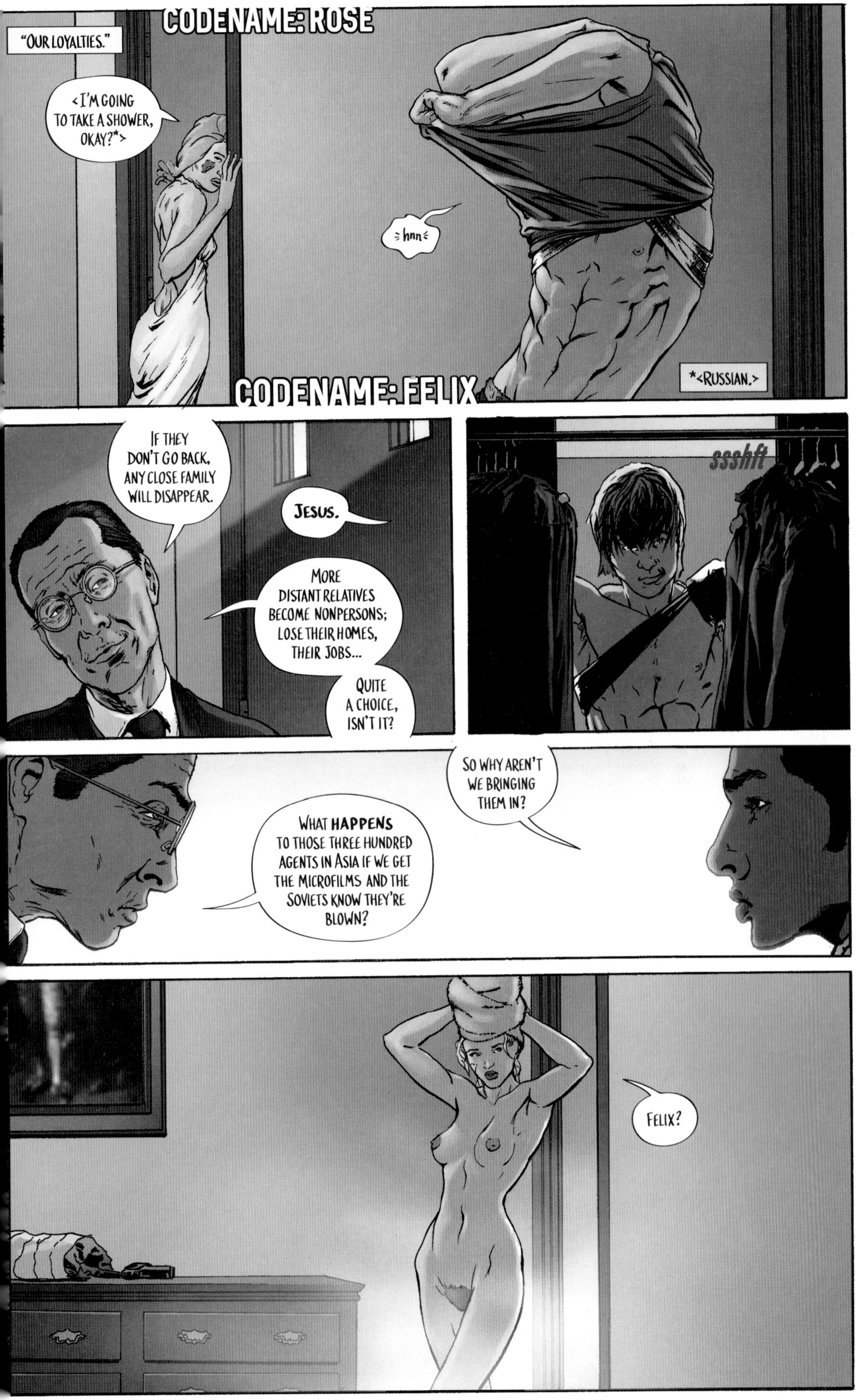
"OUR LOYALTIES."
CODENAME: ROSE
<I'M GOING TO TAKE A SHOWER, OKAY?*>
hnn
CODENAME: FELIX
*<RUSSIAN.>
IF THEY DON'T GO BACK, ANY CLOSE FAMILY WILL DISAPPEAR.
JESUS.
MORE DISTANT RELATIVES BECOME NONPERSONS; LOSE THEIR HOMES, THEIR JOBS...
QUITE A CHOICE, ISN'T IT?
ssshft
SO WHY AREN'T WE BRINGING THEM IN?
WHAT **HAPPENS** TO THOSE THREE HUNDRED AGENTS IN ASIA IF WE GET THE MICROFILMS AND THE SOVIETS KNOW THEY'RE BLOWN?
FELIX?

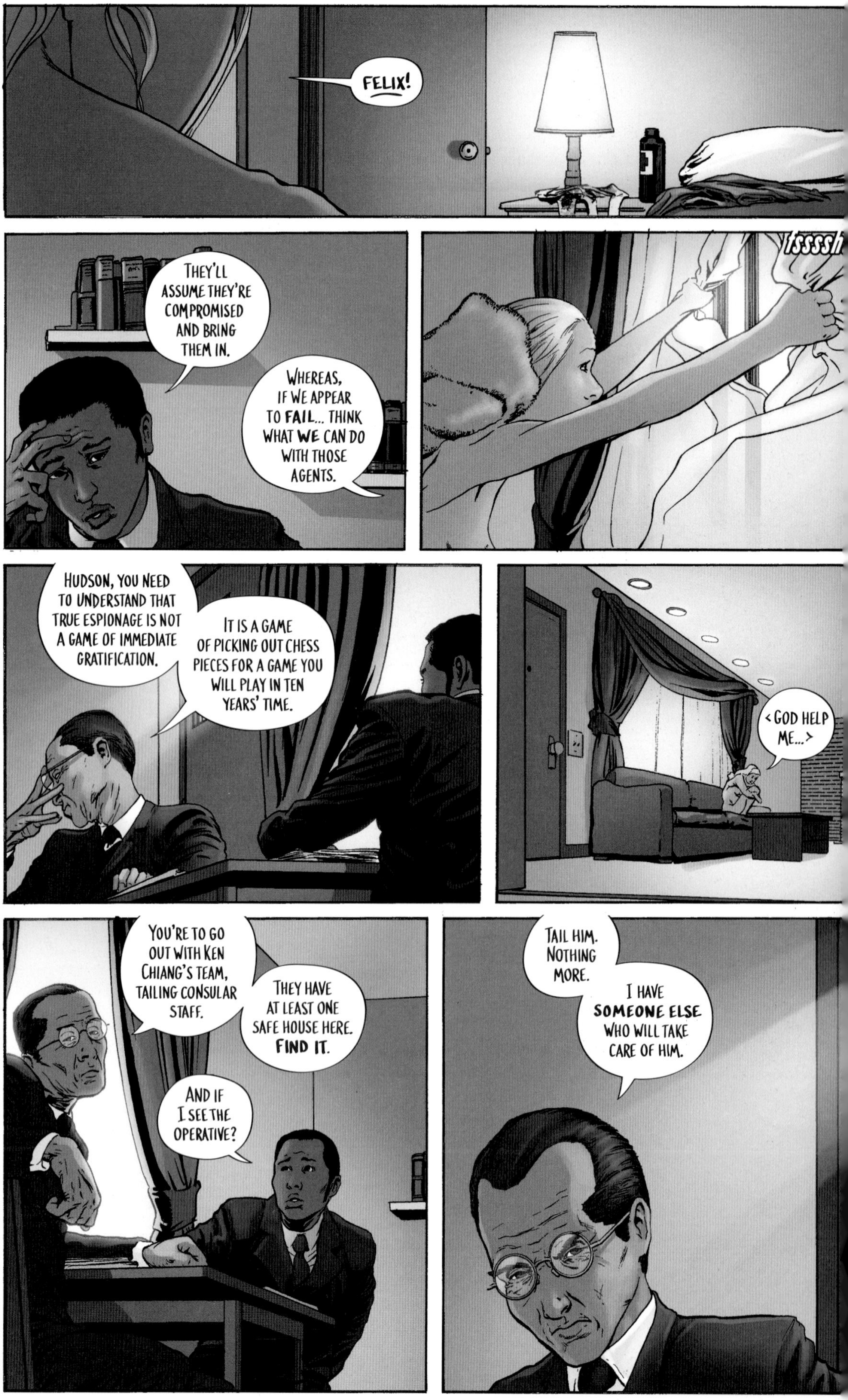
FELIX!
THEY'LL ASSUME THEY'RE COMPROMISED AND BRING THEM IN.
WHEREAS, IF WE APPEAR TO **FAIL**... THINK WHAT **WE** CAN DO WITH THOSE AGENTS.
fssssh
HUDSON, YOU NEED TO UNDERSTAND THAT TRUE ESPIONAGE IS NOT A GAME OF IMMEDIATE GRATIFICATION.
IT IS A GAME OF PICKING OUT CHESS PIECES FOR A GAME YOU WILL PLAY IN TEN YEARS' TIME.
<GOD HELP ME...>
YOU'RE TO GO OUT WITH KEN CHIANG'S TEAM, TAILING CONSULAR STAFF.
THEY HAVE AT LEAST ONE SAFE HOUSE HERE. **FIND IT**.
AND IF I SEE THE OPERATIVE?
TAIL HIM. NOTHING MORE.
I HAVE **SOMEONE ELSE** WHO WILL TAKE CARE OF HIM.

"WHEN I HAD VIENNA STATION, I DEVELOPED A YOUNG AGENT, **CKVIGIL**.

"HE WAS TRANSFERRED HERE, TO THE REZIDENZ.

... FRANK ZAPPA, "THE GUMBO VARIATIONS"

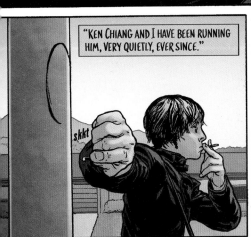

"KEN CHIANG AND I HAVE BEEN RUNNING HIM, VERY QUIETLY, EVER SINCE."

skkt

WE'VE HAD TO KEEP HIM SECRET. TOO MANY MOLES.

BUT THIS HAS BEEN A VERY **FORTUITOUS** DISASTER.

NOW WE HAVE A SINGULAR OPPORTUNITY TO SCORE A MAJOR INTELLIGENCE COUP AND DISCREDIT ALYOSHKIN, MEANING THEY WILL PROMOTE OUR ASSET IN HIS PLACE.

CAN I—

NO.

fwip

MAKSIM ALEXEYEVITCH MARKOV, LINE KR, K.G.B.

< THEY ARE AT THE SAFE HOUSE. >

< TIME TO LOSE OUR F.B.I. FRIENDS, VANYA. >

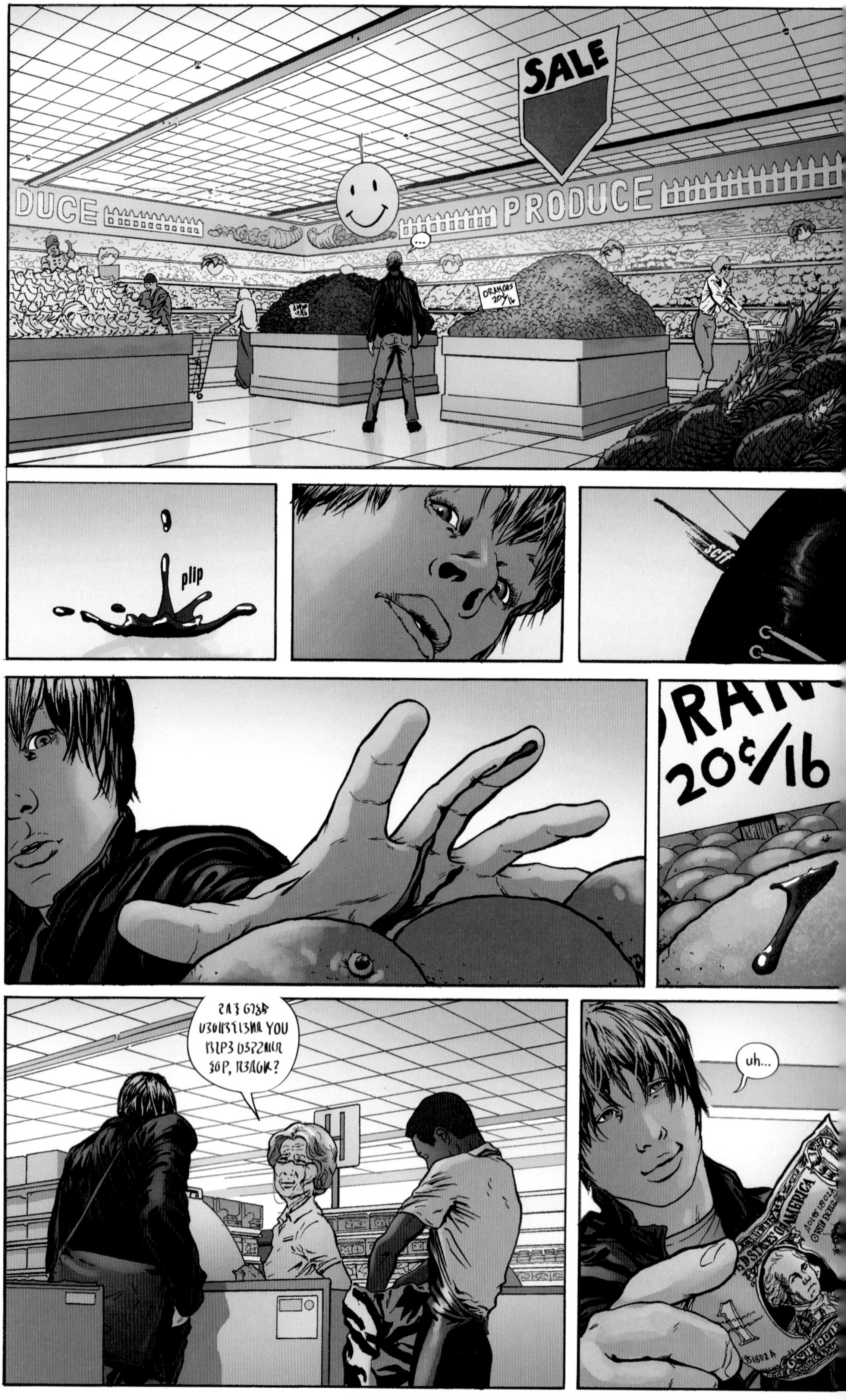
SALE
DUCE
PRODUCE
...
ORANGES 20¢/lb
plip
scff
ORAN
20¢/lb
uh...

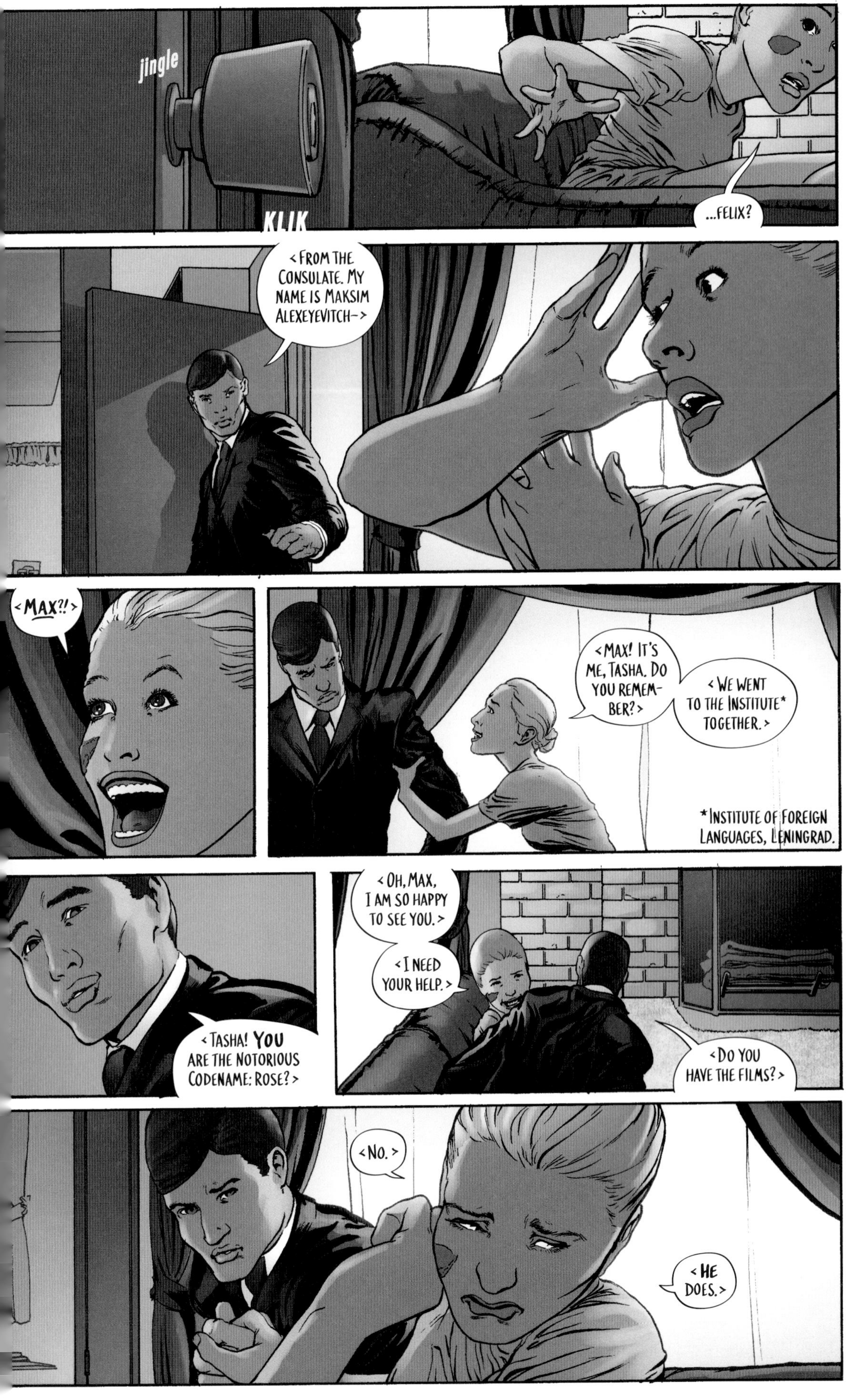
jingle
KLIK
...FELIX?
<FROM THE CONSULATE. MY NAME IS MAKSIM ALEXEYEVITCH–>
<MAX?!>
<MAX! IT'S ME, TASHA. DO YOU REMEMBER?>
<WE WENT TO THE INSTITUTE* TOGETHER.>
*INSTITUTE OF FOREIGN LANGUAGES, LENINGRAD.
<TASHA! YOU ARE THE NOTORIOUS CODENAME: ROSE?>
<OH, MAX, I AM SO HAPPY TO SEE YOU.>
<I NEED YOUR HELP.>
<DO YOU HAVE THE FILMS?>
<NO.>
<HE DOES.>

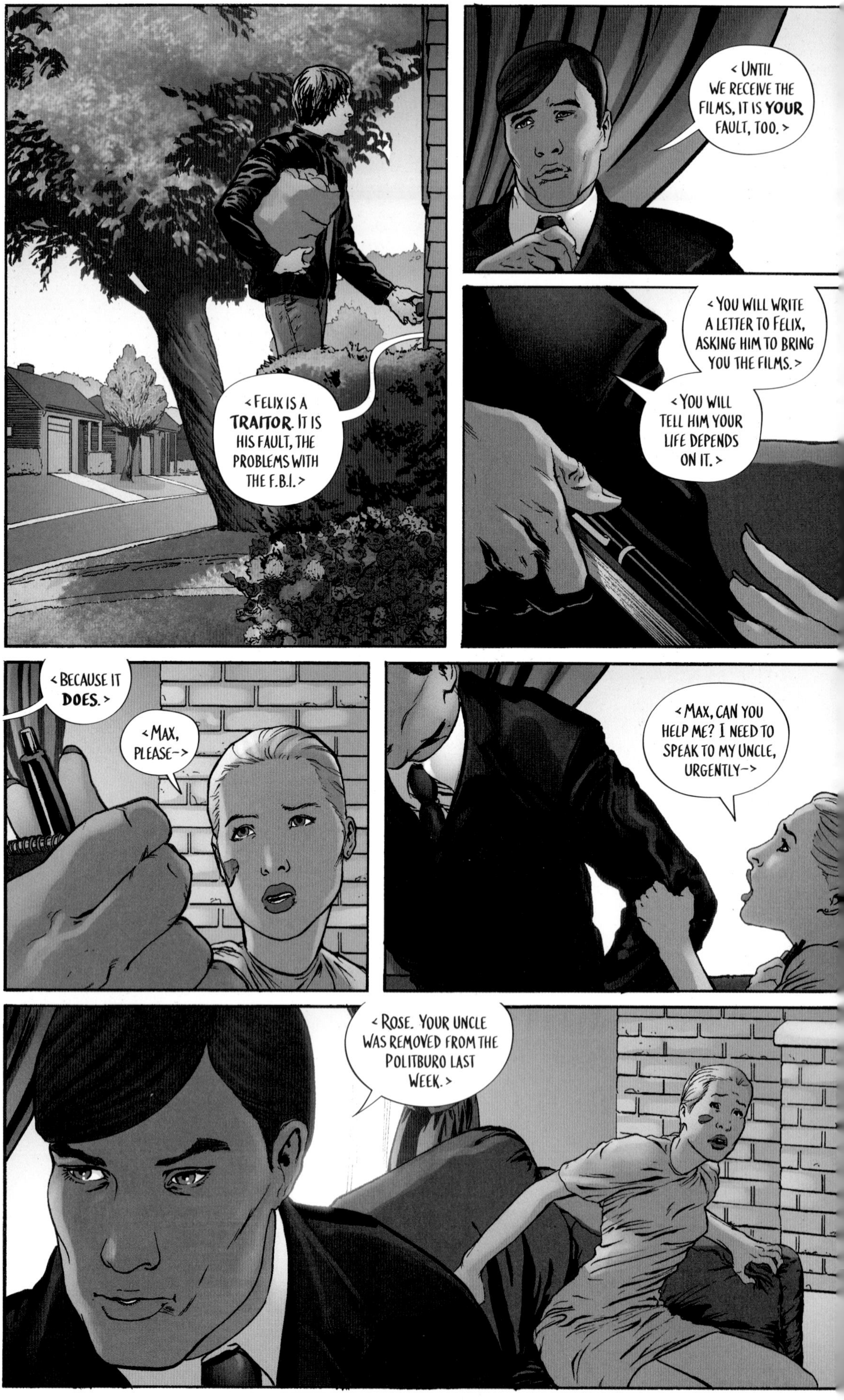
< FELIX IS A **TRAITOR**. IT IS HIS FAULT, THE PROBLEMS WITH THE F.B.I. >
< UNTIL WE RECEIVE THE FILMS, IT IS **YOUR** FAULT, TOO. >
< YOU WILL WRITE A LETTER TO FELIX, ASKING HIM TO BRING YOU THE FILMS. >
< YOU WILL TELL HIM YOUR LIFE DEPENDS ON IT. >
< BECAUSE IT **DOES**. >
< MAX, PLEASE-- >
< MAX, CAN YOU HELP ME? I NEED TO SPEAK TO MY UNCLE, URGENTLY-- >
< ROSE. YOUR UNCLE WAS REMOVED FROM THE POLITBURO LAST WEEK. >

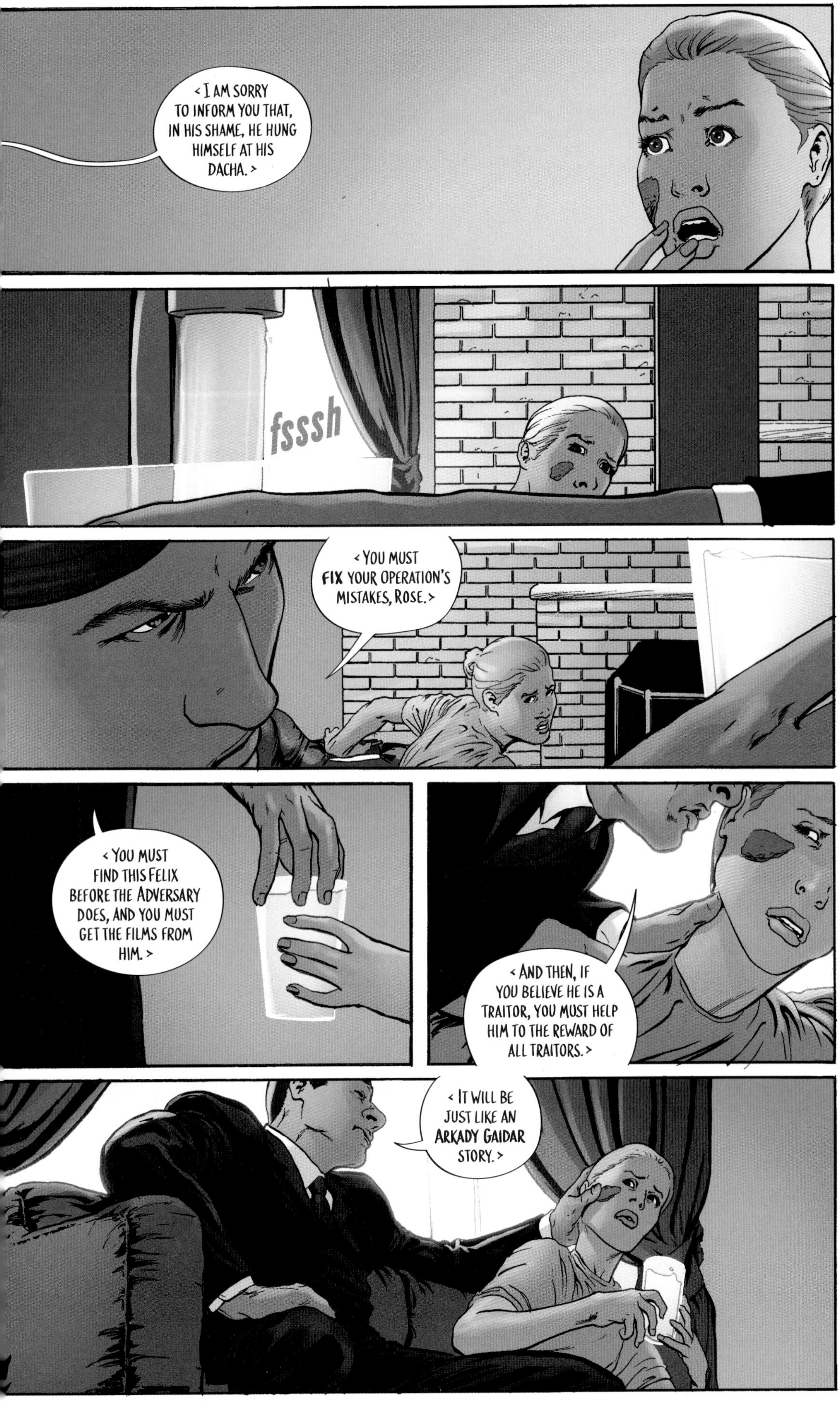
< I AM SORRY TO INFORM YOU THAT, IN HIS SHAME, HE HUNG HIMSELF AT HIS DACHA. >
fsssh
< YOU MUST FIX YOUR OPERATION'S MISTAKES, ROSE. >
< YOU MUST FIND THIS FELIX BEFORE THE ADVERSARY DOES, AND YOU MUST GET THE FILMS FROM HIM. >
< AND THEN, IF YOU BELIEVE HE IS A TRAITOR, YOU MUST HELP HIM TO THE REWARD OF ALL TRAITORS. >
< IT WILL BE JUST LIKE AN ARKADY GAIDAR STORY. >

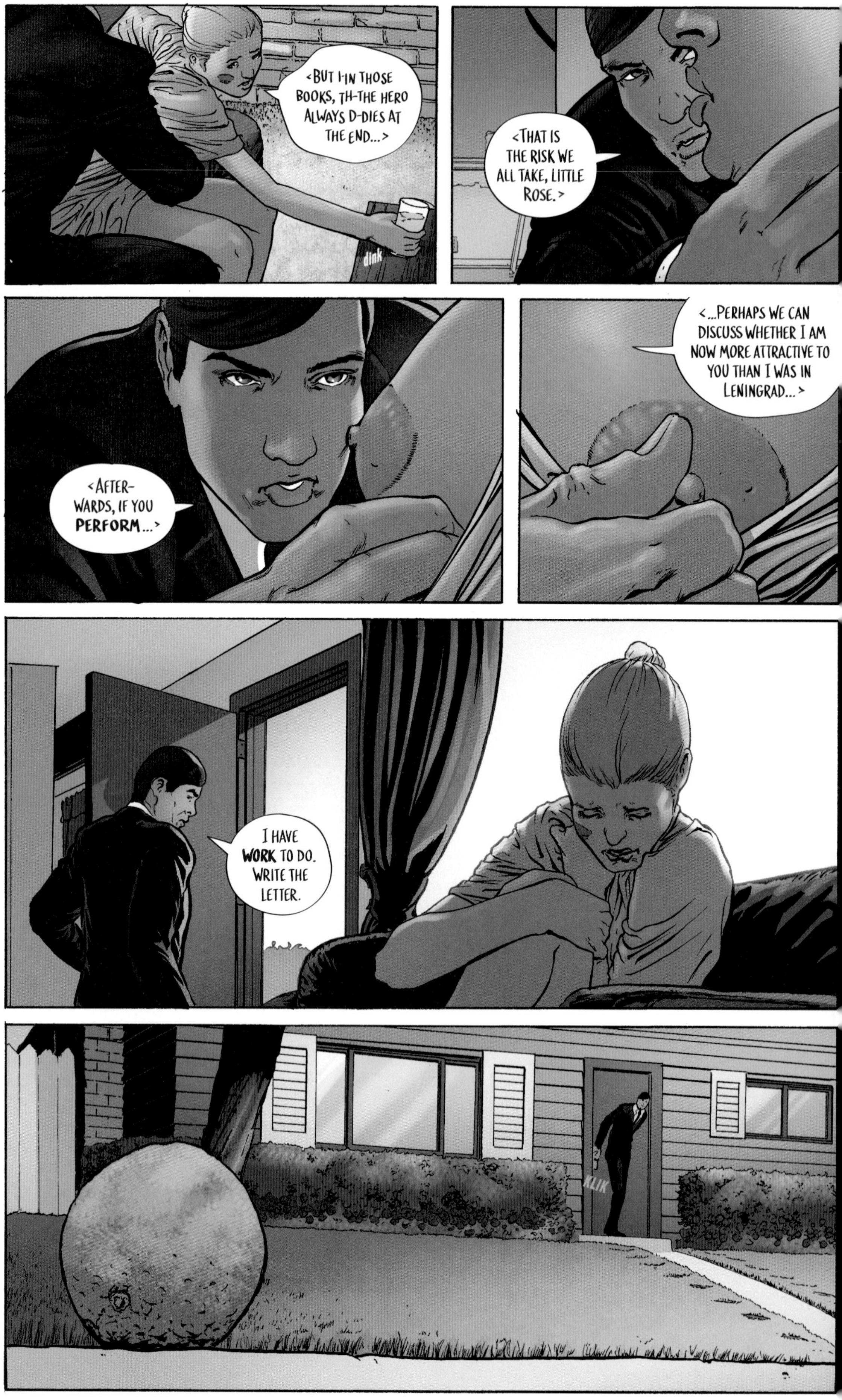
<BUT I-IN THOSE BOOKS, TH-THE HERO ALWAYS D-DIES AT THE END...>
dink
<THAT IS THE RISK WE ALL TAKE, LITTLE ROSE.>
<AFTER-WARDS, IF YOU PERFORM...>
<...PERHAPS WE CAN DISCUSS WHETHER I AM NOW MORE ATTRACTIVE TO YOU THAN I WAS IN LENINGRAD...>
I HAVE WORK TO DO. WRITE THE LETTER.
KLIK

... THE LAST POETS, "TIME"

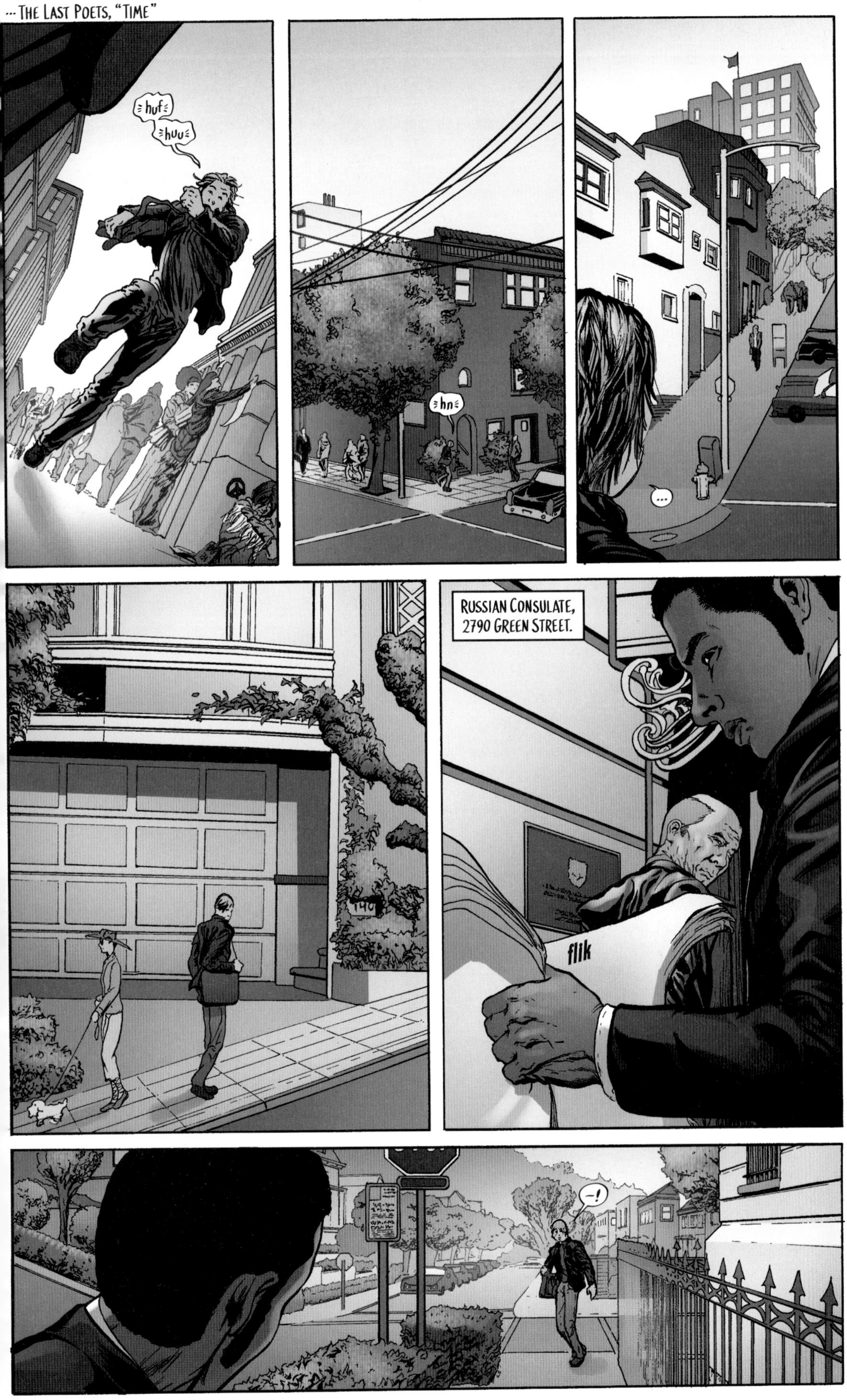
huf
huu
hn
...
RUSSIAN CONSULATE, 2790 GREEN STREET.
flik
–!

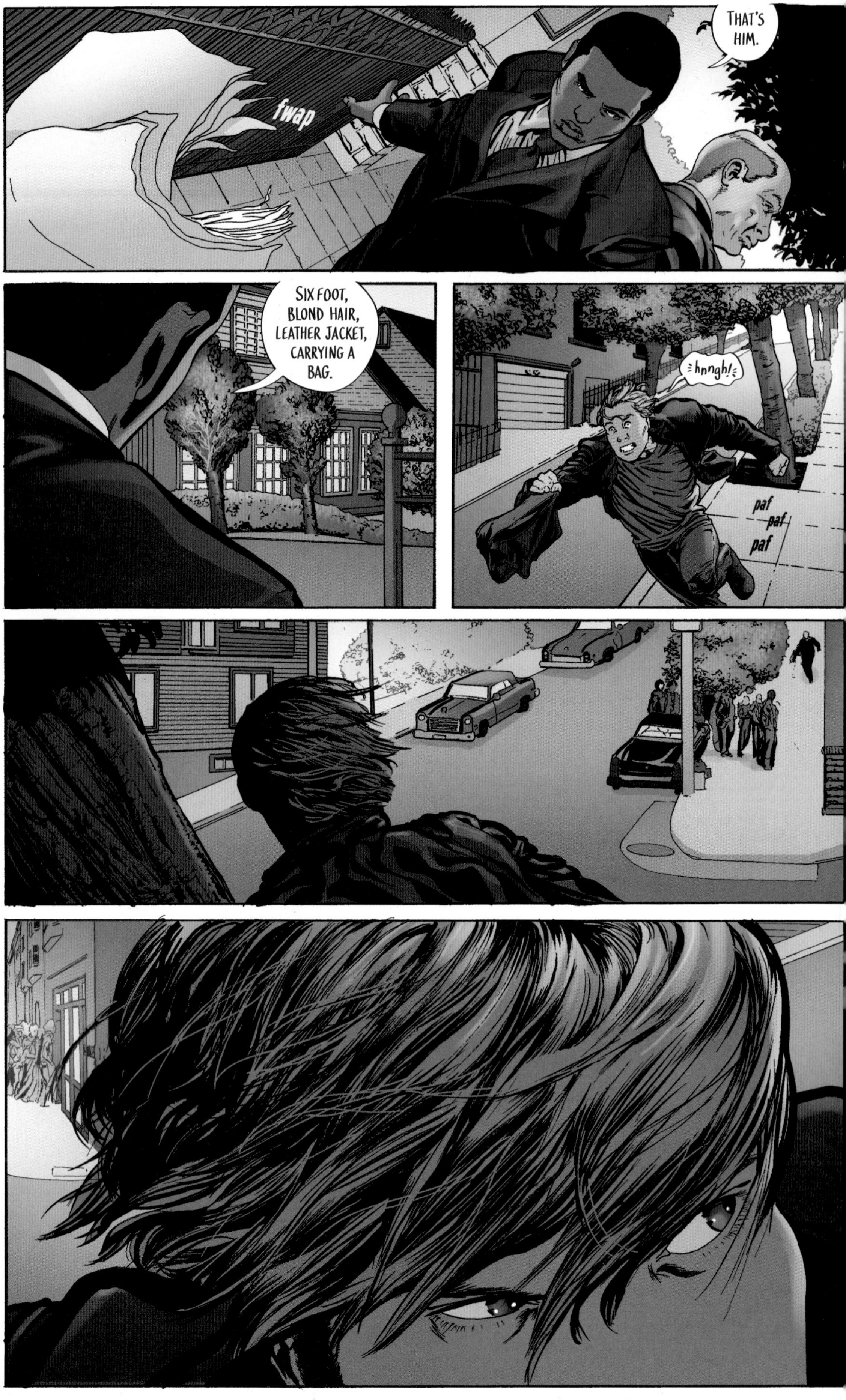
fwap
THAT'S HIM.
SIX FOOT, BLOND HAIR, LEATHER JACKET, CARRYING A BAG.
hnngh!
paf
paf
paf

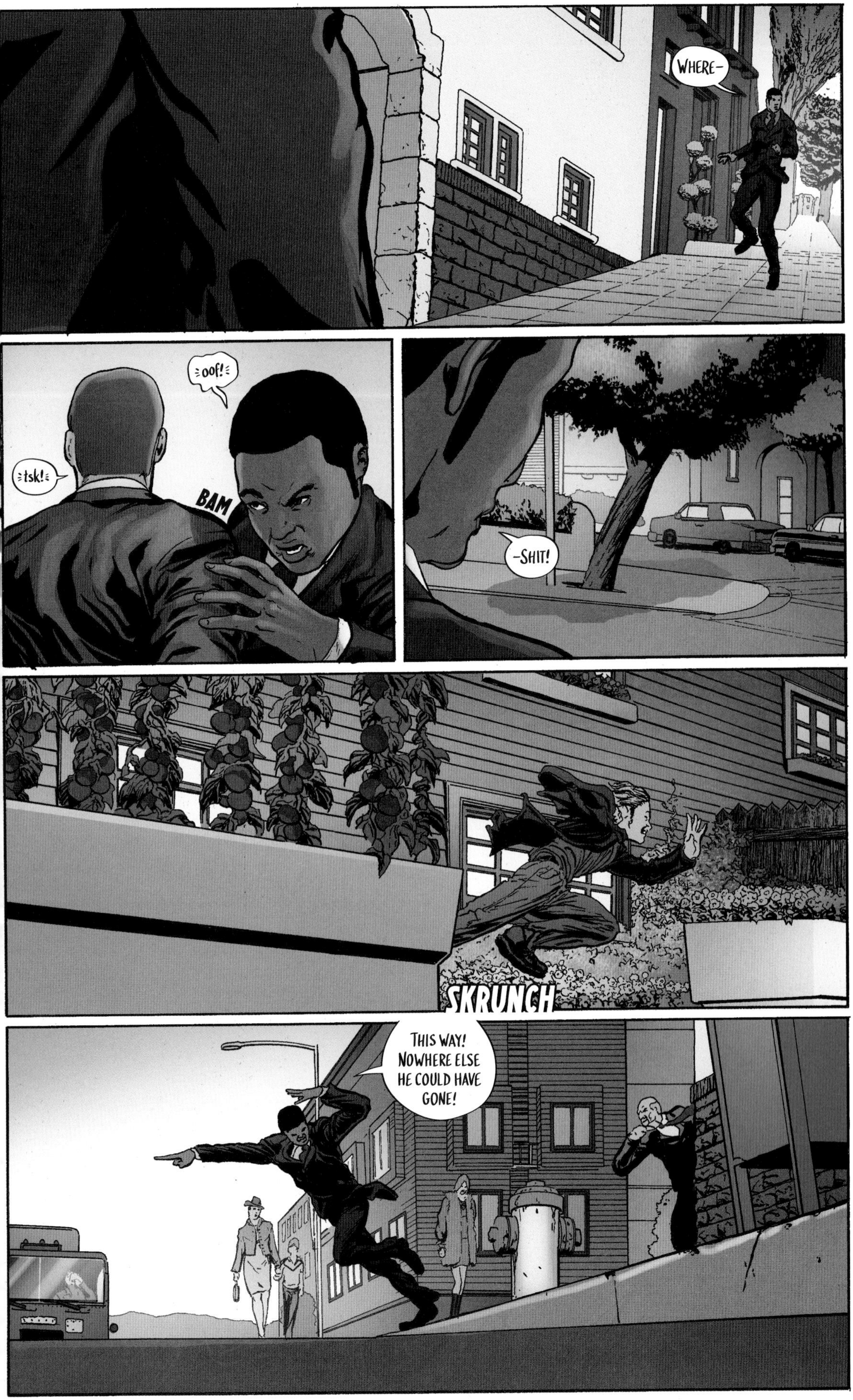
WHERE–
≡oof!≡
≡tsk!≡
BAM
–SHIT!
SKRUNCH
THIS WAY! NOWHERE ELSE HE COULD HAVE GONE!

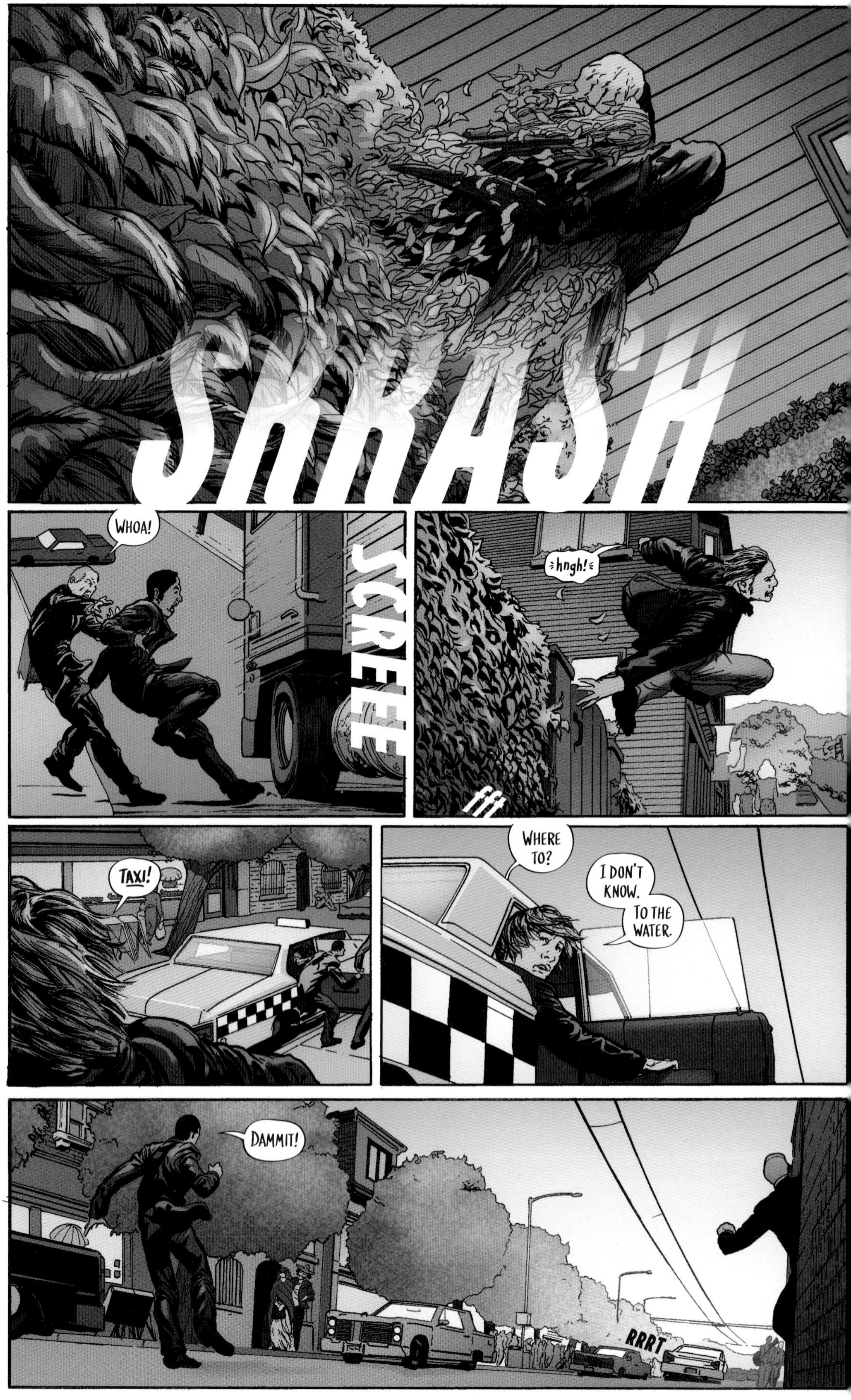
SHRASH
WHOA!
SCREEE
hngh!
fft
TAXI!
WHERE TO?
I DON'T KNOW. TO THE WATER.
DAMMIT!
RRRT

HEY! YOU RUSSIAN?

NO–

ME TOO!

< WHERE ARE YOU FROM, PAL? WE WENT FROM MOSCOW TO CZECHOSLOVAKIA AFTER THE REVOLUTION. >

THEN CAME HERE, AFTER THE WAR.

< I WAS BORN IN STALINGRAD. >

< WHAT WAS LEFT OF IT. >

< DAMN. I'M SORRY, KID. DID YOU EMIGRATE? >

< ...OR DO YOU WORK AT THE CONSULATE? >

< I'M JUST VISITING. >

< HEY, YOU KNOW WHERE I CAN BUY DRUGS IN THIS CITY? >

< OH, YOU WANT THE HAIGHT, FOR HIPPIE STUFF. >

< OR THE MISSION, FOR EVERYTHING ELSE. >

< NO HIPPIES. >

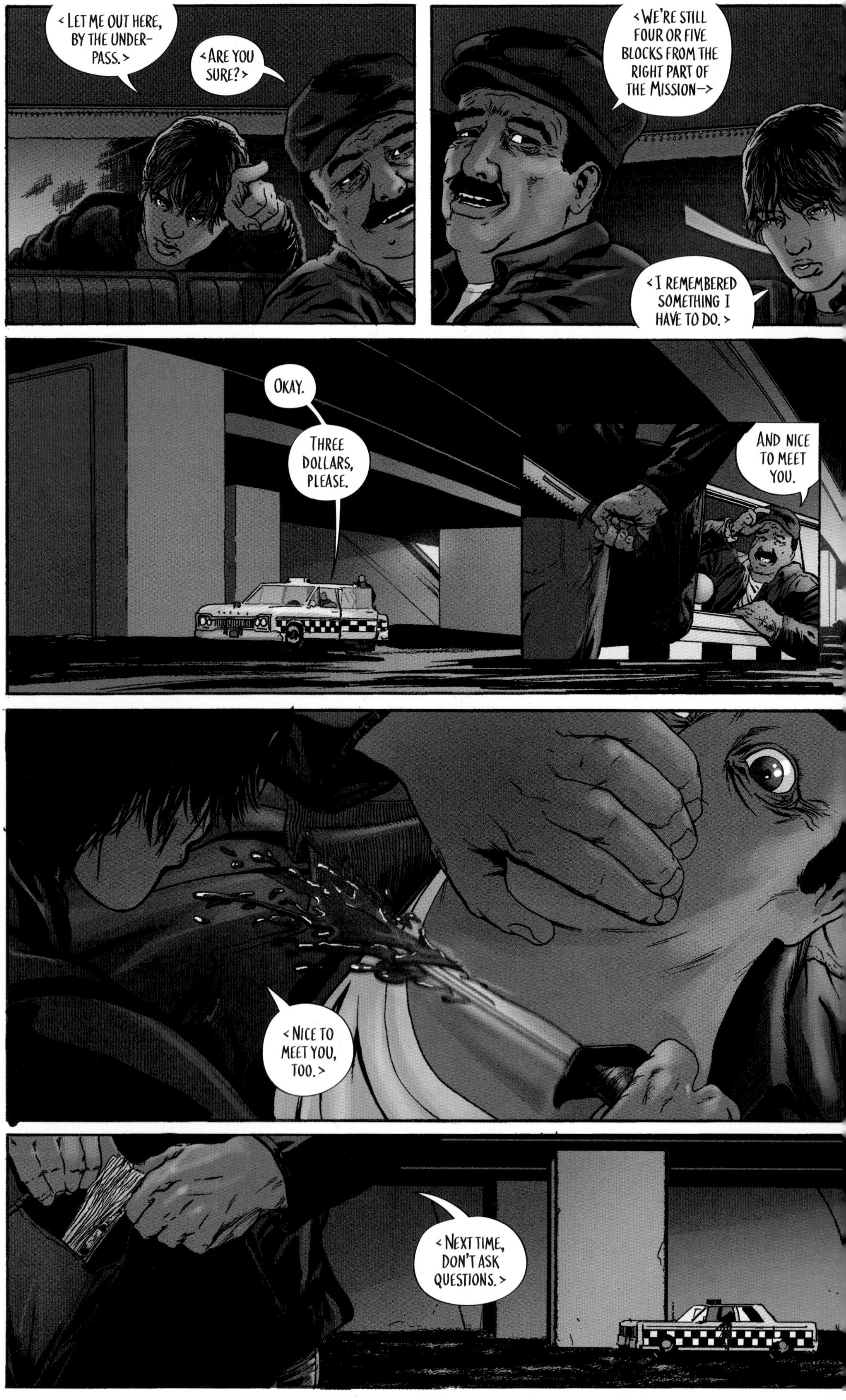
< LET ME OUT HERE, BY THE UNDER-PASS. >
< ARE YOU SURE? >
< WE'RE STILL FOUR OR FIVE BLOCKS FROM THE RIGHT PART OF THE MISSION—>
< I REMEMBERED SOMETHING I HAVE TO DO. >
OKAY.
THREE DOLLARS, PLEASE.
AND NICE TO MEET YOU.
< NICE TO MEET YOU, TOO. >
< NEXT TIME, DON'T ASK QUESTIONS. >

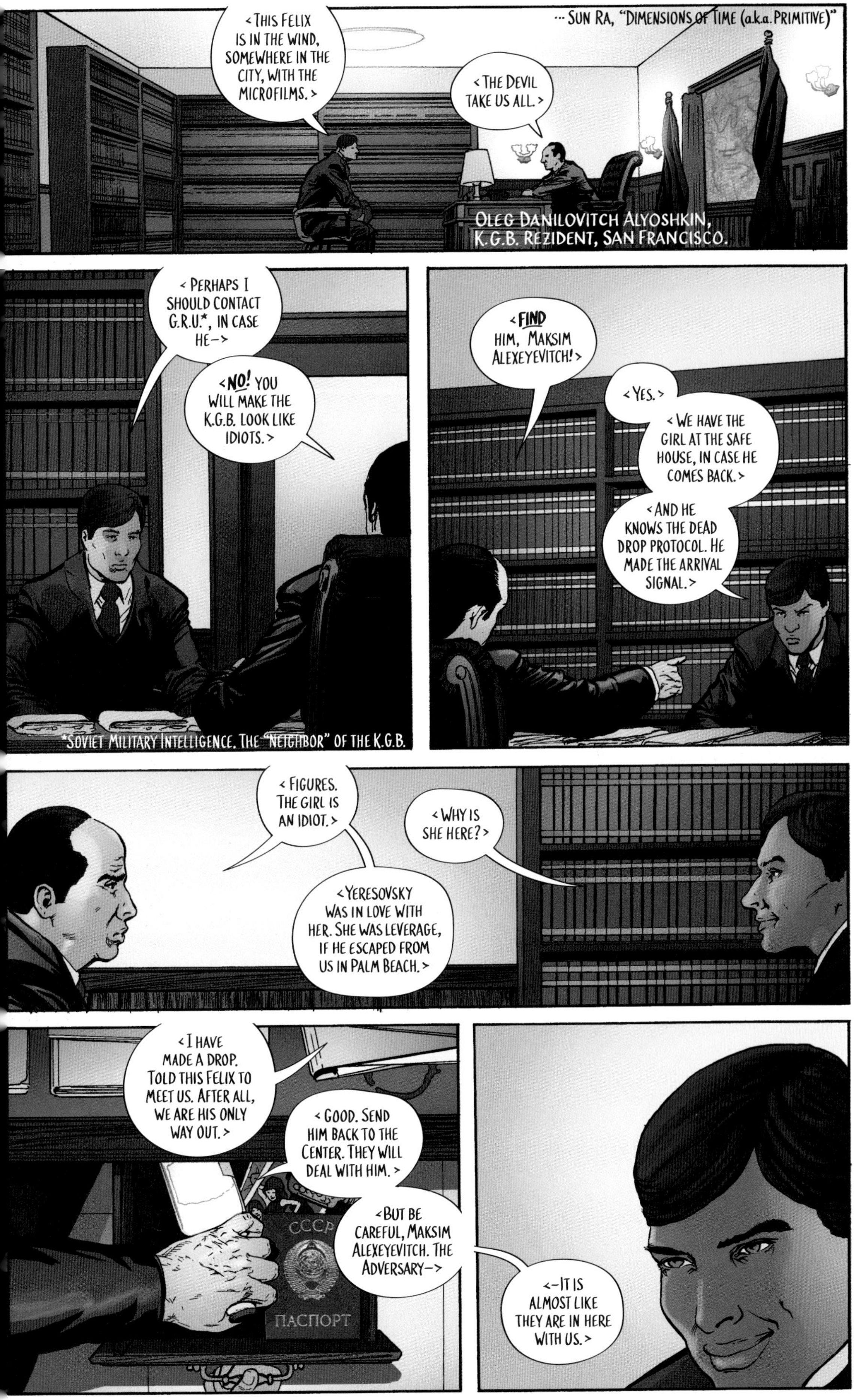
... SUN RA, "DIMENSIONS OF TIME (a.k.a. PRIMITIVE)"
< THIS FELIX IS IN THE WIND, SOMEWHERE IN THE CITY, WITH THE MICROFILMS. >
< THE DEVIL TAKE US ALL. >
OLEG DANILOVITCH ALYOSHKIN, K.G.B. REZIDENT, SAN FRANCISCO.
< PERHAPS I SHOULD CONTACT G.R.U.*, IN CASE HE— >
<NO! YOU WILL MAKE THE K.G.B. LOOK LIKE IDIOTS. >
*SOVIET MILITARY INTELLIGENCE. THE "NEIGHBOR" OF THE K.G.B.
<FIND HIM, MAKSIM ALEXEYEVITCH! >
< YES. >
< WE HAVE THE GIRL AT THE SAFE HOUSE, IN CASE HE COMES BACK. >
< AND HE KNOWS THE DEAD DROP PROTOCOL. HE MADE THE ARRIVAL SIGNAL. >
< FIGURES. THE GIRL IS AN IDIOT. >
< WHY IS SHE HERE? >
< YERESOVSKY WAS IN LOVE WITH HER. SHE WAS LEVERAGE, IF HE ESCAPED FROM US IN PALM BEACH. >
< I HAVE MADE A DROP. TOLD THIS FELIX TO MEET US. AFTER ALL, WE ARE HIS ONLY WAY OUT. >
< GOOD. SEND HIM BACK TO THE CENTER. THEY WILL DEAL WITH HIM. >
< BUT BE CAREFUL, MAKSIM ALEXEYEVITCH. THE ADVERSARY— >
СССР
ПАСПОРТ
< —IT IS ALMOST LIKE THEY ARE IN HERE WITH US. >

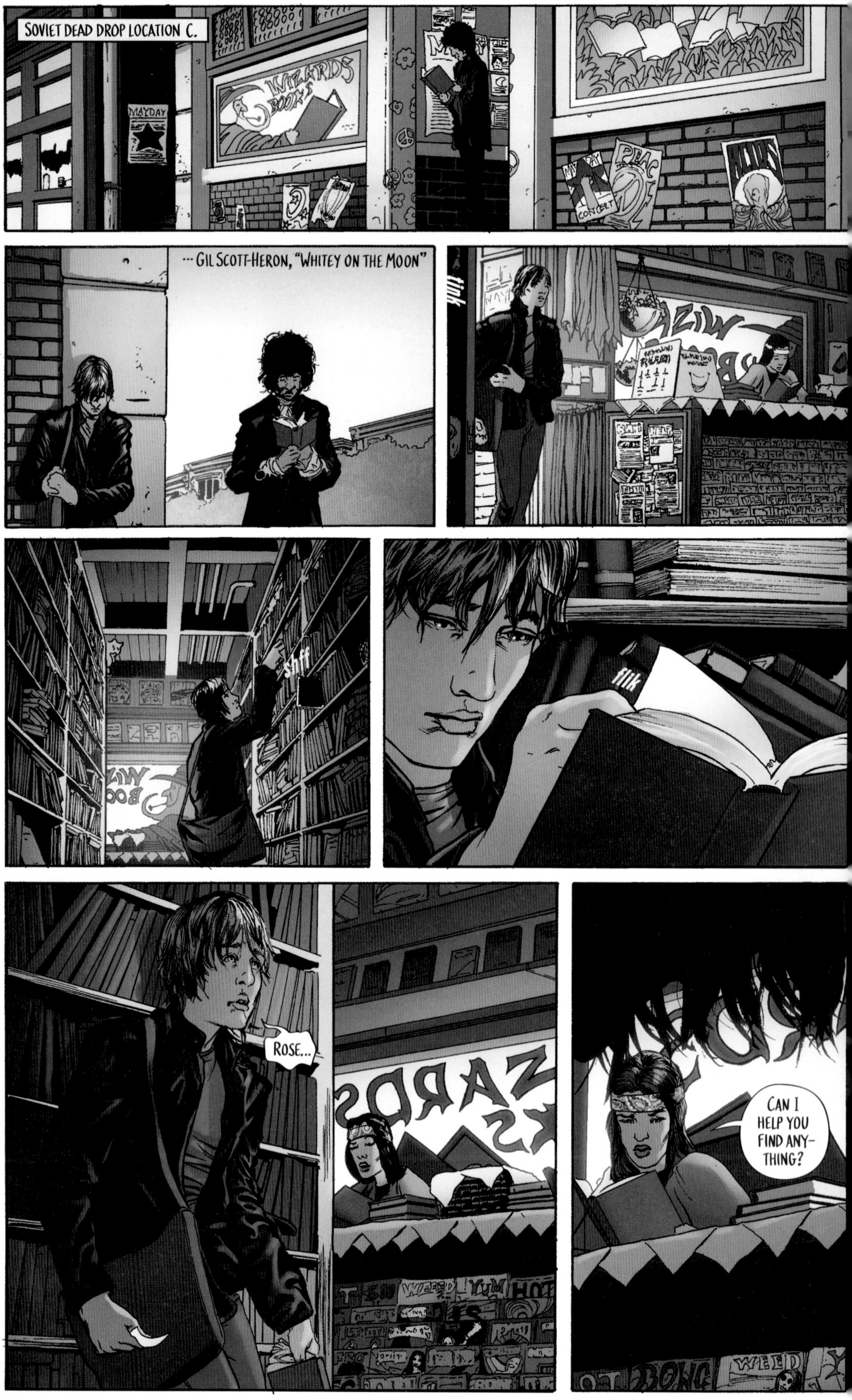
SOVIET DEAD DROP LOCATION C.
WIZARDS BOOKS
MAYDAY
... GIL SCOTT-HERON, "WHITEY ON THE MOON"
flik
shff
flik
ROSE...
CAN I HELP YOU FIND ANYTHING?

≥hm?≤

V3ЧᴖⅡ ФⴏϨЬ Ⴙ ⴏЧϨϬᴖ BOOK Рⴗϡ ЯϨⴖCⴝ?

I'M SORRY. DO YOU HAVE A PHONE?

skrunch

SURE.

BEHIND THE ГⅢНЧЬϨР ⴖϨⴕCⴝϨ.

HEY MAN, WHERE YOU FROM?

ME?

AUSTRIA.

MAGICY NECKLACE

< THIS IS FELIX. I AM REQUESTING THE KOMSOMOLETS PROTOCOL. >

THAT'S ФϨР Оⴗϡ!

HOW LONG ARE YOU IN TOWN?

BECAUSE THERE'S A ФϨЧЬϨРⴖ SATURDAY IN THE PARK. I COULD—

SORRY.

tink

WELCO FELL

I AM LEAVING TOMORROW.

DAMMIT, SANDRA...

skht

I SAW HIM. HE LOST US, THOUGH.

≥hmph≤ LET'S SEE HOW GOOD YOU ARE WITH A ONE-TIME PAD, HUDSON.

CKVIGIL HAS THINGS TO TELL US.

25191 11024 85371 46635
09512 78154 60921 51171
32218 91622 78183 40401
11711 35210 60220 47119
26433 91101 19017 03824
04613 78210 88213 50609

kof!

<NO.>

<NO, I CANNOT SAY THAT.>

skrunch

THERE'S GOING TO BE A HANDOVER.

skritch

TOMORROW. HIGH NOON.

WHERE?

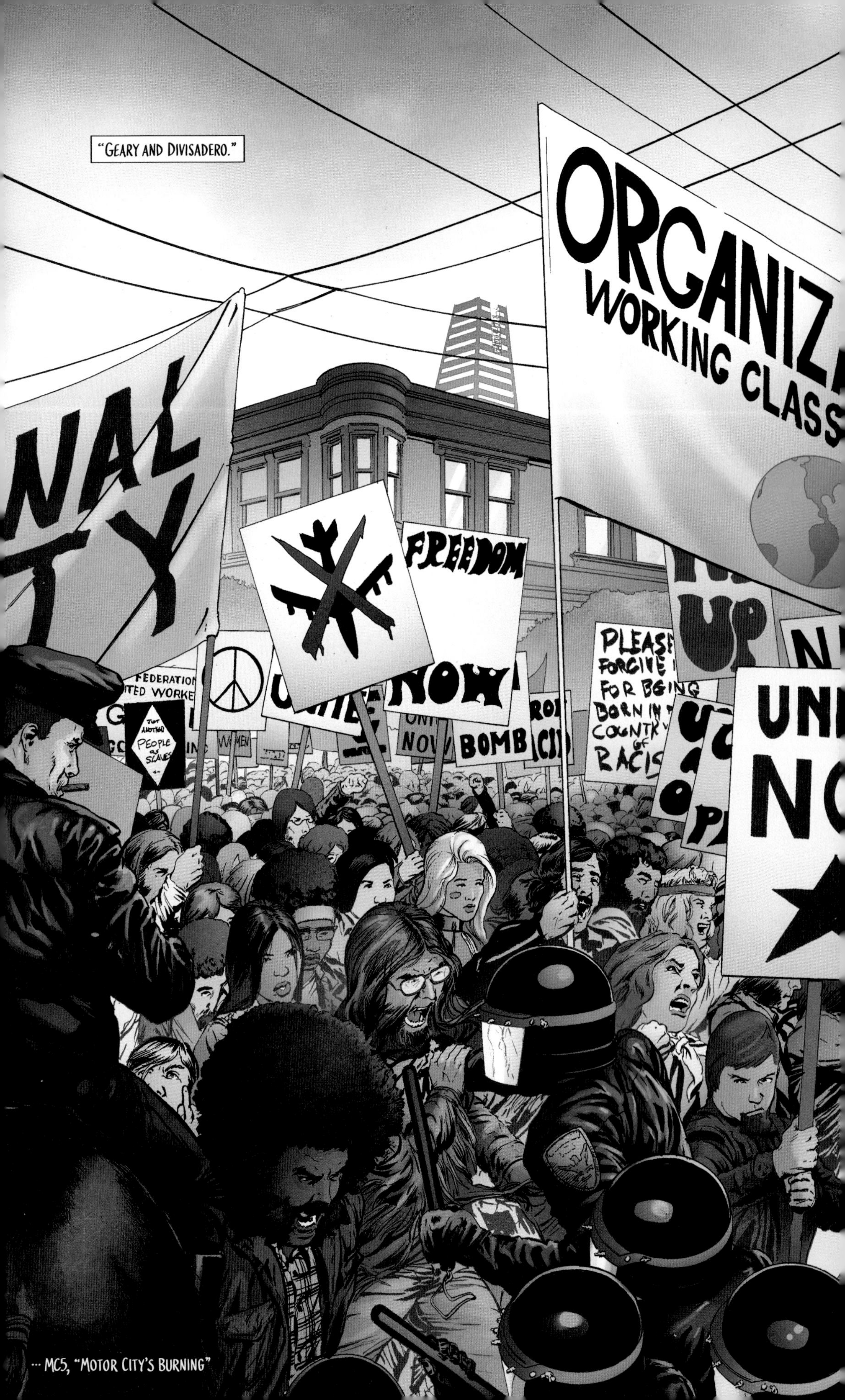
"GEARY AND DIVISADERO."
ORGANIZ
WORKING CLASS
NAL
FREEDOM
NOW
FEDERATION
BOMB
PLEASE FORGIVE
FOR BEING
UP
NO
... MC5, "MOTOR CITY'S BURNING"

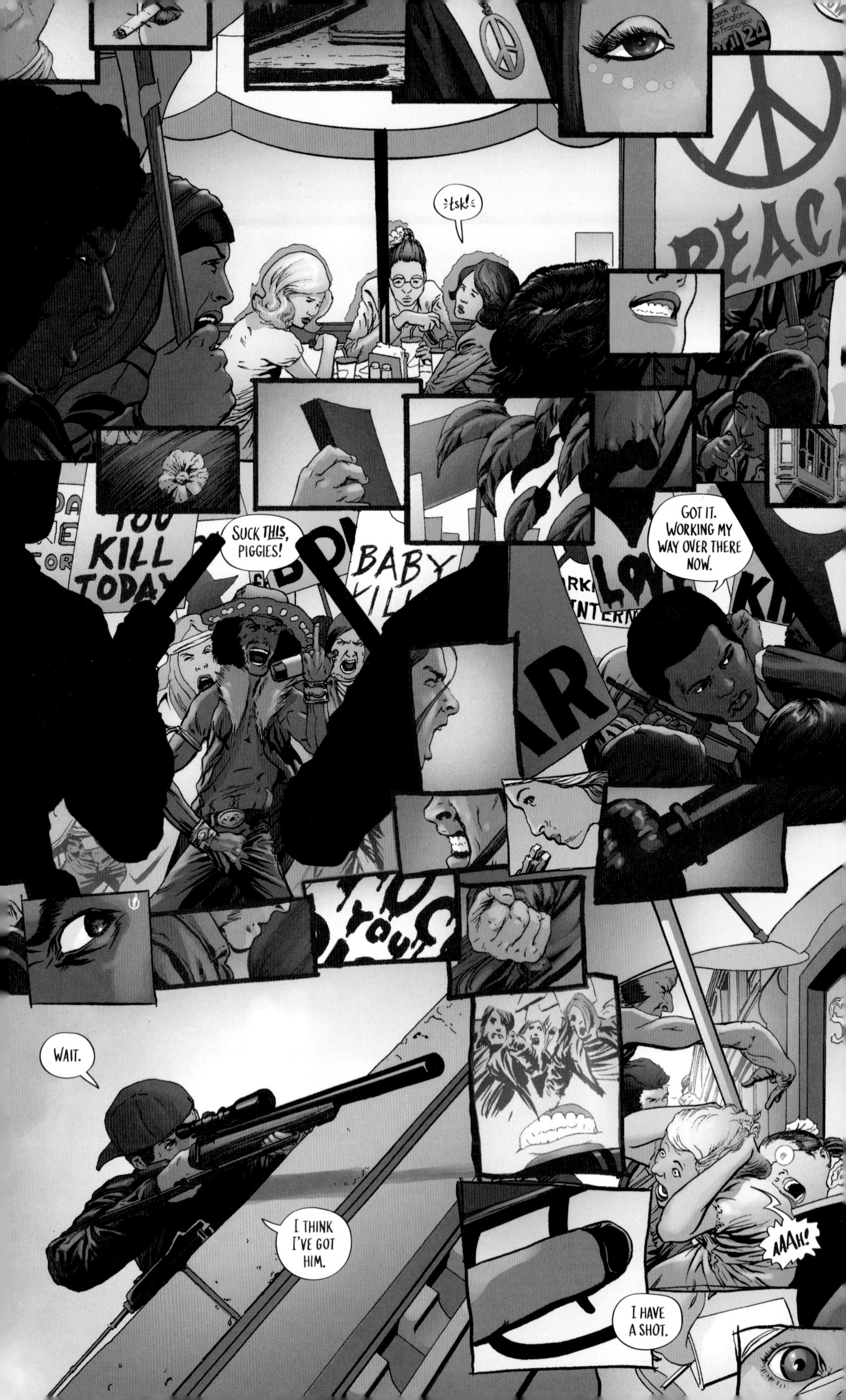

tsk!
SUCK THIS, PIGGIES!
GOT IT. WORKING MY WAY OVER THERE NOW.
WAIT.
I THINK I'VE GOT HIM.
AAAH!
I HAVE A SHOT.

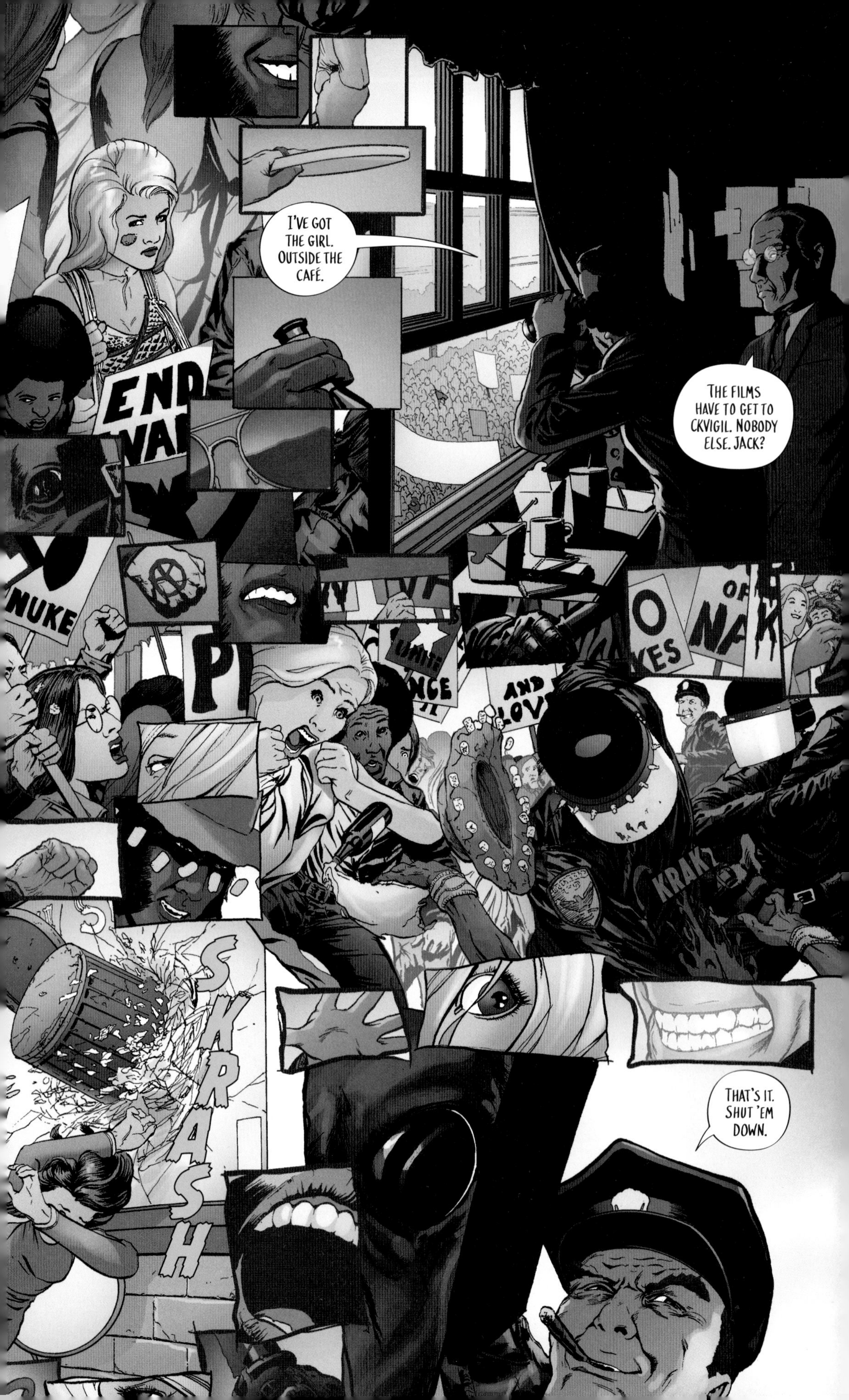
I'VE GOT THE GIRL. OUTSIDE THE CAFÉ.
THE FILMS HAVE TO GET TO CKVIGIL. NOBODY ELSE. JACK?
NUKE
SKRASH
THAT'S IT. SHUT 'EM DOWN.

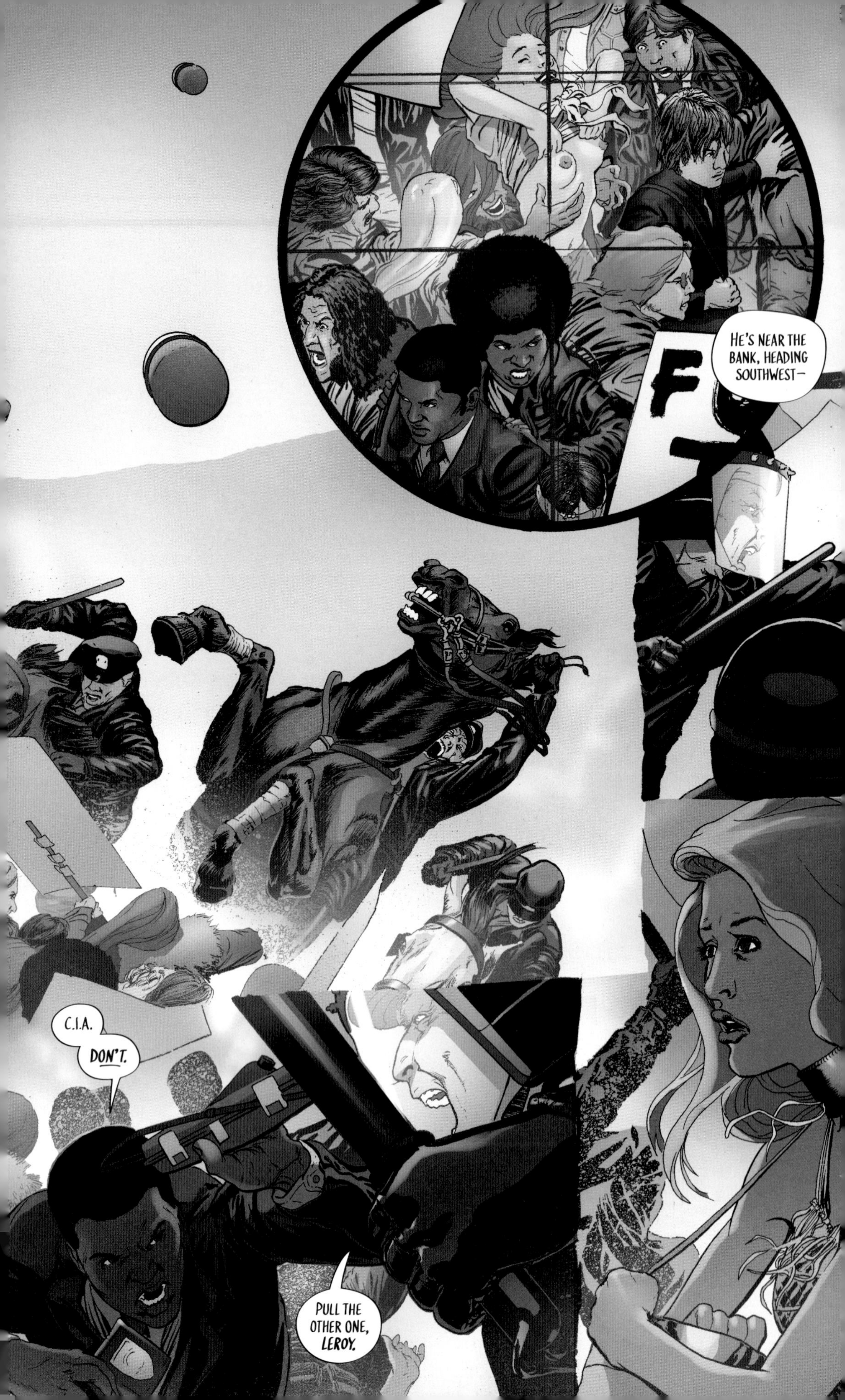
HE'S NEAR THE BANK, HEADING SOUTHWEST—
F
C.I.A.
DON'T.
PULL THE OTHER ONE, LEROY.

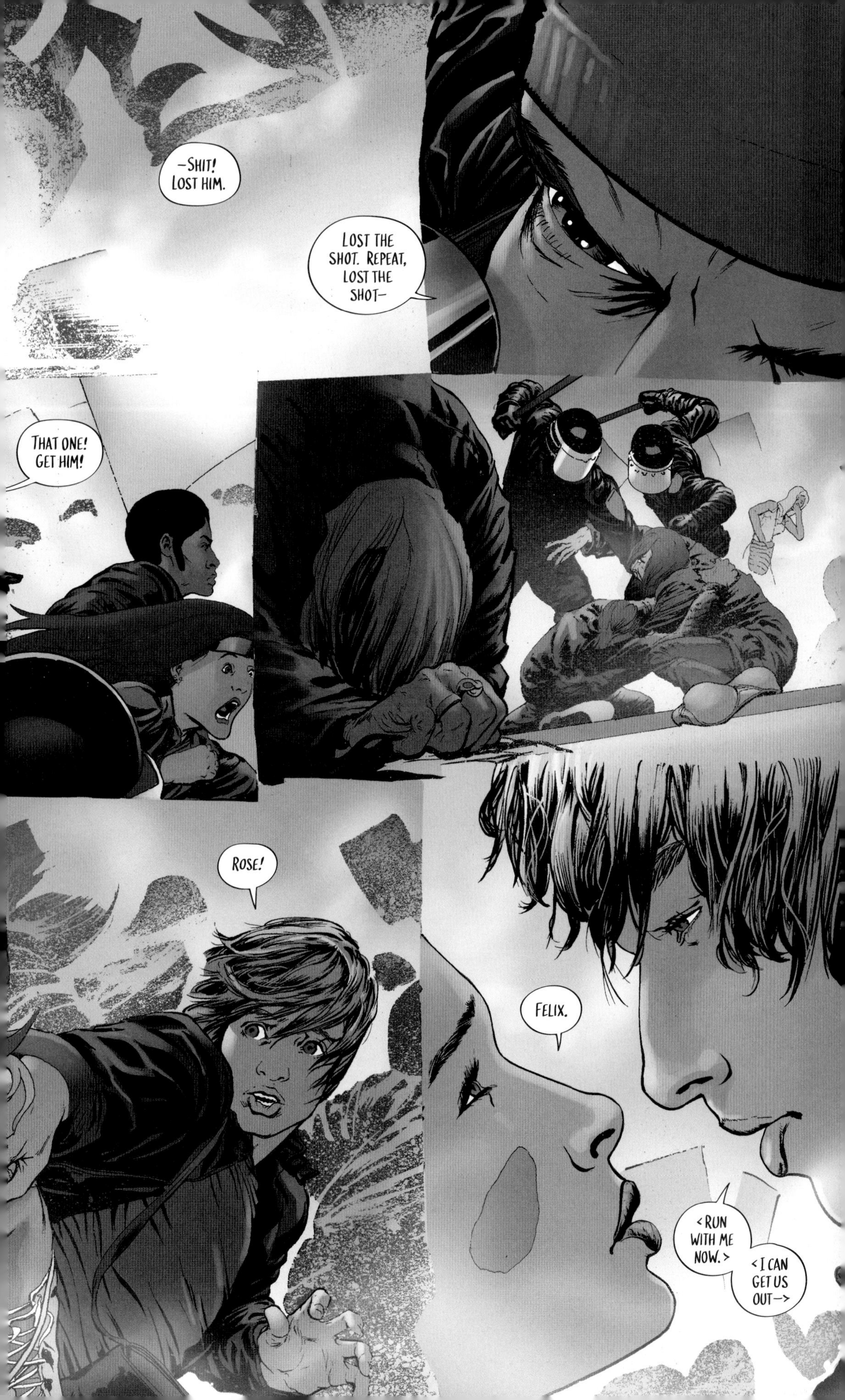

—SHIT! LOST HIM.
LOST THE SHOT. REPEAT, LOST THE SHOT—
THAT ONE! GET HIM!
ROSE!
FELIX.
<RUN WITH ME NOW.>
<I CAN GET US OUT—>

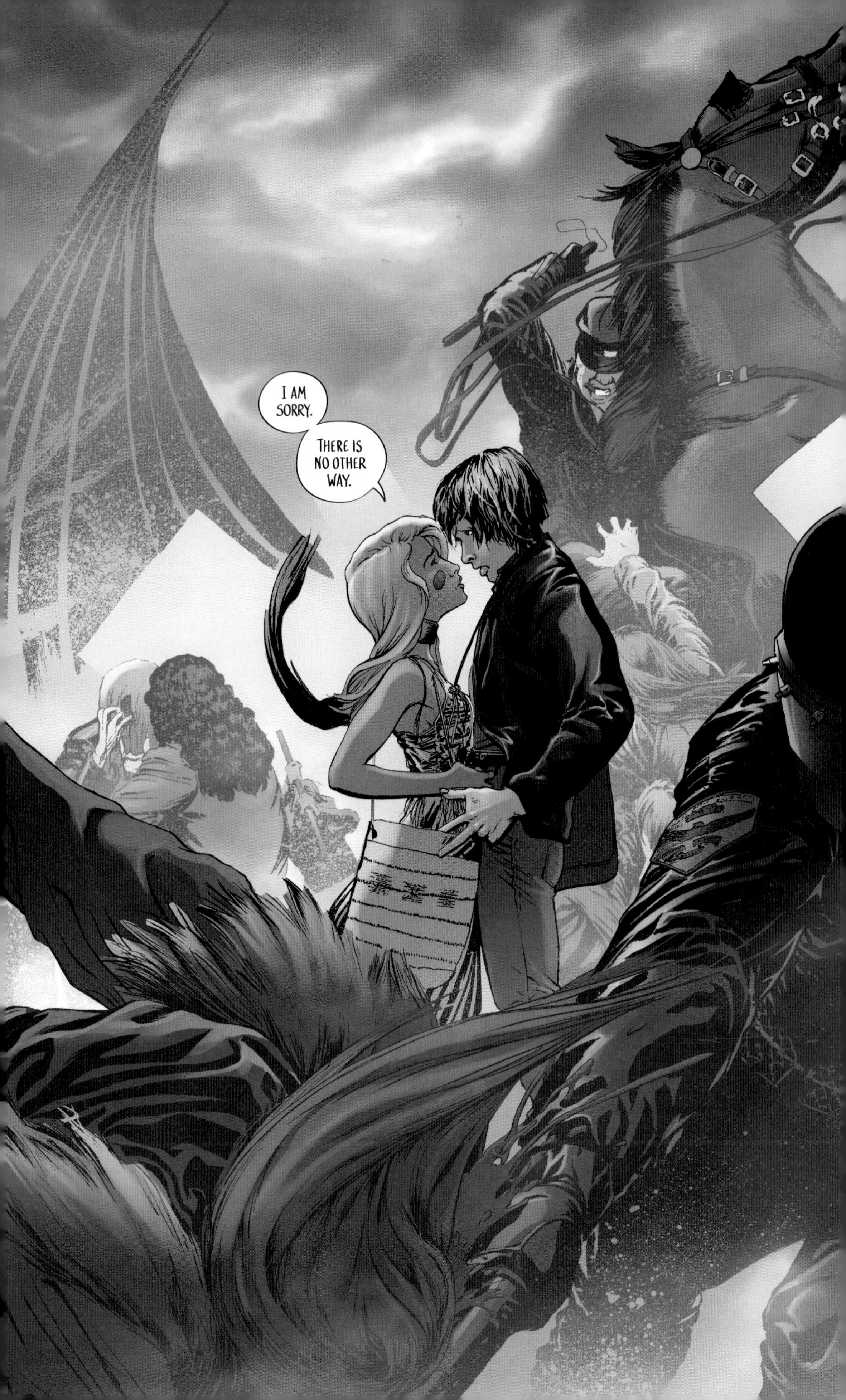
I AM SORRY.
THERE IS NO OTHER WAY.

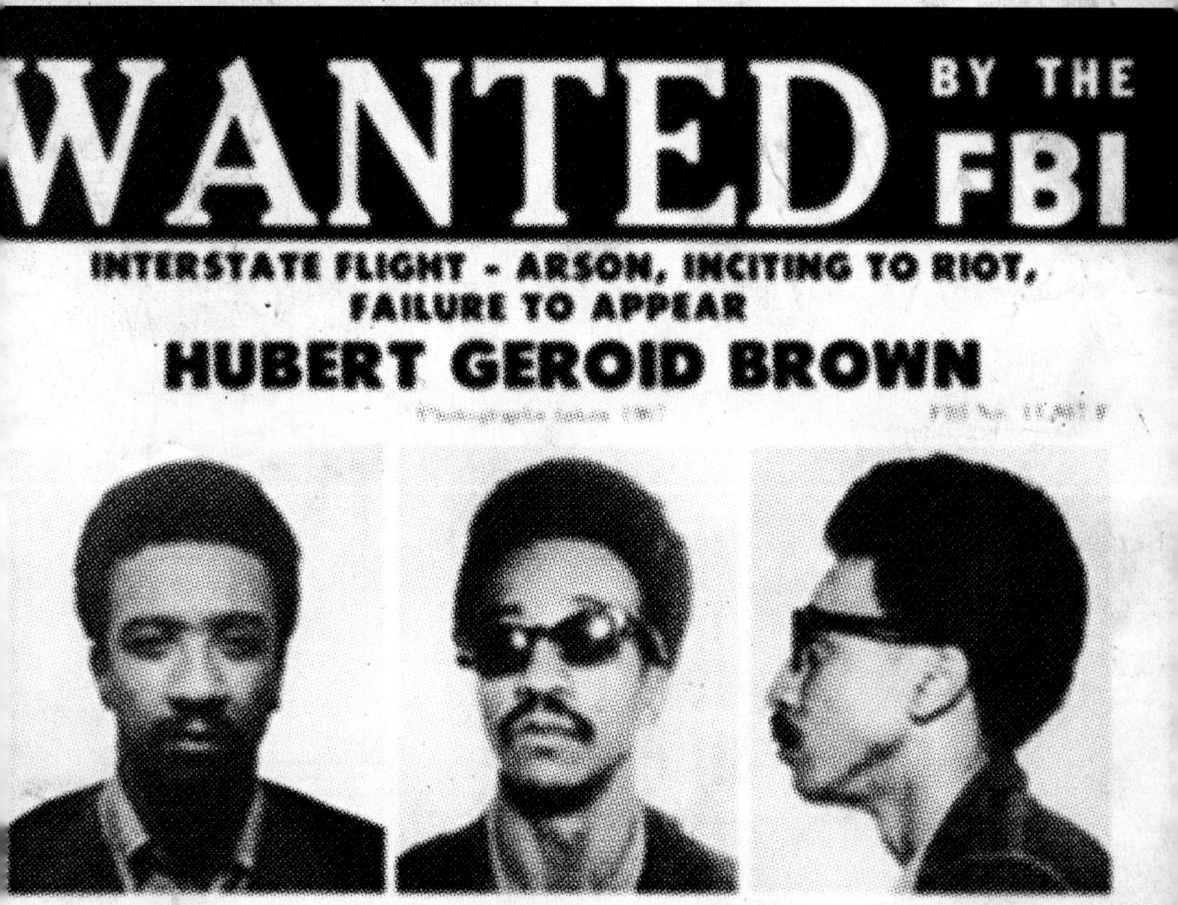
WANTED BY THE FBI
INTERSTATE FLIGHT - ARSON, INCITING TO RIOT, FAILURE TO APPEAR
HUBERT GEROID BROWN

"This is a very unforgiving country when you show this country its warts, when you hold the mirror up. If you happen not to share their beliefs, they'll kill you."
Imam Jamil Al-Amin (formerly H. Rap Brown), 1969

FIVE

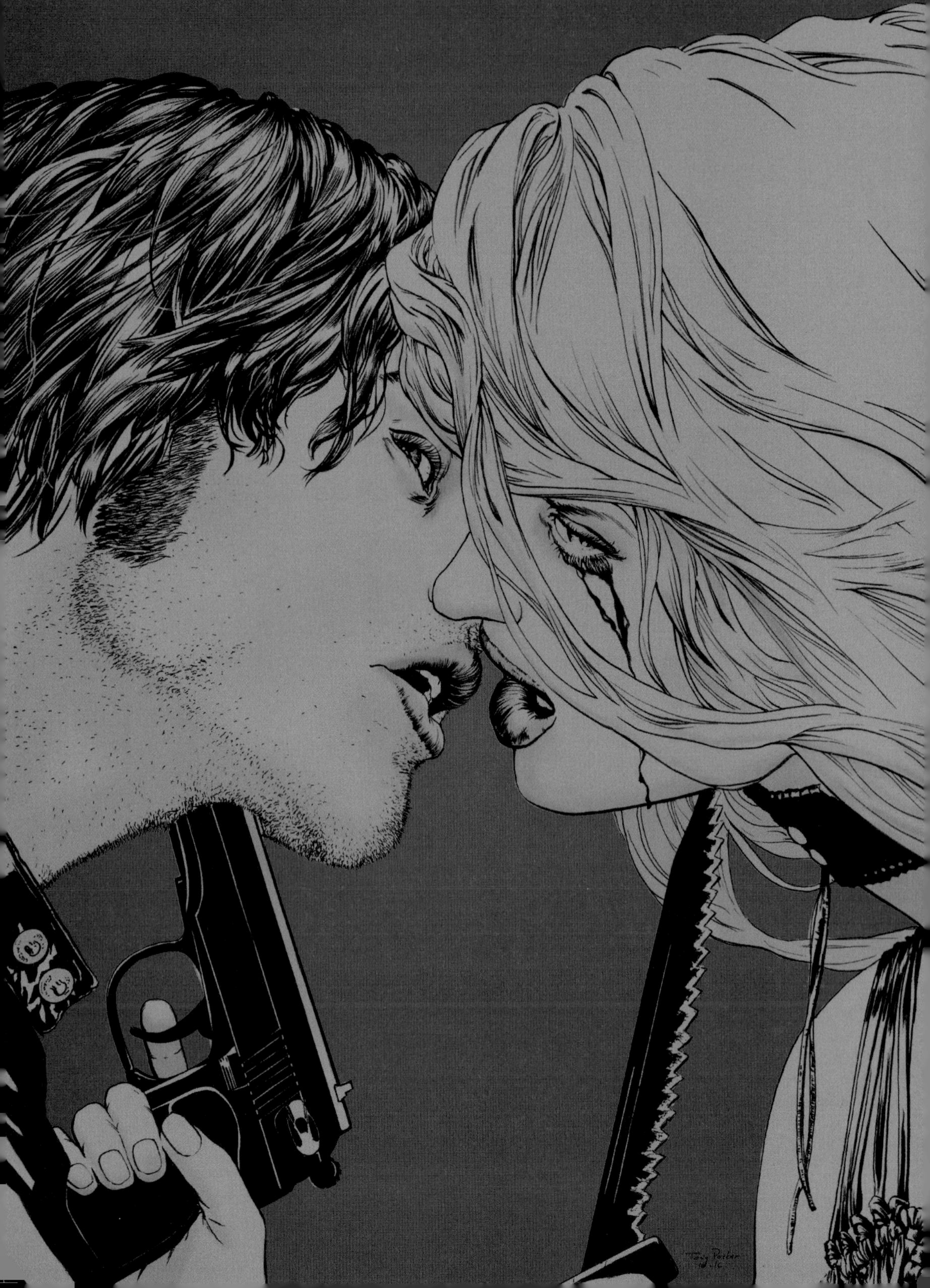

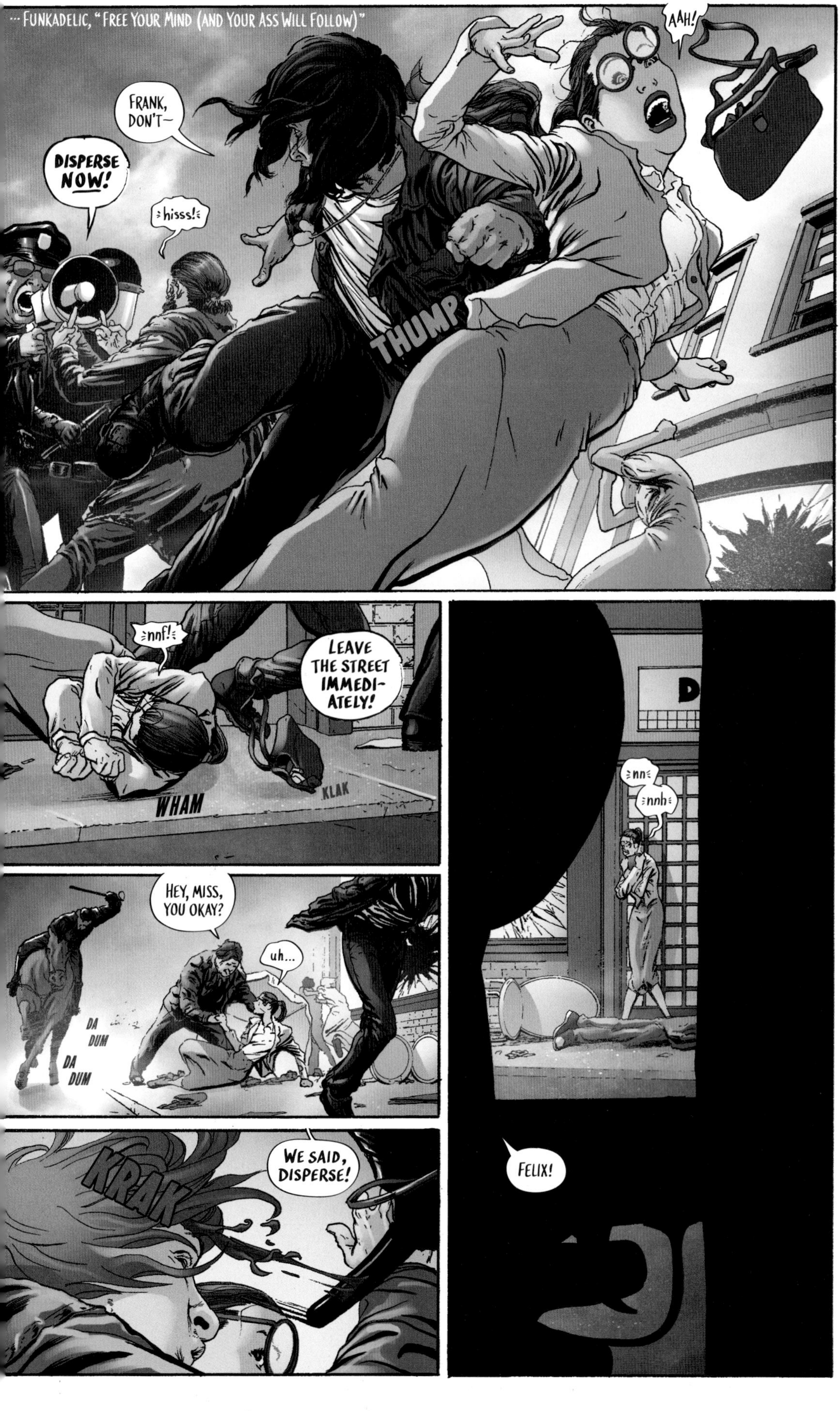
… Funkadelic, "Free Your Mind (And Your Ass Will Follow)"
AAH!
Frank, don't—
Disperse now!
hisss!
THUMP
nnf!
Leave the street immedi-ately!
WHAM
KLAK
Hey, miss, you okay?
uh…
DA DUM
DA DUM
KRAK
We said, disperse!
nn
nnh
Felix!

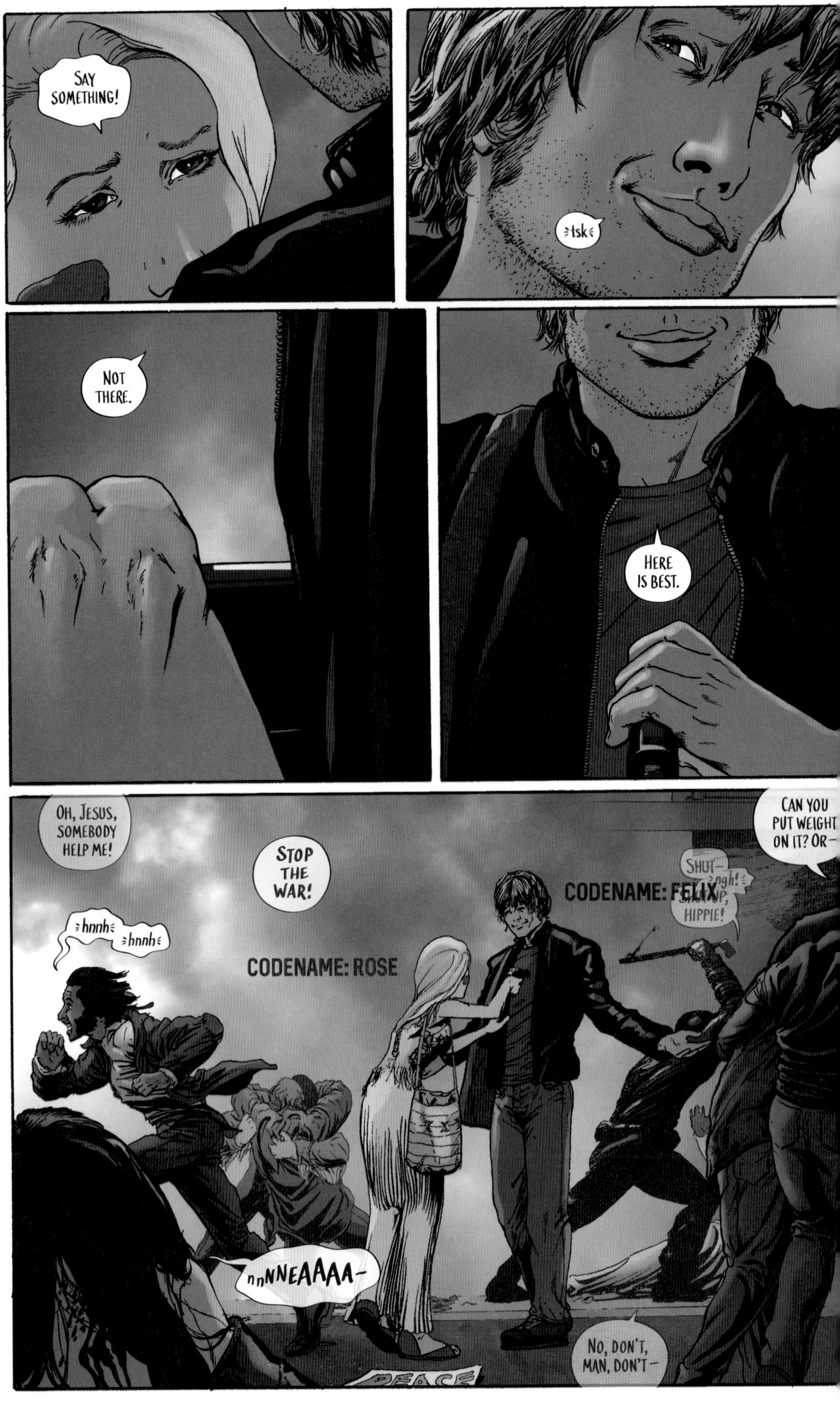
SAY SOMETHING!
tsk
NOT THERE.
HERE IS BEST.
OH, JESUS, SOMEBODY HELP ME!
STOP THE WAR!
CAN YOU PUT WEIGHT ON IT? OR—
SHUT—
ngh!
HIPPIE!
CODENAME: FELIX
hnnh
hnnh
CODENAME: ROSE
nnNNEAAAA—
NO, DON'T, MAN, DON'T—

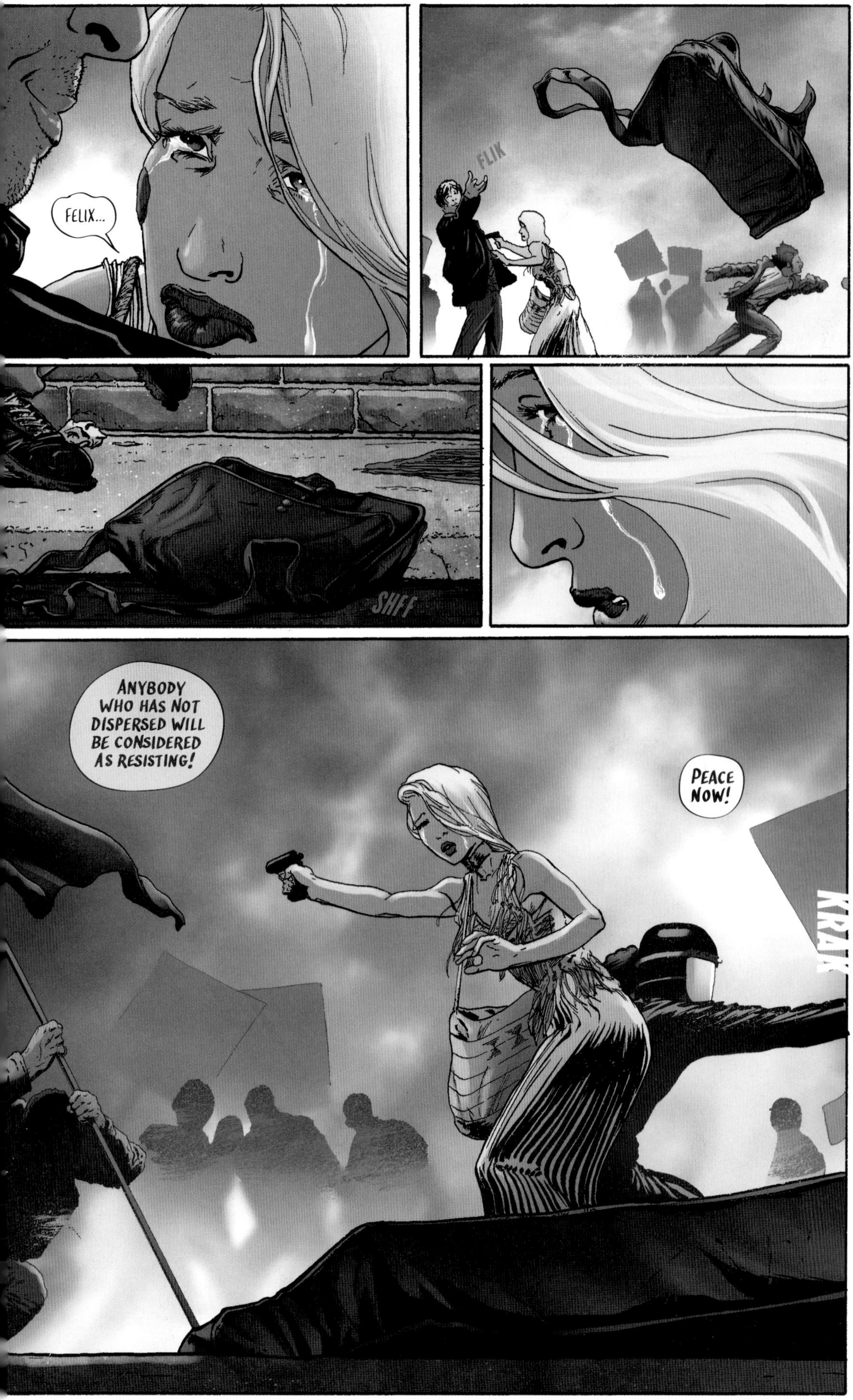
FELIX...
FLIK
SHFF
ANYBODY WHO HAS NOT DISPERSED WILL BE CONSIDERED AS RESISTING!
PEACE NOW!
KRAK

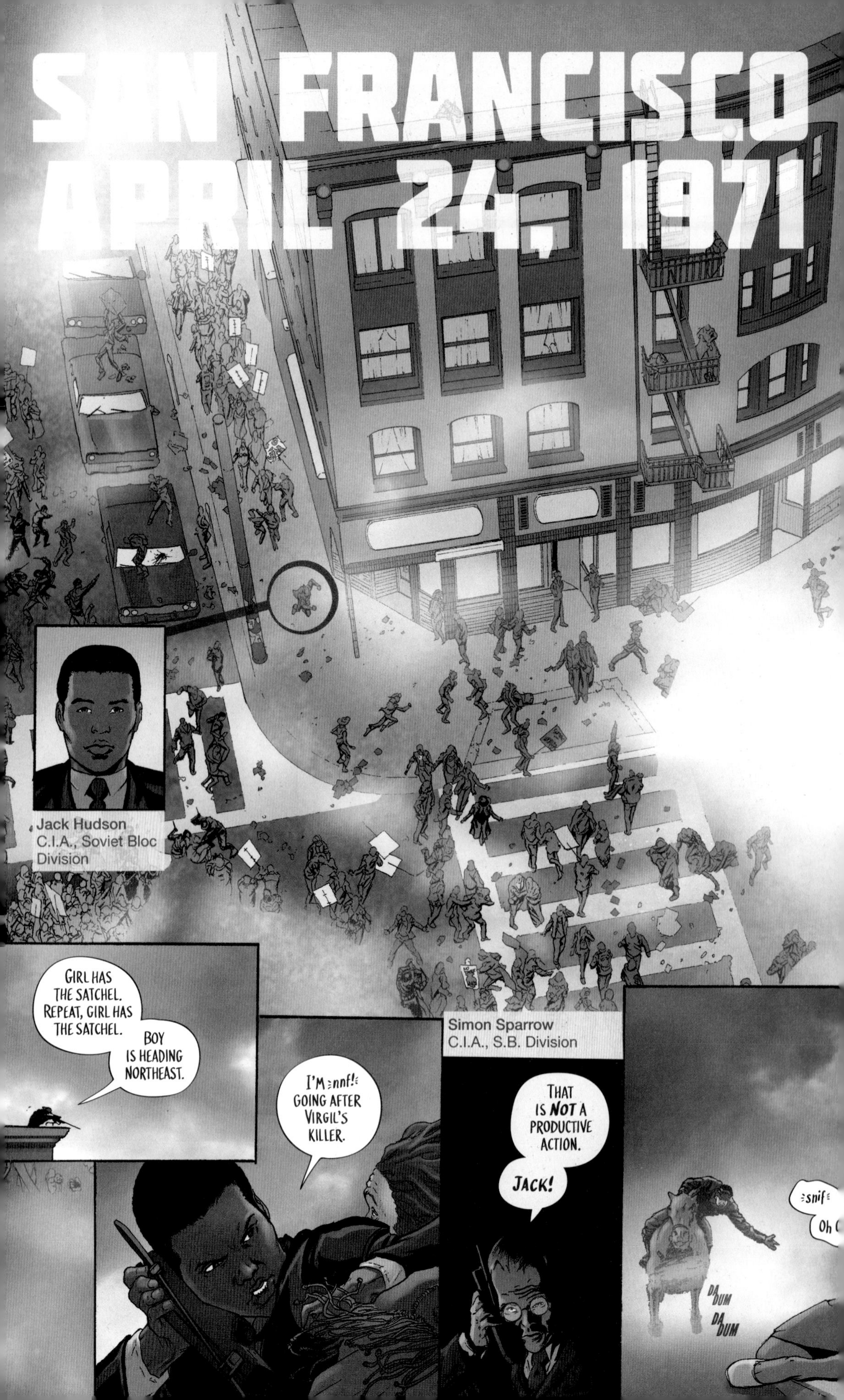
SAN FRANCISCO
APRIL 24, 1971
Jack Hudson
C.I.A., Soviet Bloc Division
GIRL HAS THE SATCHEL. REPEAT, GIRL HAS THE SATCHEL.
BOY IS HEADING NORTHEAST.
Simon Sparrow
C.I.A., S.B. Division
I'M nnf! GOING AFTER VIRGIL'S KILLER.
THAT IS NOT A PRODUCTIVE ACTION.
JACK!
snif
Oh
DA DUM
DA DUM

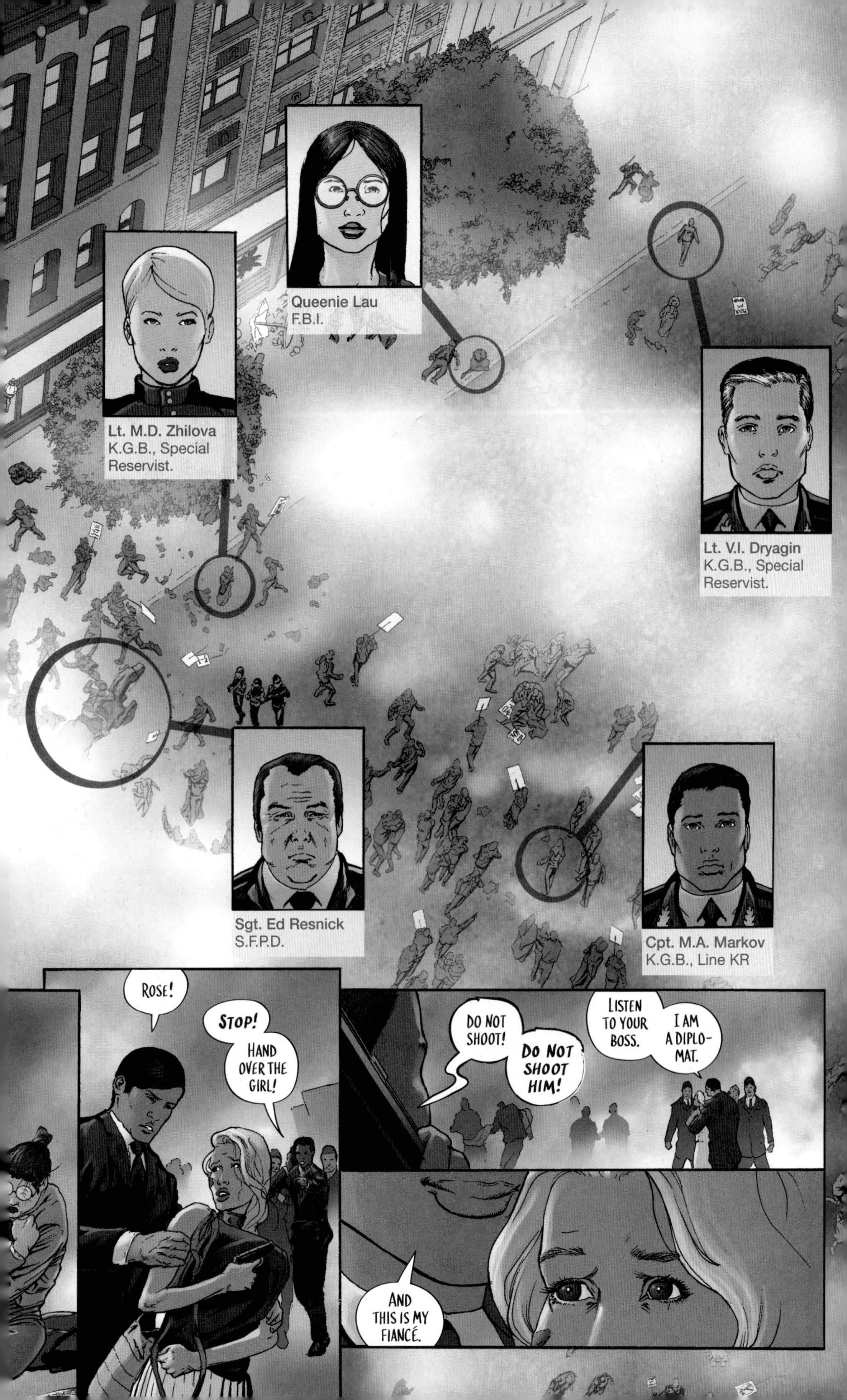

Queenie Lau
F.B.I.
Lt. M.D. Zhilova
K.G.B., Special Reservist.
Lt. V.I. Dryagin
K.G.B., Special Reservist.
Sgt. Ed Resnick
S.F.P.D.
Cpt. M.A. Markov
K.G.B., Line KR
ROSE!
STOP!
HAND OVER THE GIRL!
DO NOT SHOOT!
DO NOT SHOOT HIM!
LISTEN TO YOUR BOSS.
I AM A DIPLO-MAT.
AND THIS IS MY FIANCÉ.

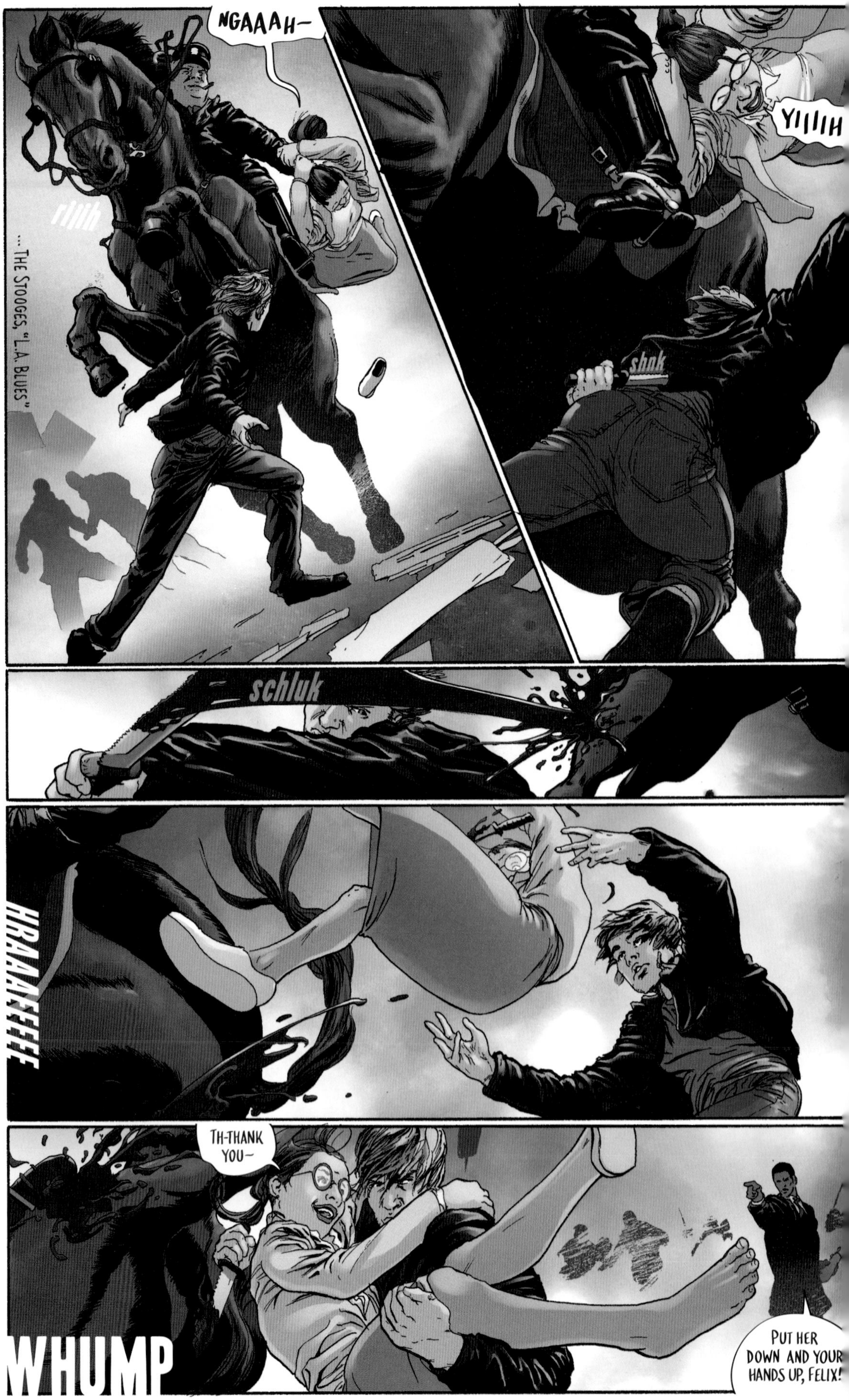

NGAAAH—
rllllh
...The Stooges, "L.A. Blues"
YIIIIH
shnk
schluk
HRAAAAEEEE
TH-THANK YOU—
WHUMP
PUT HER DOWN AND YOUR HANDS UP, FELIX!

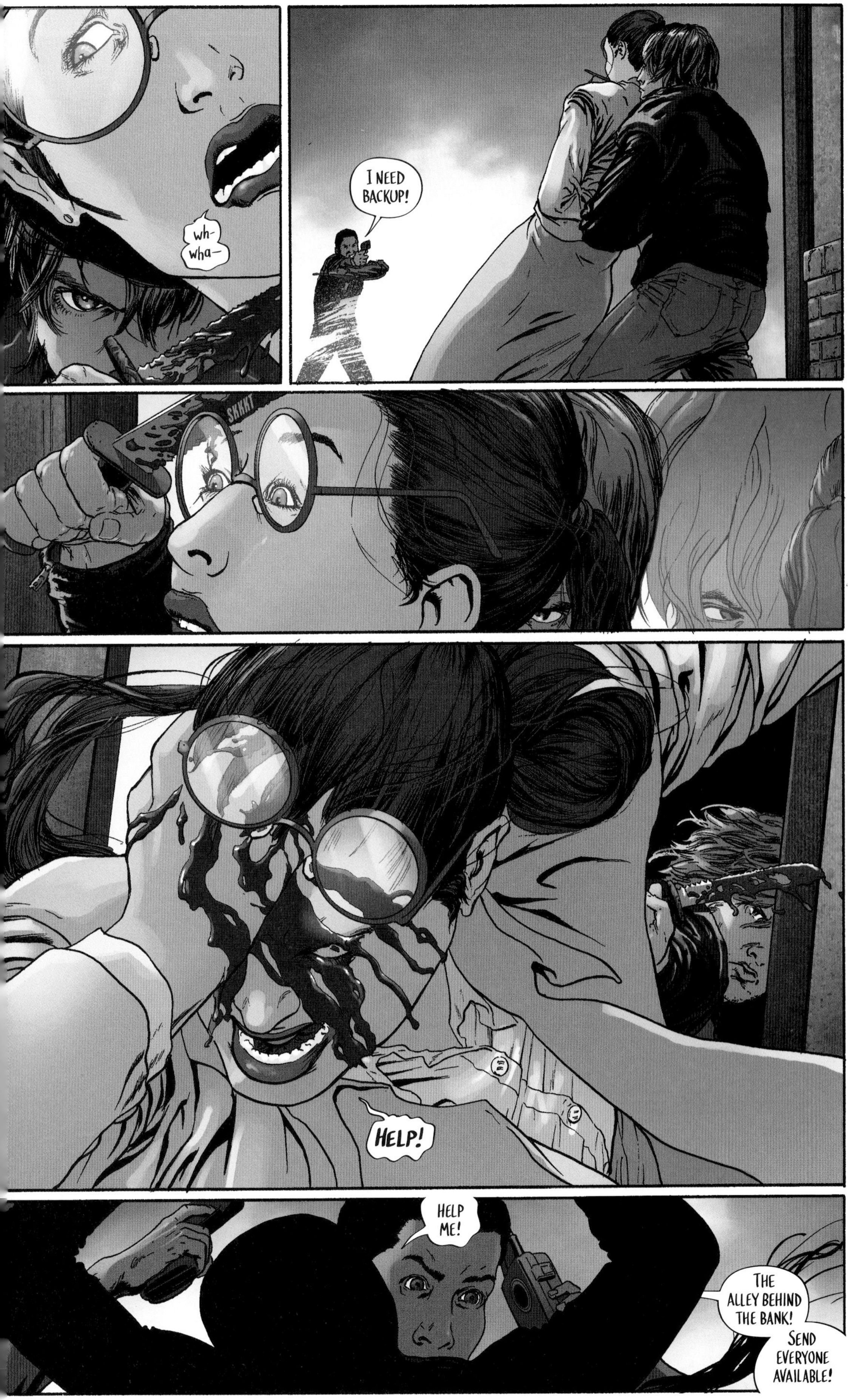
wh- wha-
I NEED BACKUP!
SKKKT
HELP!
HELP ME!
THE ALLEY BEHIND THE BANK!
SEND EVERYONE AVAILABLE!

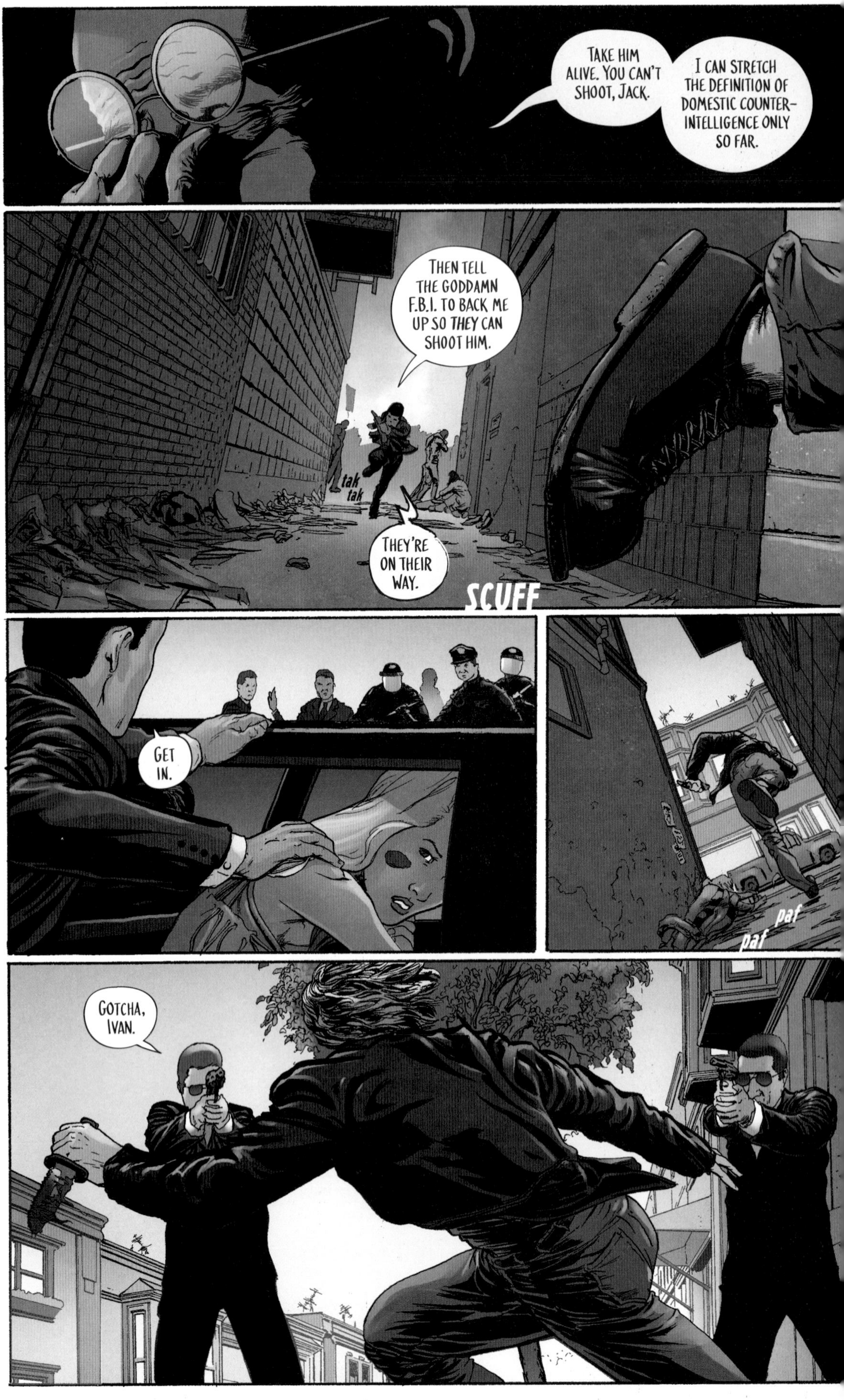
TAKE HIM ALIVE. YOU CAN'T SHOOT, JACK.
I CAN STRETCH THE DEFINITION OF DOMESTIC COUNTER-INTELLIGENCE ONLY SO FAR.
THEN TELL THE GODDAMN F.B.I. TO BACK ME UP SO THEY CAN SHOOT HIM.
tak tak
THEY'RE ON THEIR WAY.
SCUFF
GET IN.
paf paf
GOTCHA, IVAN.

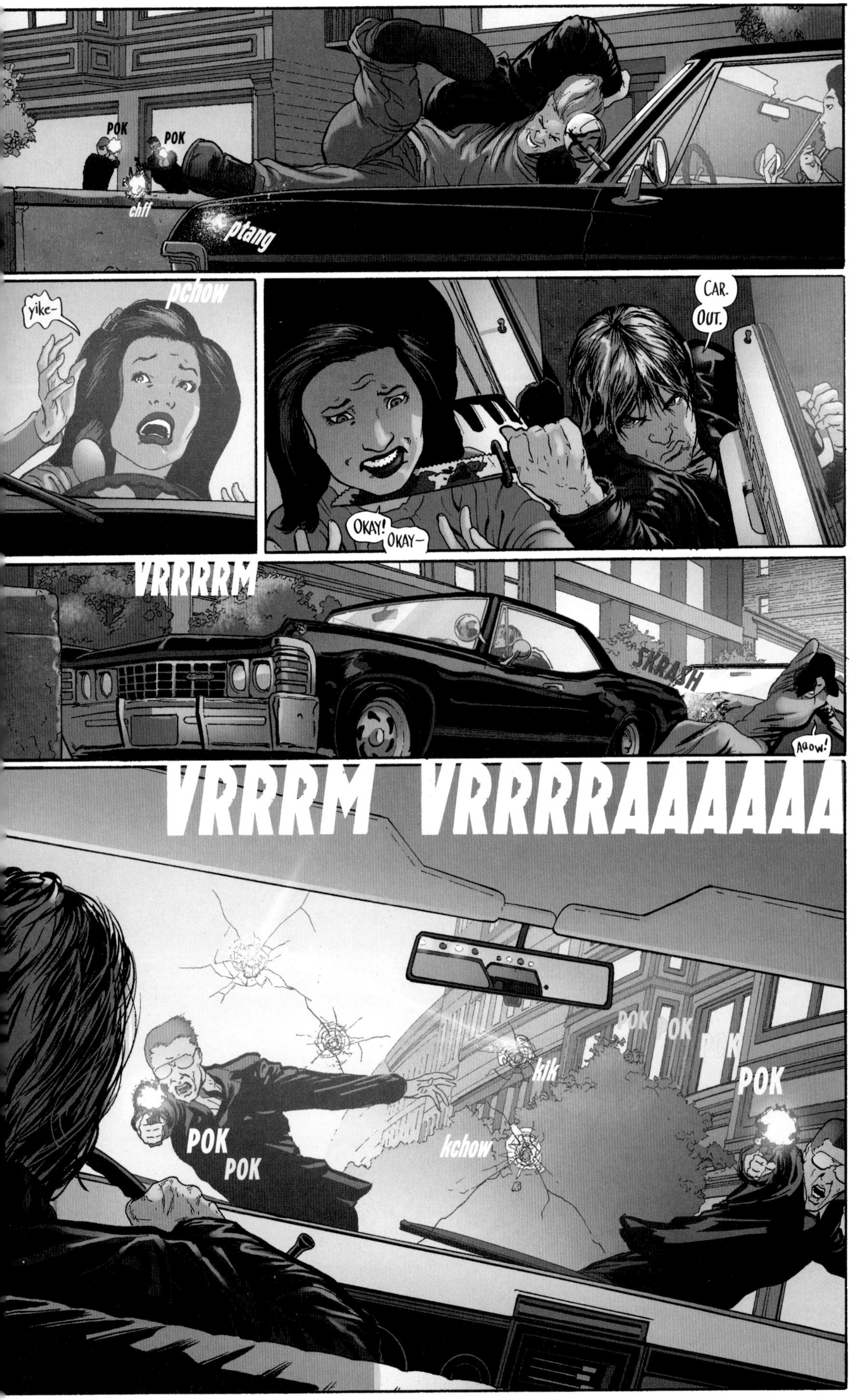
POK
POK
chff
ptang
yike-
pchow
CAR. OUT.
OKAY! OKAY-
VRRRRM
SKRASH
Aaow!
VRRRM VRRRRAAAAAA
POK POK POK
POK
kik
POK
POK
kchow

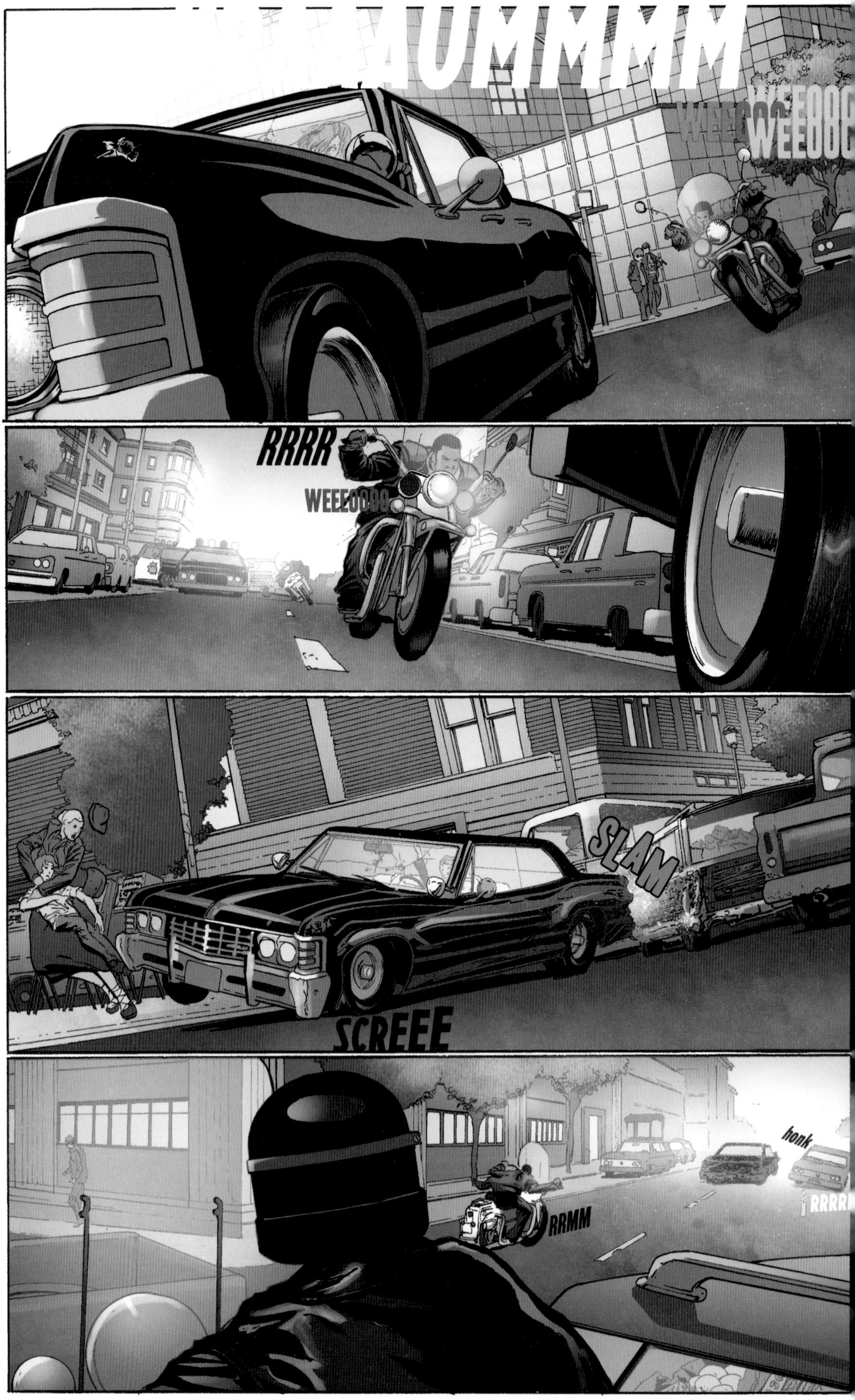
AUMMMMM
WEEOOO
WEEOOO
RRRR
WEEEOOOO
SLAM
SCREEE
honk
RRMM
RRRR

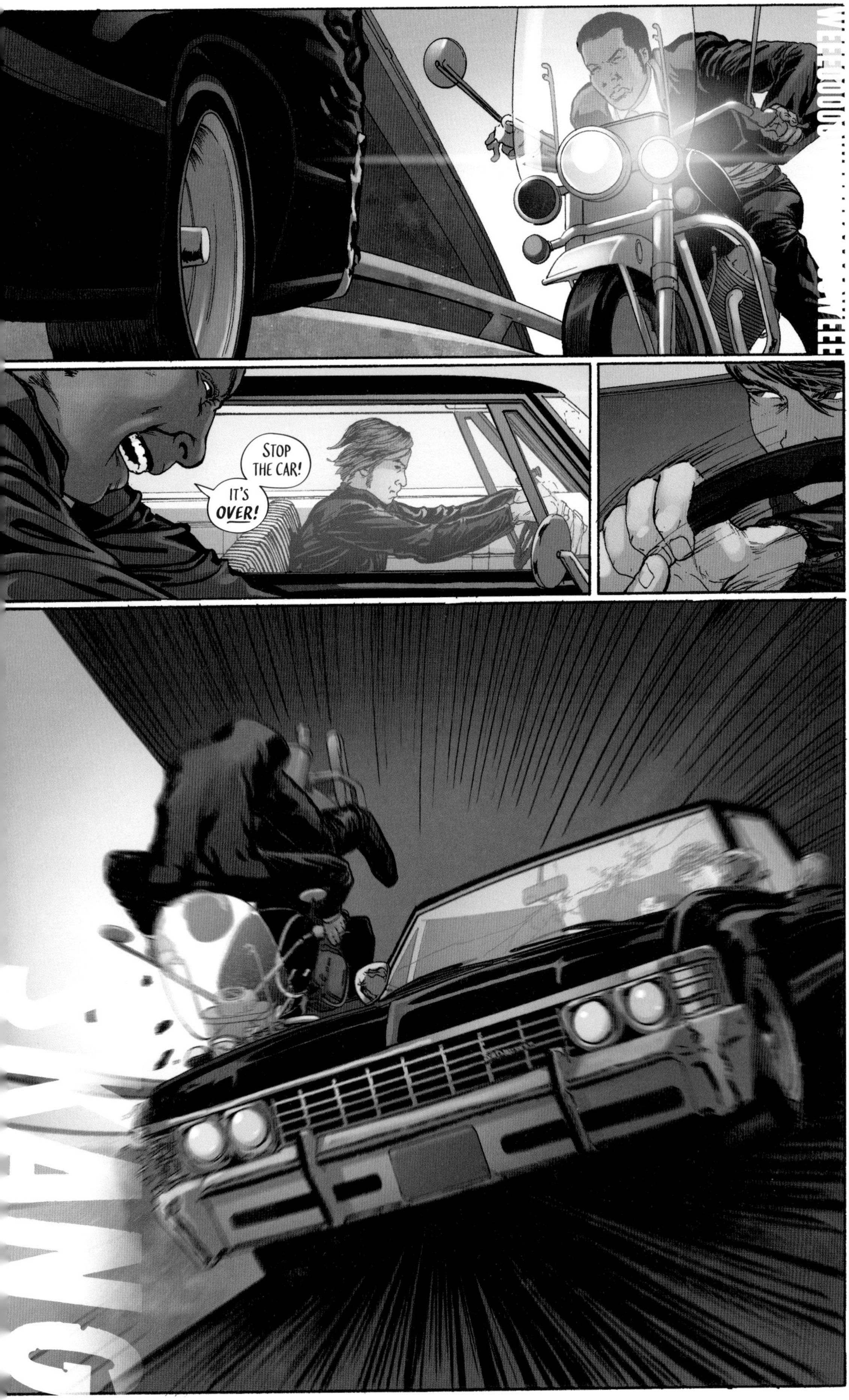
STOP THE CAR!
IT'S OVER!
SMANG

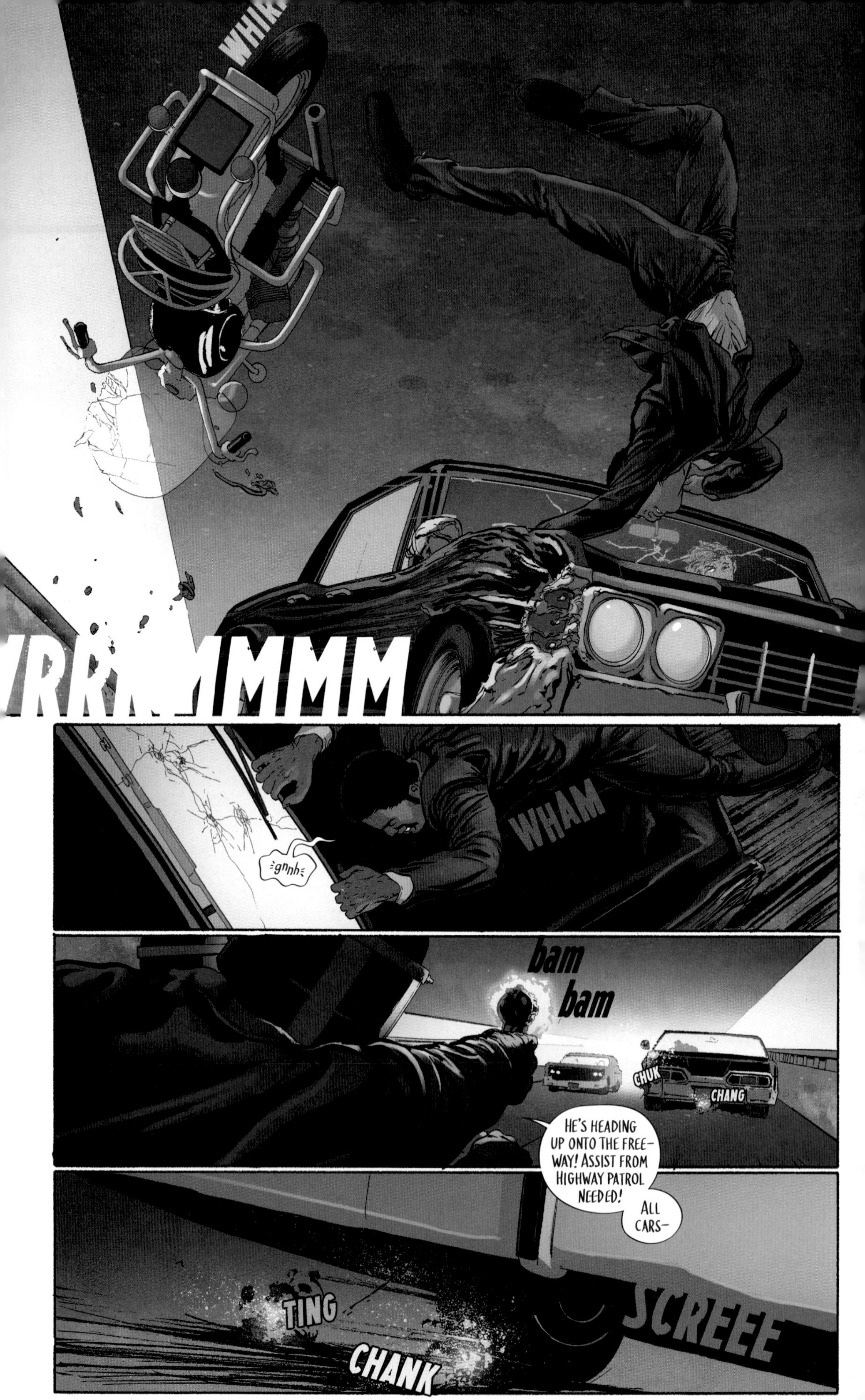
WHIR
RRRMMMMM
gnnh
WHAM
bam
bam
CHUK
CHANG
HE'S HEADING UP ONTO THE FREE-WAY! ASSIST FROM HIGHWAY PATROL NEEDED!
ALL CARS–
TING
CHANK
SCREEE

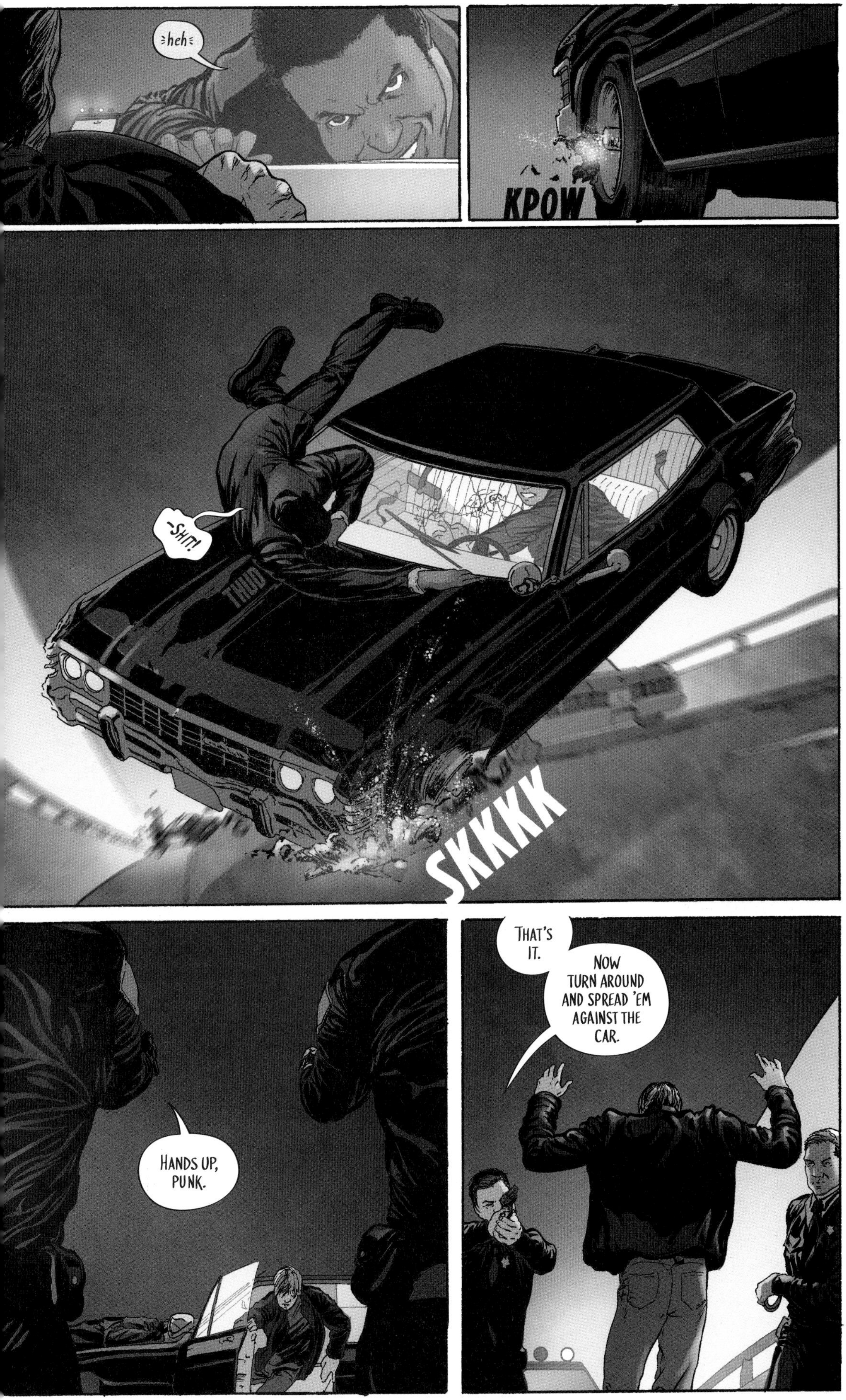

heh
KPOW
-SHIT!
THUD
SKKKK
HANDS UP, PUNK.
THAT'S IT.
NOW TURN AROUND AND SPREAD 'EM AGAINST THE CAR.

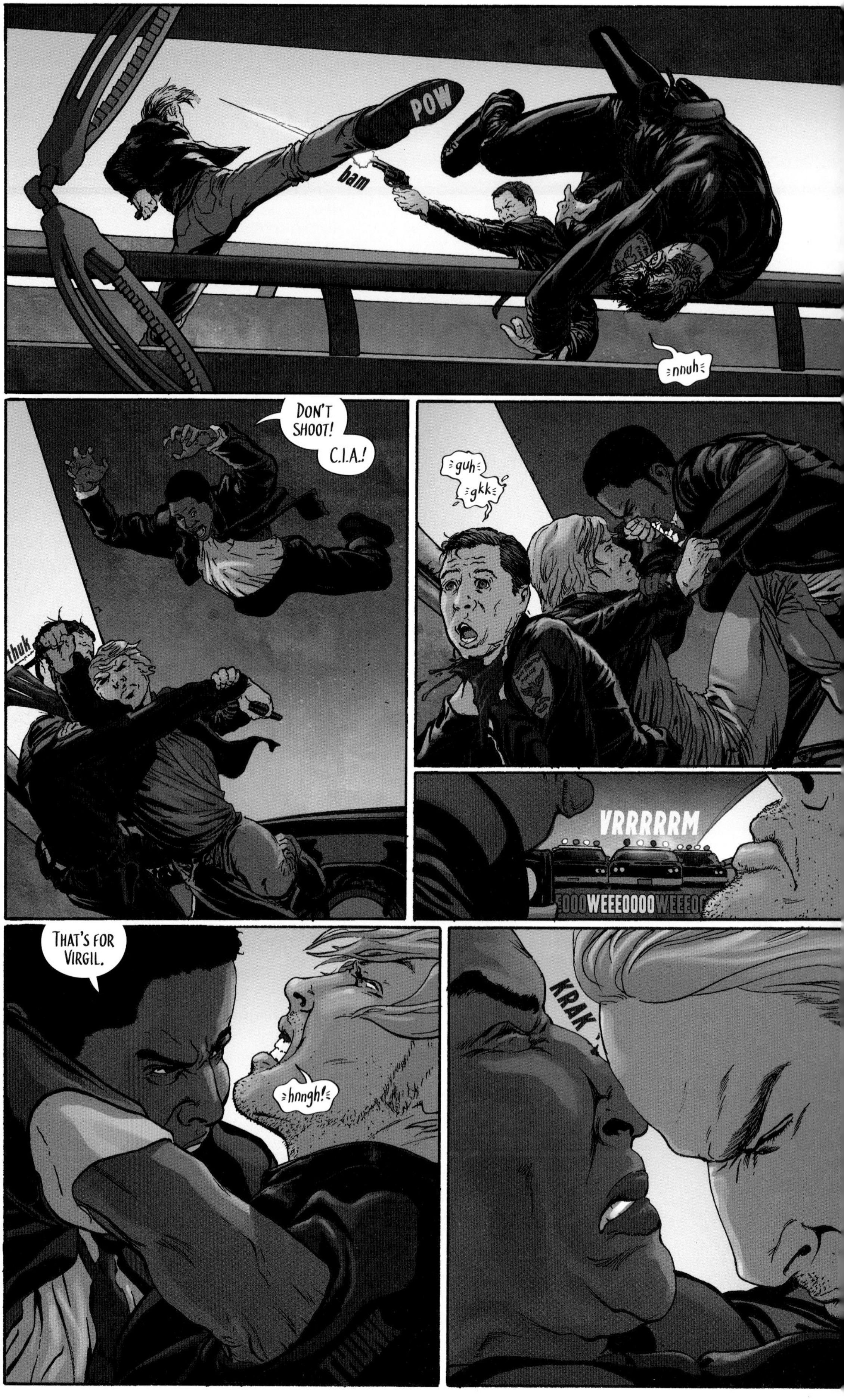
POW
bam
nnuh
DON'T SHOOT!
C.I.A.!
thuk
guh
gkk
VRRRRRM
EOOOWEEEOOOOWEEEO
THAT'S FOR VIRGIL.
hnngh!
KRAK

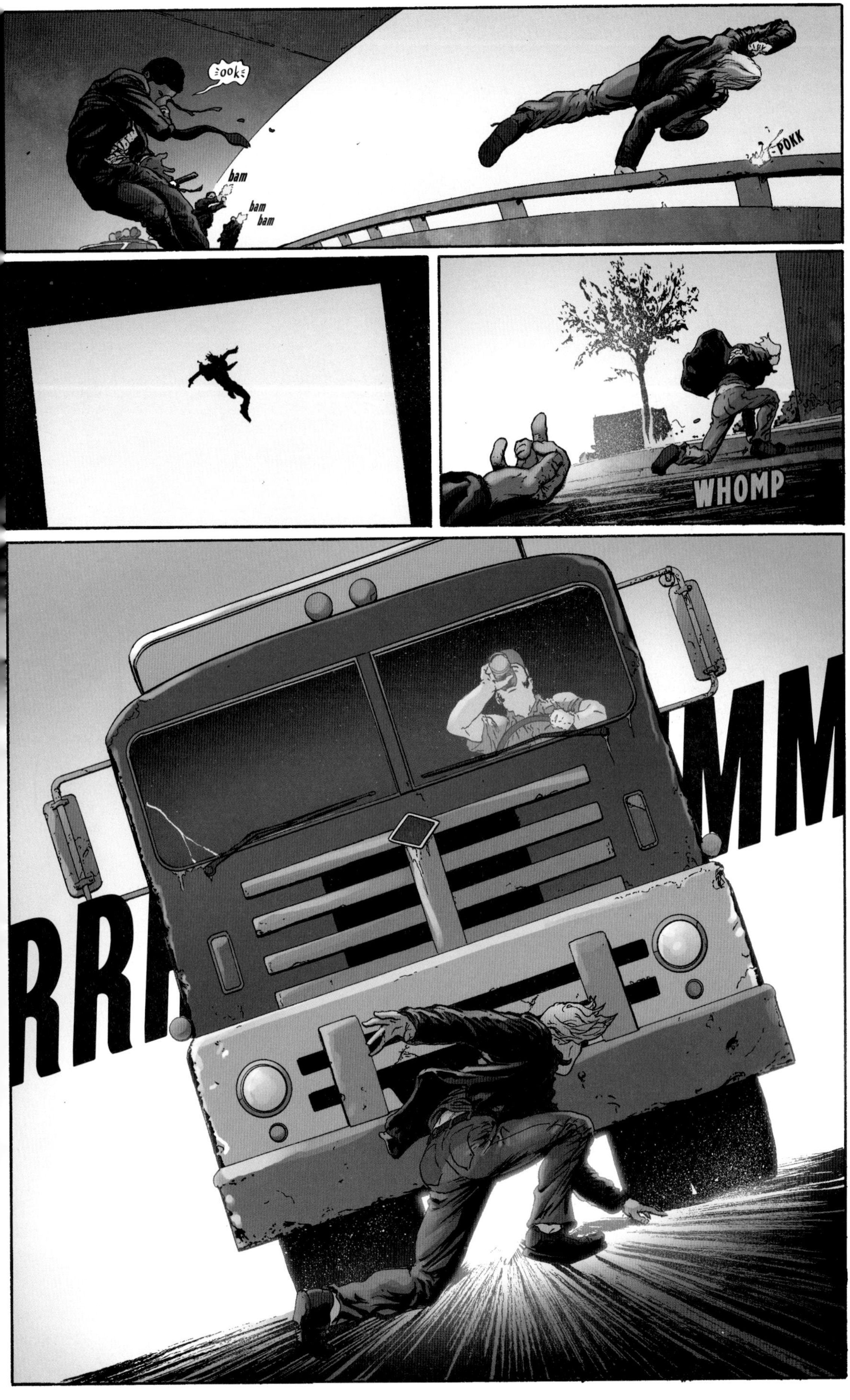

OOK
bam
bam
bam
POKK
WHOMP
RRRMMM

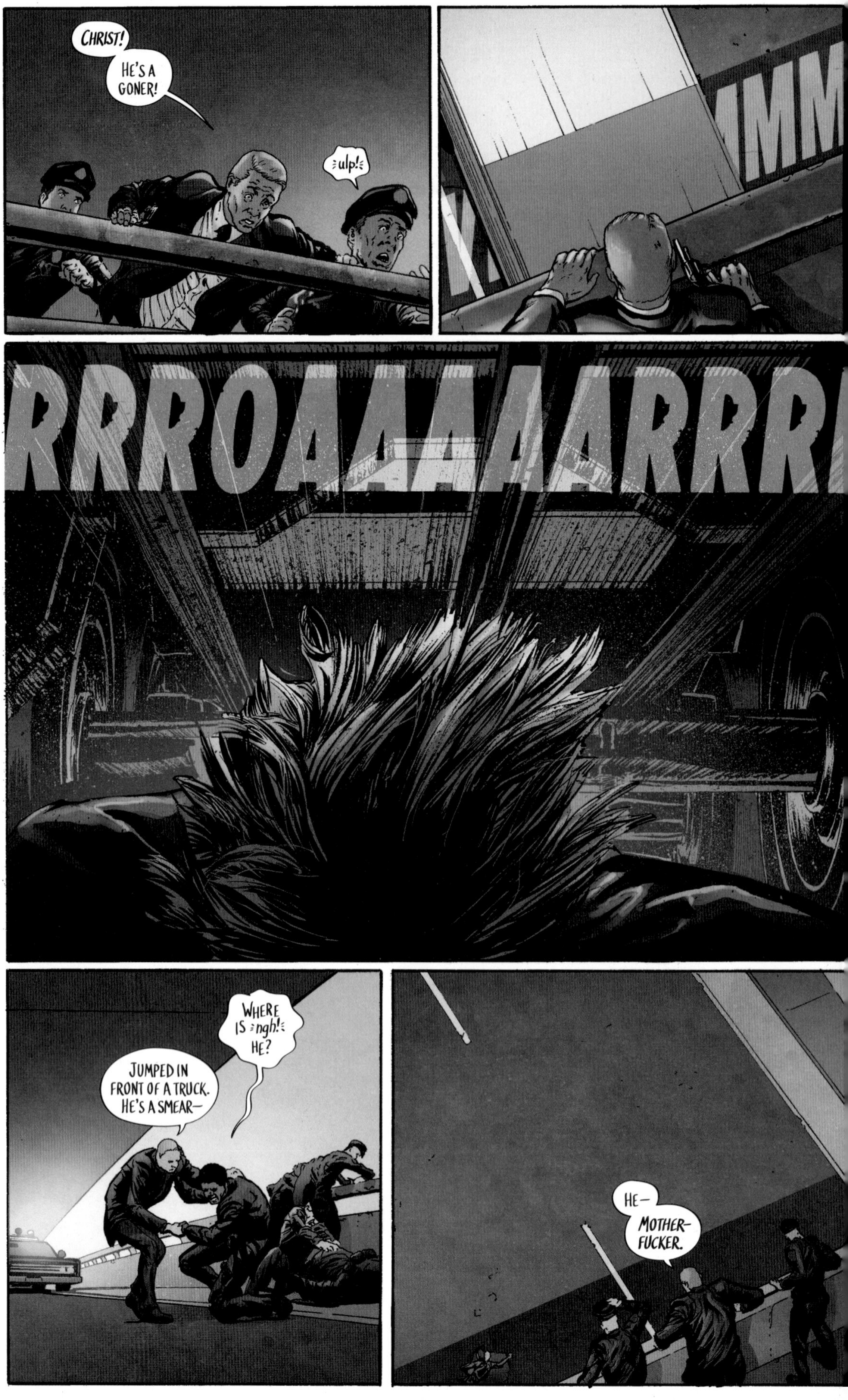
CHRIST!
HE'S A GONER!
ulp!
MMM
RRROAAAAARRRR
WHERE IS ngh! HE?
JUMPED IN FRONT OF A TRUCK. HE'S A SMEAR—
HE—
MOTHER-FUCKER.

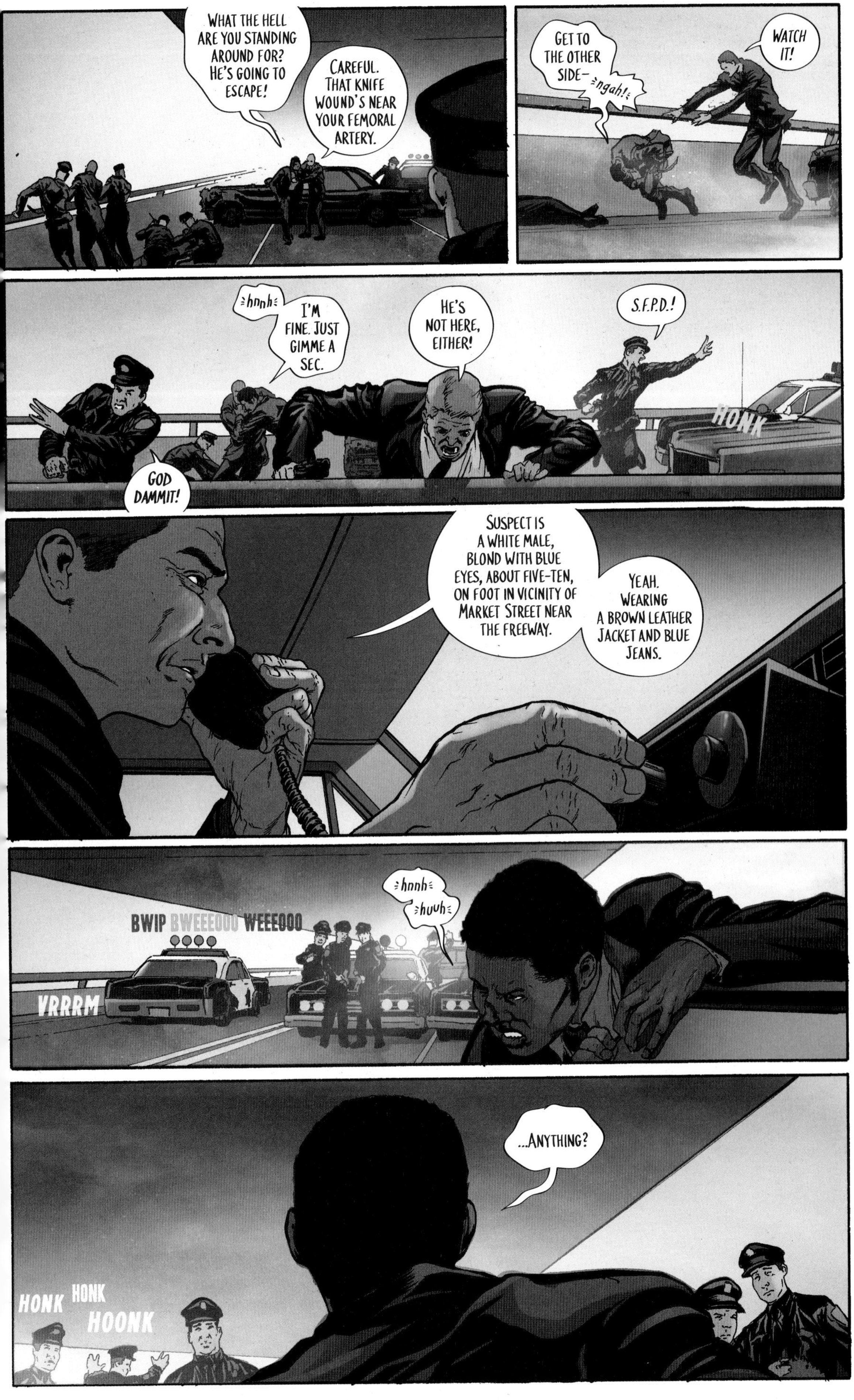
WHAT THE HELL ARE YOU STANDING AROUND FOR? HE'S GOING TO ESCAPE!
CAREFUL. THAT KNIFE WOUND'S NEAR YOUR FEMORAL ARTERY.
GET TO THE OTHER SIDE-
ngah!
WATCH IT!
hnnh
I'M FINE. JUST GIMME A SEC.
HE'S NOT HERE, EITHER!
S.F.P.D.!
HONK
GOD DAMMIT!
SUSPECT IS A WHITE MALE, BLOND WITH BLUE EYES, ABOUT FIVE-TEN, ON FOOT IN VICINITY OF MARKET STREET NEAR THE FREEWAY.
YEAH. WEARING A BROWN LEATHER JACKET AND BLUE JEANS.
BWIP BWEEEOOO WEEEOOO
hnnh
huuh
VRRRM
...ANYTHING?
HONK HONK HOONK

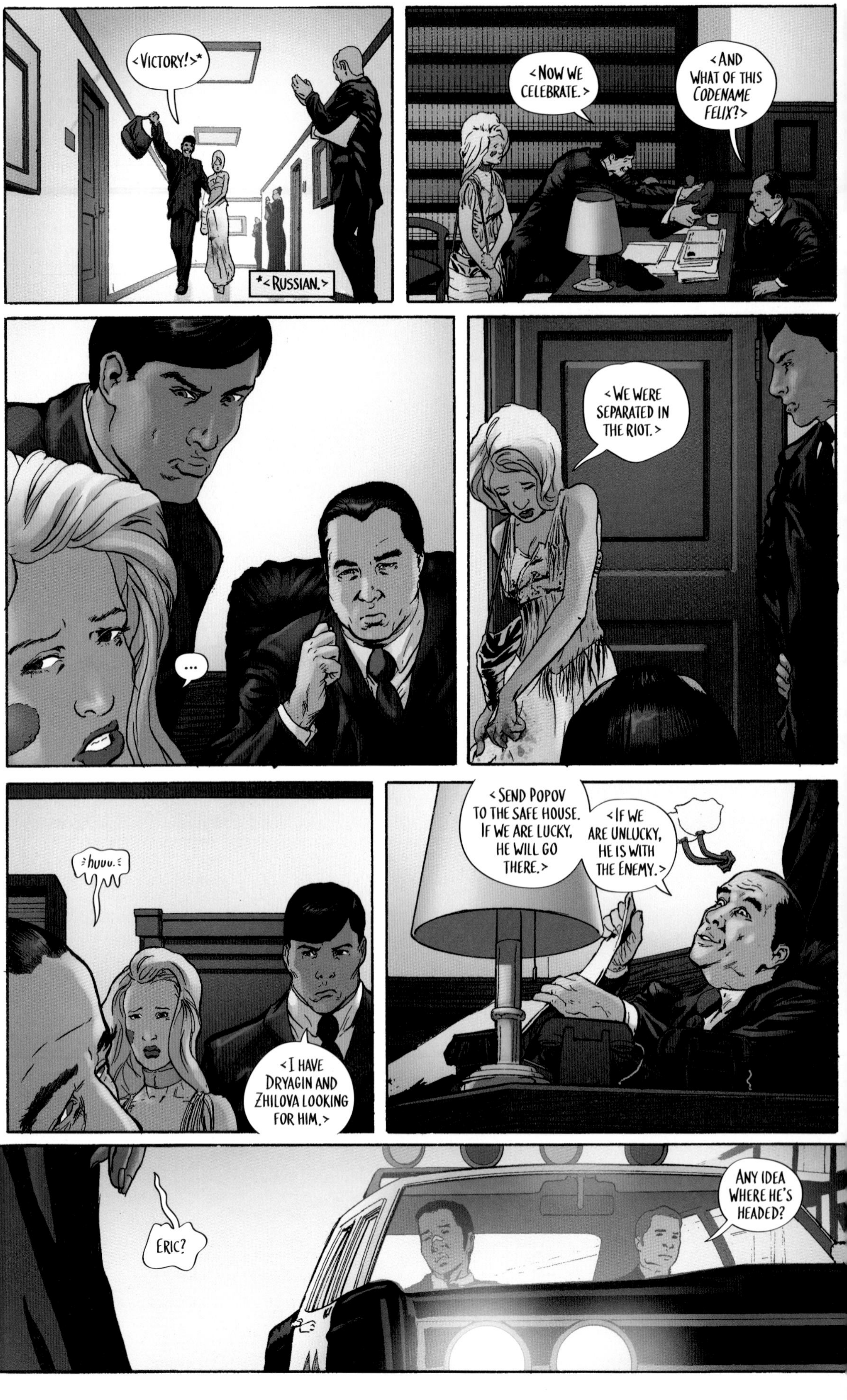
<VICTORY!>*
*<RUSSIAN.>
<NOW WE CELEBRATE.>
<AND WHAT OF THIS CODENAME FELIX?>
...
<WE WERE SEPARATED IN THE RIOT.>
huuu.
<I HAVE DRYAGIN AND ZHILOVA LOOKING FOR HIM.>
<SEND POPOV TO THE SAFE HOUSE. IF WE ARE LUCKY, HE WILL GO THERE.>
<IF WE ARE UNLUCKY, HE IS WITH THE ENEMY.>
ERIC?
ANY IDEA WHERE HE'S HEADED?

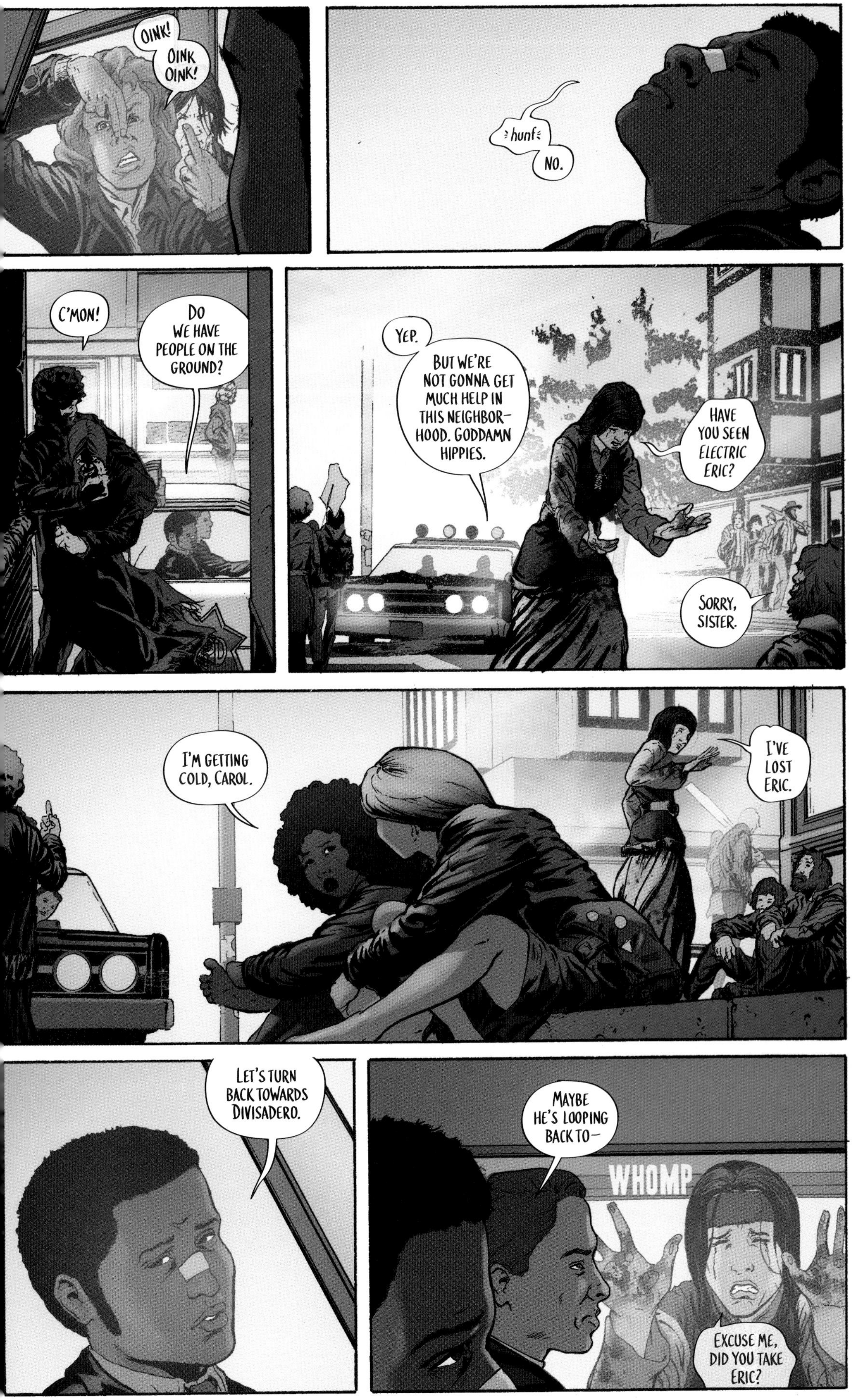
OINK!
OINK OINK!
hunf
NO.
C'MON!
DO WE HAVE PEOPLE ON THE GROUND?
YEP.
BUT WE'RE NOT GONNA GET MUCH HELP IN THIS NEIGHBOR-HOOD. GODDAMN HIPPIES.
HAVE YOU SEEN ELECTRIC ERIC?
SORRY, SISTER.
I'M GETTING COLD, CAROL.
I'VE LOST ERIC.
LET'S TURN BACK TOWARDS DIVISADERO.
MAYBE HE'S LOOPING BACK TO—
WHOMP
EXCUSE ME, DID YOU TAKE ERIC?

... NICK DRAKE, "BLUES RUN THE GAME"

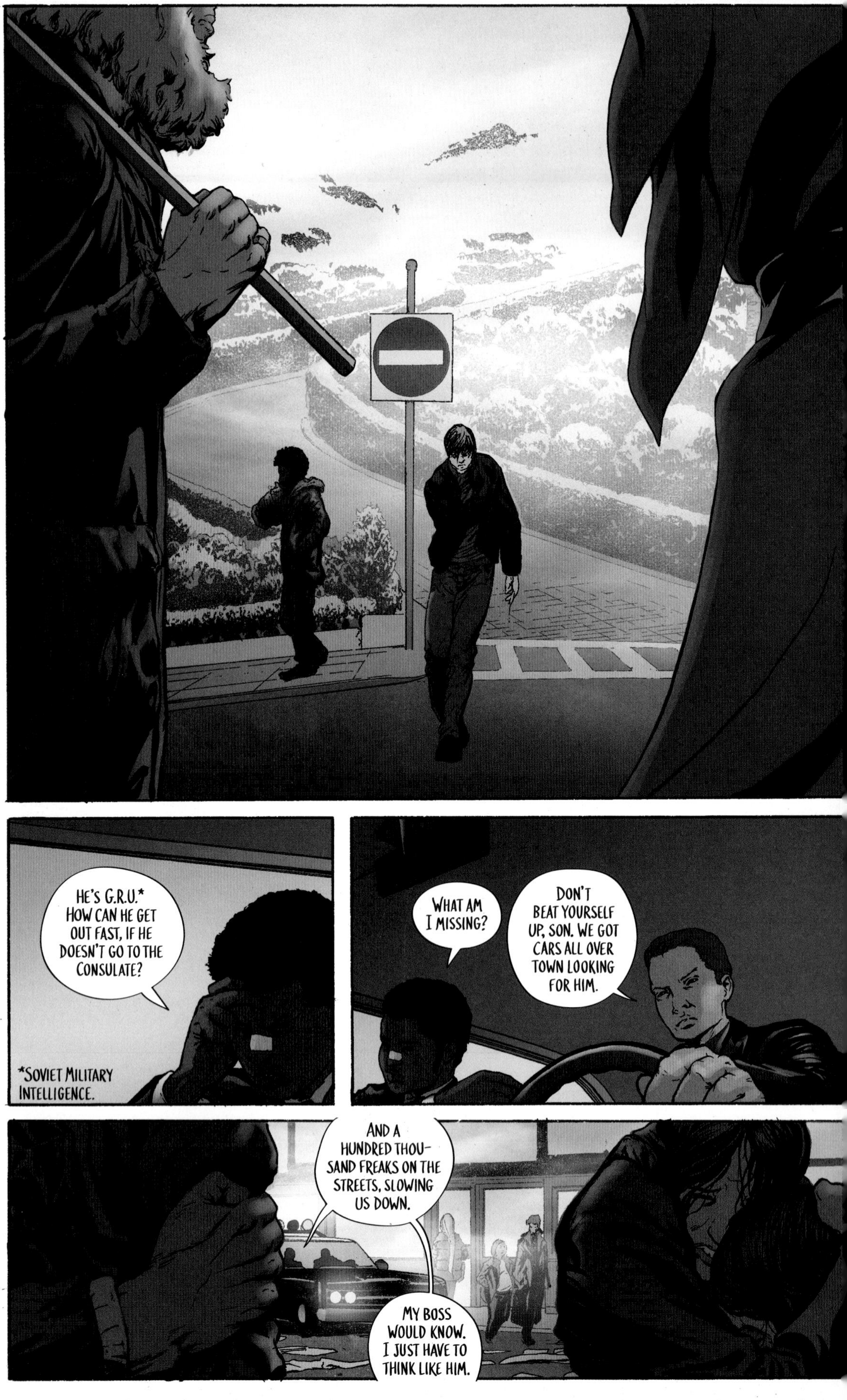
HE'S G.R.U.* HOW CAN HE GET OUT FAST, IF HE DOESN'T GO TO THE CONSULATE?
*SOVIET MILITARY INTELLIGENCE.
WHAT AM I MISSING?
DON'T BEAT YOURSELF UP, SON. WE GOT CARS ALL OVER TOWN LOOKING FOR HIM.
AND A HUNDRED THOU-SAND FREAKS ON THE STREETS, SLOWING US DOWN.
MY BOSS WOULD KNOW. I JUST HAVE TO THINK LIKE HIM.

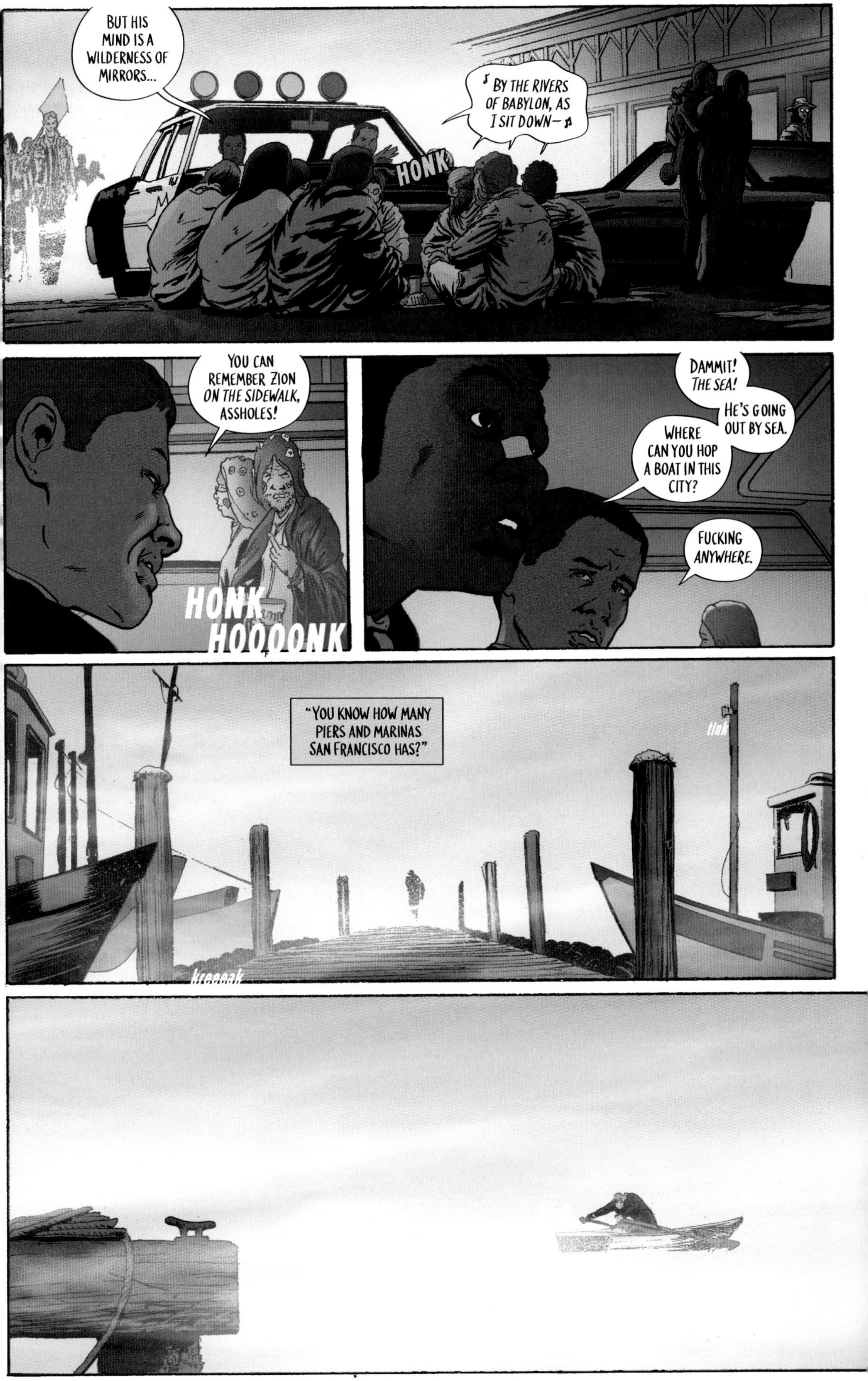

BUT HIS MIND IS A WILDERNESS OF MIRRORS...
♪ BY THE RIVERS OF BABYLON, AS I SIT DOWN— ♪
HONK
YOU CAN REMEMBER ZION ON THE SIDEWALK, ASSHOLES!
HONK HOOOONK
DAMMIT! THE SEA!
HE'S GOING OUT BY SEA.
WHERE CAN YOU HOP A BOAT IN THIS CITY?
FUCKING ANYWHERE.
"YOU KNOW HOW MANY PIERS AND MARINAS SAN FRANCISCO HAS?"
tink
kreeeeak

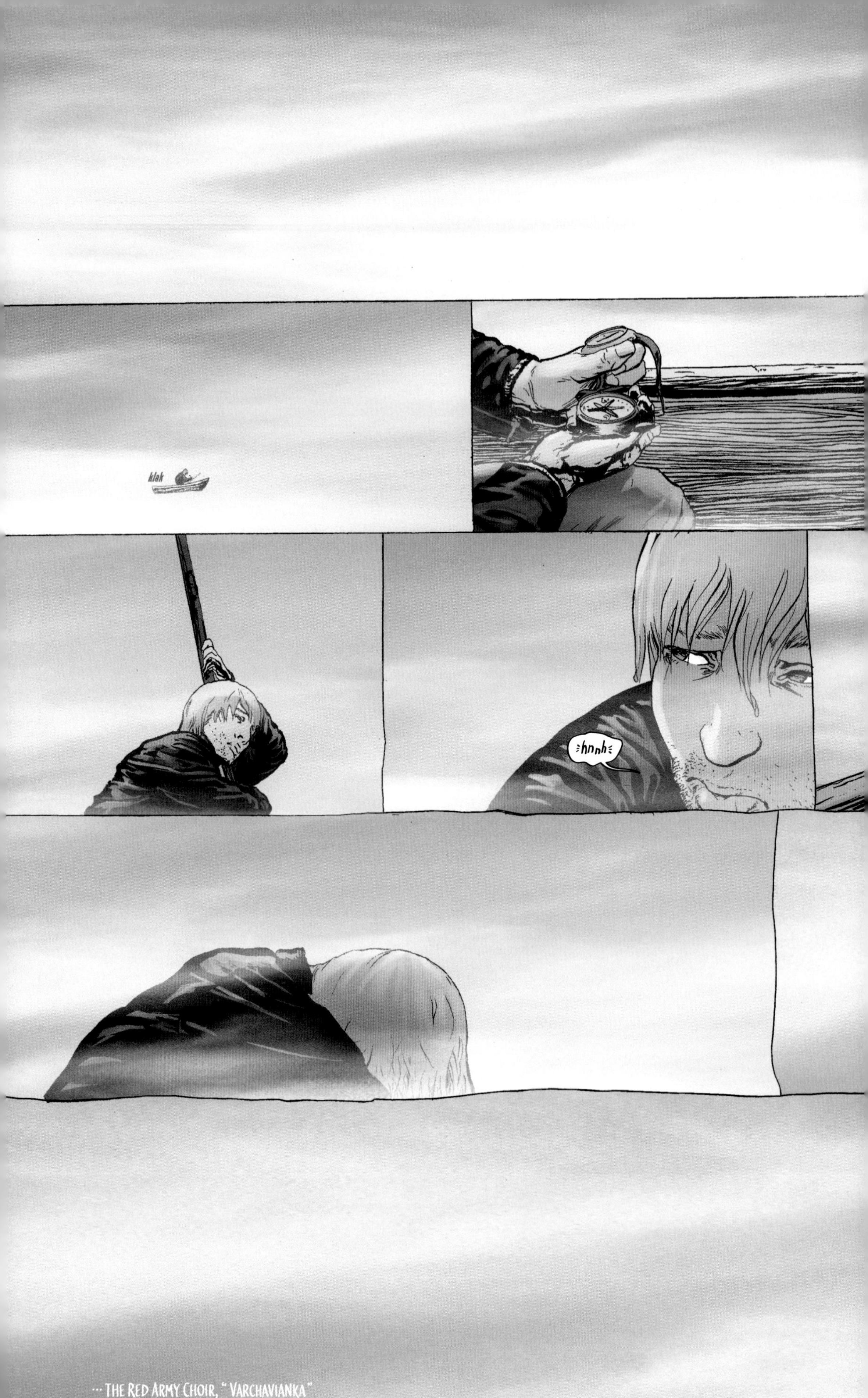
klak
hnnh

... THE RED ARMY CHOIR, "VARCHAVIANKA"

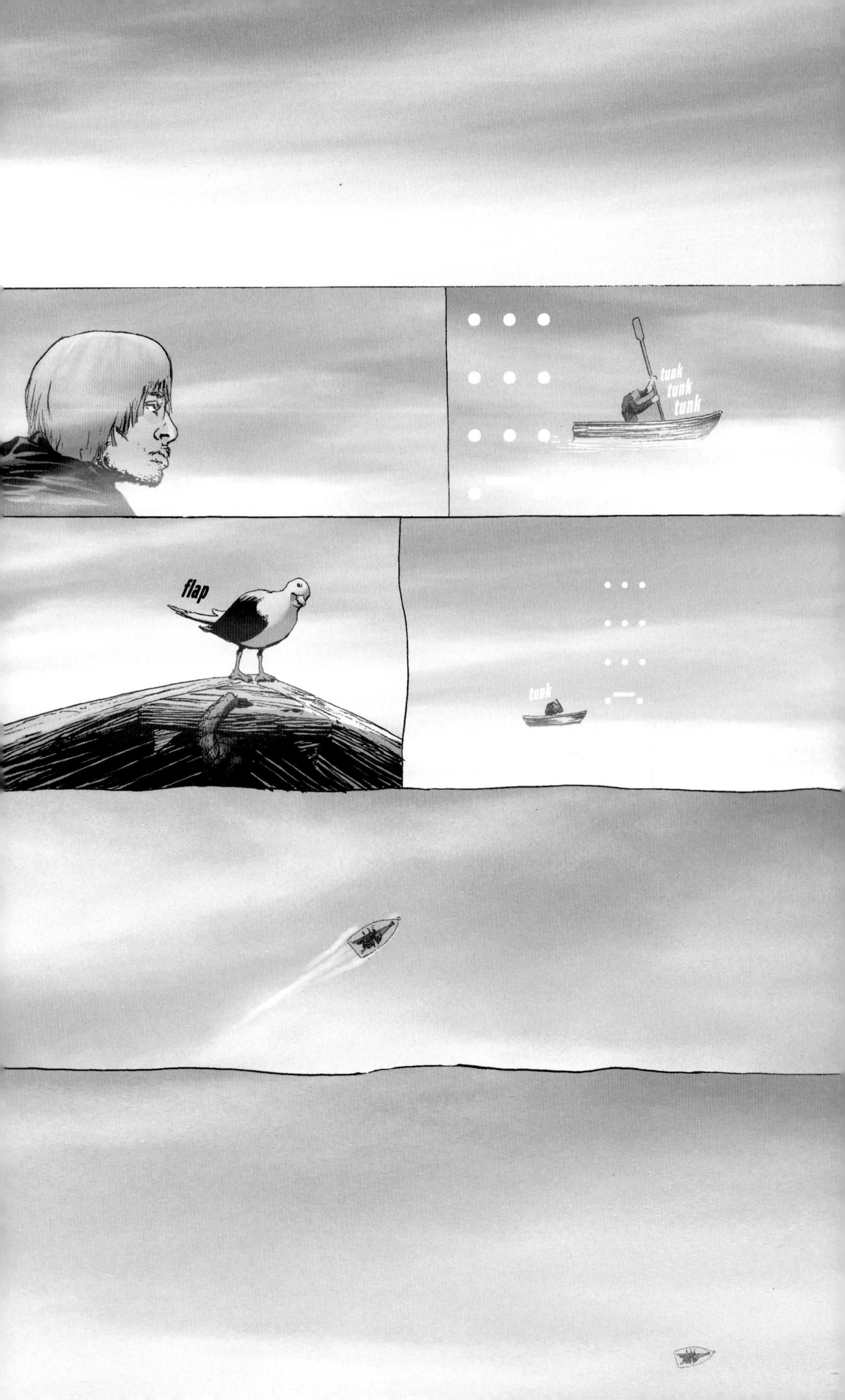
tunk
tunk
tunk
flap
tunk

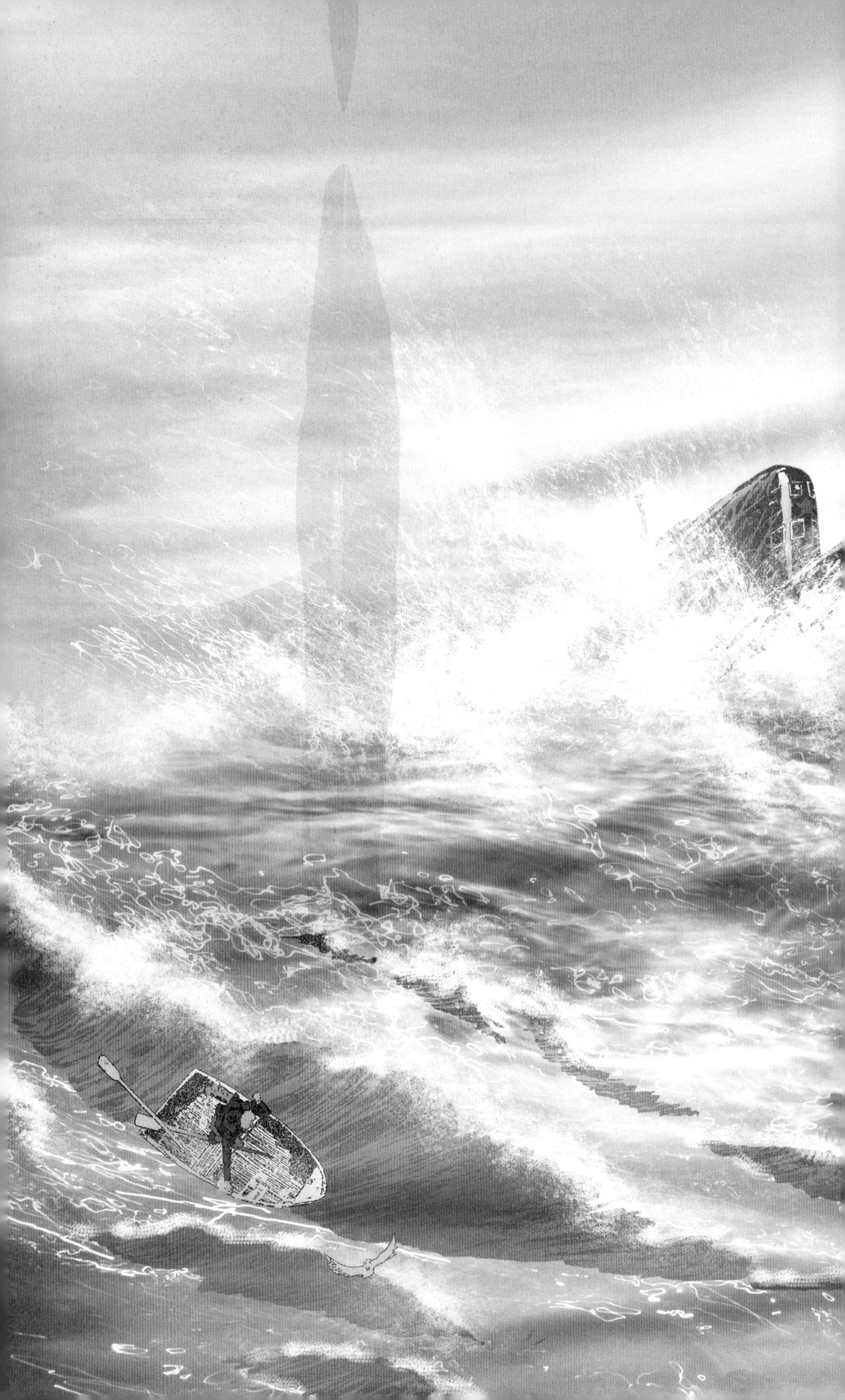

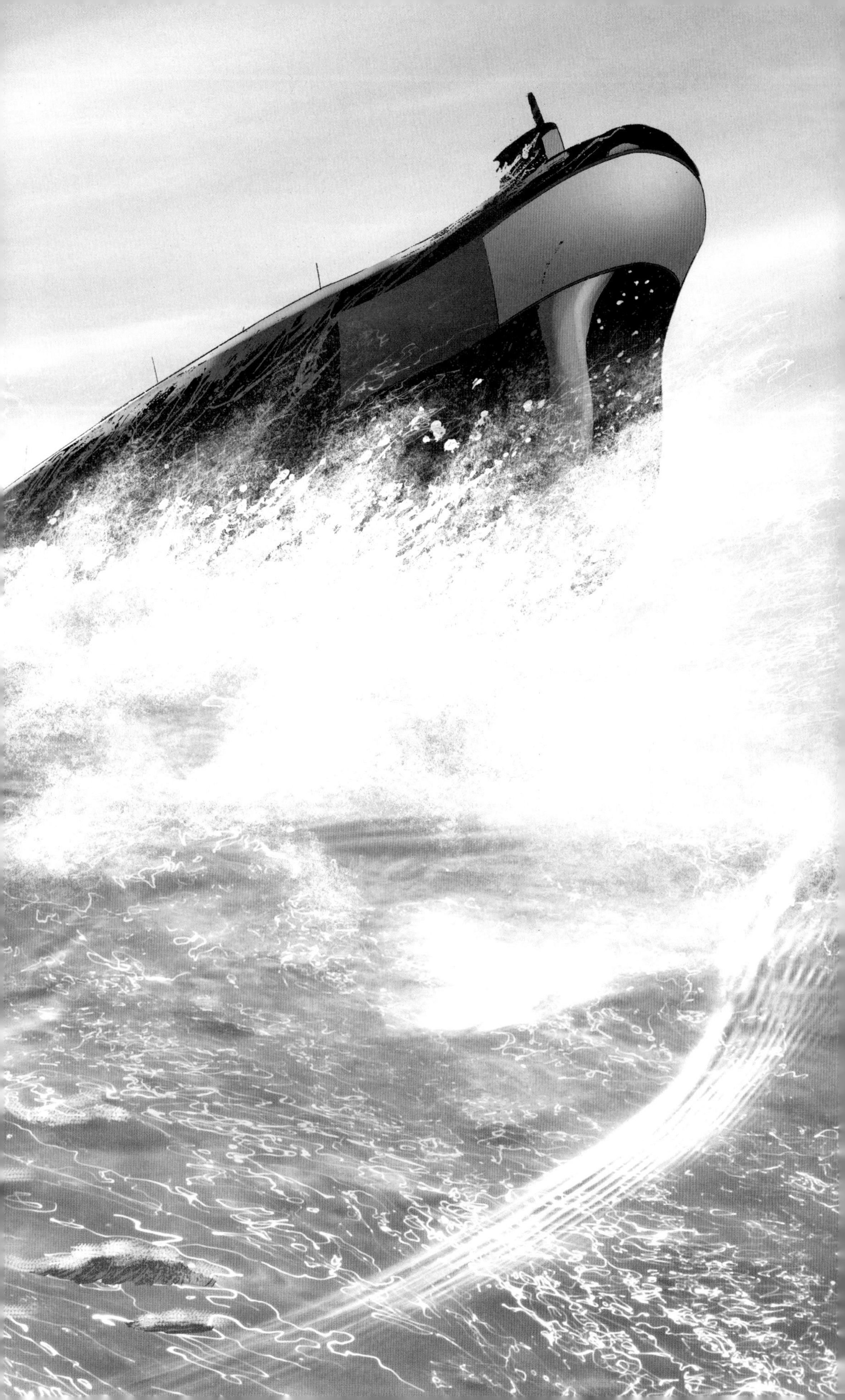

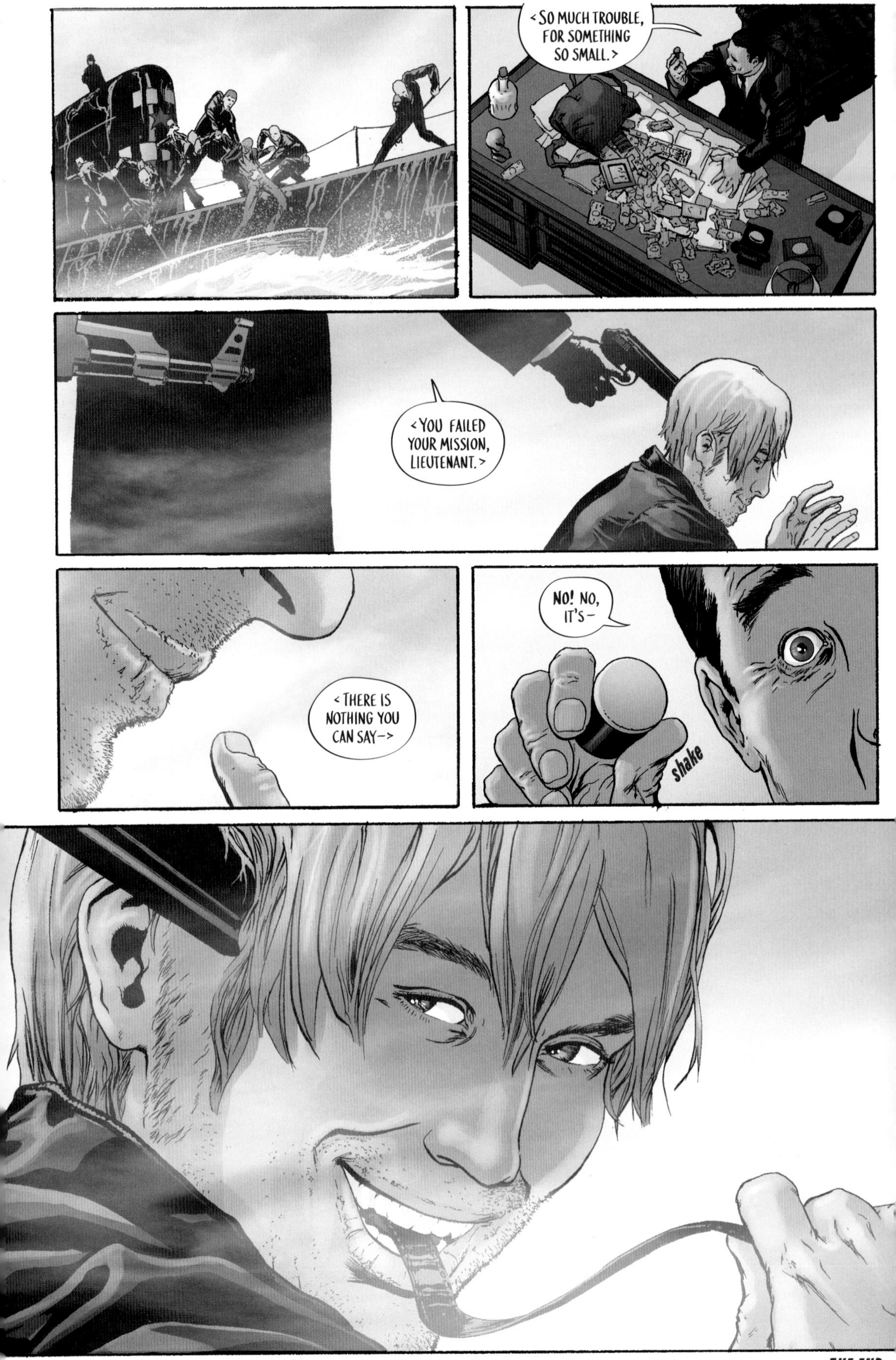
<SO MUCH TROUBLE, FOR SOMETHING SO SMALL.>
<YOU FAILED YOUR MISSION, LIEUTENANT.>
<THERE IS NOTHING YOU CAN SAY–>
NO! NO, IT'S–
shake

THE END

" If it takes a bloodbath, then let's get it over with.
No more appeasement."
Gov. Ronald Reagan on Berkeley student protestors, 1970

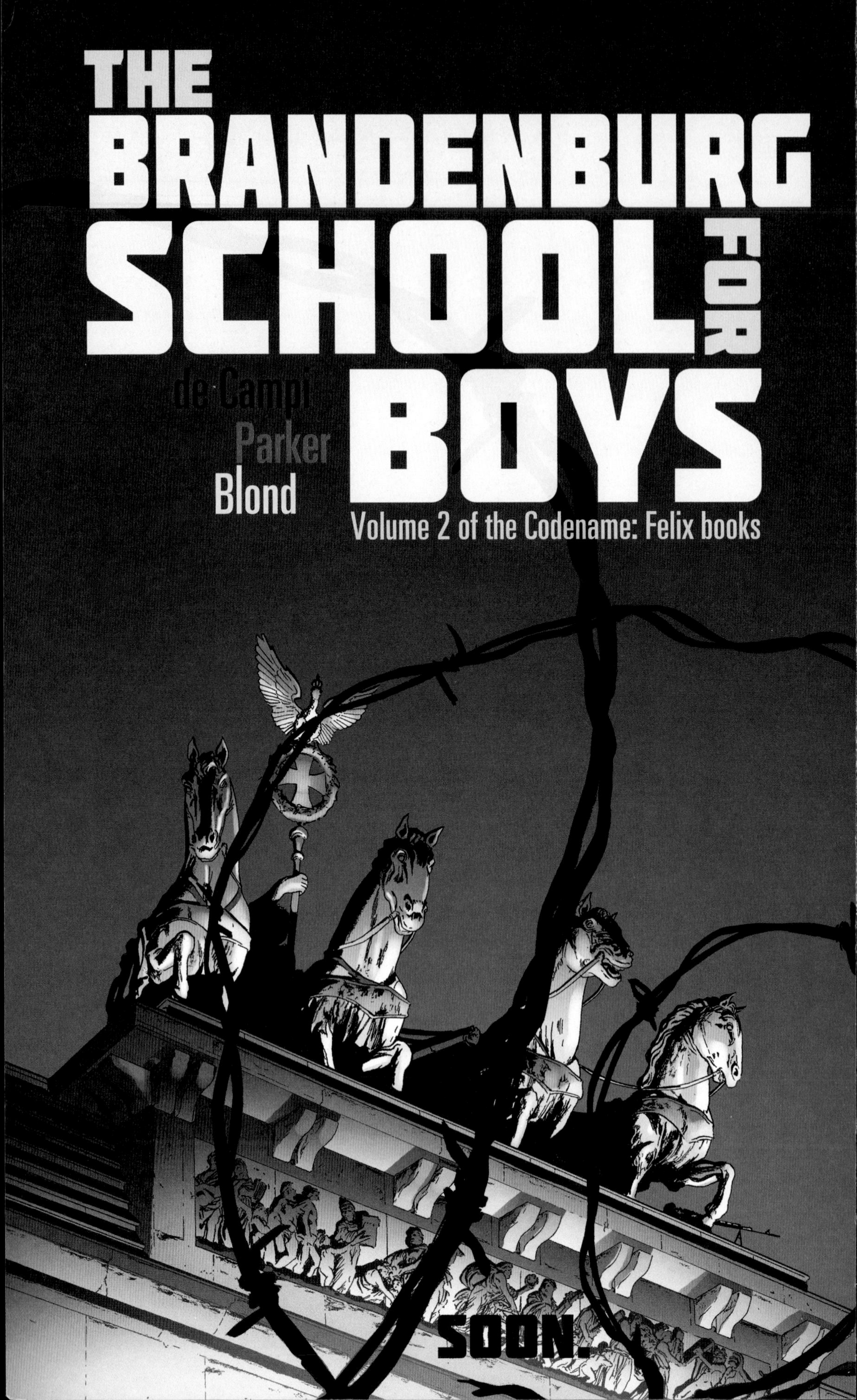
THE BRANDENBURG SCHOOL FOR BOYS
de Campi
Parker
Blond
Volume 2 of the Codename: Felix books
SOON.

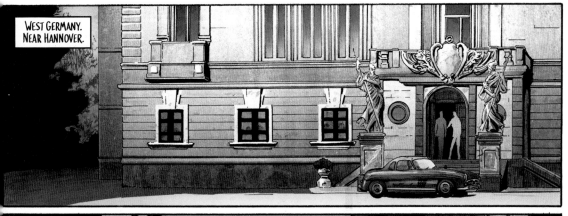

WEST GERMANY. NEAR HANNOVER.

thuc

FRANZI!

WHO—

FREIHERR VON DESENBERG.

I HAVE COME TO TALK TO YOU ABOUT *STALINGRAD.*

NO! DON'T SHOOT! I—

DO NOT WORRY, OLD MAN.

FOR YOU, I HAVE A *KNIFE.*

shnnnnk

DESIGN SKETCHES

FELIX AND ROSE

This was my introduction to the feel of the series. I had everyone in *Get Carter/Dirty Harry* suits, and was completely wrong. My revision of Felix was based off of a hitchhiker news pic, and Rose was from some Jane Fonda movies.

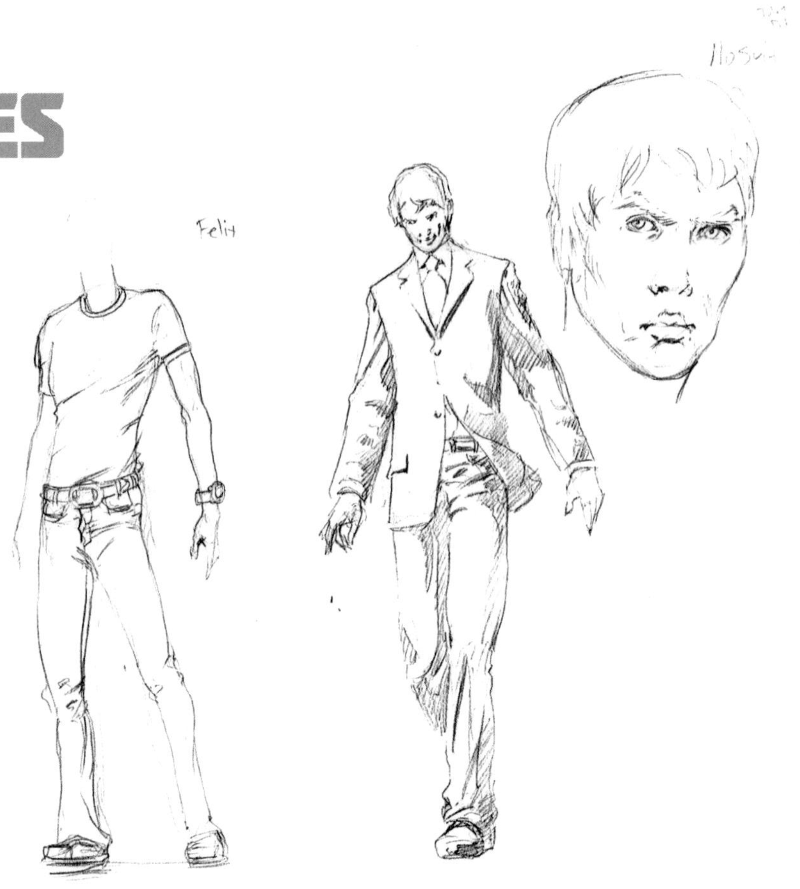
Felix

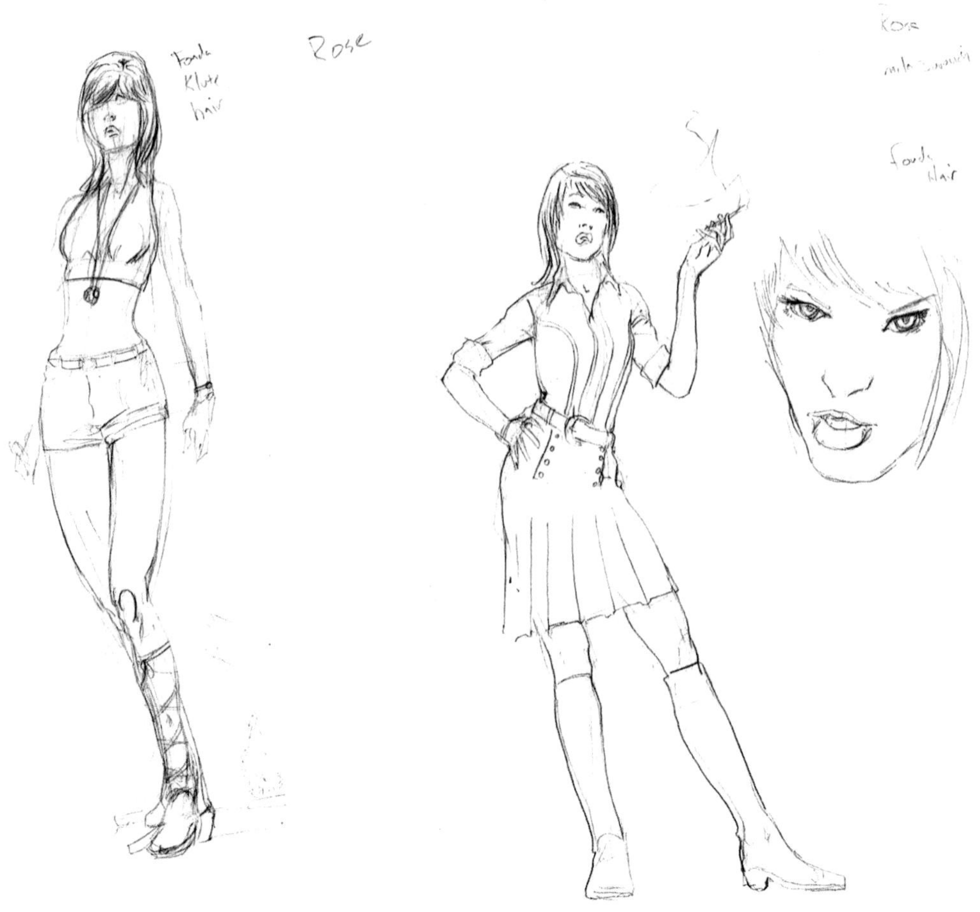
Rose
Fonda
Klute
hair
fonda
hair

COVER PROCESS ISSUE THREE

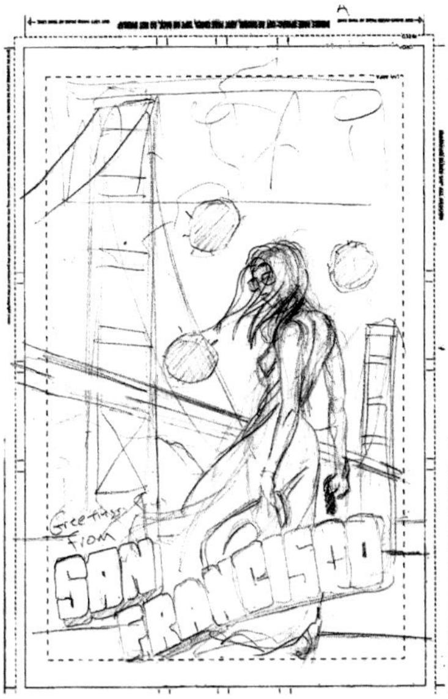
Greetings from
SAN FRANCISCO

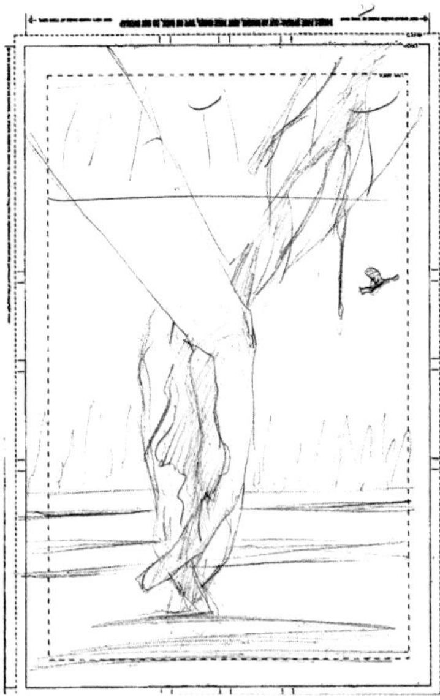

I'm a Huge Robert McGinnis fan, so this was my opportunity to fill that wonderful, pulpy void. I tried different pulp themes, and we went with a postcard (which I had mislabeled as San Francisco) with bullet holes in it. Once completed, Alex suggested against the postcard lettering, and let the image stand on its own, and it works better that way. This shows the ink wash completed physical piece, and the digitally colored final version. We ended up using a version of one of the layouts for the issue 5 cover, and I love how that ended up as well.

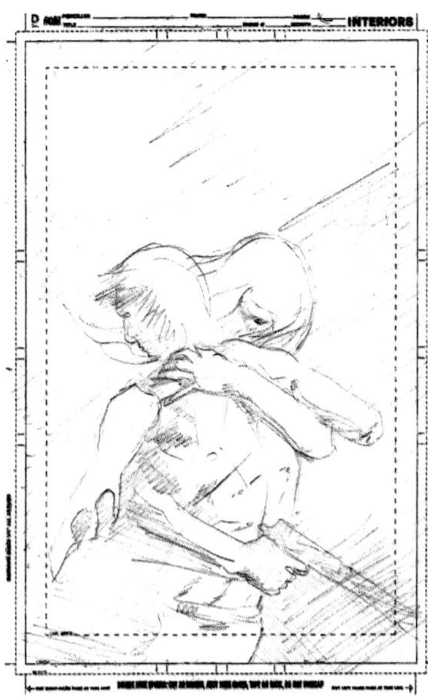
INTERIORS

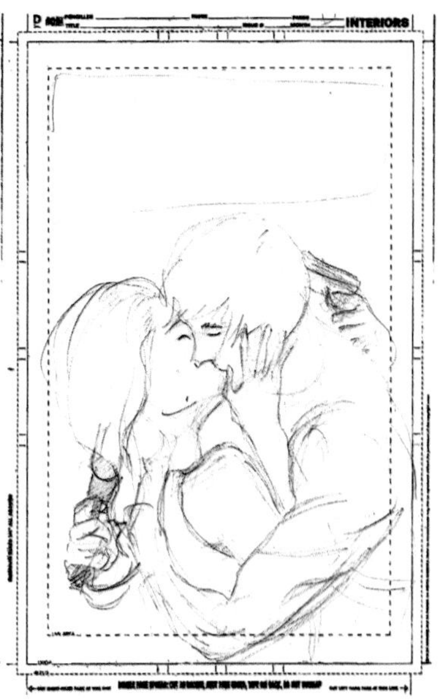
INTERIORS

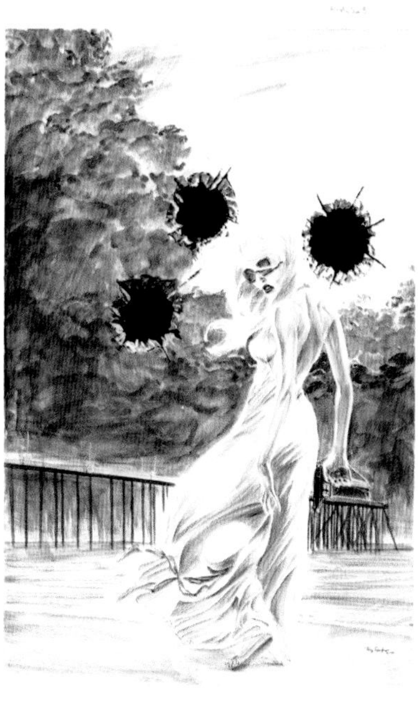

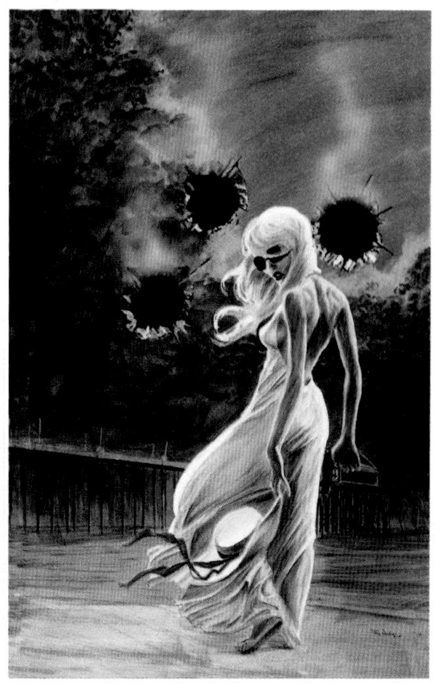

Pages 24-25

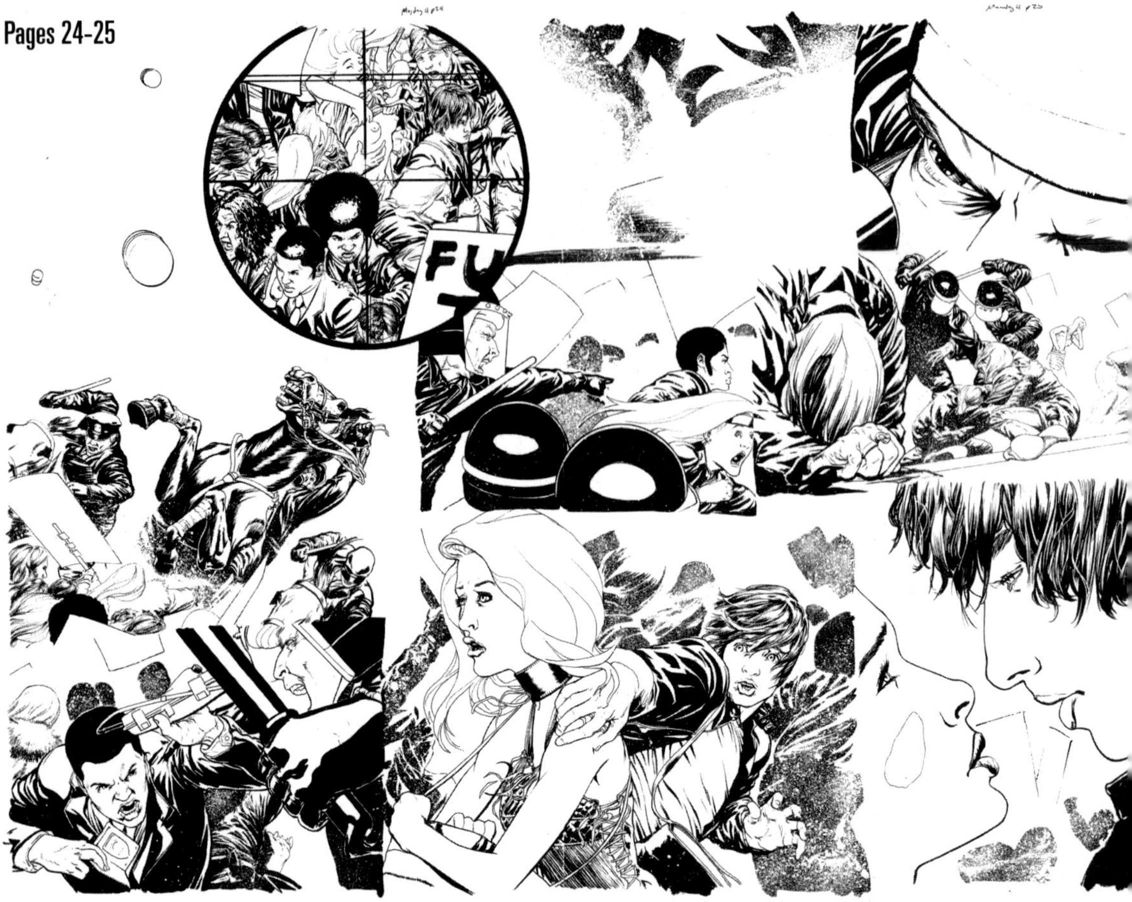
FU

UNCOLORED PAGES
ISSUE FOUR

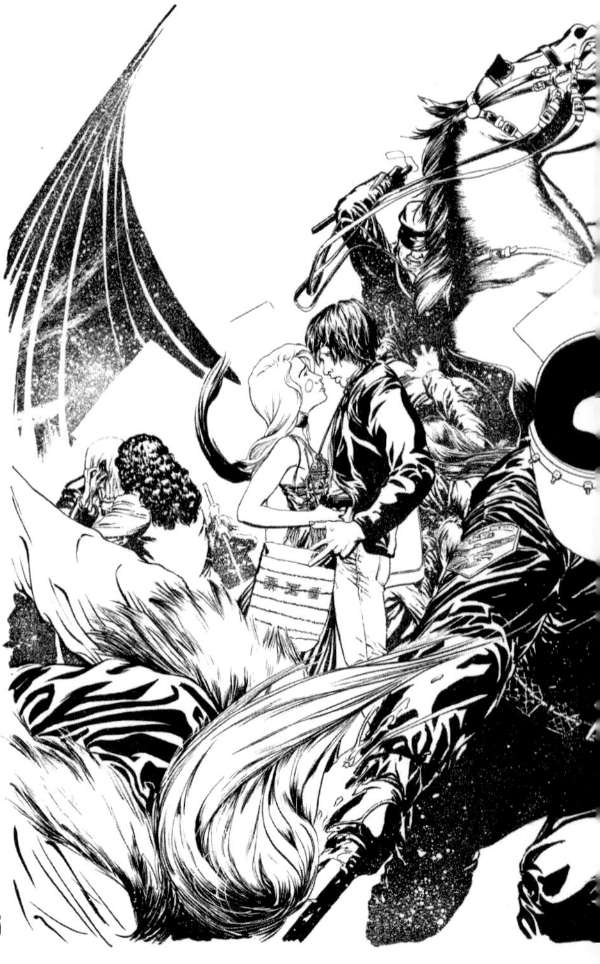

Page 26

Page 21

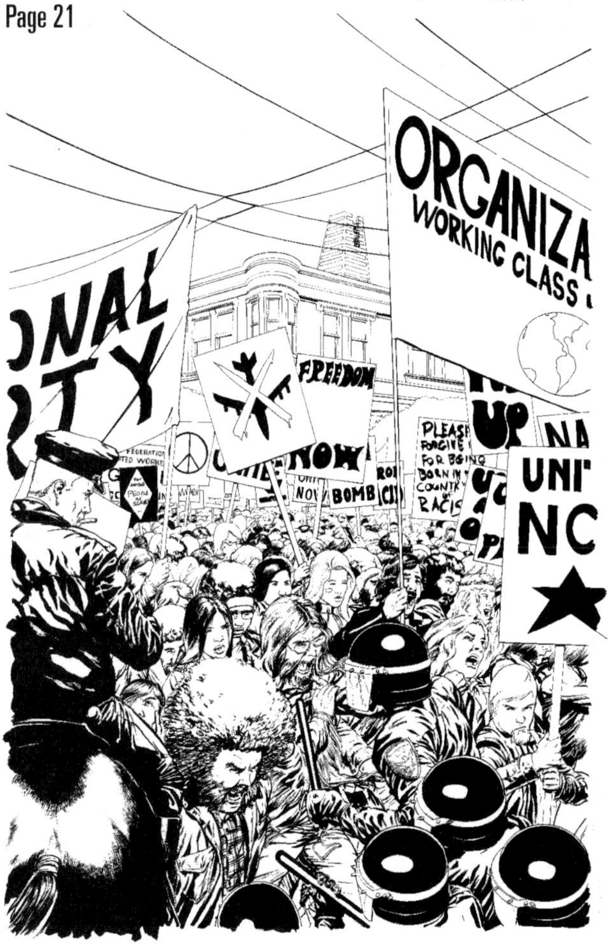
ORGANIZA
WORKING CLASS
FREEDOM
NOW
BOMB
UP
UNI
NC

Oh, just all the chaos and crowd scenes. This was a sequence where I wanted to give the reader the sense of tension and anarchy that happened that day, building up to the riot. I pulled many news photos of the event and tried to pull inspiration from the actual participants. I put in 53 panels (if I counted correctly) in that riot tension double-page splash, combined with unique protest signs and clothing for all the participants. Alex also told me that the TransAmerica building was only partly constructed at that time, so that detail helped tremendously to add to the feel of the work.

Pages 22-23

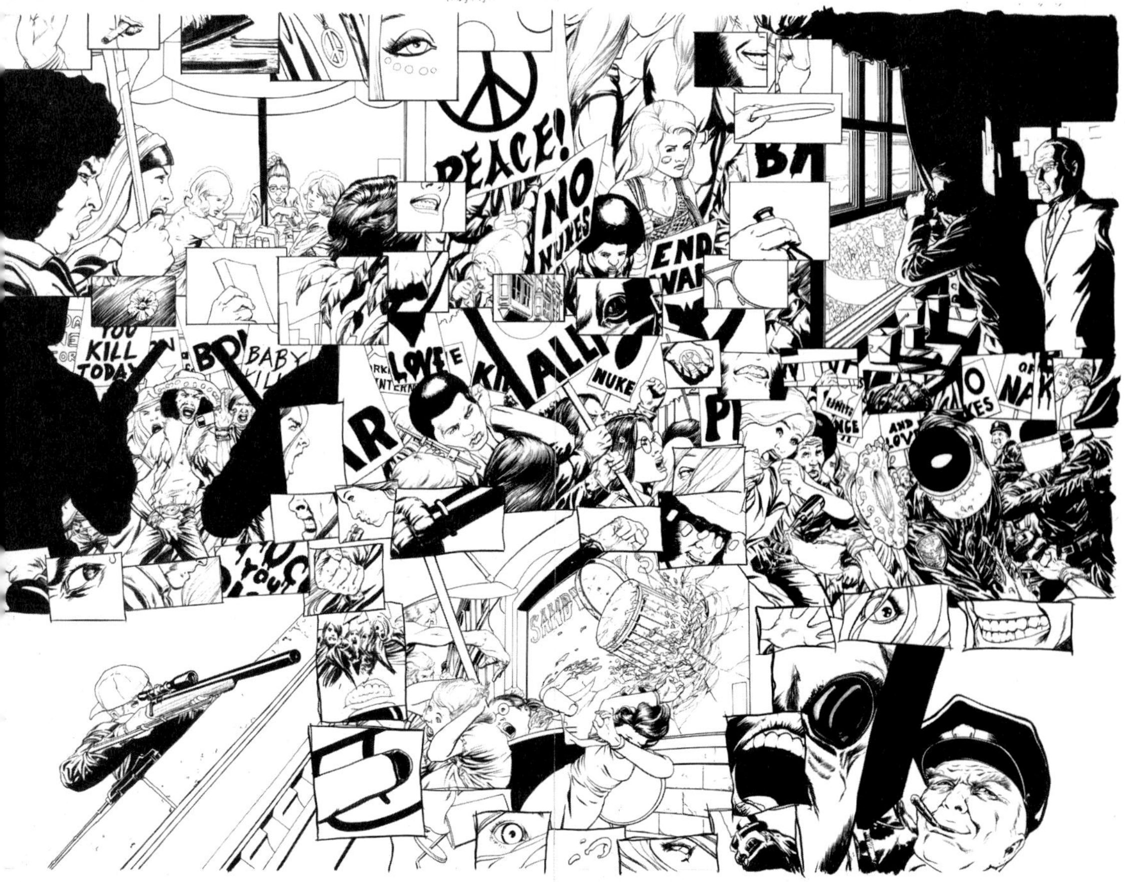
PEACE!
NO NUKES
END
YOU KILL TODAY
BABY
LOVE
NUKE

MAYDAY. First printing. May 2017. Published by Image Comics, Inc. Office of
publication: 2701 NW Vaughn St., Suite 780, Portland, OR 97210. Copyright
© 2017 Alex de Campi & Tony Parker. All rights reserved. Contains material
originally published in single magazine form as MAYDAY #1-5. "Mayday,"
its logos, and the likenesses of all characters herein are trademarks of Alex
de Campi & Tony Parker, unless otherwise noted. "Image" and the Image
Comics logos are registered trademarks of Image Comics, Inc. No part of this
publication may be reproduced or transmitted, in any form or by any means
(except for short excerpts for journalistic or review purposes), without
the express written permission of Alex de Campi, Tony Parker, or Image
Comics, Inc. All names, characters, events, and locales in this publication
are entirely fictional. Any resemblance to actual persons (living or dead),
events, or places, without satiric intent, is coincidental. Printed in the USA.
For information regarding the CPSIA on this printed material call: 203-595-
3636 and provide reference #RICH—736902. ISBN: 978-1-5343-0157-3.